COURT OF TREACHERY

AN EPIC ROMANTASY SAGA

EMPIRE OF BLOOD AND MALICE
BOOK TWO

MEG COWLEY

to the elven Realm of AURAURIA
TIR-NA-ALATHEA
(THE LIVING FOREST)
THE HIGHLANDS
THE LOWLANDS
Pelenor
Eyre

The Great Sea
Summer Palace
Kingsguard Academy
Tournai
PELENOR
PLAINS
Well of Life
Asirheim
Himmelheim
Keldheim
VALTIVAR
DRAGONTOOTH MOUNTAINS

READING GUIDE

Dear Reader,
It's important that you have a wonderful reading experience.
In light of that, please take note of the content guidelines of
this book if you have any reading preferences or aversions
pertaining to violence, trauma, or romantic content. Full
content guidance for this series can be found on the author's
website.

It is also advised to enjoy the series in order for all events to
flow coherently.

Warmest wishes,

Meg Cowley

THE STORY SO FAR: A RECAP

Heart of Shadows

In Heart of Shadows, we meet Harper, a young woman who lives the bleak existence of a penniless orphan with an unknown past in the mortal land of Caledan. In the midst of a storm, she finds a legendary Dragonheart, and when she touches it, it transports her to a faraway land full of fantastical magic—Pelenor.

There, she meets legendary elven thief Aedon and his companions—Aerian winged warrior Brand, dwarf Ragnar, and nomad Erika—who are curious about this strange young woman carrying such a powerful magical object. The companions are already tangled up in adventure—they flee the consequences of stealing a secret item from the kingdom of forest elves, Tir-na-Alathea in the form of a ruthless pair of wood elves who hunt them. Lost and alone, Harper has no choice but to ask for their help, even though she is highly suspicious of this group of outlaws. Aedon and his friends take Harper under their wing as she finds her way in this strange new land where magic rules in an elven court, dragons are real, and adventure awaits her.

The Dragonheart she found is an incredible magical artefact—but she discovers that it has been stolen from the King of Pelenor's vaults, somehow ending up in Harper's hands, and he will stop at nothing to get it back. He sends his dark and dangerous spymaster Dimitrius on the hunt. Harper encounters Dimitrius one day in the forest as he stalks through the shadows of the world trying to locate the Dragonheart. He is a powerful elven mage with the ability to evanesce through the world at speed. She is no match for him, but she squares up to him all the same, armed with a bow and arrows. Her companions rush to her defence—they have history with the Spymaster. They manage to repel him.

Unknown to Harper, it is Dimitrius who stole the king's Dragonheart. He is determined to use it to resurrect an old adversary of the kingdom Saradon, who was defeated five hundred years before, in order to overthrow King Toroth. Dimitrius cannot afford for the king to discover his duplicity, for the merciless king will execute him in a heartbeat, and so he must dance a careful line of appearing to help the King find his Dragonheart, whilst making sure in the end, he takes it for himself.

Between avoiding Dimitrius's pursuit and that of the vengeful wood elves, Harper delights in the adventure she finds herself upon. She discovers she is in fact from Pelenor and has elven blood running in her veins, but that the charm bracelet that she's had for as long as she can remember bears the Mark of Saradon, which in Pelenor is a grave treason.

All of this adds more questions to how she ended up so very far from Pelenor, across the veil, in the mortal lands, and who her family was. Even more exciting for her, is the realisation that she possesses magic, and, the longer she is in Pelenor, the more power she will be able to access.

Harper, however, is determined to use the Dragonheart—the only thing of value she has—to barter for her way back to her home country of Caledan, where she left behind her oldest friend Betta. The woman rescued her from the slums as a girl, and Harper feels honour-bound to care for the woman in her approaching old age. She is deeply worried that as winter approaches in Caledan, that Betta, who grows ill and infirm, will not be able to survive on her own, and this guilt and worry colours Harper's decisions.

With no choice but to continue with the group for now, she grows closer to her new companions—and Aedon in particular—because the outlaws prove to be incredibly noble and principled individuals who use their skills and infamy for good. Aedon uses his charm to try and determine if Harper is somehow a threat to his group, but can find nothing ill about her. She, meanwhile, becomes infatuated with the noble yet roguish elf, unable to resist Aedon's attention, handsome looks, and infectious personality.

His group stole a cure from the wood elves, and she joins them as they journey to the village that needs it, where a sickness spreads—but the wood elves have not given up. They ambush Harper and she manages to withstand their attack, giving time for her companions to rush to her aid. They fight the wood elves, who retreat—but then Dimitrius arrives. Luckily for Harper and her companions, he is now so worried by the threat of the wood elves knowing about the Dragonheart, he immediately departs to take care of them—leaving Harper and the companions shaken.

The companions take the cure to the village, but so many

are now sick, there is not enough to cure them all. They know that the Dragonheart could be used to make the potion go further—but they keep this concealed from Harper—however, they need the knowledge of how to do that, which lies in the capital of Pelenor, Tournai. This aligns with Harper's goal to return the Dragonheart to the king in exchange for passage home. Of course, the companions cannot let the Dragonheart go. Erika attempts to steal the Dragonheart and Harper parts with the companions on bad terms. She makes her own way to Tournai, where she is immediately arrested and accused of stealing the Dragonheart. She uses the only bartering chip she has—to call for Dimitrius.

Dimitrius is terrified that he is about to lose his Dragonheart and more importantly his head—because the young woman could implicate him in the theft. He quickly decides to make her his asset and claim to the king that she had infiltrated Aedon's group on his orders to obtain the Dragonheart. Harper, having no other way out, agrees to this ploy. Dimitrius saves her from the prison and takes her to his own quarters. There, he encourages and allows her to bathe, gets her fresh clothes, feeds her up, and gives her safety and somewhere to sleep for the night. Harper has never seen so much luxury, but she is not naïve enough to trust the spymaster.

The king is furious but is convinced of Dimitrius's story. Whilst the king once more has the Dragonheart, Dimitrius is glad his ruse has worked—for now. He and Harper are unlikely allies as they work together to survive. He finds himself consumed by this fierce young woman, the first person he's met who doesn't fear him, who openly challenges him, who will not submit to him no matter that he could crush her in an instant. He is drawn to and enamoured by her fire—even when she tries again to kill him and escape.

Harper is enthralled by the darkly delicious spymaster too—he is the most alluring and attractive male she has ever encountered, and the depth to him fascinates her. She feels like the more time they spend together, the more she can slide past his defences and see behind the masks he wears, to something softer and more vulnerable inside that fascinates her. However, she is not sure which side of him is real—only that all of them pose a danger to her.

Harper is still dangerous to Dimitrius, however, because she knows he has been seeking the Dragonheart and knew of its location, and of course, she was never his asset—and he cannot risk this leaking to the king. However, he cannot do what is necessary and silence her to protect himself. Instead, he concocts the perfect solution—he goads Aedon into coming to rescue Harper from the king's clutches and steal a Dragonheart for their own ends. Using their escapades as cover, Dimitrius will obtain one for himself too.

The plan is a success. Aedon and his companions liberate Harper and attack the vaults, having already infiltrated the archives to obtain the knowledge of how to use the Dragonheart to make more of the cure they need. Aedon uses powerful fire magic to steal a hoard of Dragonhearts—from which Dimitrius steals one. However, the Kingsguard attack.

Aedon is forced to use the energy of the stolen Dragonhearts—all bar one—to defend them and stop the king's magic wards exterminating them. In the attack, Harper is in grave risk and about to die. Unbeknownst to her and her companions, Dimitri watches from the shadows with his stolen Dragonheart. He holds back the king's wards to help them—because he can only hide his theft if they succeed— but when he sees Harper attacked and about to be killed, he steps in without thought. His magic chokes, smothers, and kills her assailants, giving her the break she needs to pull through.

Dimitrius vanishes, now he has what he came for—and the companions escape, separating to boost their chances of survival. Brand and Harper go up to the highest towers of the keep, where Brand will fly away with Harper and the Dragonheart to safety. Dimitrius finds them at the top of the tower—and Brand steps in to defend Harper and their prize.

However, Dimitrius speaks directly to Harper, who confronts him. She doesn't understand this mysterious and dark elf who one minute threatens and the next minute helps her. His agenda is a mystery, and whilst he has been so protective of and kind to her, she is under no illusions that he is anything other than manipulative and dangerous. She expects the king's spymaster to capture or kill them—but he does neither. Instead, Dimitrius commands her to leave—to escape with her prize. Because, if she stays, the king will execute her—and he could not bear that. There is so much unsaid between them, and turmoil in both their hearts—but time is up. Harper and Brand flee.

They meet the others late that night. Now they have everything they need to help the sick villagers: the remaining cure, the Dragonheart, and the knowledge. Harper decides that this is the adventure she's always dreamed of—and with no way back to Caledan, she will look forward instead.

She joins the companions now as one of them, having earned her place. They will flee the capital, the king's wrath, and Dimitrius to do what they do best—deal noble justice and help the needy in a kingdom where the rich and magical, and the poor and mortal are worlds apart. Harper will seize the opportunity to learn about and grow her elven magic and discover more about her unknown past. One thing is for certain—she is determined never to cross paths with the

King of Pelenor again. Or his spymaster. For Dimitrius is dangerous both to her safety—and her heart.

Dimitrius flees the capital too—to Saradon's tomb, which he has located. He uses his Dragonheart to raise Saradon from a magical stasis. Together they will break the wheel and build a new Pelenor from the ashes.

Continue reading in book two, Court of Treachery...

1
DIMITRI

The stench of carrion on the warm, moist air clogged Dimitri's nostrils. Dimitri took shallow breaths through his mouth to avoid the worst of it. He resisted the urge to flinch away from the denizens prowling around them, darting forward and back to test the boundaries. Dimitri and Saradon turned with them, never revealing their backs to the scavengers surrounding them. The threat of their elven power kept the goblins at bay.

Saradon seemed unperturbed by the nature of their hosts. He stood tall and uncowed by the numbers that faced them, unbothered by the shrill chatter that echoed around the caves. It peppered their ears with harsh clicks and guttural shrieks that Dimitri wished he could silence, because they grated on his very bones. His head pounded. But it would not do to offend the goblin horde, for Saradon had brought him here to seek their help.

Dimitri wished he had never mentioned them. Never fed Saradon the information that they massed in rebellion against the dwarven kingdom of Valtivar. He had meant to seed instability in Tournai, not inspire Saradon to seek a new ally. They were even worse in person than he had feared, and for the first time, he wondered how any of the reports had ever made it back, for the goblins were not shy about their murderous intent.

How could these creatures be an ally? More importantly, how would they, a strife-loving species, bring a peaceful vision for Pelenor? Misgivings lurked in Dimitri's mind, but he pushed them aside.

At the subtle beckon of Saradon's curling finger, Dimitri stepped forward, bearing the small chest. A bribe. It had been easy to take from the king's horde unnoticed, so trivial it was to Toroth. But the goblins' shrieks intensified at the sight as he flipped the lid back to reveal a nest of cut and polished gems. Immediately, it was snatched from his grasp by warm and unpleasantly clammy hands. Knobby calluses and broken nails scraped across his skin in their haste. Dimitri clenched his jaw and forced himself to slowly lower his hands to his sides. He longed to recoil and cleanse himself, his skin crawling with the ghost of their touch.

Squabbling amongst themselves to touch the stones and carry the chest, they hauled it to the goblin *pascha*, their leader, biting and clawing each other out of the way. Torn, dark rags of mismatched leathers, skin, and furs fluttered about them as they fought. Like so much else of theirs, it seemed cobbled together with whatever scraps they found or took, having no protection against the seeping cold of the stone underfoot.

Dimitri wondered fleetingly how they coped, scrabbling around barefoot, before realising that he cared not—he just wanted to leave. It took four of them to lift the chest, so bowed and stunted were they. If they stood tall, they would have come to Dimitri's chest. Their advantage laid in numbers and feral abandon, not in training or strength.

These goblins were bigger than the *tikrit*, the lowest goblins of all. Those thigh-high creatures hovered around the fringes of the gathering, as was their place, too lowly and puny to dare enter the presence of the *pascha*.

The *pascha* hissed with anticipation, showing his filed, yellowing teeth. "Sssssssspeak," he growled as he scooped up handfuls of gems and let them flow through his splayed fingers. He spoke the Common Tongue with difficulty, as if his mouth struggled to form itself around the words. His sibilant voice echoed, and the host around them quieted at his orders, their attention shifting to Dimitri and Saradon. Shadows flickered on the wall, thrown by the huge pyre in the centre of the cave. It was a constant grotesque dance, the host's shadows cavorting behind them, each form distorted on the rough-hewn stone.

Dimitri stirred and inclined his head, though not too much. The goblins needed no opportunity to think he and Saradon were weak or subservient. "Announcing Lord Saradon Ettrias Thelnar of House Ravakian."

Hisses arose and the frenzy around them intensified, until a glare from Saradon and a guttural bark from the *pascha* silenced them.

"I know that name," said the *pascha*. He bared his teeth at Saradon. "It cannot be. He is dead."

"I was never dead," Saradon said and stalked forward. He spread his hands wide and turned in a slow circle, inviting them all to look at him. "I am Lord Saradon, and I will take my dues. I bring my blade, as proof of my claim." Saradon drew his sword with a metal hiss, holding it high. The slim, river-steel blade shimmered with its own glow in the dark cavern, and the ruby pommel blazed with a bloody light. The instant outcry of shrieking and chattering confirmed that the goblins indeed knew the legend of his blade that, before he had come to wield it, had slain many of their kind in the hands of his forefathers. "You will help me, and I will raise you from this pitiful hole in the ground to where you desire."

The chatter crescendoed around them, the undercurrent of energy shifting from hostility to a thrill at the sight of that blade. Dimitri snuck a glance around the cave. It was much as their underground passage had been. Once great, carved, dwarven halls under the hills ruined by the vermin now inhabiting them. Pristine carvings had been battered and chipped away until they were unrecognisable, and the walls ran red with daubed blood. Whose, Dimitri did not care to dwell on.

The dwarves had abandoned it, albeit reluctantly, with the ebb and flow of their race's dominion over the land as they chased the seams of mineral riches through the mountains. The goblins had been only too eager to seize the location and strip it of any association with its former masters. The dwarves had closed ranks to defend their remaining strongholds, abandoning the occasional tunnel network or spent mine.

The goblin's location was but a small part of the dwarven realm of Valtivar, but the rift between the races ran deep. Ever had the goblins loved the caves and fought the dwarves for control of their territory. Inexorably, with their failure to present a unified force, and instead fractured by infighting amongst clans, they had been pushed back and, as in the case of the *tikrit,* enslaved by the dwarves for their own ends.

It was the only incentive Saradon could offer that they would have been tempted by. He had chosen wisely, as much as Dimitri disagreed.

The *pascha* bared his teeth in a feral smile. "You will take

Valtivar with us?" Dimitri saw the greedy gleam in his eyes at the prospect.

"We will. After you help me take Tournai," Saradon clarified. His tone was dark with the threat of revenge for those who had wronged him. Dimitri felt it, too. "As it should have been five hundred years ago, so it will be now. I will rule Pelenor. You may have Valtivar. I care not for the dwarves. Do what you will with their strongholds."

Dimitri stiffened. He could not have heard him correctly. Why would Saradon make such a generous offer, one that involved the fall of their own, most desired kingdom? Surely Saradon would not ally Pelenor with their historic enemies.

The *pascha* clicked, hissed, and chattered in his strange tongue to his chieftains, who lurked behind him. They were all dressed in the finest garbs, taken and re-shaped from dwarves, men, and even elves, judging by the patterns on their robes. Dimitri swallowed his distaste.

"We will consider it," the *pascha* said eventually. "Leave us."

To Dimitri's surprise, Saradon did not challenge the lack of respect, but turned on his heel without a further word and strode out, Dimitri quick to follow. *Tikrit* bounded through the wide halls, close enough to snatch at their heels, though they did not dare to, scattering away on all fours as soon as they got too close. The goblin-kin surrounded them, stampeding down the halls in chaos.

Saradon refused to be hurried. Dimitri matched his confident stride through the seething mass of bodies. Dimitri could bear the moist, fetid, rotting air no longer. It pressed down upon him like a physical force. As the first caress of outside air touched his cheek, he hurried forward until they burst through the shattered dwarven doors into the cool night air to breathe in deep, fresh breaths.

A heartbeat later, they raced side by side through the ether of the world. Dimitri had been unsurprised to learn that Saradon could travel as he did, unseen through the shadows of the world's essence. Little surprised him about Saradon now... except his deal with the goblins. Had Saradon learned his skills at the same hands as Dimitri? Hands teaching arcane ways in a secret order that did not exist? One that had inspired Dimitri's own dreams of defiance and creating a new order, but one that, in the end, he had been desperate to escape.

As they stopped, stepping from the void into Dimitri's chambers in Tournai, the royal city of Pelenor, Dimitri turned to Saradon. "Lord Saradon, you cannot be serious about dealing with such..." He could not find a word that fit how lowly and scum-like the goblins were, how beneath either of their notice. This was not the new order he wanted to create.

Saradon barked with laughter as he grabbed a crystal tumbler and helped himself to the contents of Dimitri's finest drink before he answered. "They are a means to an end. Fear not, Dimitrius." Saradon sank onto a couch before the roaring fire, then beckoned for Dimitri to join him.

Dimitri drew closer but did not sit.

"For now, I must take my allies where I find them. And it will do us good to sow fear and discord. If the king thinks I have united the goblins against him, he shall hesitate in his own machinations. Yet the common people who know we act for them will be unperturbed by it."

"You hope."

Saradon shrugged. "It will be what it will be. No one will know of our involvement with the goblins until such time as it befits us. All Toroth will know is that his empire is threatened from within and without." Saradon smiled at the prospect.

"What of afterward? After Toroth is gone and Pelenor is at peace? To what end does it serve us to have such blood-thirsty, unpredictable, hostile neighbours?"

"They shall not be hostile if we are allied with them. Of that you can be sure. Besides..." Saradon smiled a wolfish grin. "Who said they had a place in my peaceful lands?"

Dimitri raised an eyebrow. "You will betray them?"

Saradon shrugged. "Whatever it takes to ensure peace—for all lands. If there are even any goblins left after the battles ahead are won."

Dimitri paused in thought, but he could not see how Saradon could ensure, by agreement or force, the goblins kept peace. He had a sneaking suspicion Saradon meant a far worse fate for the goblins. Would they decimate themselves for his cause? He could not see it. As much as Dimitri could not deny he would gladly see them eliminated, it niggled at his conscience. This was not the vision he sought to build. He was not so naïve as to think that compromises would not need to be made—after all, nothing could be gained without sacrifice—but would it really require the alliance of such unsavoury creatures and the sacrificing of his principles to succeed?

"Do you think the *pascha* will accept your proposal?" Dimitri asked eventually.

Saradon's response was instant. "Without a doubt."

"And if they do not?" Dimitri's voice was brittle. So much was at stake. Too much to trust creatures such as the goblins.

Saradon's sly smile curled up once more. "A willing subject is far more biddable, but whichever way they choose, they shall serve me."

A prickle ran down Dimitri's spine. Saradon would bind

the goblins to him using dark magics if they did not choose to serve him. It could not be so. Dimitri had seen the visions of a green and pleasant Pelenor, prosperous and free from corruption. This did not match that.

"Surely the moral goal of our crusade will be enough," Dimitri suggested, keeping his tone light. "We do not need to bind others to our cause through force."

Saradon almost snorted out his fine wine. "You would trust a goblin's conscience? Come now. Do not be a fool. I am not naïve enough to hope for such things. I was foiled once before—I shall not see it done again. I will do anything it takes to succeed, and I shall take no risks, for there will not be a third chance." Saradon stood, drained the crystal glass, and nodded to Dimitri as he set it upon the table. "Return to court, Lord Ellarian. We both have work to do." With that, Saradon vanished into the ether.

For a long while, Dimitri stared at the spot where Saradon had stood, as the flames died in the fire before him and the lamps burned out, wondering at Saradon's plans— and what he did not know of them.

That evening, King Toroth's unceasing tirade at Raedon, master and general of the Winged Kingsguard, continued. Dimitri slunk back into the shadows, for it would not do to catch the king's ire himself. Raedon's hunched shoulders and bowed head said he had long given up on trying to protest his position.

Dimitri smirked. He had foisted blame upon the Kingsguard for the Dragonhearts' disappearance. It would only appear so. The Kingsguard had faced Aedon and his companions in the vaults yet failed to stop them. To his relief and glee, Dimitri had not been connected to any of it. To the disappearance of the Dragonheart—or to Harper's vanishing. In the king's ire, he had quite forgotten about her. Dimitri pushed away the ache that sat in his chest at the thought of Harper. The one that told him how painfully vulnerable he was to the threat of her allure. How she had challenged and fought and excited him—and how she could have damned him. She was gone. She could not incriminate him. That was what mattered, he told himself firmly.

The king had seized the first poor fool he could punish for the loss of his greatest treasures. For Raedon, general of the Kingsguard and the most fearsome warrior in the king's service, the failure and the punishment were his to bear—and Dimitri shouldered none of it. Dimitri did not know what the king would do to Raedon, so angry was he, nor did he care. Raedon was an even bigger ass than his brother, Aedon, the king's former golden boy. *Maybe Toroth will exile Raedon, too*, he thought hopefully. Mind, there would only be another jumped-up, arrogant prick to fill his place. There always was when it came to falling in and out of the king's fancy.

Toroth's face reddened and spittle flew from his mouth as he stormed around the room, gesticulating wildly with vicious jabs of his fingers. "*Get out!*" he thundered. Raedon, after the briefest of bows, fled. Dimitri melted farther into the darkness. He did not wish to be the king's next victim.

Only Dimitri knew what had truly happened. That Aedon had burned through the stolen pile of Dragonhearts, using up their stores of magic to save his companions until only two were left in their possession—the one they had stolen to cure the village's sickness, and the one he had taken to raise Saradon. The rest remaining in the compromised vault had been removed and taken somewhere so secure, Toroth would tell no one of it.

Dimitri suppressed a grudging respect for Aedon and his ability to control such magics. He had tenacity, that was certain, and was resourceful, but Dimitri still resented that life had bestowed such powerful capabilities and privilege on Aedon.

No one knew Dimitri had let Aedon and his companions walk free, either. Why had he done it? If he were being honest with himself, it was because of *her*. Harper. He had allowed himself to grow overly familiar until compassion stung him. Nothing would have pleased him more than to abandon Aedon to his fate, but she had stopped him. Stopped him even thinking of it.

For a moment, he saw the tall, winged Aerian warrior, Aedon's companion, standing on the parapet before him, with Harper clutched in a burly arm. Exhausted, afraid, yet defiant. Her eyes wide, but the set of her mouth so determined as she stared him down. He still thought of her more than was good for him. Who she was in all of this. There was no chance it could be coincidence, but with the work yet to do, he could not dwell on it. All the same, he regretted not keeping a watch on her. Now she was... heavens knew where.

Dimitri pushed away all thoughts of her, Aedon, and his band of outlaws, and allowed himself to savour the moment, and the maturation of his plans and long-held wishes to topple the establishment. All the moving parts were about to align. He allowed himself a smug grin.

2

HARPER

The water *glowed*. Harper drew closer to the azure pool, cocking her head this way and that. The pure, clear waters captivated her. The strange light they emitted had nothing to do with the sun far above them. She would have called glowing water impossible, yet so much had happened to defy all logic and reason that Harper had given up questioning.

Around her companions the forest loomed, a watchful protector of the secret place. The canopy created a cocoon of fire, the leaves in a symphony of colour before their impending shedding. Birds trilled and creatures rustled in the distance, along with the gentle peal of animals' bells as they grazed on the last of autumn's bounty in meadows far away across the valley. But, it was silent where they stood, and a strange kind of watchfulness prickled her skin.

Their horses, stolen from the Kingsguard of Tournai and now tethered to the great trees, were happy to pause in the shade and nibble the grass—and Harper was glad for the break. They had ridden hard for weeks with the threat of

11

King Toroth's wrathful pursuit, first for the village, where they had used the stolen Dragonheart's magic and knowledge from the royal archives to cure the remaining villagers, and then south and east, past the long reach of Pelenor's capital, Tournai. The days, at first fraught and with the frisson of fear ever-present, had eased. Harper had been glad to run free—from Toroth, at least.

As for the spymaster Dimitrius, those feelings were altogether too complex. The hair on the back of her neck always prickled at the thought of him, as though his violet eyes were still upon her. He had let her escape—more than that, actively pushed her to—but she had seen the arcane manner in which he could travel through the world, slipping unseen from shadow to shadow, and she did not entirely trust to be out of his machinations yet. With every fresh stop on their journey, she found herself searching for him in the shadows —to no avail. Did she want to see him? For the curl of unease in her at the thought of him was part apprehension and part something else entirely opposite.

However, they had fled, and seen nothing of the king's men—or the spymaster—and now? Now, they were here. Wherever 'here' was. Harper had not quite believed Aedon's promise that all would be revealed. She looked to him, and something pulled low in her belly as he grinned, mischief sparkling in his eyes, and beckoned her. He had promised her the climb would be worth it, but as beautiful as the pool was, hidden deep within the forested valleys up the foothills of the mountains, it did not seem worthy of a visit. Harper gasped as Aedon disappeared into the cliff. A moment later, his head popped out between fronds of greenery that Harper thought clung to a solid rock face. "Come on!" he called.

She followed him through the vegetation flanked by her companions, pushing the heavy web of ivy aside. A concealed cave sat beyond the fissure illuminated by small patches of light—and darkness beyond. There, the waters that fed the pool babbled across an invisible streambed. It was cooler in the cave, and chills crawled across Harper's skin. She rubbed her arms, grateful for her cloak. Aedon's hands and face illuminated before her as he conjured a faelight to guide their way, but as Harper's eyes adjusted, she realised it was not as inky black as she had first thought. The faintly glowing stream wound into the distance up a slight incline, but tiny motes of light danced down it.

Ahead of their companions, Harper followed Aedon eagerly, though her stomach tingled. Was it with faint apprehension, or the curling of magic deep inside her? She could not tell. In her weeks in Pelenor, since the Dragonheart she found had magically transported her from her homelands to this wondrous and strange place, that tiny seed of energy in the pit of her being had swelled into a trickle of ever-present energy—one that she could feel, but not yet harness.

"Come on," Aedon urged, and she sped up. The darkness felt inviting, not intimidating, though Harper could not explain why. Ahead, the light grew, as well as a humming sound that Harper could not source, until they stepped into a tall, wide cavern. It held a vast pool that disappeared into the gloom in the distance under the mountains.

Harper could deny it no longer. Glowing specks of light swirled lazily through the water and air—and pure magic formed them. Somehow the motes moved, though the air was still. She tingled with the energy of it all. This place felt like touching Aedon's raw magic, but a thousandfold more powerful. It had been alluring to feel his shared power coursing through her as he attempted to coax her sleeping elven magic forth, but this was *intoxicating*.

The hair rose on the back of Harper's neck, but not from

the temperature. It was neither cool nor hot now, but somewhere comfortably in between. No, her senses pricked at the watchful, benevolent presence of something greater that held court there. It was as though the entire cave held its breath with her.

"What is it?" she whispered.

Aedon drew closer. "You'll see. Follow me."

To her surprise, he took off his boots and walked toward the water. Picking his way down the rough, rocky shelf, he padded into the shallows. Aedon turned toward her, smiling reassuringly, as his faelight soared lazily above them all, illuminating marble walls, slanted at an angle, that ran with lines of a vibrant rosy colour.

"Take your boots off," he instructed.

Her attention flicked to the water—too deep to see the bottom after a short distance, nor anything that inhabited it. She clamped down on the rising feeling of panic. He would not ask it of her if it were dangerous, she reasoned, and he was already in the water. She cast her attention over him—utterly at ease. She stepped forwards, despite the seething unease lurking in her belly.

Moments later, her boots stood next to his—and then her cloak atop them. Harper slowly advanced, glancing into the swirling, glowing waters with a frown. Aedon grasped her hand the moment she stepped in, pulling her with him. She gasped, expecting the shock of cold—but it did not come. To her surprise, the water was warm, as comfortable as his hand on hers, and buzzed against her skin.

He strode out farther until submerged to his waist and tugged her with him, so she had no choice but to follow, despite the tingle of fear that now stroked her spine and the catch of her breath as it threatened to stall. The water flowed around her, billowing her shirt, as the fingers of a gentle current tingled across her skin. What lay in the strange waters? It unnerved her to not be able to see her feet or where she stepped. She suppressed visions of sinking into deep, ink-black water, never to be seen again, and fought down the wave of panic clutching at her chest. Aedon grasped her other hand, lacing her fingers through his as he moved to stand before her. Harper blinked away the blackness and focused on his laughing green eyes. The glowing motes bobbed around them, swirling in a sedate dance on their invisible currents.

"Drink it."

"W-what?" she spluttered.

Aedon's lips broke into a wide grin as he beheld her confusion with mirth. "Trust me, Harper. Drink it. I promised you all would be revealed."

Slowly, Harper pulled her hands from his and lowered them into the water. For a long moment, she enjoyed the gentle tug of it passing between her fingers, the sensation grounding her. Each mote of light brought her a slight tingle as they drifted into her in the air and water. Aedon nodded his reassurance.

She cupped the water in her palms, brought it to her mouth, and took a tentative sip. Her eyes widened. "It's so sweet!"

Emboldened, Harper took a long draught, draining the liquid in her hands. She cupped them in the water twice, then thrice, savouring the rich sweetness as it tingled down her throat, leaving her stomach full of butterflies. It was a refreshing quench of her thirst after a long ride, soothing her dry mouth and throat—but more than that, this water tasted of energy and life.

"What is it?" she whispered, though she already had an inkling. She had felt the sensation before when Aedon had shared his magic with her. Already, she sensed it bubbling up inside, a spring waiting to burst forth.

"Magic," he confirmed, and his grin widened. "Welcome to the Well of Life."

Harper observed her surroundings. Hues of pinks lined the walls as layers of marble, carved by time and water, undulated around them. The water glowed, reflecting a rosy hue, as the golden motes swirled into the depths and distance, and so high above them was the cavern that Harper could not see the ceiling.

"What is this place?" Her voice was hushed, reverent. She knew nothing of this place, but it was clear it was special.

"A Wellspring. One of a few areas where the river of magical energy that flows through the world unseen intersects with the physical plane. This is one such place... A literal spring of magical power."

It sounded fanciful, but Harper nodded. She could feel the truth of it humming through her.

"For me, it feels like the comfort of coming home, but for you, it is the storm after a drought. Drink. Take your fill."

She did, hungrily, until her belly hurt from the volume of water and she could take no more. The power building within her welled from the tips of her toes to every hair in her head. Harper realised with a cry that she floated, hovering in the water away from the bed of rock beneath them and now inches taller than Aedon. She flailed in the air, panicking—until Aedon grasped her hands in his to become a reassuring tether to the solid rock below.

He grinned. "Be calm—you are safe, I promise. Magic has missed you, it seems. Allow it to fill you up like an empty vessel."

Harper closed her eyes, revelling in the feeling of pure energy coursing through her, intense and pleasurable as it welled from her core to her extremities. She laughed with delight as she opened her eyes to realise that her very skin glowed with magic. She splayed her fingers before her, marvelling as golden light arced from each fingertip, bouncing upon the water's surface to join the swirling dance of magic and energy around them. What was her potential now? With a thrilling rush, she realised the magic at her fingers sparked at the slightest hint of her will.

Her glow was reflected in Aedon, who laughed at her, sharing in her joy—and Brand, Erika, and Ragnar, who watched with smiles from the rocky shelf. Now Harper knew what he spoke of—the truth of it that she had doubted until now. She was no mortal, but of elven blood, and she had *magic*. Her innate powers, so long slumbering, charged through her like a mount who refused to be contained or tamed. Inside, she could feel it longing to burst free. Her mouth split with a joyous grin to match Aedon's as she revelled in the power and potential.

More, her body urged. *More*.

Aedon reeled her in, pulling her back to the rock. Her hands found his shoulders and his slid around her waist. The surprise of his touch shocked her for a moment, for her body felt so overwhelmed by the intensity of the magic swirling through her. She waded away and staggered out of the water to their waiting companions, who watched with curiosity. Despite the strange warmth of the place, Harper's clothes clung to her with cool wetness.

With half a thought, she wished to be dry. A moment later, all trace of water had vanished from her clothes, leaving her pants as crisp and fresh as the day she had first worn them. Harper gasped.

Aedon chuckled. "Very nicely done."

"Can I do anything just by thinking it?"

"Not quite. You find yourself blessed by the uncommon bounty here, and that was no doubt an accident of happy chance. You might find yourself able to do the strangest things with a thought, but magic is like a muscle. A thread to pick up and twist and pull, to weave into what you wish. It takes years of honing to become capable of great deeds, and you cannot exceed your own will and strength to perform it. But you can certainly do minor magics with ease now. It's instinct. You must use it well, however. Magic is not a whim to be used whenever one desires, upon whatever one fancies. With magic comes responsibility," he warned.

Harper looked to her hands once more, turning them over and back in wonder. She watched as the glow faded into her skin. "Can anyone else do that?" Harper glanced at her companions, who looked toward the exit, hasty to leave, she reckoned, by the way they shifted.

"No, lass," replied Ragnar. "We could drink from the well, yet it would be nothing more than sweet water that quenched our thirst. Only those of elven blood may take magic from the wellspring."

"Come," said Brand. The Aerian warrior towered over them all, though even he was dwarfed by the cavern. "We are still not far enough from Tournai to be safe from the Kingsguard."

"Nor the elves of Tir-na-Alathea," Erika warned them, already down the tunnel and scouting the way ahead.

And Dimitrius, Harper added silently. She shivered and hurried after Brand, pushing all thoughts of the raven-haired spymaster from her mind.

Aedon scoffed but followed, chivvying Ragnar and Harper before him. Harper turned for one last look at the cave, trying to imprint the vision of the rose-lined walls, swirling golden motes, and glowing water upon her memory. Never had she seen a place like it before.

She pinched her arm. The nip hurt, and she quickly rubbed the skin to soothe it. No matter how many times she tried it, she still had not woken in her own pallet in Caledan. *It's truly not a dream. This is my life now*, she told herself again. Each time, she said it with less regret, thoughts fading of what she had left behind. This time, a thrill ran across her skin, sparked by the magic coursing through her. She had left so little behind after all and found so much. Magic was yet another question she now sought an answer to. With a huge grin, she broke into a jog and bounded after Brand as the gleam of sunlight bloomed ahead.

3

DIMITRI

"Do not promise that which you cannot deliver," Lord Thaeus scoffed at Dimitri, who stood before him, unperturbed by his lack of faith.

"Quite, quite," Dimitri replied, nodding at the older elf, who far surpassed him in rank. "I promise nothing. What can be promised in such times? Only more of the same. Fear, rumours, instability. I merely *offer* an alternative. One where you are rewarded more justly for your endeavours in fair Pelenor's name."

Lord Thaeus scoffed. "Harumph! And you think Toroth will take this on his back? I think not!"

Dimitri suppressed a smirk. "I hardly think it, but there is far more at work than what you realise. You are not the sum of these machinations."

Thaeus raised an eyebrow. "And *you* are?"

"Nay. All of us are mere parts. And yet, I know what will unfold. It will be the greatest change in our country's history, and you had better be on the right side of it if you wish to see your House and name preserved." He fixed Thaeus with an unflinching glare that exuded his conviction of that.

Thaeus swallowed. "S-Surely not," he stammered. "I mean, you would need an invading army to topple the king."

"Would we really?" Dimitri asked, though he thought to the goblin forces that Saradon wooed to do exactly that. "Toroth has grown himself a nation of folk—common and high alike—who despise him. Why, he has grown his very own rebellion."

Thaeus dabbed a dank cloth to his forehead, then tucked the handkerchief away once more. His eyes darted around, as if the very walls had ears, and sweat beaded on his forehead.

The walls did have ears—and they belonged to Dimitrius. "Fear not, Lord Thaeus. You are safe with me."

"Forgive me if I do not trust the king's spymaster." The reply came with the usual injection of hostility and suspicion.

"I suppose I might deserve that. Yet... Did you ever wonder why you never did get arrested, or charged with the embezzlement of taxes from all the landed goods that were never declared in the port at Eyre this last decade?" Dimitri asked casually, picking imaginary specks from his nails. He had waited patiently to play that card.

Thaeus stilled, but Dimitrius saw the flare of his nostrils, the bob of his throat, and the slight widening of his eyes. "I don't know what you're talking about."

"Of course you don't," said Dimitri smoothly, leaning toward him to clap him on the shoulder conspiratorially, winking. "It never happened, did it?"

"Certainly not," replied Thaeus, even though Dimitri knew it most certainly had. *Such a flea-bitten coward.* Dimitri truly despised them all, for the court was rotten to the core.

Each of them was more self-serving than the last. They cared not for how the realm bled.

Dimitri knew he had Thaeus cornered. All the long years of gathering information, not all of which had been for the king's benefit, would finally pay dividends. And, one way or another, he would ensure they all received their comeuppance, too, when all was said and done. He needed them to break the wheel, to remake Pelenor to his and Saradon's visions, but he did not need them afterward. Not in their current form. They, however, did not need to know that.

"Excellent. Then I look forward to working very closely with you, Lord Thaeus."

"Quite, Lord Ellarian." Lord Thaeus's watery eyes followed Dimitri as he strode away.

It marked the end of a long day of plotting, and the last noble Dimitri would blackmail, bribe, or curry favour with… for now. He considered he had collected enough of them for one day. His neck was now over the parapet, especially when he infiltrated the guilds. It would take just one of them to betray him, but he knew they would not. In implicating him, they would also damn themselves to certain death at the king's hands. He did not know any one of them who would be so brave as to sacrifice themselves for that.

Still, Dimitri's heart hammered as he strode to the safety of his chambers, and a wave of anxiety rushed through him when four red cloaks turned the corner, walking toward him. He forced himself to stride past the Kingsguard with his usual arrogant grace, glaring at them as he passed, then flicking his attention away as though they were beneath his notice. They did not so much as dare look at him and not one uttered a word. It was only when he returned to the safety of his own warded rooms that he at last let the mask slip and let out a great, shuddering breath of relief.

"Are you quite all right, Dimi?" Emyria asked, her greying brow raised in question.

"I shall live another day perhaps, Emyria," Dimitri replied. A yawn swallowed his next words.

Emyria tutted and stood on her tiptoes to unfasten his cloak, sweeping it over her arm before she hooked it upon the stand. "Well, dear, sit. I shall bring you a warm drink and your slippers."

"What would I do without you, Emyria?" Dimitri flashed her a tired, grateful smile and slumped onto his most comfortable couch.

"No doubt get into a lot more trouble," she said, glaring at him with pursed lips and mock sternness. She had been a mother of sorts to him. Her brown, greying hair was pulled back from her kind face and swirled into braids that bobbed as she worked to pour him a sweet infusion.

"I don't doubt it. How long have you been here now?" The years blurred into one another, sometimes. How long *had* it been?

"With you? As well you know, sir. In Tournai, it will be nigh on a hundred years now."

A hundred years serving the king's will. Did the time fly or drag? It could not have been a century—and yet in the same breath, it also felt like an eternity. He shuddered at the thought, though he had been there almost as long, albeit in a different way. "I hope I am a better master than the king was."

"You know the truth of it." Her voice soured with each clipped word. Neither of them had ever truly spoken about what he had rescued her from, and she did not like to dwell on it. Unlike him, she had just the barest hint of elvish blood in her line, and thus was destined for the lowliest forms of servitude and station in her prolonged life. The gift and the curse of her heritage.

"I'm sorry, Emyria. I did not mean to dredge it up. I suppose I have been wishing for better circumstances for us all."

"I thank you, Dimitri. I know you will deliver us through these testing times." She had already thanked him many times over the years for sheltering her, for giving her a comfortable life where she barely had to lift a finger, unlike her former slavery. Deep in thought, he watched her leave.

As much as he orchestrated this for himself, he also did it for the likes of her, too. Nowhere in his new Pelenor would there be bonded servants. It made him feel uncharacteristically noble, momentarily washing away the slime of the court and all its shadows, but the moment quickly passed. First, he had a mire to wade through and a realm to overturn.

4

HARPER

"Where to now then?" Harper asked. They had fulfilled their task to find a cure for the sickness sweeping the remote village. Now that that obligation had been fulfilled, her thoughts had once more strayed to Caledan and Betta—with not a small amount of guilt at what she had left behind, no matter how impossible it would be to return. The group looked to Aedon, the unspoken leader of their mismatched troupe.

Aedon blew a long exhale and spread his arms wide. "We have a whole world of potential. Now we wander until we find our next calling, as we always do—but far from Tournai." He grinned and winked.

Warmth bloomed in Harper's chest at his infectious optimism. They had left the village a much better place than they had found it, cured of the spreading sickness that had ailed the folk there, although there had been no time to enjoy the hospitality insisted upon by the villagers. They dallied far too close to the Winged Kingsguard's might—and none had forgotten the threat of the Tir-na-Alathean elves that haunted their steps. Their ways had parted, but neither Aedon nor his companions trusted that the wood elves had given up their hunt. Harper and her new companions had fled south, past the heart of Pelenor and toward the spur of mountains that cleaved the kingdom apart, and within which sat the dwarven realm of Valtivar.

"We can find shelter in the mountains. And perhaps even some respite at Keldheim or another hold," Brand suggested, though his gaze darted to Ragnar when he mentioned the dwarf's homelands.

"We would be safe from Toroth's reach there," acknowledged Aedon.

"If they will have us." Ragnar's quiet voice caught them all.

"You are not an exile or a criminal, as the rest of us are," said Aedon gently. "You are welcome there."

Ragnar scoffed. "*Welcome* is not the word I would use."

Aedon pursed his lips. "Perhaps. But we must lay low for a while. Tir-na-Alathea is closed to us now, and all in the realm of Pelenor or near it, save for the dwarves of Valtivar, are loyal to the king and his riders. There is nothing for us in the wilds beyond the mountains. Not with the coming of winter."

"I did not say I disagreed with the logic of it," Ragnar said, an uncharacteristic snap to his voice.

Harper looked between them. Ragnar had once told her he missed his home, and his sadness had been visceral. Yet he did not want to return? The outlaws' histories were as complex as a woven cloak. She wondered at his reluctance to visit Keldheim, the dwarven stronghold.

"We do not have to go if you do not wish it." Aedon's tone was sympathetic, though his sharp eyes watched Ragnar for any trace of his will. "It just means we'll have a rougher exile this time than what I dare say any of us fancy!" His roguish grin returned. "Not that we're not used to the splendour of nature's bed, of course."

"Mmm… Rocks and roots in my back. I love it so," said Erika with an eye roll.

Harper chuckled at the nomad woman's rare humour.

"No. We shall go. If I—*we*—are to visit Valtivar at all, I must present myself in Keldheim," Ragnar said, though the grim set of his mouth said he did not want to at all.

"Then it's done!" Aedon grinned and clapped him on the back. Ragnar glowered at him. "Oho. I have missed dwarven feasts. And the drinks! Oh, especially the drinks. Come, come. There's not a moment to waste!" He scurried off.

Harper raised an eyebrow and looked at Brand. "Are we close to Valtivar?" she whispered to him. He bent to hear her, ruffling his wing feathers. The way Aedon had scampered off, it seemed as though they would be there in no time.

"Depends how you define 'close'." The Aerian pursed his lips. "If you have a dragon, then yes. If you're a mere commoner like us, some weeks."

"*Weeks?*" Harper gawked at him.

"Yes."

She groaned—already fed up after weeks in the saddle, and besides which, her body had still not recovered from her ordeal in Tournai. With a sigh, she hefted her pack, a gift from the grateful villagers, onto her back and followed her companions down the winding trails of the forested foothills.

Now they had left the village and the Well of Life behind, there was little to gossip about around the fire. Harper swallowed. She had not dared broach the subject yet. But her curiosity had only grown with her mountain of unanswered questions. How had he summoned such a magnitude of power?

"Aedon?" she said in a small voice.

"Yes?" Aedon blinked at her, as if surprised she had spoken at all, for they sat in a comfortable silence about the fire, all staring into the abyss of the flames, surrounded by a circle of thick trees. Their attention flicked to her.

She cleared her throat. "I wondered... The fire in the vaults. What was that?" Heat seared her cheeks, and she felt certain he would tell her to mind her own business, but Aedon simply stared at her. She did not break her gaze and he stirred, meeting her scrutiny with an imperturbable expression.

After a long pause, he sighed. "I suppose I ought to tell you the truth. That was a special gift of mine."

The others looked at him, then hurriedly looked away, as though they invaded on a private moment. Harper did not speak, waiting.

"It was a gift from my dragon," he added in a soft, pained voice.

Harper's eyes widened. *A dragon?* Surely, she had misheard.

"Valyrea," he said, even more softly. He had not spoken her name in such a long time, but it still cut him. She could see the pain etched into his face. He shook his head, and his hands balled into fists. "She was the most beautiful soul I have ever known. I have never loved anyone so fiercely as I loved her. She was my partner in heart and mind. Together, we were one. Together, we ruled the skies. I was the youngest general of the Winged Kingsguard of Tournai who had ever ascended. I was the strongest, the best, the smartest."

Harper's lips parted. First a dragon, now… she could not reconcile the outlaw criminal with one of the red-cloaked and dragon-mounted members of the Winged Kingsguard. *Aedon?* It made no sense.

His voice soured. "I was young, arrogant, and foolish. Thought I could take on the world. Together, we were so strong, who could overcome us? Certainly not goblin scum." He spat upon the fireside at the word. "I was wrong. I should have returned to Tournai, sought backup. But I did not. We flew into battle alone. Valyrea was strong, but she was not invincible. She died, yet I lived. I think this is the greater torture, a punishment I deserve, for leading her to her demise. Every day without her is agony. I have a few of our bonded gifts, including affinity with fire, to thank her for, but I would rather have her instead."

Harper's mouth hung open. "I had no idea," she breathed, barely audible. "I'm sorry."

Aedon shrugged, a tight, sharp jerk of his shoulders. "You were not to know."

"Is that why you were exiled?" she dared to ask.

Aedon shook his head. "That was the beginning, but no. For that, I was not exiled, merely disgraced. My elder brother now holds the position of general. He's welcome to it. If nothing else, I'm glad to have no part in Toroth's business."

Harper fell quiet, her mind alight. Aedon had been a dragon rider—one of the Winged Kingsguard of Pelenor— and their leader, no less. He had never given the barest hint of a clue, and the revelation was shocking. Unease curled within her. If her companions held secrets of this magnitude —what else remained untold? Could she trust them as much as she thought? She dared not spread her attention around her new friends. For as much as they had saved her life on several occasions, she had to remind herself that she still did not really know them enough to trust them intimately.

Life was very different in Pelenor. With each passing day, it only seemed more so. She looked to the dell of trees sheltering them, keeping the dark night at bay. There was so much more out there. For all Aedon's sorrow, she could not help but feel a thrill of anticipation and anxiety at the thought.

As they stirred to make their resting places for the night, Harper stepped close to Aedon and placed a gentle hand upon his. "Thank you for sharing that." Her heart thundered so loudly, she could barely hear her own whisper. He was just as handsome with grief, though in a different way. To her own annoyance, her attraction to him had only grown after their adventures, though she berated herself for it every time she thought of him with infatuation—for he was nothing like the thrill of *that* pair of violet eyes and the sharp sneer that she so desperately tried to distract herself from.

His fingers squeezed hers in silent thanks, and he smiled sadly as his green eyes, golden in the fire's light, met hers. "Good night, Harper," he said softly. She wanted and hated the way that her stomach swooped at his words.

5

AEDON

rand watched Harper bed down for the night, then his stern gaze flicked to Aedon, who stood brooding into the fire.

"A word." It was not a request.

Face blank, Aedon followed him away from the others, but annoyance seethed under his skin. He knew that face.

"Stay away from her," Brand growled.

Aedon scowled. "I beg your pardon?"

"Harper. Stay away from her. I can see a mile off the girl has an infatuation with you that you ought not encourage."

Aedon drew back, then puffed out his chest with indignation. "Who says it's any of your business?"

"The fact we all live together, for one." Brand scowled at him.

"I can do, or not do, whatever I please."

"Stay away from her," he growled again. "I've seen it time and again with you. You let these casual romances throw themselves at you, then leave them broken-hearted because you're too scared to open your heart again. Not Harper. She's one of us now, and she needs us. I won't have you breaking her, too, for she'll be truly lost and alone then."

"Well, I—"

"Promise me."

"I don't reall—"

Brand stooped to his level and shoved his face, bared teeth and all, toward Aedon's. *"Promise me."*

"I promise I won't be irresponsible, if it'll make you feel better." Aedon recovered some of his customary swagger and rolled his eyes. "I didn't know you were the sentimental type." He dared to pat the giant Aerian atop his head of tangled hair.

Brand snapped his head back, away from Aedon's reach, and glared at him. "It's not a joke. I'm serious."

Aedon glowered back at him. "If you're so serious, sort out your own love life before preaching to me."

The feathers on Brand's wings flared. "What's that supposed to mean?"

"You know exactly what I mean. You two must think we're all blind. You need to take your fucking further into the woods if you think to keep it a secret, brother." Aedon considered the Aerian a brother and the nomad a sister, for they had been through so much together that deeds bonded them deeper than blood. Whilst he judged neither of them for what they decided to do together, he didn't need to hear it—nor be reminded of his own lacking love life.

"That's none of your business. Don't change the subject, *elf.* Keep your word." Brand ruffled his wings, turned away, and strode back to camp.

Aedon watched him go but lingered in the shadows at the edge of camp. His attention fell upon Harper's form, still wriggling in her cloak to try and find a comfy nook in which to sleep.

Her piercing grey eyes—that insolent, curious stare—swam before him. The determined set of her delicate jaw. He sighed. It had been a while, and he had missed the thrill of the chase. Surely it was harmless? Brand didn't know what he was talking about. *Bloody Aerian.* Aedon pushed all doubt from his mind.

6

DIMITRI

imitri's eyes snapped open. His bedroom was
cool, dark, and silent—as always. But a tingle
wormed its way down his spine. He lay immobile,
holding his breath, opening all his senses to the world
around him. What had awoken him?

Nothing seemed amiss, but tension coiled within him, the
silent voice of instinct speaking. He slid from the smooth,
silken sheets and stood, curling his bare toes in the thick fur
of the pelt beneath his feet. The cool air chilled his bare
torso, for he had only worn bed trousers that night. He
padded toward the door, his feet silent across the ornate
wood parquet, and pressed his ear to the wood.

Silence. Yet still, it niggled at him. He opened the door,
preparing a barrage of magic, just in case, even as he berated
himself for such silly fears in his own quarters.

"I can hear you, Lord Ellarian."

A sheet of unbidden terror—followed by the snap of
unbridled rage for the invasion of his personal space—seared
through him as he recognised the intruder. The deep, cool

voice was unmistakable. Dimitri let out a deep exhale, and some of the tension drained from him—but not all. To what did he owe the pleasure of such a late, unannounced visit? Besides which, he was not so naïve as to trust that his ally had his best interests at heart. A healthy distrust lurked within him.

Snagging a shirt, which he hurriedly threw over his head, Dimitri rushed down the corridor to where the dying embers of the hearth threw tall shadows around the room. Saradon stood before the fire. To Dimitri's distaste, he swore he could smell the stench of the goblins upon Saradon, but he made no comment on it.

"Lord Saradon? I did not expect you."

"Dimitri, is that you?" Emyria's voice quailed up the corridor. Dimitri froze.

"I have company. You are dismissed," he ordered, more haughty than he would normally speak to her, but she knew the role he had to play in public and never rebuked him for it. It kept them both safe.

No reply came, and he suppressed a sigh of relief. "Do not worry. We shall not be disturbed, Lord Saradon." He threw extra wards around them, just in case.

"Do not call me that here. There are too many wanton ears for my liking."

"Are you certain it is not too dangerous for you to be here? It is too soon to act." Dimitri quickly sketched his progress since their last encounter.

"You have done well, but yes, we are not in a position to move yet. I come to unleash my most powerful weapon."

Dimitri stilled and waited, filled with anticipation.

"You shall see." Saradon smirked once more. "Come."

They were soon in the bowels of the castle, striding down the quiet corridors with purpose, though Dimitri could not fathom their destination. Every footfall seemed too loud, a jarring clatter that would attract unwanted attention, but Saradon shrouded them so they could pass unheard and unseen by all. It seemed he wanted to wander the halls of his former home, but Dimitri did not think it was borne of nostalgia.

Past the red cloaks at every checkpoint they went, and true to Saradon's word, none stopped them or even seemed to perceive their existence. That instinct still prickled uncomfortably underneath Dimitri's skin.

Down into the depths of the mountain they went, heading straight for the catacombs that held the bodies of past rulers and their families... including Saradon's own mother, Karietta. Dimitri had not wanted to return there, but he steeled himself for it, for he knew Saradon would not turn his path now. Dark recesses passed them by. Doorways through the crypts leading to chambers, all filled with tombs. It was pitch black but for the amber faelight Saradon guided them with. Now, Dimitri could smell no goblins, but instead, the cool air filled his lungs with slow decay, of dust and dead things long passed.

It felt like a repeat of his previous trip. Indeed, he could still see the faint outline of scuffed tracks in the dust from his last visit, for no one else visited those who rested there. Saradon led the way straight to Karietta's tomb, raised from the floor with her likeness in stone atop it. She stared, unblinking, into the unending night around her. As Saradon's faelight bloomed, filling the chamber with warm light, Dimitri leaned closer. The last time he had ventured there, he had not dared such light. He had missed the finest of details upon the tomb—the embellishing of metal, the subtle details of the stone.

"Stay back."

Saradon's low voice startled him, and Dimitri dropped back to hover at the edges of the small antechamber, where the walls, hewn from the mountain itself, seeped freezing cold into his back.

Saradon shook his hand free of his obsidian cloak. The ruby signet ring gleamed upon his finger. He slipped it from his hand and approached Karietta's tomb. Dimitri waited, barely breathing with the anticipation of it. When Saradon pressed the ring to the stone lips of his mother's likeness, Dimitri could feel it building—a hum of magical energy from Saradon himself. In a low, dark voice, he crooned in a language Dimitri had only heard within the dark Order he had deserted… and it set the hairs all over his body on end. Somehow, the language made the magic grow, as though it controlled the power, but Dimitri was of elf blood, just like Saradon. Magic was instinctive. It did not need words to control it. More than that, it was abhorrently *wrong* to form magic by force, to contain and push it within the construct of words. Saradon knew that as well as anyone.

The tales had always said Saradon had no magic until his uprising. Now, Dimitri knew there to be truth to the stories that Saradon had long denied—that he had schooled in dark arts to come by his powers, and perhaps done far worse to acquire them. Once more, Dimitri thought of the Order of Valxiron. Saradon was connected to it somehow. What did he want with them, and they him? A sharing of power?

For a moment, it was as though Dimitri found himself in the chamber under the mountains raising Saradon again, for the warmth flaring within the room and the metallic tang of strange magic searing his tongue were of the same ilk. Most of the energy swirling around them seemed to flow from the ring, not Saradon. Dimitri wondered at it. The trinket had seemed so innocuous, though it was now clear the ring was something far greater. It unnerved Dimitri, but there was no time to think, for a wave of energy, heat, and light flashed through them. At the height of the inferno of noise, a crack echoed through the air as the tomb split asunder before them, the stone fractured and smoking. The magic was gone again in an instant. A sweet, cloying smell overlaid the dark, musty decay of the tomb.

"What was that?" Dimitri asked in a hushed tone.

Saradon turned to him, his face still grim with concentration. "That was the sum of our machinations, Dimitrius. My curse is once more released. This time, I shall not fail."

His curse! The bottom dropped from Dimitri's stomach as an icy fear shot through him. He knew the lore. Knew how Saradon's Curse had decimated the magic of the court until even the dragons could not stand before him.

"Come now. You had no such qualms when we made our pact," Saradon said, his eyes narrowing.

Dimitri composed himself. "Indeed. You are quite right. There is a price to pay for peace. But this… It will not affect innocents?"

"I shall make sure of it. Only those poisoned by the greed and sin of the court shall be afflicted," Saradon said quickly. "You are safe, of course."

Dimitri nodded, though he was not convinced by such easy words. "What will come to pass?"

Saradon's smile was slow and wide, savouring the thought. "Magic will leech from the court until I possess it all." He bared his teeth in a wild grin.

Dimitri suppressed a tingle of dark premonition at Saradon's words. He spoke of darker magic than even Dimitri knew, for he had turned away from that path before learning such ways.

"The court will crumble. As they weaken, I shall

strengthen. Toroth and his ilk will be as easy to shatter as glass, and Pelenor shall be mine. No one can stand before me. I have only to wait a short while before I can reach out and take what ought to have been mine. Now," Saradon added, without waiting for Dimitri's reply. "I must go. Our savage allies will not manage themselves." The goblins had accepted Saradon's proposal. The realisation slid down Dimitri's spine, cold and jarring. "I shall return when it is time. I expect you to continue our good work, and report to me in person."

Saradon vanished into the ether, leaving Dimitri in the dark as Saradon's faelight vanished with him. He looked toward the exit. He did not fancy walking all the way back, so he conjured his own faelight and faded from the living plane. A few heartbeats later, Dimitri stood in his own chambers once more, gratefully taking deep breaths of the sweet air. Troubled, he sank onto the couch. *"The court will crumble,"* Saradon had promised with grim glee. Dimitri would be watching to see how it manifested.

What had Saradon unleashed? Dimitri could not help but feel as though he had involved himself in machinations he did not understand, which only added to the coil of tension winding tighter in his belly.

7

LANDRY

Landry sucked the froth from the fringe of his moustache before taking another swig of his tankard. The Dragon's Horn was their usual meeting place. The landlord gave them the best price per pint for their custom, as well as use of the back room. Away from prying eyes. The guilds of Tournai valued that, and their reward flowed as golden as his brews.

That night, the back room with its clouds of tobacco smoke wafting, held only complaints as the guilds congregated to bemoan the king and his rising taxes, which bled them all dry, even as their trades dwindled with the closing of all passes east over the mountain, thanks to the goblin troubles.

Landry stroked his beard, nodding as the Master of the Guild of Bakers looked at him, the chair of the proceedings. "Yet he will not act! How are we supposed to feed His Majesty when we cannot procure any of the fine flours from across the mountains that he demands we use in his breads?"

"I understand your concern, Aberon," Landry said, his

voice even and measured. It was his duty to remain neutral, though he shared their frustrations. With his responsibility, he supped his drinks at half the rate of his peers, who grew more rowdy and malcontent with the bottom of every tankard they reached. He had a sore enough head from the hammering at the forges all day long without adding drink to it.

"Yet you do nothing about it!" snapped Aberon. "Do your forges not grow cold without dwarven ores to supply them?"

Landry frowned. "They do indeed, yet anger will get us nowhere, Masters."

As Master of the Guild of Metalsmiths, dwarven ores were the lifeblood of Landry's business. He was indeed running short of the ore he needed to forge new armour for the Kingsguard, new shoes for their horses, and all manner of accoutrements the city folk required of him. Yet the goblins were far from home—and a problem they could not solve.

He glanced around their assembled company. The masters of the craft guilds on one side, the merchant guilds on the other. He had only been elected by the craft guilds' weight of numbers, for the merchants sneered at those who dirtied their hands to earn a living. With a hand blackened by a day of forging, Landry set his now empty tankard upon the table and laid his hand flat on the uneven wood. He was not ashamed of his craft.

"All roads east through Valtivar are closed with the goblin troubles, it is true. That ought to only seek to unify us. We are all in this predicament together. None of our wares or materials may pass the eastern borders." His gaze lingered on the merchants. Frowns covered their sneers. "We need the king's help. We can only plead with him to address the issue, for—"

Aberon scoffed at him, and the merchant leaders tittered. "*Plead*? Plead with him? He will not help us. He has made it very clear that the goblins are not his problem to bear. He cannot be reasoned with! Did you not see the traitors burning?" Aberon demanded. Their company shuddered at the memory of the burning pyres that had blighted the plains before the city and a rumble of discontent laced with the charge of fear chased around the room. Aberon jabbed a finger at Landry and scowled. "That will be the fate of any who ask for aid from *him*."

Landry pursed his lips. "I can agree. Our chances are slim, but what do you propose?" He held his arms wide and looked about, challenging them all. "What can be done? Are we not all old men, moaning bitterly into our tankards, with no hope of recourse?"

And thus, the meeting of the guild masters descended back into complaints and squabbles, for no one had a solution. Exasperated, Landry slipped out and left them all to it, until their next formal meeting, where he hoped they would come with more hope in their hearts. It was their only weapon.

Landry meandered up the winding, cobbled streets to the lower middle levels of the city, on the border between the poor districts and the wealthy. His forges were near the lower end, of course, for the fine folks did not like smoke clogging their clean air. Now, however, with the dark of night blanketing all, his forges were dead and cooling, his men gone after a day of hard work.

Landry admired their work—piles of helms and breastplates for the Kingsguard—as he checked the forge, just as he did every night to ensure they were safe. His men were careful—the ashes cooled and the embers dead already. The stone houses still contained enough wood, thatch, and flammable materials for just one stray ember to damn the entire neighbourhood.

With his checks complete, he ambled up the stairs, tiredness dogging each step, to the home above the forge that he shared with his wife, Aislin, three boys, and young daughter. With a squeal, Shayla ran to greet him as he entered, throwing her arms around his legs. He scooped her up into a hug, kissing her forehead, his beard scratchy. At her protests, he deposited her upon the floor once more.

Aislin, the slender, elven beauty he still did not know how he had won, slid her arms around his giant torso and placed a soft kiss upon his lips with a loving smile, before walking back into the kitchen to finish cooking. Her twinkling green eyes caught his gaze before she turned away. Shayla tugged him toward the dinner table where the three boys awaited. It was the only time the boys were ever early for anything.

"Evening, Fa," chorused the twins in unison, drowning out their younger brother.

"Evening, boys," Landry replied and sank into a chair with a grateful groan. He washed his face and hands with the wet cloth, as he did every night, slowly teasing every last piece of grime from between the lines of his skin, under his nails, and in the corners of his face, until he gleamed, and the cloth ran sooty and black.

Dinner was soon before them—as was Aislin's wooden spoon, rapping whichever of the boys dared try to sneak a scrap before Landry blessed the dinner and took his own cut. Once he had, the boys were permitted, with a nod from their mother, to partake, but at the warning glance from Landry, they held back—though barely—until Aislin and Shayla had taken their own portions. The twins squabbled raucously over the best cuts, as they did every night, whilst their little brother sneaked out the choicest pieces as they were preoccupied. Landry hid his smile in his beard.

"Anyone would think we starved you," tutted their mother.

"Or that we had raised a pack of animals." Landry glared with mock sternness at Fergus and Finn, who grinned at him and continued their tussle. It was all in good fun. Landry had once been the self-same with his own brothers. The twins were burly boys, nearly men. They would take over the forge when he was too old to lift the hammer.

Only their younger brother took after his mother. He was slim, willowy, unsuited for a life in the forge. Like Shayla, he had inherited their mother's figure—and her magic. The forge ran strongest in the twins' blood, despite their half-elf heritage, but the younger two had their mother's elven magic and looks. It was not them for whom he worried. He hoped their blood would send them straight to the academy for the Winged Kingsguard. The twins, however… Landry sighed, earning him a concerned look from Aislin. If his business ceased, their future would also be lost.

"Are you quite all right, Landry?"

He brushed her off with a tired, warm smile, but he knew he did not fool her.

That night, when the children were asleep under the eaves above them, he tugged her close in their own bed, folding her frame into his and taking comfort from her arm encircling his waist and her head tucked under his chin. "I worry that we might not be able to sustain trade soon if this continues.

Then where will we be?" Landry said after he had told her of the shambles of the meeting.

"You have never failed us before, love," she murmured reassuringly. "We will weather this storm, if one is to come, as we have weathered all that have come before us."

He kissed the top of her auburn head. "What did a city wretch like me do to deserve the likes of you?" he murmured into her hair. Aislin had forsaken her family to marry him, a lowborn mortal in their eyes.

She let out a quiet chuckle and leaned up to kiss him on the tip of his ruddy nose. "You were yourself, my love, and that will always be good enough for me. Worry not what the morrow brings. The answer will present itself in time, and whatever it may be, we shall face it."

Landry was glad for her faith and confidence, her strength in holding him up, even in times of doubt and despair. Yet he was not so sure he could be as optimistic as she, knowing the storm that could be coming to them both within and without the guilds, caught between the king's iron will and the goblin uprising. Landry could only hope the king had mercy upon them all and would fight to open the trade routes safely once more. Without that, the country would falter, stumble, and crumble. But Landry knew Toroth, and he knew aid would not come from the king. Despite Aislin's assurances, Landry did not sleep, but stared long into the black of night, hoping for answers.

8

HARPER

edon had a dragon. The thought hounded her. Harper longed to ask more, but the hurt in Aedon's eyes did not invite prying and stilled her tongue. It was also a reminder that they were worlds apart. Not only an elf and a powerful magical being, but also a dragon rider? Against her, a commoner, even if of elven blood with slight magic of her own, it was a paltry comparison.

Her magic had become a distraction of sorts. Harper turned her hands, watching golden sparks arc and dance from fingertip to fingertip, a smile tugging at her mouth. Now magic bubbled fiercely within her, a little spring unable to be quelled. It was the fourth time that day that she had glanced down to see her fingers alight with it. In the weeks since she had been in Pelenor, she had, true to Aedon's promise, already seen the tips of her ears lengthen and point ever so slightly.

"Very pretty, Miss Harper," Ragnar said as he sat next to her upon the fallen tree. In his hands, he held his own magic —a carving. Harper had only recently noticed that all of his

46

chatura pieces were hand-carved. No wonder his fingers were stiff with the wear of it.

She grinned at him. "What are you carving?"

"A king," Ragnar said and held up the piece. Already, the delicate head and half of the cloaked, armoured king was carved from the pale wood.

Harper shook her head. "I don't know how you do it. So intricate." Her own prowess at carving wood stopped at chopping logs for the fire.

Ragnar winked. "Years of practice." He pulled a little figure from his pack, a pawn, and passed it to her. "Here. A gift to start your collection."

Harper rolled the small piece—a kneeling serf upon a block—in her fingers. "Are you sure? I cannot accept this. It's—"

"I insist. It might only be a pawn in a game of kings and queens, but even the smallest person can change the course of fate."

Harper watched him return to his carving. "Don't you wish you had magic so you could do it easily? Maybe even in an instant?"

Ragnar frowned at her. "Never. Where would the fun be in that? I derive my joy from making them, from each little shaving and cut, from the improvement of my craft. There would be no joy in making one with just a thought."

Harper frowned, confused.

"Would you want to go hunting and kill an animal upon a wish?" Ragnar pressed.

She recoiled, appalled. "No!"

"Precisely. Why?"

"Because the animal deserves the honour of a death bought with skill, not, not… *sorcery*."

Ragnar nodded. "It is the same for me. Each piece deserves my craft."

"A noble craft it is, too!" said Aedon, appearing behind them and clapping each on the shoulder. "Your *chatura* game pieces are the finest in all Pelenor and Valtivar."

"You're just saying that because you'd like a new set," said Ragnar, turning to fix him with a pointed stare.

Aedon grinned without apology. "You see right through me, master dwarf. Whom else should I ask but the finest carver around?"

"I'm the *only* carver around. Someone's got to take no mischief from you, laddie."

Harper giggled.

"Would you like to see what you *can* do with magic, Harper?" Aedon asked, an impish twinkle in his eye. "We'll have to teach you how to stop that." He nodded to her hands, which still sparked.

"Really? Yes!" She scrambled to her feet and followed him to the babbling stream near the camp. Aedon leapt with uncanny agility onto a flat rock in the centre of the stream. Harper followed suit but wobbled as she landed. Aedon's strong hands grasped her wrists and pulled her away from a watery fall. Instead, she found herself crumpled to his chest as he laughed at her, his arms around her waist. Her breathing stalled.

"Almost!" he said.

"Thanks." She looked up to find his intense green gaze upon her, so close that his lips were mere inches away. Harper froze.

Slowly—slower than he ought to—Aedon let his hands fall. His fingers skimmed down the fabric of her sleeves. Harper let out a shuddering breath at the contact, something uncoiling deep inside her. It had been far too long since she had enjoyed the touch of another—or allowed herself to be anything other than cut off and uncaring.

Aedon stepped away, and cold flooded in where his warmth had just been. He sat on the rock at its highest end, where the ledge-like stone jutted out above the water. She swallowed, taking a moment to compose herself before she followed him. Harper joined him, dangling her feet over the edge, inches away from the brook swirling around them.

She cast sidelong glances at him as he gazed out over the vista, at the stream winding through the pale trees and into a silvery pool that reflected the steel of the sky. *He belongs with nature*, Harper thought. His very form seemed a beautiful reflection of nature's bounty around them, though now it was on the steady decline into winter. Already, the ground was a carpet of fire and the trees upheld little to the sky above them.

"Autumn is my favourite season," he murmured.

She glanced at him, waiting for him to continue.

"The world never changes more than in the autumn. Nature turns to rest, and all goes in a blaze of glory as though it wishes to make itself known, so none will forget it until spring returns." He snatched a fire-coloured leaf from the stream as it floated past. "Isn't it beautiful?"

He handed it to her, and she traced the blood-red veins across its surface. It was unlike the autumns in Caledan. A greyer, darker, wetter season than the rest of them, save winter. There were no golden carpets there. No blaze of glory. She nodded. Seemingly of its own volition, the leaf danced from her palm and up into the air, where it hung, swirling, before slowly floating down to the water once more. There was no breeze. Harper raised an eyebrow.

"Child's play." Aedon winked at her. "Come. Try it. Wish

for it to fly." He plucked another leaf from the stream and placed it, wet side down, upon her palm.

Harper furrowed her brows and willed the leaf to fly. The spring bubbled up inside her, eager, yet the leaf did not move. "I don't understand."

"As I mentioned before, magic is a muscle you need to train, like any other. Just because you have the ability does not mean you possess unlimited power. You must condition your focus and strength of will to control the magic within you. Try again."

Harper tried again. And again. And again.

By the time Brand's shouts called them back to eat, Harper had barely made the leaf wobble on her palm—and she was not sure if it was her doing or the stray breeze that had picked up. Yet she had somehow mastered how to keep the magic from bubbling out through her fingertips.

Even though she struggled to make sense of it, the prospect was still exhilarating. With power came freedom. Her thoughts strayed back to the tavern she had worked at, and the lecherous drinkers therein. They would not dare touch her if they knew she had such strength. No longer would she be helpless in the world. It was a pleasing thought.

Tired, hungry, and disgruntled, she stood, her limbs stiff from such long stillness. Aedon rose smoothly, as graceful as always, and offered her his hand, pulling her across the water. He caught her scowl and laughed. "Harper, don't worry. It will come. I promise. Let me show you."

He slid behind her, his front pressed to her back, and reached his arms along the length of hers until their fingers intertwined. She stiffened at his touch, and bit down on a groan at the warmth of him seeping through her back. She did not dare move, to lean back into his touch, to betray herself.

"Relax!" he chuckled. "Look."

She felt his magic flow through them both and erupt from their fingers. At once, a maelstrom of leaves arose from the ground, as if battered by an invisible gale. Up they soared, coalescing into a giant, swirling, elegant dance. Harper relaxed at last and sank back into Aedon's chest, laughing at the feeling of magic rushing through her, and the beauty before her as oranges, golds, and reds cascaded through the air in a tumbling dance.

Aedon twirled her around to face him, his back straight. Harper knew his posture would be from his past days as a dragon rider of the Winged Kingsguard. He whirled her around in time with the leaves, somehow compensating for her ungainly steps—Harper had never danced a day in her life—until they were both flushed and laughing.

Closer they twirled until his warm arms encircled her, their faces inches apart. The way he stared at her—it was as if the rest of the world fell away. Gone were the twisting leaves and the slight nip of the cold air. Gone were the woods, and the stream, and the sky. There was only him.

Harper looked into Aedon's green eyes. She could now see they were not just green, but flecked with blue, yellow, and amber, gleaming iridescent with their usual sparkle of mirth and mischief. Aedon leaned closer. Harper's breath caught as she tilted her face toward his, his breath rolling hot across her lips.

"Harper! Aedon!" Brand's thundering voice snapped across them both. The leaves fell to the earth as the magic ceased in an instant.

9

HARPER

Warmth receded and cold rushed in as the spell of the moment between them shattered. Harper twisted to face Brand, her cheeks burning, words tangling in her throat, and frustration rearing. Why did she feel shame at being caught? She was a grown woman. She could do what she liked. Her attention snapped back to Aedon. The elf stepped back, his eyes flashing with uncharacteristic anger as he looked at the giant Aerian striding down the bank toward them.

"Camp. Now," Brand growled at Aedon.

Aedon bristled. "I—"

"*Now.*" His tone brooked no argument.

Still catching her breath—both from the dancing and the almost-kiss—Harper stood frozen, glancing between them. To her surprise, Aedon's mouth set in a thin, grim line. He did not look at her as he strode away, fists balled. Harper's frustration evaporated as cold flooded into her. What had just happened? She had never seen Brand order Aedon thusly or seen that dynamic between the two of them. She looked at

Brand, confused and a little scared by the huge warrior looming above her, a prickle of fear lurking in her belly. What had brought on his sudden anger?

Brand's gaze softened as he saw her wide eyes. "Are you all right, Harper?"

She nodded mutely, resisting the urge to bring a trembling hand up to her lips. Brand moved closer, and Harper angled herself defensively, lowering her weight so she could run if needed. She did not fear Brand as the hunter and warrior she knew he could be, but Harper knew something was afoot, and it set alight her instinctive desire to flee.

Brand stopped and held up his dark palms. "I don't mean you any harm. I'm sorry to intrude, but it's for your own good." He looked away and rubbed his hand across the back of his neck.

Harper frowned. Was he… *embarrassed*?

"You ought not to have such dealings with Aedon," he said awkwardly, still not meeting her eyes.

Harper felt both intrigued and indignant. "It's not your business," she uttered rebelliously, though embarrassment sent a blush to her cheeks.

"Yes, it is. You both travel with us. That *makes* it our business. But more than that, you are our companions. We care for you. It's best for both of you if you do not become involved."

"Why?"

Brand paused and chewed on his lip. He still would not meet her gaze. "When Aedon lost Valyrea, something within him broke. It has never healed, and he has never been able to truly love anyone or anything. Of course, he has dallied with maids from here to the blue seas—"

Harper spiked with a sudden dark rush of emotion that stung as it blitzed through her.

"—and never has he left anything but broken hearts in his wake. I will not allow that for you, and I will not see him hurt himself once more."

Harper did not know what to think of that. It was not what she had expected.

"Will you heed my advice?"

She looked at him as he met her gaze at last. "I'm not a child," she eventually said, and raised her chin to him. "I appreciate your care, but I make my own choices, whatever they be."

She could not forget the way Aedon's warm, glowing skin surrounded his bright green eyes, or the way his hot breath felt against her lips, or the way the promise of his kiss had made her stomach flutter. She would not lie to Brand, or herself, and promise to walk away.

Brand's shoulders slumped with a mixture of disappointment and resignation, but he nodded. "Come, Harper. Back to camp. Our meal is ready."

It did not have to be anything serious, she thought. She had never needed a man before, and nothing had changed. She would be damned if she denied herself a little fun.

Aedon kneeled at the fire, glowering as much as the logs he stoked. Ragnar and Erika sat in tactful silence.

"Oh good. We're ready for you," Ragnar said with a rush.

"Sorry for the delay," Brand mumbled. He sat next to Erika, who offered him a choice morsel skewered on a sharp stick from the fire. He took it gently, his fingers brushing hers, and murmured his thanks.

Erika stiffly picked up her own stick and ate, not looking at anyone. Refusing to, Harper realised. She glanced between Brand and Erika. How had she never noticed it before? The way they gave to each other in silent appreciation. The strong bond they had when sparring. The close camaraderie

—closer than they had with any of the others—a silent affinity. The way they disappeared into the woods alone sometimes—but returned together. Or vice versa. Harper wondered if there were anything more to it. The corner of her mouth quirked up in a small smile.

When they rose simultaneously after finishing their food to go and train down near the stream, Harper was almost certain of it. She could have laughed. Brand had no call to question her or Aedon's actions if he performed the same dance with Erika.

"Yes. The irony isn't lost on me, either," said Aedon darkly as he caught her watching them leave.

Ragnar looked between the two of them in confusion.

"Brand and Erika... The not-so-secret romance," Aedon clarified for him.

"Ah, yes. And the irony?"

"Oh, nothing," Aedon said breezily—as he did, Harper had realised, when purposefully avoiding answering. "Harper has finally twigged."

Ragnar pursed his lips. "They're a funny pair. Never known anyone like them."

"*Funny* isn't the word."

"What do you mean?" Harper asked.

"Oh, just the two of them. You've seen how they are, together and apart," Aedon said, gesturing a hand after them. "Not exactly *normal*. Both running from their pasts and what haunts them, always dancing around each other. It makes me want to bash their heads together and tell them to get on with it and be happy already."

Ragnar snorted with laughter.

"Brand told me a little about himself... and Nyla."

Ragnar's mirth faded. "Yes," he said sombrely. "To this day, he blames himself, and her death haunts him. I don't know that he'll ever let go of her—and put her to rest enough to move on."

"But… It wasn't his fault that she died, was it?"

"Honestly, we cannot be sure. I think only he knows the truth of what happened. But he has always taken it upon himself."

"And Erika?" Harper dared to ask. She still knew almost nothing of the reclusive nomad woman.

"If she has not told you, it is not ours to tell," said Ragnar, glancing at Aedon, who nodded. "Suffice it to say, she has endured far worse than us all."

He left it at that. Harper hung onto the cryptic clue, wondering how Erika's past could be worse than Ragnar's exile from his people, the death of Aedon's soulmate dragon, and the murder of Brand's heart.

Still so many questions. Every time she made headway, finally feeling like she began to understand, she found herself tossed into the gale like a leaf again. Harper could not help but rekindle that swell of something warm in her chest at the thought of leaves dancing in the wind and the feeling of being within Aedon's arms. She wondered if either of them would heed Brand's tense warning. Harper glanced at Aedon, but his gaze was on the fire once more, brooding.

10

SARADON

It was the darkest hour of the night. Afnirheim, the dwarven stronghold to the east of Valtivar's capital, Keldheim, slumbered, unaware of the nightmare that was about to unleash itself upon the dwarven city.

The last sheaf of rock crumbled away, opening a fissure to what lay beyond. It was only slightly less pitch black than where they stood. Saradon detested the cramped tunnel, but he bore being hunched over without complaint. It was time to show his goodwill to the goblins, fulfilling his end of the bargain, so they would serve him when the time came. Around him, they shrieked and chattered with excitement as the rush of cool, fresh air whooshed past them. Saradon breathed a sigh of relief. Even his wards had not been able to shut out the most permeating of the goblins' stench.

Behind him, the horde awaited the *pascha*'s signal. They filled the honeycomb of roughly hewn and hacked passages, which tunnelled through the rock, like a rot creeping from the depths to snare the roots of what grew above, for that was what they were. A plague that would consume

Afnirheim from below. It had taken every tooth and claw at the *pascha*'s command, along with Saradon's own magic, to bind them. Goblins did not work in unity, but Saradon forced them—otherwise, surprise and success would not be theirs, and both were crucial to his machinations.

At the *pascha*'s screeching command, the goblins surged forward into the lower levels of Afnirheim. It was so far into the kingdom of Valtivar, and the dwarves had no idea they were there. Saradon allowed his face to split into a wide grin as the feral beasts surged past him. Like a tide, they swept through the caverns where the dwarven goblin slaves, the *tikrit*, were kept. All were freed from their bonds and hauled from the grill-covered pits to join the horde. And join it they did, gleefully. They could now exact revenge on their dwarven masters.

They took the settlement by surprise. Against the undiminished battle rage of the goblins, the slumbering dwarves stood no chance. It was not long before the air was tainted with the iron tang of blood, the cool quiet of Afnirheim riven by an ear-splitting, crescendoing cacophony of goblin shrieking and dwarven screaming.

Saradon had neither love nor hate for the dwarves. They were simply a necessary casualty—and their deaths were on the goblins' hands, not his own. War was coming. They would be the first of many to die. After all, the wheel had to be broken before it could be rebuilt. Saradon did not need to stay to see what transpired next. By the bloody dawn, Afnirheim would belong to the *pascha*, and the *pascha* would belong to him.

11

DIMITRI

Queen Idaelia never missed the Samhain festivities. As autumn turned to winter, the queen, who was winter incarnate, brought cold and slumber to the land. Without fail, she sat atop the dais in the king's own place as a living embodiment of the mother of all nature, a symbol of the turn of the year.

Tonight, the throne was empty.

The king did not deign to sit upon it, though it was his own, for he would not break tradition and risk cursing the changing of the seasons. Instead, it was Rosella who arrived, late and flustered, to sit in her stepmother's place. She was radiantly beautiful, but a sham, and all who dined within the hall knew it.

There were other notable absences that no one could miss. Thaeus, pleading illness, had already fled, as had some others. It created a flurry of rumours to circle around the room in whispers the king, dining with his sons and daughter at the top table, could not hear. *Illness* was some of the whispers. *Treason* others.

"Did you know Lord Khyrion hasn't been seen for two weeks?"

"Dead and buried already, I hear."

Dimitri let them gossip. He knew full well that Khyrion, one of his own now, had fled, also under the pretence of illness, to avoid the king's wrath, spooked that the king would somehow discover the very crimes Dimitri had black-mailed him with.

Toroth brooded at the top table, where a cloud of dark-ness held court. The conversation quieted around him, for his foul mood dared anyone to speak just one word he did not like. Dimitri sat in silence, too, listening and observing—as Toroth had intended, but for his own ends. It was clear Saradon's Curse was at work. Some of the absences were the result of cowardice, nothing more. Other ailments were inexplicable, including the queen's. She had never been struck down by any malady. Dimitri knew what would happen next, if Saradon, and the tales of his first rising, were to be believed.

Idaelia would wither away, her magic dwindling until, at last mortal, she would die. Elfkind could not survive without magic in their blood, so intimately were the two bound. It had been easy, at first, to imagine death changing the court. But faced with those he knew dying, whether he liked them or not, Dimitri did not entirely know how to feel.

Dimitri caught the subtle beckon, the curl of Toroth's finger, to attend him. He hurried to the king's side, bending toward him. "Yes, sire?"

"I like it not. All these missing faces? It is no coincidence. Who plots what, Dimitrius?"

"No one before you, sire." Dimitri's words held truth, in a way, for he stood *beside* the king, not *before* him. He suppressed a grin at his duplicity. "They are fearful of the rumours of a sickness sweeping the city. They can talk of little else."

Toroth clenched his jaw. "I would know more. This is unlike ought I have seen before. Never has my court been so empty when all are ordered to remain by my side. You must ascertain the truth of the matter, Dimitrius."

"Of course, sire." Dimitri bowed. Glee bubbled up inside him—Toroth had no idea he had orchestrated it all, and he would have no idea what struck him.

12

DIMITRI

The hood shadowed Dimitri's face as he hunched in the corner of the tavern. It had been a long while since he had ventured out under such guises. No one approached him. He exuded hostility. He was quite looking forward to finding out the lay of the land, listening to the reports Rook and his other associates usually fetched. Rook, displaying a prominent limp, edged over to join him. They sat in near silence, breathing in the stale, smoky, sweaty air. There was much talk of discord, but little of war, and none of rebellion. The common peoples were not naïve. They knew the king's men had ears everywhere. That was as telling as anything. Dimitri stirred. *If they're not discussing war and rebellion here, where* are *they discussing it?* He had caught a few grumbles about the king's rising tithes from the group of mortals propping up the aged bar, but those had been swiftly quashed.

They moved through the city to even more unfavourable locations and ever worsening beer, until their tankards were just for show, their contents too bitter to stomach. The mood was noticeably sourer there. Right by the walls of Tournai, this inn held the lowest echelons of Pelenori society, and they were none too pleased with their load.

"If they raise those damnable tithes one more bloody time." One of the men swore.

"Saradon-cursed greedy pig swill," another growled.

Dimitri sidled closer to the group.

"Steady on, Fen," one of the man's companions said, having a strong southern accent from the farmlands. Unbeknownst to them, he was Dimitri's man, Raven. "Ain't no good mouthin' off 'gainst the king like that. His rats are everywhere! Yer want to watch yer tongue."

"Says who?" Fen challenged, drawing himself up tall.

"Ah, nobody, lad. That's who. I ain't no better off than th' lot o' ye, but if ever I knew a thing, Saradon would ha' brought us more fortune, goin' by th' old tales."

A spike of appreciation rose in Dimitri. *I could not have worded it better myself.*

Fen looked around nervously. "Don't be saying stuff like that in this city, man. The king *will* have you for that."

"Not afore he 'as you! I tell thee, Saradon would ha' brought us better luck." Raven muttered darkly to himself, almost unheard by the rest of them. They drew closer to listen. "Th' ol' tales say Saradon wanted peace for this land, but not the *king's* version."

Dimitri nodded to Rook—a signal. The man slid to the opposite side of the tavern, behind Raven.

"Hear, hear!" cried Rook in a city accent, then moved to one side before anyone could note him. "I've heard it. Tis true," he said again, now with a sharp, stern voice.

"That's codswallop," said Fen dismissively, batting at Raven with a giant hand. Raven stepped back to avoid the clumsy Fen, jostling someone, who spilled his pint over the sticky, stone floor. Raven was repaid with a punch to the jaw, much to Dimitri's regret. Before he and Rook could intervene, the entire tavern descended into a riot, with fists and furniture flying. None shouted in defence of the king, to Dimitri's pleasure, but all were keen to affirm their true knowledge of the legend of Saradon—and claim recompense for the number of spilled pints soaking them all. Dimitri, Raven, and Rook dodged through the mess outside and into an alley, where Dimitri stopped, bent over in laughter. "Oh my. I forgot how much fun that sort of thing was."

Raven grumbled, rubbing at his jaw.

"M'lord?" Rook raised a brow.

"Oh, lighten up, Rook. It's not all treachery and treason. Sometimes, a good, old-fashioned fight is enough of a solution." Dimitri grinned at his nonplussed associate. "Come on. We have other places to spread this malarkey before our night's work is done."

"I don't follow, m'lord." Raven's dark brows creased with confusion.

"And you don't need to. The king thanks you for your service," reassured Dimitri. He dismissed Raven, who still grimaced and rubbed his jaw. As the man walked away, Dimitri beckoned to Rook, who followed him back into the higher levels of the city, to the tavern where he knew the guildsmen were to meet to discuss their latest business at home and farther afield. When they entered The Dragon's Horn, the front of house was packed from wall to wall with a mass of bodies. Dimitri held back a gag as he pushed through their sweaty, unwashed ranks to the back, where he then settled by the open arch that led to the back room.

Inside it crowded more men, but the ale was thin between them, and they spoke of business and affairs beyond the ken of the drunkards on the other side of the wall. Dimitri and

Rook lurked outside their ranks, the solid line of backs facing them, listening with care to what passed within. Dissent was clear within the merchant and craft guilds. It seemed none could escape the effect of the goblins closing Valtivar's trade routes. Dimitri shared a meaningful look with Rook upon hearing that. Their unruliness grew with the flowing beer until their presiding head, the blacksmith master Dimitri could not name, stood and raised his hands to quiet them.

"I hear your concerns, my fellow guildsmen. Know that I respect all your views, and all said herein is held in confidence between us, as brothers in trade. Valtivar's troubles are our own, it is true. Yet we cannot continue to pay the king's tithes as our businesses wither." His gaze passed across them all as they listened, waiting for what he would offer them in hope. Dimitri and Rook shuffled closer, peering over the shoulders before them.

"I will speak with the head of the Kingsguard," the blacksmith offered. "I'll tell him of our troubles, and ask that he escalate it to the king's ears." He was drowned out momentarily by a round of disgusted murmurs. "I know. I know, brothers. We have no love for the red cloaks, but might I remind you, they are a hearty source of business for us all."

His warning glare raked over them, then flicked to the back of the group, catching sight of Dimitri and Rook lurking. His eyes narrowed, before he glanced away and continued. "I will also ask him the best way that we might approach the king most humbly to beg for his assistance with this matter, since it affects us all. I can only imagine that if the trade routes remain closed, the kingdom will struggle over winter at a time we need provisions more than ever."

It was well-worded. *Carefully* worded. Dimitri wondered if the smith had recognised him. If he had, well-worded indeed. Discontent still rumbled through the sullen ranks, mutterings of the king's greed and laziness, as well as their own complicit meekness in not acting more strongly. Yet a vote was taken and cast, and the smith's words chosen as their way forward. Dimitri slipped away before the guilds dispersed, buzzing with euphoria at the prospects. *The trade routes are closed.* Pelenor would be crippled by the winter solstice if they were not to reopen, if the king did not act. It was another weapon to arm himself with.

By the end of the night, six taverns had erupted in riots over the king's tithes, Saradon's name ringing in curses upon Toroth and his greed. Moreover, Dimitri now knew the guilds might be receptive to his work, if it would allow them to continue trading in prosperity. It had been a productive night, Dimitri reflected as he sank gratefully into his sumptuous bed as the sun rose, with orders to Emyria for no one to disturb him.

Dimitri received little respite, however, for his brothers and father would not be denied.

"I don't care that he's been up half the night, probably skulking around with some whore. How dare you talk back to me, servant scum!"

Dimitri roused from sleep at once at the sound of his brother striking Emyria, who cried out in pain. He leapt from the bed and charged down the hall.

"Unhand her at once!" he thundered.

His brother released Emyria, who rose to her feet, gave Dimitri a reassuring nod that she was all right, and fled to her quarters.

"You are not welcome here," he said flatly. "I will not have you in my home, manhandling my staff. Get out, Dahir."

Dahir smirked at him. "Father orders you attend him at once."

"*Father* can shove his orders up his arse." Dimitri turned away. "Get out, or I will see you cast out on your backside."

"You cannot defy him, Dimitrius. He is the head of our House." Dahir did not move.

"A House that *my* hard work gained him, let's not forget." Dimitri's lip curled. "I'll think about it. I need to sleep. Unlike you, I have a job to do. Get. Out." Flames flickered to life in his palms.

Dahir scowled at him, but stuck his hands into his pockets and strode away, like he had owned the situation. They both knew he did not have the strength to match Dimitri. *Scum*, cursed Dimitri as the door slammed shut behind Dahir so hard that the room seemed to shake. He would attend his father—and make him squirm—but he would make Damir wait. First, sleep.

13

DIMITRI

His brothers and father awaited in silence and irritated boredom in the drawing room of Damir's quarters in a lavish four-storey townhouse in the upper circles of Tournai where the nobles had their city homes. His wife, Dimitri's stepmother, curtseyed and left at his arrival, regarding him with a flat, cold stare that he replied to in kind.

Dimitri glanced at his brothers. Dahir, the middle brother, who scowled at him. Hadir, the eldest, who utterly ignored him. And Namir, the youngest, who glowered openly at him. Dimitri fixed them all with casual boredom, as usual. The mask he always wore for them. They could not hurt him anymore. The boot was now upon the other foot, and all of them knew it. He leaned against the grand, stone hearth, the fire warming him through, waiting for one of them to speak.

"Thank you for coming, Dimitrius," his father began.

Dimitri raised an eyebrow. *Thank you? What does he want?* Damir never had manners with Dimitri unless he had need of him. He looked at them closer. *Fear...* He did not know what they feared, but he could scent it upon them, see it in the nervous dart of their gazes, sense it in the flicker of anxious movement in their hands. He smiled lazily.

"We need news. Trouble is brewing. We've all felt it for some time—both here and at home." Damir meant the lands surrounding Eyre, the lands of their House, far in the south of Pelenor. "The goblin raids on the east of Pelenor, near our lands, have ceased, but I do not trust the quiet. I fear more is at work than we can see. The scum were getting bolder, yet to suddenly vanish? It makes no sense."

Dimitri said nothing, waiting for his father to continue.

Damir spread his arms wide. "And here! The queen is ill, and others besides. More use this mystery ailment as an excuse to flee, but why? For what? Others have disappeared without a single word. The court is afire with rumours, but no one knows the truth of the matter. It unnerves me to hear such things. If anyone knows, we reckon it to be you, Dimitrius. And if anyone will keep our House safe, we know it can be trusted to you."

Our House? Trust? Dimitri nearly scoffed, but curled his lip instead as he eyed them, filled with disdain. *Are they so fearful they think pandering to me will help them? Very well.* He would beat them at their own game. He would not tell them what he knew, however, or that he was behind it all. They would love a chance to grab more power for themselves, but he was under no illusions. They were not worthy of his trust. He would enjoy this. Damir worried at the signet ring upon his finger as he waited for his son's response.

"Of course," Dimitri replied smoothly. "My sources say the goblins are massing. It is of concern that they will strike the south." At Damir's lands. Damir paled at the thought. "It is a possibility. Some of my scouts have not returned... and I do not think they will now." Dimitri let the implications sink in before he shrugged and pushed off from the hearth to stroll to the tall windows that overlooked the city. "I understand your fears. By comparison, our House is as new as drying ink."

"And we are grateful for your help in acquiring our fortunes," his father said cautiously.

Dimitri stalled, his eyebrows raising as high as they could go. Had he heard that correctly? *Another thank you?* They were truly doomed if his father was so desperate as to be pleasant. It had been Dimitri's doing, though inadvertently. In exposing the old lord of Eyre and his House's treason, which had damned them all to death by dragonfire at the king's orders, a power void had left only one choice. Damir, the then steward of Eyre. He had gladly and greedily taken the reins, proved his loyalty to the king in weeding out any remaining dissent, and promptly been granted all land and titles associated with the House whose name they had acquired.

He pursed his lips. "Yes, *your* fortunes. I take no part in them." *Not as an illegitimate child.* Not for the first time, he wished his father would reveal which mistress had birthed him, but Damir had never strayed from being tight-lipped on the matter.

"That might well be the case, but we are indebted to you all the same. Aren't we?" Damir prompted Dimitri's brothers, who grumbled their assent. Dimitri had never before managed to make them all beg for his assistance. They soon would, he reckoned.

Dimitri sighed and turned back to his father, who waited expectantly. "Fine. If I hear any whisper of the goblin's movements, I will inform you." *Maybe.* Damir's shoulders sank with relief. "As for the rest of it, keep your noses out of trouble and none will find you."

"But what of the mystery of the illness? And the disappearances? The withdrawals from court?"

"Keep yourself distanced from it all," Dimitri said coolly, fixing his father in a stare. "Do your duties." His gaze flicked between his brothers. They looked away. He knew as well as they did that they had shirked their duties for quite enough time now. The king would notice, eventually, and punish them for it. It was an irony not lost on Dimitri that as the king's informer, it was his duty to pass on such knowledge. He would spare his brothers—for now. They visibly squirmed as they realised he held their fates in his hands. *Not so nice to be the one tormented now, is it?* Dimitri thought, viciously pleased with their predicament.

"Take no part in any rumour or gossip. There is more here than you know," he hinted, piquing their interest, but he would not feed them more than that. "It is critical you are above reproach in all eyes. If you do that, I will ensure we make it through the storm that is to come."

His father paled at his words. "What storm?" he asked, aghast.

Dimitri shook his head. His expression was serious, but inside, he coiled with suppressed glee at their discomfort and upset. "I will say no more. Heed my words."

And with that, Dimitri left them all sweating upon their fate.

14

HARPER

The days ate up the long distance, and the Dragontooth Mountains, which had been a low, hazy smudge in the distance, soon soared so far into the heights that their summits were lost. Harper craned her neck, trying to see them as they rode. Today, she rode with Aedon once more, as Ragnar and Erika each took their own horses and Brand soared above them.

Still, the lurching movement of the horses unsettled her, and she was glad she did not have to figure out how to ride one herself. Her arms encircled Aedon's waist firmly as she rode behind him, clinging on for dear life and looking forward, as ever, to dismounting that night, for the sake of both her sore legs and bottom.

It was as close to time alone as the two of them had—for Brand put paid to any privacy between them, lurking nearby at all times, it seemed. Harper did not know whether to be irritated or touched to begin with, that the gruff warrior had taken her wellbeing so to heart. Her gratitude waned in the face of his oppressive presence everywhere she turned, until she longed to scream with the feeling of being stifled. Aedon's silence on the matter irritated her too—he made no more moves towards her, to shed clarity on breaking things off, or to stake his claim upon her. She did not know whether she wanted him to or not—but anything would have been better than his limp avoidance. That only bred disdain in her, Harper found.

Disdain did not elicit any of the consuming inferno of feelings within her that she had only ever found in the dangerous presence of one certain spymaster whose violet gaze and domineering presence stalked through the edges of her dreams. And, when she made the mistake of falling asleep during the long rides, it was all too easy to reckon, in the disorientating moments between sleeping and waking, that it was *his* waist her arms encircled, and his unyielding muscled back she rested against. That shocked her awake quickly without fail as she suppressed the thoughts with brutal savagery.

They made for quicker progress than on foot, however, so she was ultimately glad for the horses. A sore bottom, chafed thighs, and private embarrassment were a worthy payment, or punishment, against miles of walking, Harper reasoned. Even with the lure of her magic to experiment with, it was hard to distract herself from the misery of the saddle as the days stretched on.

As the mountains neared, Ragnar, who led them, altered his course toward a giant rift in the peaks and a great valley hemmed in by sheer cliffs. The gorge penetrated deep into the range until it was lost in the twisting, turning valleys between the peaks. Harper wondered how long it would take them to get there, because the mountains were so large, they never seemed to draw any closer.

A rising wisp up ahead caught her attention. "What's that

smoke?" she called to Aedon as the wind rushed past her face, beating her hair against them both.

"A full stomach!" he said, and she could hear the smile in his voice. "It's the Maiden's Beard. The final inn on the road before we cross into the dwarven realm of Valtivar."

Harper snorted. "The Maiden's Beard? What kind of name is *that* for an inn?" In her home county they had names like 'The Anchor', 'The Crown', or perhaps at most exciting, 'Knight & Dragon'. Tam's inn, where she had worked, was called 'The Hound & Barrel'.

Aedon threw her a lop-sided smile. "Well, you've never met a dwarven woman have you?"

Harper stared at him. "They have beards?"

"Their beards are better than mine, let me tell you, lass," sniffed Ragnar, looking indignant as he palmed down the length of his braided beard. "*Luxuriant* tresses with not half the maintenance I have to keep on my wiry bush. Lucky buggers."

Harper stifled a giggle. Her heart lifted at the prospect of food—a hearty, hot meal, with any luck—and their impending crossing into Valtivar. She hoped reaching the dwarven realm meant soon reaching shelter for a longer period. Already, she missed her shack more than she thought would be possible. Her pallet back in Caledan seemed like a kingly bed compared to the cold, packed earth and open elements. Even though Aedon had now taught her how to spell against the cold and shroud herself with a blanket of warm air, she could not conjure a soft place to lay, no matter how much she wished it.

It grew dark by the time they reached the inn, which sheltered against a bluff. Harper realised that, to her surprise, the inn was a single storey dwelling of timber that seemed embedded within the very hill itself. The chimney rose through the grass above, and the warm glow of firelight danced through the small, diamond-paned windows. They picketed the three horses in the lean-to with the other patrons' mounts, where fresh hay was stacked against the most sheltered wall. The horses seemed to be as glad as they to be out of the elements, for they strained at their tethers at once to graze.

Heat blasted Harper as she stepped across the threshold of the inn and onto a rush-lined, stone-flagged floor. The heat tingled through her as she removed her cloak and flexed her fingers to ease the stiffness and chill within them. For a lone inn situated in the middle of nowhere, it was busier than she had anticipated. After the silence of the outdoors, apart from the thundering drone of horses' hooves as a constant companion, the noise was unexpected. Now, conversations assailed her from all sides, in all manner of strange tongues. Dwarves, men, and elves filled the inn, but it was a far cry from Tam's inn back in Caledan.

Here, she saw merchants, warriors, and rangers, not drunks and layabouts. Here, the air did not smell of stale sweat, pipe smoke, and worse, but musky woodsmoke, pine, and rich food. Here, the patrons seemed uninterested in the serving girls—at least before their sustenance—being more than content to flick them a coin for their service before tucking into steaming plates. Despite her appreciation of this place, smelling the familiar scent of ale upon the air gave her a pang of almost homesickness when she thought of Betta. *You can't return*, she reminded herself. *Betta will be fine*. She hoped the weathered old battle-axe would manage to survive the winter without her help.

Wooden pillars supported the low ceiling elaborately carved with nature scenes. Some were carved from giant, living root systems that descended from the trees growing above the tavern, continuing down into the earth below. Harper brushed her fingers across the smooth wood as they passed, winding through the stools and tables to the bar at the head of the room.

Flames crackled from the twin fires at either side of the surprisingly large space. One to warm the patrons, the other to cook bubbling pots of stew and a boar upon a spit. Harper's mouth started watering as the smell of meat and woodsmoke twined its way into her nose alluringly.

"Can we have some of that?" she whispered to Ragnar, tugging on his sleeve.

"I should think so," he answered, sounding offended at the prospect of not doing so.

"What can I get for yer?" the barkeep asked, flicking a practised gaze over them. Harper noticed every snag of his eyes upon their various weapons.

"Ales and your meat stew all 'round, please," Aedon said, counting coins from a purse hidden within his cloak. Harper eyed the money. She had still not figured out what Pelenor currency entailed.

The barkeep nodded and swept the coins from the counter-top in one swipe. "Wait for yer drinks. Maid'll bring yer food." He poured the fizzing, honey-coloured liquid from a cask into wooden tankards, sliding the full vessels across a bar worn smooth with age.

Once each had their drinks, they made their way to a corner near the fire where they begged enough spare stools from neighbouring tables to form their own circle around a barrel. Brand stooped, his wings crumpling against the ceiling, and he huffed a sigh of relief as he perched upon the stool, which was comically tiny under his bulk, able to ruffle his feathers once more.

"Cheers to another mission well done," Aedon said, raising his tankard.

The group followed suit—Harper scrambling to copy them—before supping deeply from the ale within. Harper groaned on the first mouthful. It was far sweeter than Tam's sour brews. She gulped another mouthful eagerly.

"Steady on, Harper, or you'll be drunk before we eat," Aedon said, laughing. She grinned at him, emboldened, but he only laughed harder.

Their ales were almost gone by the time their dinner arrived—chunks of boar meat and vegetables in a bowl of steaming stew, and a hunk of bread. The companions fell into silence, each tearing through their food as quickly as they could chew. Harper savoured the rich, honeyed bread— only a day old and hardly stale—dipped into the stew. Juicy. Tender. Rich. Hot grease ran down her chin as she tore from a particularly large chunk of meat. It dripped into the stew below. She closed her eyes in bliss.

When Harper finished, she threw her meagre scraps—a chunk of bone with a shred of meat remaining—to the hounds sprawling before the hearth. They fought over it, cracking the bones and gobbling up the leftover marrow within. The companions collectively slumped back in their chairs with satisfied groans, nursing refilled tankards, as the swell of conversation flowed around them.

"Are we safe here?" she dared to ask, keeping her voice low. Though Brand and Erika constantly scoured their surroundings for the first sign of any threat, Harper had never seen the four of them so relaxed.

"As safe as we can be," Brand murmured in reply, continuing to examine the closest patrons. "The Kingsguard turn a blind eye to these places, so they're frequented by the likes of us—and worse—as well as honest traders. They're good places for us to come. We hear a lot more out here than we do in the cities, where we're hounded by the red cloaks."

Harper nodded and glanced around. Now she could see their fellow patrons up close. Their cloaks were on the tattered end of their lives, and under each bristled a hint of weapons—the bottom of a scabbard, the haft of an axe. Long, tangled hair was restrained in braids and ties, pulled back from faces that bore shadows and scars.

"I can't understand half of them," she said, annoyed. Their voices were hidden amongst their own cacophony, and it seemed half of them did not speak the Common Tongue.

"If you spoke Pelenori, you would understand most of it. It matters not. We can listen and hear what you cannot, but I reckon you will still find many interesting titbits. Plenty of folk speak in the Common Tongue. Keep your ears open."

Harper did as Brand suggested, listening to snippets of conversations—when she could understand them—whilst nursing her second tankard and trying to still her wandering mind, freed by the drink. All spoke of looming war, the closure of trade routes south through the mountains to the dwarves and beyond, and the threat of a dark force, but Harper could understand no more of their words.

When conversation turned to Tournai, an icy fear shuddered through her, and she stiffened. It would not do to dwell on Tournai, what had happened there—or a certain spymaster. But they did not speak of Aedon, or her, or the missing Dragonhearts, or even Dimitrius. The latest preoccupation was the weakening of the very king himself. Now, they only dared speak in murmurs, and Harper had to strain her ears to hear them. From Aedon's unflinching stare into the fire and Brand's set mouth and hard gaze into his tankard, she knew they also eavesdropped.

"The king and Tournai have been cursed? It is too fanciful to believe," Erika muttered, full of her usual suspicion.

"Yet these are the most honest mouths in all of Pelenor, if only you can discern through the swill to find the truth," Aedon replied.

"If their words be true, then it is troubling for my kin," Ragnar said with a frown of worry.

"The goblins are always causing a fuss," Aedon dismissed. "I'm sure your kin have all in hand, as they usually do. You know how the goblin-kin get rowdy time and again, before your jarls put them in their place."

"Jarls?" Harper whispered.

"Dwarven lords," Brand whispered back.

"Perhaps you're right," Ragnar said, though he seemed unconvinced.

"I'm always right." Aedon winked at the dwarf.

"What concerns me more is the news from Tournai. What would be huge enough that the king be turned from seeking us for the theft of his Dragonhearts?" Erika asked with a scowl.

Aedon tempered. "I agree. *Those* are dark tidings, if they be true. What did you hear, Brand? You were closer than I."

"A curse lays upon Tournai. Those of magical blood in the court waste away daily, their powers spent and gone. The queen is gravely ill, and they say King Toroth's power wanes."

Something hollowed within Harper at those words, and the thought of Dimitri there—he had been kind to her. He had ensured she had escaped. His actions muddied the hate she was supposed to feel for him and she did not know at all what to do with that tangle. Instead, she latched onto thoughts of Emyria. Emyria did not deserve to grow sick.

"He can barely control the Kingsguard, and rumours

spread like wildfire. No one knows what passes, and in that unknown lay doubt, fear, and unrest. It is said that the common people will mass against him before too long."

The companions shared long glances. What could they say to it? Tournai was too far away for them to be concerned with.

"Well," Aedon said lightly. "At least that might turn them from our trail for a while."

"We can only hope," muttered Brand.

The merry atmosphere and raucous laughter of the inn faded into the background as they worried on this new information, until Aedon slapped the table and stood. "Come. We need to be far from here by dawn. Who knows who we may encounter upon the road if we dally too long. We stay our original course and head for Keldheim."

"We'll have to be extra careful. The goblins are sly, sneaky creatures." Ragnar's face contorted in an uncharacteristically hateful scowl. The flickering firelight threw deep shadows across the crevices of his face, making him appear even more angry. "We don't want to encounter them if they are on the rise once more."

"Duly noted. I dare say we're not planning to. What's the safest road in?" Aedon asked.

"As we planned. Take the cleft and pass Himmelheim on the dwarven road to Keldheim. The main ways will be safe and clear."

"Then it is done. Come."

They rose, and others glanced at them as they passed. Harper returned their interest with her own, taking in every detail of them. They were quick to drop their gazes against her scrutiny. They walked out into the night—bitter after the cosy warmth of the inn—wrapping their cloaks around them in a futile attempt to stave off the wind, then saddling the horses with rapidly numbing fingers. Harper tried to summon magic to keep her warm, but the best she could manage was to keep the worst of the chill from her toes.

"We travel through the night," Brand said grimly.

They nodded.

"We'll make the pass by dawn and rest then," Aedon agreed.

Harper nodded dully. With a full belly and lulled by the warmth of the fire, she had no inclination to ride through the cold dark at all. Yet it seemed they now fled a new enemy, one that skulked in the dark of night.

She drew close to Aedon, suddenly relieved to be sharing a horse—it meant his protection, too, in this strange new land. Brand took to the skies, battering them all with a gust of air as he took flight to circle above them, watchful, as ever, for the first sign of trouble.

15

LANDRY

Landry froze. His heart stuttered as the shadowy figure stalked toward him through the darkening forges lit only by their dying embers. His hammers hung from the wall by their loops, and all his tools, which could be weapons, were stored neatly away. All out of reach.

"You were at the guild meet. Why?" he blurted out.

The dark figure stopped and cocked his head. The man stepped from the shadows into the ruddy glow of the dying forge fires that cast sickening shadows and light across his face. For the first time, Landry saw who skulked. His chest tightened and his heart stuttered. He clenched a fist—a poor defence against the king's darkest servant.

"I was." The spymaster's even voice gave no answer—or hint of intention.

Landry stood ready, though he was not sure what for. What did the king's spymaster want with him? He could barely hear the cracking of the embers over the rush of blood in his own ears. Was he to be arrested? To be the latest inno-cent to be charged with treason? To be used as bait to draw out the dissent that bubbled too close to the surface? What would become of his family if he were taken?

"You need not worry. I'm not here to arrest you," Dimitrius said, as though he could read Landry's mind.

Perhaps he can, Landry thought darkly before he silenced the thought and glared at the king's spymaster with as much suspicion and hostility as he dared. "What do you want, spymaster?" Landry asked, striving to keep his voice level. His thoughts had fled—he had forgotten the man's true title, his House—but Landry was too consumed by concern at his own predicament to worry about the rigidities of politeness. He did not trust the immaculate, dark man, with his sly smile, cunning eyes, and clean hands that he reckoned had never done a hard day's work.

The spymaster flexed those smooth, unworn fingers as he stepped forward, casting himself into shadow once more. Landry took a step back. "Call me Dimitrius, Master Landry."

Landry swallowed. The king's spymaster knew everything, it was said. Sickness swooped in the pit of his stomach.

"I know you and the guilds struggle to meet the king's tithe, and other taxes, in light of the disruption to your trade routes."

Landry said nothing. He would not incriminate himself or his peers, if that was what the spymaster sought.

"What if I could help?"

Landry narrowed his eyes in suspicion.

The spymaster sighed. "I'm not trying to trap you. You may know me as the king's spymaster, but many of my duties are less… *unsavoury* than you might believe. I know the king will not listen to you. He will not aid the dwarves in defeating the scourge of goblins. But you and I are not alone in longing for a fairer country, Master Landry. The ability to live our lives in peace, good health, and fortune. Do you not want the same for your wife, sons, and daughter?"

A chill struck Landry to his core, horrified at the mention of his family. This dangerous elf knew his family in such detail? Landry's fingers twitched. He longed to feel his hammer in his hand—its strength and security—though he knew he would be no match against the powerful elf before him. Landry growled. "Do you threaten my family?"

Dimitrius held up his hands, eyebrows raised. "Of course not, Master Smith. I merely offer you... a better way forward, shall we say. I cannot promise anything, but if I could secure the trade routes once more, so the guilds could resume full, unhindered business and Tournai could remain stable over the winter, you would be amenable, yes?"

"What do you want in return?" Landry asked flatly. He was no fool. The court of Tournai did not barter in gifts. Favours were hard-won, earned through great effort, and debts were always collected when it came to the elves. He had learned that, at least, from Aislin's callous family.

Dimitrius's gaze sharpened, the affable smile fading from his face. Landry knew the spymaster had realised he could not be tricked or cajoled into whatever he plotted. "I need nothing from you, Master Smith. Nothing but your word that when the time comes, I will have your support." Dimitrius waited expectantly.

"Support for what?"

"You don't need to know that."

Landry clenched a fist. *I can neither deny nor accept him.* After a pause, he swallowed. "I will consider consulting the guilds with your proposal." He folded his arms. Unusually tall for a mortal, he was glad he stood in equal measure with the slim elf before him. He stood in silence, glaring, channelling his suspicion and fear into open distrust and dislike.

The conversation was over. *Leave*, Landry growled in his head, wishing he could utter the command out loud.

The spymaster stirred, then nodded sharply. He glanced around the forge, his eyes lingering over the curiosities within. "I will bid thee goodnight then, Master Smith. I'll return for your answer soon. Extend my *warmest* greetings to your wife and children." The spymaster's words were genial, but his eyes were hard and cold.

Landry waited until Dimitrius turned away and strode from the forge before he blew out a shuddering exhale and sagged against the wall. He hurried upstairs to where those he loved and the warm hearth awaited. There, he could shut the door and bar it against the dark of night and the spymaster's threats... and pretend they did not darken his threshold.

16

DIMITRI

Dimitri and his associates' work had been a little too effective. Riots had erupted daily in the city of Tournai over the past week. The king's curfew barely held, and it took the combined effort of the Kingsguard and Winged Kingsguard to keep a seething order—of sorts. The common folk protested the king's rising tithes, as well as the class divides between more privileged elves and less privileged mortals. In turn, the court, struck down by the mystery affliction that tore through the city and spared few of magical blood, stirred up tensions yet more, with ruthless edicts and district-wide lockdowns.

The mortals of the city took advantage of their ruler's infirmities. Shops were looted. Homes and buildings vandalised. Those of elven blood set upon and beaten—or worse. Hate toward the elves from the mortals, who had been little better than chattel to them over the centuries, ran deeper than Dimitri realised.

Rumours of instability in the king's court only fuelled the divide and the fighting. Rumours of farther afield from traders arriving in the city, of the goblin uprising sowed fear amongst the populace, fear that had been contained to the guilds so far. It seemed the goblins had already taken the roads between the dwarven cities.

No one knew fact from fiction, but caravans had started going missing at an alarming rate on the now impassable trade routes and scouting patrols simply vanished, never to return. By all accounts, a dark, brooding stain upon the dwarven lands of Valtivar was spreading. Too close to Pelenor, all whispered. Too close for comfort.

Dimitri was thrilled in a way. Here was the sum of all his machinations now fruiting into open spoils. He had barely needed to try—they roused themselves to desperate action. It seemed that Toroth had indeed grown his own hostile army, one that would eventually cast him down. The spymaster enjoyed reassuring the king whilst sowing rumours throughout Pelenor of Saradon's return in Valtivar. Before he knew it, trouble had spread through most of Pelenor, with looting and riots in all the cities, uprisings against the king, and fearful panic with the looming threat of the cursed one's return. Meanwhile, he kept his own allies as close as he could, though many had fled to their own estates and lands in fear of the mystery sickness creeping through the court of Tournai.

Instinctively, whilst the country descended into chaos, Dimitri knew it was not yet time to act. To remove Toroth would only create a power void he could not fill. Yet. But it was time to finally hint at what was to come. The mystery illness was already being called, albeit in hushed whispers, Saradon's Curse, thanks to insidious hints from Dimitri's associates. His own father and brothers dithered, desperate to flee to their own lands, but Dimitri commanded them to remain. To their growing frustration, he would tell them nothing of his plans or what he knew, only ordering them to trust him to see them through the ruin that was to come. Damir, his cowardly father, did not like being blind to the threat. Dimitri could not have cared less. There was no love or loyalty toward them. They were another tool, nothing more. And he would use them all to the bitter end.

17

HARPER

When dawn broke, giant cliffs soared on both sides and a carpet of evergreens marched across the valley mouth, herding them into a narrowing valley. After the open plains, it felt oppressive and dark to fall under their shadow. Harper craned her neck up until it hurt, yet she could not see the sky, so tall and thick were the trees there as they entered.

Her faelight hung next to Aedon's, bobbing beside them as they travelled. It was a pale imitation of his, but the first she had managed to conjure. She was proud of it, steadily fuelling it with a small trickle of magic, much like feeding a fire. Their horses plodded along, exhausted, and eventually, Aedon bade them to stop as they came upon a small stream crossing the trail.

"We'll stop here. There's water and plenty of shelter." He yawned and rubbed his eyes. "We'd best not dally too long. We can't afford to sleep all day."

Fatigued, Harper sat against a tree, cradled in its roots, and was asleep almost immediately.

After a few hours, Brand chivvied them all to their feet. With barely a word, they mounted the horses and continued. Harper could have fallen asleep against Aedon's warm back as she clung to him in the saddle, but after a while, the trees thinned, and a welcome breeze blew. Mountains passed on either side, soaring out of sight, and the ground slowly rose as they delved deeper into the mountains.

By the following week, they took winding tracks up through forested foothills, where breaks in the trees now showed the plains far below them, just visible through the foothills. Aedon told Harper that they were truly in dwarf country now, and Pelenor was far behind them. The countryside looked much the same to her.

That night, they stopped in a small clearing beneath a rocky overhang, surrounded by the dark trees. The valley was narrow, the trees unnervingly quiet. A small waterfall rushed nearby—the only sound—collecting in a small pool before it continued its journey down the mountains. Harper gratefully drank. It was the freshest water she had ever tasted; sweet and cold.

"That's melt water from the glaciers far above us," Ragnar said. "Soon, it will not flow, for all will freeze. We are lucky the first storms of winter run late this year; otherwise, some of the passes would already be closed to us."

Harper nodded, regarding Ragnar curiously. The dwarf seemed nervous and tense to be in his homelands once more, not enthused as she might have expected, but she dared not pry as to why. He had already been uncharacteristically snappy with Erika that morning and disappeared to sleep as soon as they had eaten their evening meal, not even staying awake for his customary game of *chatura* or to carve his latest game piece.

Erika and Brand slunk off for their customary evening sparring session, leaving Aedon and Harper alone around the fire. Aedon grinned at her. She answered with a small smile of her own, one tighter and more guarded. He stood and stretched. "Come on. Time to practice." Aedon had had her hone her magic skills daily in their travel, no matter how tired the pair of them were.

It seemed he too distanced himself from revisiting the intimacy Brand had disturbed all those days ago. A part of her wanted it—wanted the distraction of him, of *anything* to wipe thoughts of the spymaster she was supposed to hate from her mind. The handsome elven thief was an easier choice, after all—though perhaps no less foolish. A part of her was relieved not to have the choice before her at all.

Again, he laid out an array of rocks, twigs, and small objects of varying sizes before her, and as usual, she did her best to lift them. A few lifted easily, wobbling in the air a few feet above the ground. Others remained stubbornly frozen. Some flew through the air a few feet before they tumbled to the ground as they lost momentum.

She stopped when it felt as though all her energy and concentration had been leached from her. "Why does this make me so tired?" She groaned. Aedon seemed to not even break a sweat when he did significant magic. Aedon grinned as he sent leaves and pinecones tumbling around her. Scowling, Harper batted them from the air.

He laughed and released his hold on the objects, all of them tumbling to the ground. "I keep telling you. Magic is a muscle. Think how tired you are after walking or spending a day in the saddle. This is the same. It takes strength to perform magic. Why do you think you cannot move mountains? If it were as easy as that, all mountains would be upon their heads!"

Harper snorted at the ridiculous thought. "How long does it take to be able to do, well, *interesting* things with magic?"

"The more you train, the faster it will be," replied Aedon, but he would not say any more than that. He suddenly stood. "Come. I'll show you something else since we're here."

Curious, she followed him from the clearing along the cliff until they came upon the waterfall. Somewhere in the distance, the muffled sounds of weapons clanging filtered through the trees—Brand and Erika.

"Water is easier to manipulate, for it loves to move. Want to see what a little magic can do?" Aedon asked, eyes twinkling at her mischievously. She nodded. He reached out and pulled her toward him, her back to his front. Her breath caught as he encircled her in his arms—and she let him, her pulse skittering. What was this dangerous line they danced on? What was this precipice she dangled over?

Harper had not wanted to admit that she found him attractive, but it had been so very long since her dalliances with Alric, the tanner's son. As much as she had never desired the commitment of being Alric's wife—or anyone else's—there were other parts of his company she missed. Aedon's magic rushed through her, winding with hers, and then the waterfall no longer cascaded down the rocks. Jets of water arced from the sheet, twining and twirling through the air, until it cocooned them. Ribbons of water raced around them like a spider's web, catching the starlight, the full moon's glare, and the last light of the dying day.

"Can you feel it?" Aedon whispered, his breath caressing the side of her neck. It grazed her ear, awakening something deep in her core.

"Yes," she breathed. It was an intoxicating rush that

consumed her blood. She felt his want for the water to be free. She added her will to his own, her slivers of magic to his, and the water twisted and turned even more, until it seemed they were alone, standing in a bubble in the middle of a waterfall rushing around them.

Aedon's fingers stroked her arm as he turned her to face him. He dipped his head toward hers. Her gaze dropped to his mouth. Want and warning warred within her—the need for some escape, some release, and the risk of complicating everything. Her breath hitched as his arms tightened, but before she could decide, his lips met hers.

His kiss was fire, racing through her body as her eyes slipped shut. She opened her mouth to him, sliding her hands up his chest. Around them, the rushing of the water continued, or was it the sound of blood in her own ears? She could not tell. His sweet tongue gently teased hers, and she yielded to it with a moan.

More.

But in her mind, it was not Aedon who stood before her, but the spymaster she pictured, fighting herself with want and disgust at how fallible she was to his dark charm. His hands planed up her back. Tangling one in her hair, he caressed the nape of her neck with an idle thumb and deepened their kiss, making her moan in anticipation. And yet... no. It was not Dimitrius, but Aedon before her.

Harper stilled and pulled away. She could not—this wasn't what she wanted. The thought crushed her. She did not want the charming elven rogue, tempting as he was, easier though it would be to fall for his ready smiles and smooth words. She could not fight that she wanted precisely who she was not supposed to—someone she ought never to see again, for her own safety.

"Harper?" Aedon's magic dissipated and water crashed to

the ground around them, drenching their cloak hems. All that desire crashed with the illusion of their magic, but the drenching of disappointment and bitter shame shattered into cold shards of fear that shredded into her, for inhuman shrieking echoed off the cliffs. Chattering in a harsh tongue jarred her ears, magnified as it came at them from all directions.

Harper opened her mouth, but Aedon swore in a tongue she did not know and shouted, "Goblins!"

He grasped her hand and broke into a run, pulling her behind him. They sprinted to camp, just as the first missiles struck the rocks above their heads. Ragnar was already up, brandishing the axe he usually kept belted at his waist. He turned to them, raising it with a snarl, but halted when he saw them.

"We cannot outrun the filth," he said, his teeth bared.

A moment later, Brand and Erika burst into the clearing, faces flushed.

Illuminated by the fire's light and the moon's gleam, shapes raced down the cliff face. Harper blinked. There was no way anything could run down a sheer cliff face, but there they remained. Glints of armour and tangled limbs, churning over one another. No trace of pleasure remained within her. Nor shame. Only terror. Claws, teeth, and death raced for them.

18

HARPER

"To me," Brand bellowed. Harper surged with her companions to form a small arc placing the fire to their backs, and drew their weapons. Aedon hurled magic at the advancing tide of darkness. The blast knocked several screeching goblins off the cliff. They landed with a sickening crunch—and Erika darted forward to dispatch them without mercy.

Harper drew her dagger, Aedon's gift, with a shaking hand and brandished it before her. Erika crouched beside her with her twin blades dripping black blood. Brand flanked Harper on the other side, holding his giant, two-handed blade before him.

"Goblins hate fire, iron, and magic," he growled. Harper nodded, but her throat had closed, cutting off the scream that threatened to tear free, and she could not form a reply.

Now, the chattering of the goblins was a deafening cacophony. Their tongue was hard and savage, their shrieks even more excited as they found their prey for the night.

Goblins leaped from the cliff face and scurried towards the group, hemming the companions until they were surrounded.

Harper could not look away from the horror they posed as a current of raw fear screeched through her. They wore odd armour over their strange figures. Mismatched leathers and sparse metal plating or chainmail adorned them as they ran in a crouched position, almost on all fours, brandishing an odd assortment of weapons, from knives, to axes, to spears with cruelly pointed and serrated blades.

There was no more time to decide how she would defend herself, let alone attack, for the handful of goblins fell upon them, dozens more racing down the cliff. Brand cleaved left and right with his blade, slicing through their paltry armour. They died, squealing, at his feet. Some dodged and met Erika's mercy—a quick, silent death. Others avoided the pair and made for Ragnar who held his own against them, wielding the giant axe with more skill than Harper realised he possessed. Aedon held them back with blade and magic, but more kept coming.

Harper panicked, dithering, filled with shame at lurking behind her friends, but knowing with a deep instinctive dread that she was as good as dead if she stepped forward— and as much the same if her companions parted before her. They stepped before her on purpose, she realised, with a rush of gratitude that was complicated with yet more shame that they compromised themselves on her account. Goblin faces, distorted by hate and bloodlust, snarled at her as they approached, only to be cut down by her companions.

Pointed, filed teeth were covered in blood, which had splattered over their faces, matching the bloody handprints and gory, daubed decorations of their clothing and armour.

Their shrieks were only outdone by the terrified screaming of the horses as the goblins set upon them. Their brays punctured into silence—and Harper knew the worst had happened. She let out a ragged sob. They were caged. No chance of running.

In the darkness with the firelight throwing cavorting shadows around them, the goblins became demons of the night. Harper trembled as her companions thinned and she was forced to raise her meagre blade to fend off attack. There was no time to think as she dodged blows and struck out with her dagger, surviving on luck only. A goblin shrieked as he slipped on a pinecone from the plentiful litter on the ground. A rush of a different kind swept through Harper. She dodged to the fire's edge, where their woodpile lay.

Remnants of Aedon's magic still swirled within her and she grasped for it, pulling it together with the last dregs of her own strength. Bolstered by the desperate rush of battle, she hoped she could manage what needed to be done. Harper sheathed her dagger and gathered an armful of pinecones, thanking the skies for dry weather in recent days.

Lighting one at a time in the fire and shielded by her companions for precious few moments, Harper darted between them to throw pinecones at the goblins, sending them on their way with her own magic and willing the fire to spread. After a few attempts, the pinecones flew true, snagging in the goblins' clothing. Fire took hold in their fabric and fur trimmings. Harper crowed with renewed vigour as she became the flames, using her magic to tease them across the goblins to leap and take upon their neighbours' garments.

Aedon backed her, shooting her a fierce grin. She felt his

magic envelop hers, stoking the flames and sending them wild. The distraction was enough. As the goblins fell into disarray, trying to avoid the fiery missiles, her friends advanced, hacking them down where they stood, until the tide receded before them. A last wave of goblins swarmed from the cliff. Harper realised their vulnerability—her companions were protected by the fire, but too spread out.

Harper threw blazing pinecones until her shoulder ached with the strain, but her meagre magical reserves were almost spent and she was entirely unprotected by the fire as the fight ebbed from around her. A goblin broke through—and charged. Harper tossed her last pinecone at it, but it bounced harmlessly away before she could coax the fire to jump hosts.

Her magic sputtered. She was unarmed. Unable to draw her dagger in time. She froze in terror. The goblin was upon her, his gleeful snarl wide. His pointed teeth in her face, the stench of rotting meat rolled over her, clogging her lungs. Harper could not even draw a breath as death descended for her.

Crunch.

Eyes wide, the goblin fell to the ground as Aedon withdrew his blade and stood shoulder to shoulder with Harper. The shouting, screeching, and crashing of metal drowned out her tremulous thanks. Giving a sharp nod, he turned back to their companions, who had retreated before the onslaught, and together, they gave one last push against the goblins.

As the goblins finally fell back, Ragnar stumbled and tumbled to the ground with a strangled yell. The horde pounced upon him with relish, clicking, hissing, chattering, and screeching at their prize. Grabbing Ragnar before his companions could rally, the goblins dragged him back up the cliff face, screaming and hollering from in their midst. Brand took to the sky in desperation, but even he was too slow. The rabble disappeared into a fissure in the rock and the darkness of the mountain.

Soon, their din was lost. The silence was deafening. Ragnar was gone.

19

LANDRY

Landry hurried through the dark streets of Tournai with his cloak and hood pulled tightly around him against the driving wind and lashing rain. Normally, the rain did not bother him, but that night, shadows and the threat of the king's wrath nipped at his heels.

It had been an unproductive meet of the guilds, and worry settled in his belly. The threat of arrest was enough to terrify anyone, but their own had now been targeted. Two guild masters were missing. Their wives had already beseeched Landry for help. He knew they had been arrested, though not what for. They had committed no crime he knew of, which worried him even more. As leader of the guilds, Landry worried he would be next to suffer the king's wanton moods.

He was only glad that he remained free… for now. The spymaster's dark presence dogged his steps. He still worried that it was some elaborate trick of Dimitrius's. He still had given no answer to the spymaster, who had not approached him again. Landry felt like a dead man, waiting for the axe to fall. The promise of Dimitrius's return was a threat that grew worse for the waiting.

Aislin threw herself into his arms the moment he entered their home. She had clearly been dithering, waiting for him to return.

"Oh, thank goodness you're home. You're so late. I worried…" She bit her lip, not wanting to say what she had worried, but he knew.

That I was not coming. His chest seized as his heart splintered. To protect her—his family—was his purpose and to know he could not do so in the face of greater power than his own threatened to break him. "I'm fine. Don't worry, my love," he said in a voice lighter than he felt, but she looked at him with creased brows, her green eyes flashing with worry.

She searched his face. "You're *not* fine, though, are you? I heard. Aberon has been arrested now, too, hasn't he?"

Face ashen, Landry could not deny her.

"You must turn from this madness, Landry. I cannot see it happen to you, as well. I fear what the king will do to all those he has arrested. I could not bear it if you were taken."

"I shan't be taken, Aislin. I pro—"

She stepped back. "Do not promise what you cannot keep!" she warned.

Shayla sidled from the kitchen, eyes wide. "Papa?"

Landry straightened at the little girl's presence, and Aislin blanked the consternation and frustration from her face.

"Good evening, my little ember." Landry smiled as warmly as he could. "Where's my evening hug?" Shayla dashed forward to be scooped up into his arms for a scratchy kiss. "Now, go see that the boys are ready to eat."

Shayla scrunched her nose in distaste as she wriggled free and ran up the stairs, shaking dust from the ceiling above her parents with every thunderous step as she raced to fetch her brothers for dinner.

Landry met Aislin's concerned gaze once more. His wife stood with her arms folded. That was never a good sign. "You need to keep your head down, for the sake of the children and I," she said in a low voice.

"I know what I must do," he said, more gruffly than he intended. "I am not so foolish as to act, no matter how riled up and scared everyone else is. Half the guilds are for supporting the spymaster, half against. Thus, I shall act neither way."

Indeed, half had wanted to accept Dimitrius's offer in their haste to secure the trade routes once more, but Landry was glad that enough shared his own trepidation at trusting the shadowy spymaster. It marginally lessened the pressure to act.

"But you don't feel safe?" Aislin echoed the fear he did not name.

Landry shook his head, sighing. "I'm considering sending you and the young ones away. I'll keep the twins with me, I need them to keep the forge going, but Shayla and her brother are too young for any of this." His voice dropped to a whisper. "And you are too precious."

"I'm not going anywhere." Her eyes narrowed in defiance, before flicking upwards. Above them, the house rumbled and shook as their four offspring barrelled down the stairs for supper.

"If it gets any worse, you must. I know you don't want to, but your family will take you in, if needed," Landry said.

"It won't come to that," she hissed as their children ran between them to the table.

Landry hoped she was right, but misgivings lurked in his stomach, and as he sat to eat, he chanced a look through the window. Another building in the city burned. The looters were out again.

I cannot send her away. I cannot let her stay. I cannot remain. I cannot leave.

The food tasted like ash in his mouth, and the walls felt too thin to protect them from the threats that lay too close to their door.

20

DIMITRI

Thick, choking smoke clogged the city. The plains before Tournai were blackened. From the upper reaches of the city, Dimitri watched the pyres burn, shaking with anger. Toroth had shown his hand. It only fuelled Dimitri's desire to crush him. Hundreds from all walks of the city, from lords right down to the half-elf who owned the tavern by the gate, had burned. All for treason—and all innocents. All for rumours of Saradon, or criticism of the king's own failures to keep the trade routes open.

The king had shown how fear and insecurity consumed him. Mere rumours and slights had doomed all those now who burned before the city. Despite Dimitri's careful assurances that no direct names had been found, that the city was loyal to him, the king had gathered up anyone he had seen as a fitting target and condemned them. Death by dragonfire for all. The great, black dragon still wheeled above the city, as if surveying its handiwork with pride.

The full force of the Kingsguard flooded the city to keep peace, for the people revolted in their open fear, anger, and hate of the king. With the troubles, food was scarce—though not at the king's table—and the mood volatile. A spark, ready to burst into flames. Dimitri only felt regret that ordinary folk—the downtrodden like him, who he had done all this for—had so far suffered more than the blasted king. He wondered whether the guilds would stand with him now. Soon, he promised himself. It was almost time. He could not wait for Saradon to sweep in and kill the king.

As he walked toward the great hall to attend the king, Raedon stormed the same way, visibly seething. No doubt because responsibility to keep the peace fell upon his shoulders, yet it seemed to be an evermore impossible task. Inspiration struck him.

"General!" Dimitri called across the courtyard, for Raedon strode so quickly, head down, that he had not noticed the king's spymaster. Raedon stopped and looked up. His scowl deepened when he saw who had summoned him, then he turned away, striding off once more.

"Wait."

Raedon did not stop, and Dimitri was forced to run after him, much to his annoyance. He stepped in front of Raedon, forcing the general of the Winged Kingsguard to halt.

"What do you want, spymaster?" growled Raedon. "Get out of my way." His voice carried across the still air.

"Meet me in the rose garden at the next bell if you want to find out," murmured Dimitri.

He strode away without looking back. He did not need to in order to know Raedon was hooked by curiosity, because he had not moved. He would come. Dimitri was certain of it.

Raedon stalked between the bushes. He had removed his distinctive red cloak and ceremonial garb, and wore only his usual scuffed, working leathers. He cast a striking contrast to Dimitri's smooth, black robes. Tousled, sweaty hair, fresh from his patrol of the city, compared to Dimitri's coiffed elegance.

"What do you want?" His voice was flat as he stood a healthy distance away, arms folded, eyeing Dimitri with distaste.

Dimitri ignored his rudeness. Relief prickled between his shoulder blades that the general had heeded his summons, but safety was not his yet. "The Kingsguard is struggling. I hear attacks upon the red cloaks have increased this week. I am correct, no?"

Raedon's deepening scowl was his only answer, but it was enough.

"Worry not. We are warded. This is a conversation that ought not be overheard." Thick rose bushes enclosed the small, round, paved courtyard in a cocoon of privacy. None would see them there.

Raedon frowned, but he did not speak. Dimitri surmised Raedon was curious enough to at least hear him out.

"The king is not himself," said Dimitri evenly. "You have noticed, yes?"

Raedon did not move for a long moment, then nodded sharply.

"And, naturally, it is your job to clean up this mess. It will get worse after today, you know." Dimitri referred to the burnings.

Raedon gritted his teeth and muttered something under his breath, his hands flexing as though they longed to clench into fists.

Dimitri leaned forward. "Hmm?"

"*Fool*, I said. Damned bloody *fool!*" Raedon seemed to feel better for being able to curse the king aloud—and now his hands were fists, and they shook.

"Yes. It was ill thought out. I did what I could to prevent it, but of late, he sees threats where none exist. It's as if he thinks the very shadows are out to get him." At Raedon's incredulous look, Dimitri nodded. "I swear it. I tried to avoid this, but you know how wilful he is. Once an idea takes him, a dragon could not pry it from his grasp."

Raedon grumbled his agreement. "What do you want, Spymaster?"

"I extend an offer of alliance toward you, General. We might not like each other, but we can work together."

Raedon's eyes narrowed sharply, filled with distrust. "For what end?"

"That depends. I seek a Pelenor that is peaceful and prosperous. What do you desire?" Dimitri hoped he was right to voice such things aloud to the general. He would not hesitate to punish him in Toroth's name. He hoped he had the measure of Raedon right. That he, too, grew disillusioned with the king. Raedon's eyes narrowed further. "It's not a trick question."

"Then you ought to know I desire that, too. I am duty-bound to make it so."

"Of course—and the situation we find ourselves in at present could not be further from that. Could not be moving further away from that," he added pointedly, meeting Raedon's glare.

"What are you proposing?" the general asked guardedly.

"If the king is not fit to rule..." Dimitri left the sentence unfinished, the words hanging in the air.

"You are an idiot if you think I will help you—"

Dimitri scoffed in disgust, cutting him off. "I do not want

that. Don't be ridiculous." He might have wanted power and security, but he was not foolish enough to desire a throne. "Who are you bound to serve, General? The people and the land… or the king?"

"I won't betray my king," Raedon said stubbornly.

"A quality to be admired, to be sure." Dimitri paced around the area, like a predator circling prey. He stopped to admire a rose. "Yet where has it gotten you? Over the years, you have followed orders you did not agree with. I know precisely what you have done."

Raedon scowled again. "I don't need *your* judgment. You've done far worse, no doubt. I've done my duty. I am bound to serve."

"As are we all. But maybe that doesn't need to be the case. Maybe we can serve without compromising everything we stand for."

Raedon scoffed.

Dimitri allowed himself to chuckle. "Yes, quite. Not under the current paradigm. I will give you that." He shrugged, fingering the rose and letting it drop. "All I'll say is, with the current troubles in the city, which my reports tell me are spreading across the realm, and the illness that seems to be striking down half the court, including our own queen, I do not think Pelenor will hold much longer without some hope. We need a strong, fair leader to navigate us through this mire. To see Pelenor through to the other side, intact. I do not think Toroth is that elf."

Dimitri slyly examined Raedon under the pretence of admiring their surroundings. He could not miss the slight straightening of Raedon's shoulders. The spark in his eyes. The general had always wanted to be powerful, and there was only one position more powerful than the leader of the Winged Kingsguard.

"What would you have happen?" Raedon asked cautiously. They both knew what Dimitri suggested was tantamount to treason. But Raedon was cautious enough not to voice it.

"Just think on it, General," he said. "Who are you bound to—king or country—and what is your duty?" Dimitri turned and left, his smile hidden. It was child's play manipulating egos.

When Dimitri returned to his quarters, a note waited amongst his daily post. It was written in a charcoal stick, partly smeared by the hand that wrote it, upon a rough, dirty parchment scrap that had been torn from a bigger sheet. This had come from a smithy. Dimitri held up the crumpled paper.

"We will stand."

He smiled, the satisfaction seeping through him in a wave of warm elation. The guilds were his.

21

HARPER

arper stared at her companion's pale faces as they stood in the deafening silence. Nothing stirred but the fire. Each spun slowly, taking in the clearing. It looked like a battlefield. It *was* a battlefield. Dead goblins littered the ground, and black blood pooled upon the dirt and grass. The bodies of the horses were most forlorn of all. The goblins had brought the beasts a cruel death they did not deserve. Harper could not look again. She had already vomited everything in her belly. Now the goblins had Ragnar.

Aedon voiced their worst fears. "We cannot hope to rescue him, can we?" he asked dully.

Brand shook his head. "If we found our way in, we would not find him or our way out."

"What will happen to him?" Harper asked. It emerged as a whispered croak, for she had gone hoarse with shouting during the fight.

Aedon's eyes darkened. "I dare not imagine. At the very

least, they will torture him for sport. I doubt they will give him a swift death."

"We need help to hunt them, before the worst happens." Erika was more grim than usual. She stared up at the rift in the rocks, as if she could will Ragnar from the mountain's bowels.

"Yes," said Aedon heavily. "Now we have ever more need of the dwarves. And no horses."

"How far away are we from Keldheim?" Harper looked between them all. Brand and Erika looked to Aedon, who answered.

"A few hours from the road, then less than a day of hard travelling."

Brand ruffled his wings. "I can fly quicker. Forewarn them."

Aedon nodded jerkily. "Yes. They will act. Goblin uprising or not, their pride will suffer for it, regardless of Ragnar's position—that should aid us further."

Position? Harper wondered. There was more to Ragnar's story than she knew, but their cryptic clues made no sense.

"I'll leave at once. You, too?" He looked to the rest of the group.

Aedon nodded.

"They will return," said Erika darkly. "If we want to live through the night, we must go. We need to be far from here by the time they return."

Harper glanced up at the dark fissure apprehensively as shivers crawled down her spine. She did not want to meet a goblin ever again. That was certain. Could she still hear their chattering, or did it simply still ring in her ears? Hands shaking, Harper grabbed her pack from where it rested—and promptly dropped it. The contents spilled out and she let out a strangled curse, flexing her hands and willing herself to pull together. They had no time to waste, and the back of her neck prickled as though the goblins watched them from the cliffs. She roughly re-packed it and hoisted it onto her back. Her companions followed suit, then Brand, with a short nod and a glance at them all, launched himself into the air.

"Fair winds to you, my friend!" Aedon called. Brand raised his hand in salute and wheeled into the sky.

"Come," said Erika, striding away from the destruction. Her hard voice held a sense of urgency, and Harper followed at a jog. The woods felt darker and more menacing with only the three of them. Harper already missed Ragnar's steady, reassuring presence and Brand's protective bulk.

They travelled as swiftly as their aching, tired bodies would allow. The rush of battle faded, and Harper hurt from head to toe. She did not complain but pushed harder, chased by the threat of goblins snapping at their ankles. Erika led, blade drawn, guided by Aedon's tiny faelight. He kept it dim, for they wished to pass unseen, as he brought up the rear. Harper did not dare walk with her dagger out, for the treachery of roots under their boots had already tripped her once. Aedon's long strides followed Harper, making the shadows stalking behind them feel slightly less threatening, as they all stared into the night, tight-lipped for the first hint of any trouble.

Travelling in the dark was painstakingly slow, for they had such little light to go by, only a tiny game trail to travel, and Aedon's and Erika's memories of the way. It was impossible to journey silently as they stumbled through bushes and over roots. Even their quiet passage sounded like they wantonly crashed through the night. On high alert, her senses scanning their surroundings, Harper was certain they would be found by the goblins. She strained her ears to hear the first sound of their chattering approach.

With a cry of relief, Aedon pointed ahead. Harper spied the pale ribbon of stone winding through the trees. A few minutes later, they emerged onto the road. Lined with pale, flat, octagonal stones, it was a road the likes of which Harper had never seen before.

"Dwarven craftsmanship," Aedon said with a tired smile that was more of a grimace. "It'll make our passage easier. Come." He set off at a jog, followed by Erika.

Harper groaned and followed them, but her legs were so stiff that she grew farther and farther behind. Aedon turned and noticed her falling back. He stopped, waiting for her to catch up, whilst Erika continued forging ahead.

"I'm sorry," she gasped. "I can't push any harder."

"It's all right," he murmured. He grasped her hand. Through his warm palm, she felt his magic travel to her. It filled her with a warming glow that pushed aside the least of the aches and banished a little of the tiredness. Her knees threatened to buckle all the same. "Come on," he said, tugging her with him.

They broke into a jog. She was relieved to keep pace with him now. They jogged behind Erika, who did not slow. Trees passed as the steady *thud, thud, thud* of their boots on the stones ate up the distance.

By the sun's rising, Harper had lost track of time, having no idea how long they had been going. With the sun finally clear of the horizon, Aedon stopped and stretched. Erika halted at his bidding, though she seemed reluctant. The moment Harper stopped, she collapsed to the road, her legs seizing with cramps that sent shocks of pain through her body.

"We must halt for a brief respite. The sun is up. The goblins will not assail us now. We can afford to rest for a couple hours," said Aedon.

Harper needed no encouragement, for she was hollow with weariness. Aedon left the road and Harper crawled after him to a cleft free of damp and rocks. With not another word to her companions, she fell asleep curled against the trunk of a great tree. Harper's exhaustion-laden nightmares were of goblins and dark places.

The rhythmic drum of traffic on the road woke them not long later. Aedon jumped to his feet. "Dwarves! I'd know that sound anywhere!" He rushed to the side of the road, followed by Erika and Harper, who still rubbed sleep from their eyes.

Ragnar's kin approached in lines of four dwarves abreast, all running in formation and keeping perfect step. They wore leather armour covered with metal plates and embellishments, and all had double-headed axes strapped to their backs, and a mace and knife at their waists. Helmets capped their heads, leaving their faces clear, apart from a simple nose guard, and braided beards bounced on their chests with each stride.

"Hail and well met, friends," said Aedon, stepping forward. "I bear urgent news and seek your assistance for one of your own."

Their captain stopped and gave them a once-over with no small measure of suspicion. His company came to a halt and readied themselves behind him, placing hands on weapon handles. "And you are?"

"Aedon Lindhir Riel of House Felrian. My companions are Erika of the Indis and Harper of Caledan. We were travelling with Brand of the Aerians, who even now flies to Keldheim… and also we travelled with Ragnar Dúrnir."

The dwarf's brows furrowed. "*Dúrnir*? Ragnar *Dúrnir*?"

Harper glanced between the pair of them. This individual knew Ragnar—there was something here she did not understand, and it made her uneasy.

Aedon straightened. "Yes. He was taken in an ambush by goblins to the north of here last night."

The dwarf bared his teeth. "The scum are becoming bolder, I fear. You are fortunate to meet us indeed. We also travel to Keldheim. Join us. We will see you safely there."

"I thank you, ah…" Aedon bowed, then raised his eyebrow expectantly at the dwarf.

"Jarl Halvar."

Harper's eyes widened. He was a dwarven lord.

"My thanks, Jarl Halvar. We shall not delay you any longer. Our own news requires the swiftest passage we can bear."

"Fall in," the jarl ordered.

22

HARPER

The world faded in and out once they reached the gates to Keldheim. Harper swayed with exhaustion from one step to the next, forcing her sluggish feet to move and begging her fading mind to stay awake. Before her, a sheer rock face soared into the heavens. Above, low clouds drew in and darkness settled, shrouding the summits. The rock blazed with light, embellished with metal carvings as far as Harper could see. Golden light danced from the stone, making the sea of metal glitter invitingly. Long, slim, octagonal holes punctured the rock at regular intervals, through which more light spilled from the bowels of Keldheim.

Great stone gates rose before them, complete with the same metal details. They barred the way into the heart of the mountain realm, and thudded open to let the company pass. Instantly, the rhythmic tramp of the dwarves' steps magnified tenfold, echoing as they passed along a high, wide tunnel. Harper and her companions followed the dwarves as the gates boomed shut behind them, sealing them into the mountain.

It was surprisingly light inside. Metal-and-glass lanterns filled with warming glows lined the walls and hung from high ceilings. Harper breathed a sigh of wonder as they stepped from the tunnel farther into the mountain. It was as if the entire interior was hollow. Buildings and ways climbed the rock, but none were open to the sky, though far above them all, a great orb of light cast the muted glow of a sunset upon them.

Ducts—some carrying flowing water, others roads and paths—spanned the space upon giant columns that disappeared into the depths. Harper dared to look over the side of the bridge they had emerged onto, but her stomach swooped as she saw just how far down the dwarven city went.

Ragnar wasn't joking, Harper thought as she recalled how he had told her that Keldheim was vast and sprawling, only a little of it above the level of the ground outside the mountain. Jarl Halvar led them across the terrifying abyss, under which the mountain continued down, filled with dwarven dwellings and buildings built into the very mountain itself. They took another turn onto a sloping ramp that led down one level and then another, until Harper was entirely lost—and when she looked up, could not see where they had entered the mountain.

"Dismissed," Jarl Halvar called to his troops. They sped up with an extra spring in their step as they broke formation. "You may follow me," he added to Aedon, Harper, and Erika, his troubled gaze flicking between them. He removed his helmet, revealing a slightly balding head of wiry hair, turned, and led them to a grand pair of doors.

"This is the königshalle, the king's hall," he added for their benefit, and Harper was glad. Her companions might already have been familiar with the place to any degree, but already, she felt as though she was drowning, swept away in a tide she could not fight against, into this new place. What ought she to expect here? Would this court be as dark and terrible as Tournai's? Would the dwarven ruler be as cruel and dangerous as the King of Pelenor? Her nails bit into her palms as she staggered after Aedon with the last of her strength.

At Jarl Halvar's bidding, guards in uniform much like his own, though with different colours and embellishments woven in, heaved the doors open to reveal a great hall. Tall slits, placed where windows would have been, were filled with what seemed to be a starry night.

"Elven magic," Aedon murmured to Harper as he walked with her and Erika. "Our gift to the dwarves in ages gone past. Have you met a dwarven king before?"

Harper shook her head. *What a preposterous question.* She did not have the energy to voice the thought.

"Dwarves respect strength, not delicate flouncing like the elven courts. Fist to your chest when he greets you. Bow at the waist, sharp and neat. Stand tall."

Harper nodded, committing his instruction to memory.

Halvar stopped before them. They halted abruptly too, their feet crunching the neat mats of woven straw beneath them.

"König Korrin." Halvar greeted the king exactly as Aedon had instructed Harper to. The king bowed his head in response, but his attention focused upon the three of them—strangers in his domain.

Harper, keeping her eyes lowered in respect, tried to perceive him. A full head of thick, black hair. A beard that tumbled down to his knees but held back in elaborate braids threaded with more treasures than she had ever seen. Tattoos flowed along his hands and the edges of his face, hinting at unfamiliar patterns and runes—just like Ragnar's. Fine clothes and leathers adorned him, tooled with patterns that matched the gates of Keldheim in both style and metal embellishments, gilded into glorious harmony with those embellishments in his beard. Thick boots gave him a strong, unshakable stance before them as he rose from his angular, carved stone throne.

"Jarl Halvar." The king's voice was deep and booming, just like the doors to his realm. "Who do you bring before me? The elf, I recognise." He spoke in Common Tongue with fluency, but Harper could not tell by his tone if he said it with fondness or malice.

"König, allow me to present Aedon Lindhir Riel of House Felrian."

Aedon bowed to the king with his fist to his chest, then stood tall again.

"Harper of Caledan, and Erika of the Indis nomad peoples."

Harper and Erika bowed, too. Harper's heart hammered as she did so.

Jarl Halvar spoke in a formal tone. "Welcome to our realm, travellers. The realm of Korrin Dúrnir, König of Dwarvenkin and Valtivar, ninth of his name, the Goblin-Cleaver, the Jewel-Blessed, and the Defender of the Mountain. What seek you?"

Aedon looked to the jarl, who gave an almost imperceptible nod. He cleared his throat. "König, we bring grave news. My companions and I encountered goblins on our journey to Keldheim. One of our companions was taken. We know not where."

"Ah, yes," the könig said, nodding. "Your friend, the

Aerian, arrived and gave us news of this. Send for him," he instructed the jarl, who bowed and left.

"You will help us, König?"

Korrin pursed his lips and turned away to pace the hall, his hands clasped behind his back. "No. We can offer no assistance in this."

Aedon's eyes widened. "König, he is your kin. Surely—"

Korrin turned and glared at Aedon for his insubordination. "The goblins are a nuisance at present, as your own journey has shown you. Our interests do not lie in delving into their midst to rescue one dwarf. There are unfortunate casualties. Our priorities are in the defence of our strongholds and roads."

Aedon's face reddened. Harper could tell he longed to snap back, but to her surprise, he swallowed his anger and pride. "Our friend is Ragnar," Aedon said delicately. "Ragnar Dúrnir."

Korrin stiffened. His head whipped around to fix Aedon in an eagle-like stare. "*Him?*"

Something cold slithered in Harper's gut. There was something more here at play than what she knew—and Ragnar's past was not as uncomplicated as she had thought.

"Yes, König."

"What makes you think that would change my mind?" Korrin's voice was ice cold as he turned away once more.

Aedon swallowed. "I had hoped the plight of your own kin might move you, König."

Korrin gritted his teeth. "There is more at stake than you are privy to, master elf. Even my own kin does not come before the safety of my people."

At that moment, Brand entered through the great doors, shadowed by Jarl Halvar. Harper's heart leapt to see him well but stuttered at his grim expression and the dark look he cast towards Aedon that promised of things which needed to be said in private.

"Show the guests to comfortable quarters," Korrin commanded. Halvar beckoned to the three of them, who bowed to the king once more and hastened to Brand.

"Well met, friend," Aedon said in hushed tones.

"This way," said Halvar.

Brand gave Aedon a meaningful glance before switching his attention back to Halvar. "Any word from Afnirheim yet, Jarl?" he asked.

The jarl's shoulders hunched. "Not that I've heard." His tone was clipped.

"Dark tidings."

"Indeed."

"The king will send you to investigate?"

Halvar narrowed his eyes. "That is none of your business, Aerian."

Aedon raised his eyes to Brand, who nodded subtly to him—Harper understood. He had something to say, and it was not for the dwarf king's ears. Harper looked between them, nonplussed. Surely, they had failed and Ragnar was doomed. What else could they do?

Brand watched the door to their rooms close before he turned to them all. For a change, he stood tall inside, his wings unscathed by the ceiling, which towered over even him. Harper brushed her arms briskly. It was not overly cold to say they were encased in stone, but she could not shake the pervasive chill creeping under her skin. The faelights bobbing high above them bathed them in warm light, illuminating a dwelling built into the mountain. Solid walls were their only reminder that they were deep in the mountain.

"What have you found?" Aedon asked.

"It's worse than we fear. Afnirheim has fallen silent. No news from there in over a week. All those who set forth have not returned. It would seem Korrin is fearful, for he musters the dwarves in secret, yet he will not openly see fit to send a full company to investigate."

"It's impossible," said Erika as she scouted each room off the corridor with her blade out, just in case, before nodding at them. "Those disorganised savages don't have the brain-power to conquer a bucket, let alone a dwarven city filled with trained jarls and their commands."

"Naturally," said Brand. "And yet, there have been some unsavoury reports, by the sounds of it. I believe this has something to do with the goblins, but I doubt they have taken the stronghold. That *is* preposterous. However, it's entirely possible they have taken the ways, which is no good for the reputation of safe travelling through Valtivar. You can bet that Korrin worries on it."

"Then why does he dally?" asked Erika with a sneer. "I thought these dwarves were supposed to be strong and decisive."

"Because to muster any response at all means he acknowledges the threat," said Harper. The others looked at her, surprised. "I've seen it before. When I was young, pirates raided our coast. The lord would not intervene because he did not want to admit he had any weakness in the first place."

Brand narrowed his eyes. "Precisely, Harper. And even his own kin's peril may not sway that."

"Who *is* Ragnar?" she asked, furrowing her eyebrows. The others shared glances that were not lost on her. She snorted impatiently. "Oh, come on. There's clearly something everyone—except me—knows. Ragnar isn't here to answer for himself, so you might as well just tell me. There's little use keeping me in the dark now." It soured her to speak so harshly to them, but being the only one who did not know what everyone else spoke of infuriated her.

Brand pursed his lips. "She's right," he said to Aedon.

Aedon shrugged. "Fine. But don't let it change how you think of him. He's still the kind-hearted, generous, level-headed Ragnar you've come to know." His words sounded more like a warning to Harper. What could be so very bad that she did not know?

23

HARPER

"Ragnar Dúrnir is König Korrin's first cousin. Their fathers were twins, pulled from the womb at almost the same moment."

Harper raised her eyebrows, her mouth falling open. "Wait. You mean…?"

"Yes. For a time, it was considered that Ragnar would contend with Korrin for the throne. Korrin, being the eldest child of the eldest dwarf, took the throne once his father passed on. Ragnar was happy to see him do it, for he had never wanted that life, nor the life of any dwarf here in Keldheim."

Ragnar could have been king—and yet he had travelled with them as a veritable pauper? A *cook*? She could not fathom who would choose that life if given a much easier alternative. It was so ludicrously far from anything Harper had thought possible. She voiced her questions aloud.

Erika laughed, a short bark. "Not everything is about money and power, girl."

Harper rankled at the derision in her tone, drawing herself up as tall as she could and staring down her nose at the nomad, her cheeks hot and her mouth stumbling over a retort. It was not wrong to seek plenty and comfort—thank you very much—she longed to say, but she could not get the words out.

Brand stepped in. "I'm sure she well knows it. Ragnar was not made for this life." He gestured at the halls around them. The stone cut into precise vertical and horizontal lines, the perfectly flat surfaces. The oppressive, silent weight of the mountain. Harper would not want to be here for a lifetime either, in fairness. Already, she felt suffocated, longing for the freedom of the open sky above her and the wind on her face. "It might be hard to believe it, but in some ways, he prefers the life he leads with us. We ask and expect nothing of him but himself."

Harper thought on that for a moment. "He said that he did not fit in here. What did he mean?"

Brand stayed with her as Aedon and Erika flitted about their temporary abode, pulling out blankets here, earthenware bowls and utensils there, delving into every nook and cranny they could under the unwavering light of the small, faelight-filled alcoves that passed for windows in the main room. "Dwarven culture is very particular. There are expectations. The higher your class, the more there are. The same is true for all societies I have seen. Ragnar did not conform to those expectations—or wish to."

"Which are?" Harper was not sure whether she had been too bold.

To her surprise, Brand sighed. "As you might expect, dwarven culture is very different to your culture, or mine. You might be expected to wed or bear children, yes?"

Harper scowled but nodded.

Brand chuckled darkly. "I know. That's how I felt about my lot, too. Ragnar was expected, as the king's cousin, to uphold their values. To war with them, to mine with them. It is not his way, as you well know. He fights when needed but would prefer not to. Whilst he loves to craft, and perhaps might be suited to turning the products of the mines into priceless pieces that would surely be unrivalled amongst his people, as the cousin of the king, he is forbidden to follow such a profession—whilst crafting is respected here, as the king's cousin, he is far above that, you understand. Several of the mines in Valtivar, and one here in Keldheim, fell into his possession as his inheritance. He could mine the minerals, the metals, and the gems, but never enjoy and enhance their beauty."

Harper turned this information over in her mind, picking over each new facet. She understood that, to a degree. And yet, she had never wanted to work her fingers to the bone at Tam's inn, or scratch for any food she could to survive. Her sympathy for Ragnar diminished. *We all must do things we don't want to. At least he could have had a life of privilege to make up for it.* She clamped down on the harsh, judgemental thought as bitterness coated her tongue.

Her sourness must have shown, for Brand ruffled his wings and cleared his throat. "I know. Perhaps it sounds wanton to you. There was one thing he objected to above all else."

Harper waited, not expecting that he would change her mind.

"The dwarves keep slaves. *Tikrit.* They're a small breed of goblins, as dim-witted and feral as they come, but they make excellent workers when compelled with whip and rod.

They're the creatures who do the dwarves' mining, in return for meagre food and working conditions."

Harper gaped. *The dwarves keep goblins?* She shuddered as thoughts of bared, pointed teeth dripping gore flashed into her mind again, then shoved the memory as far down as she could.

Brand smiled grimly. "Yes, exactly. They're not very tasteful creatures, even the *tikrit*, which are the most miserable excuse of a goblin I've ever seen. I cannot say I agree with the practice, but it is what it is. Ragnar despises the *tikrit* and could think of nothing worse than dealing with them daily, of having them in his mines, and of perpetuating such cruelty, even on creatures so undeserving of compassion."

"What did he do?" Harper hardly dared ask.

"That, I do not know. But to say that he is *welcome* in Keldheim is not the best way to put it. They owe him a duty of respect through his rank, so they will give him that, but nothing more."

Harper chewed her lip. "Does that respect extend to rescuing him?" *Or trying to.* She dared not think about Ragnar, imagine in what state he would be, if even alive, faced by the monsters that had taken him. That made the caged animal inside her, the one that longed to lash out at the confines of this tight, airless space, quail with helpless terror.

"That's what we will find out," Brand said heavily. "For Ragnar's sake, I hope Korrin decides swiftly, and in his favour. We do not have time to dally."

Harper's stomach swooped with sickness at his words, as the constant undercurrent of worry rose in her once more. No matter his value to these people, his kin, Ragnar was their friend, and he was worth saving. She felt helpless.

It was into the next day—not that they could see the night sky far above them—when they at last sat to eat a small meal, courtesy of the dwarves. The sweet breads and unknown meats with a hint of strange spices were foreign to Harper's tongue, but a welcome change from the repetitive food of the road or, worse, nothing.

After eating, they still felt too worried to sleep. The silence was somehow weighty, as if the mountain would slip down and crush them whilst they slept. Harper wondered again how thick the stone above their heads was. They sat without speaking around the empty, cold hearth in the centre of the room. Brand could not pace any more. Erika sharpened all of her blades and cleaned them twice. Aedon simply sat, staring into nothing, his hands clasped before him across his lap. No wood had been left for them, but Harper did not mind. Despite the hole in the roof that Aedon told her was a ventilation system to circulate good air into the caves, she did not trust that they would not be smothered in their sleep.

Slowly, Brand and Erika stood. There were five rooms to choose from, each with twinned beds, some pushed together and some parted. They bade Aedon and Harper good night and strode down the hall—together. Harper pulled her cloak tighter and rested her chin on her drawn knees.

"Copper hex for your thoughts?"

She glanced at Aedon sitting across from her. He twirled a six-sided copper coin between his fingers. A copper hex, she surmised. Still, so much of this world that was new to her, felt so very foreign.

"I'm worried about Ragnar."

He did not reply but nodded gravely.

"If the dwarves don't agree to help us, can we find him ourselves? Can we save him?" *Before it's too late?*

He seemed to know what the end of her unspoken thought was, for his face softened.

"I mean, you used your magic, Brand and Erika used all their skills, yet we still just managed to fend off those goblins. How can we stand a chance against *more* of them in their own domain?"

"It's a difficult one. Honestly, Harper? I'm not sure." It was the first time she had ever seen the cocksure, carefree Aedon at a genuine loss. The great Aedon, filled with the magic of dragons. Brand, the legendary Aerian warrior. Erika, the nomad who refused to be stopped. If they did not stand a chance... Her own paltry magic was worthless too.

Power isn't everything. She could not chase Erika's words from her mind. For the first time, Harper allowed herself to imagine the worst. Every moment Ragnar was away from them was a moment that made it all the more likely he would be dead long before they found him—if he even were alive anymore.

Harper swallowed past the lump in her throat. "What if we're too late? What if our power isn't enough? What if we find him and..." She could not finish the sentence.

Aedon rose from his own chair and walked over. He sank beside her and wrapped an arm around her shoulder. Grateful for the anchor of his weight against the rising storm of worry in her, she leaned into him. But his words did not help. "I don't know, Harper. I'm sorry. I just don't know."

For the first time, she heard grief in his voice, and pitied him even more than she worried for Ragnar at that moment. Harper rested her cheek on his shoulder in silent solidarity, and he rested his forehead against hers. Despite her exhaustion and grief, his friendship provided some comfort.

Aedon shifted beside her, turning her into his chest. He brought up his hand to cup Harper's neck, sliding it up to her chin, and tugged it up. Her breath stalled, about to ask what he was doing—and then his lips met hers without delay.

24

HARPER

Aedon's touch was gentle, but the contact was a violent shock. Harper's breath stalled for all the wrong reasons as panic flooded her. As he pulled her closer, she struggled away, but he only followed her, the weight of him leaning over her as he pressed her further into the cushions and the strength in his body too unyielding to resist. Harper turned her face away, breaking his kiss. His lips fell to the nook of her neck below her ear.

"No!" She shoved him away, a palm thrusting into his chest, and pushed back to the armrest of the chair until it dug into her back. Her legs dangled uselessly off the seat, pinned by his body. Aedon braced himself above her, a hand to either side of her, and confusion filtered through him.

"What's wrong?"

Harper shook her head, bringing her other hand up to scrub her lips so hard that it rubbed them raw. "I don't want this." Her voice shook—not from fear of him, but the fear of what she did not want to acknowledge—the realisation she had had beneath the waterfall of what she *did* want. That impossibly dark, sinful, and shameful desire so deluded she could never voice it.

"What?"

She met his gaze and held her voice firm. Of this, she *was* certain. "I don't want this. Us. I don't want anything between us—only your friendship."

"I don't understand." His brows furrowed. "Beneath the waterfall. You—We—"

"It was a mistake."

He stared at her as though he was a stranger.

"I value you as a friend—nothing more. I'm sorry." She stopped the torrent unleashing. That she had longed for something more. Thought to find it in him. And instead only found a deep longing for something which she could never have—and should not want—and that she would never get. No amount of having him could replace that.

Aedon remained suspended above her for a long moment. Her spread hand still lay firmly planted in the middle of his heaving chest. He regarded her with utter confusion. And then, the pressure eased as he pulled away. His face closed for a moment, and she held herself still and silent as she watched his internal struggle. This was the part she feared—men, in her experience, did not like being told no. She had seen plenty of brawls at the tavern to testify to the result of their fragile egos being damaged by a woman's choice. But Aedon swallowed. Straightened. And looked her dead in the eye with something that resembled wary respect. "Alright. I thought there was something between us."

She shook her head and sat up, folding her hands in her lap.

His expression dropped and the colour drained from his face. "Oh Gods. And I just dived right in there. What a fool! I really am sorry—please, believe me. I would never force myself on you, or anyone. I thought you wanted this too." He ran a hand through his hair and then dropped his face into a hand, groaning into his palm.

Relief warmed her. He wasn't going to be an ass about this—a gentleman instead, in fact. "I didn't mean to mislead you—but the waterfall made me realise I didn't want this. It's for the best we remain friends, and nothing more. I'm sorry if you're disappointed."

Aedon smiled ruefully, and rubbed the back of his neck with a palm. His eyes slipped shut—before he opened one a crack and shot her a sidelong glance. "Well. I can't say this is a comfortable experience." He let out a small chuckle. "But I appreciate the honesty. You're probably right—look at what's going on. I think I wanted a distraction," he admitted, giving her a sheepish grin. "That was disrespectful of me. I'm—"

"If you say sorry one more time, I'm going to punch you, Aedon."

He laughed again—this time, spontaneous and genuine—and she warmed, smiling too with relief that this would not make things awkward between them.

"Why are you going to punch him?" Brand said, the scuff of his boot announcing his entrance a moment too late.

Aedon turned to Brand, with no hint of the animosity between them that had plagued them where Harper was concerned. "I have made a monumental ass of myself, and she is claiming rightful recompense."

Brand smirked. "In that case, allow me to deliver your justice, Harper?"

Harper snorted. The giant Aerian would knock the elf flat. "We do still need him—I think."

"Ouch," exclaimed Aedon, glaring at her with mock offence. "You wound me!"

"I think that's the point," Brand said drily, glancing

between them. "Is everything alright here?" His gaze settled on Harper, his expression impassive.

She caught the implied undertone, and stood, smoothing down her shirt. "We're good. Thanks. Right?" She looked down at Aedon, still that small coil of anxiety worried that either way, the tentative friendship that bloomed between her and the others would somehow be tarnished or worse, ruined.

But the smile he gave her was genuine, if a little withdrawn. "Aye. We're good."

"Good," said Brand with a sharp nod. "Glad to hear it."

Harper wondered if he had understood what had passed between them—or how much he had seen. But she had nothing to cringe about, she realised. She had not allowed him to take advantage of her—or allowed herself to compromise in the face of what would have been an easier indulgence, if a hollow one. She had drawn her boundary—and then she had defended it. There was no shame in that, she realised.

Harper straightened, the steel in her bolstered momentarily in the face of so much uncertainty and change. That was what she needed, she realised. The faith in herself to keep the candle of hope burning despite the storm that raged outside her. That self-assurance would help her face whatever tomorrow brought. Ragnar depended upon it.

25

HARPER

Brand retreated back down the hall and into his room, his wings scraping on the doorframe with a *ssshhh*. His door closed with a snap.

"Right. I'm going to gather the shreds of my dignity in private. Sleep well," Aedon said as he stood, cracking a small grin her way. He disappeared into his bedroom, shutting the door without another word.

Harper glanced between Brand's closed door and Aedon's. She swallowed. The ghost of his touch lingered on her skin, and it made her shudder with the wrongness of how it felt to stretch that budding friendship into something so romantically intimate. She could still taste his lips upon hers. In the silence of her solitude, she was even more deeply glad she had stopped the kiss—and averted what would have been a terrible mistake.

Harper crossed to her room and closed the door, grateful for privacy. Her pack rested beside the bed. A wave of exhaustion, kept at bay by what had just happened, engulfed her. The room moved as she swayed. She had no energy to take note of her surroundings. She slid off her boots and tumbled onto the bed fully clothed.

That night, nightmares haunted Harper. Spectres of Ragnar and the goblins, twisting and mutating into each other in the darkness. Then it shifted and the spymaster was before her—and it was him she kissed, not Aedon—for she could not escape herself in her dreams, nor find it in herself to feel shame at her desires. However, his face blurred between the two of them, Aedon and Dimitri, Dimitri and Aedon, and she fought revulsion and attraction as the conflicting feelings rolled over each other, as turbulent as rushing water.

Her rest was fitful, and in the morning, she woke bleary-eyed and with a throbbing head to the sound of running water. The faelight in the alcove above her head glowed brighter, as if daytime. Harper sat up with a groan, both at her tiredness and her aching body. She stumbled to the other room in her suite to find a bathing room similar to the one she had used in Dimitrius's quarters at Tournai—and through her dizzy exhaustion, that left her with a pang of something else she did not want to name. Here, a small trough had continuously running water flowing from one side to the other, then out through a pipe. She washed her hands and face gratefully. The cold water was a sharp relief that banished some of the haziness.

It was silent outside her room, and she surmised the others had not yet roused, so she stripped off her clothes, peeling away the last layer that stuck to her skin with sweat and grime, and dumped them unceremoniously onto the floor. Harper wrinkled her nose at the thought of having to put them back on, but there was no other option.

She ran the taps until the bathing hollow filled with hot, steaming water, and eased herself in with a grateful moan.

The heat stripped away the worst of her aches. Grabbing her shirt from the floor, she dunked it into the water, scrubbing it with the soap and wringing it out. She held it up. It looked slightly cleaner, which was better than nothing. The water turned from clear to murky as she scrubbed the dirt from her skin. After she was done, she sat for a few minutes with her knees drawn up to her chest, deep in thought as the previous night washed over her. Aedon's actions played over in her mind. His unexpected advance, her rebuttal, and the aftermath. And more than that, what it meant for her—that she wanted the spymaster.

Dimitrius.

She shuddered as she thought his name, torn by revulsion and longing that distance from him only intensified. Why was she so fixated by him? What did this desire that threatened to become an obsession make her? A fool? Or worse? Harper did not know. Perhaps mercifully, no answers returned. Her thoughts returned to Ragnar and her resolve steeled as she pushed aside her selfish concerns with a tinge of guilt. Ragnar needed them.

No one remarked upon what had transpired the previous night. Judging by Erika's silence and her curious glances between Harper and Aedon, Brand had already told her. Jarl Halvar's knock upon the door was a welcome relief from the air of anxiety that curdled any conversation between them. Harper could barely eat as it was—she felt far too nauseated at what they were to face that day.

"König Korrin will see you now," the Jarl said. It was not a request.

They made ready and followed him into the city. They

passed through long, soaring hallways, vast caverns filled with buildings carved into the rocks, and grand courtyards with skies and trees of stone. Bright faelight illuminated all, and Harper gaped at the details she had missed in the gloom of the previous night. Now, Keldheim bustled, dwarves rushing to and fro with purpose.

They were dressed much like Ragnar, though their clothes were far less ragged and patched. Some were clad in the same garb as Halvar, marking themselves as Korrin's army. Many sported tattoos upon their fingers and foreheads, just like Ragnar and Korrin, with similar patterns and designs stretching down their necks, up their sleeves, and out of sight. They marched through the streets with double-headed axes strapped to their backs and single-headed axes or maces to either side of their waists.

Halvar led them through a bustling underground market, where Harper was surprised to see men and elves trading alongside dwarves, hawking wares at the top of their voices. The cacophony echoed around the space as the companions hurried through, the scent of spices and foods wafting around them. They soon stood before the grand doors of the königshalle once more. Self-conscious, Harper smoothed down her still soggy shirt and tugged her cloak around herself to conceal it.

The warm hall was full of feasting and conversation as the dwarves of his court sat at the several trestle tables and breakfasted at leisure. In the corner, a rowdy bunch of dwarves howled a bawdy drinking song to the merriment of their kin, the words incomprehensible to Harper. They followed the jarl through the heart of the hall—the unusual mix of their company garnering the interest of all those dining—to the king sitting upon his stone throne at the far end who idly picked foods from a plate on a table next to him.

"König." Aedon greeted Korrin with a clenched fist to his breast and a bow.

"Elf Felrian and your companions, I bid thee welcome." Korrin nodded.

"Call me Aedon, if you please, König. I no longer represent House Felrian."

"Very well, Elf Aedon. I have thought long and hard this night past of Ragnar's predicament. As much as I am loathe to enter into such a foolish venture, I cannot deny that I owe him by blood."

"You will save him, König?" Aedon asked, raising his eyebrows in surprise.

"Perhaps," Korrin corrected. He leaned forward and lowered his voice, so the throng of people filling the hall could not hear him. "Afnirheim, as you may be aware, has fallen silent. No trade enters or leaves. No scouts. Nothing. It is as if they all vanished upon the road. I have no doubt the goblins are to blame. They breed worse than rodents and, once in a while, must be put back into their place. If they have grown so bold as to take my roads, I shall show them where they belong. Their domain is to the east of Afnirheim. Though they may dare to trespass in my territory, they would not dare to remain. If my cousin is still to be found alive, it will be there, in their stronghold. It is not unheard of that they capture dwarfs for their cruel sports." His lips curled in distaste.

"I will send you forth with Jarl Halvar and his scouts to discover the truth of what bars the way to Afnirheim, and there we may find some trace clue of my cousin's fate."

An ember of fear burned into life in Harper's belly.

Korrin would send them to find Ragnar—the very breath after declaring none who ventured to Afnirheim returned?

"Perhaps you may discover my cousin's fate along the way, but I will not ask my dwarves to put themselves in danger for this mission." Korrin glared at them under his bushy eyebrows, as if daring them to disagree.

Aedon bowed again respectfully. "I would be glad of the chance to discover my friend's fate. He is a dear companion to us all."

Korrin harrumphed, as if he could not believe it. "You will leave after midday meal. You may take what you need from our stores in preparation. Our roads are the finest, but they are long and hard, and my people shall not wait for you."

Harper held in a groan at the thought of having to walk even farther, but she knew there was no choice. They had to follow Halvar's scouts, for it was their only chance to find Ragnar before the worst happened. If it had not already.

26

HARPER

alvar led them to the armoury to tend to their weapons and clothing. Harper had never seen so much metal in one place before, and she gawked at the cavernous space filled with different levels, from forges on the bottom, to tooling and crafters in the middle, to stores of finished armour at the very top. The space was kept to a temperate warmth by the heat of the forges, where molten metal ran white hot.

"Take anything you need, by gift of the könig," Halvar instructed them, then eyed Brand's bulk. "We don't have anything to fit you, I'm afraid."

Brand shrugged. "It's no matter. My weapons and armour are suitable."

Halvar looked over Brand's worn leathers as if he would disagree, but said nothing to him, instead, turning to the rest of them. "We travel fast, so take only what you are sure you will be able to carry. Our light mails and leathers are over there. Weapons over here." He gestured in one and then another direction. "I shall wait by the entrance. Be swift, for we must sup before we leave." He pursed his lips, as if somewhat annoyed that he had to mind them rather than attend to his usual duties.

"Thank you, Jarl," Brand said, then made his way over to the racks of armour and weapons to admire the craftsmanship. He let out a low whistle as he fingered their chainmail shirts. "Come, look at these. I've never seen anything like it in my life."

Harper followed the rest over. She picked up a small mail shirt, immediately surprised at how small and fine the links were and how light the garment was. "Surely this won't protect anyone. It's so fine, you could stab straight through it."

To her surprise, Brand guffawed, his laugh echoing around the space. "You may think it, but I would trust my life to dwarven armour. I only wish they could make something large enough to fit me. I wager this is the finest mail you'll see anywhere this side of the Great Sea."

Harper looked back to the gleaming silver metal. It seemed impossible, but she knew Brand would not jest about such things. She unclasped her cloak and slipped the shirt on over hers to check for sizing. It was loose and fell to halfway down her thighs.

"That looks a decent fit," said Aedon.

Brand, however, cocked his head, narrowing his eyes as he looked her up and down. "It's light, but are you sure you'll be able to carry its weight for days there and back?"

Harper nodded, not wanting to seem weak, though she was not entirely sure she could manage it. She would need to if they were to encounter goblins again. A shudder chased down her spine at the thought. As casually as she could, she returned the mail vest to the racks and found a smaller, shorter one that was half the weight.

Once they had all chosen some small pieces of armour to supplement their protections, they wandered through the weapons, but nothing did they take, save some arrows to top up Aedon's small quiver, which only had four left. The arrows the dwarves made were too short for his long reach, but with nothing better, he would manage. A bell tolled in the distance, the peals booming through the rock.

"Lunch time," Brand groaned in appreciation, his grumbling stomach choosing that moment to make itself known audibly. Harper looked at him in surprise. Had it already been so long since breakfast?

"It's time," Halvar called up to them. They hastened to his side. He led them back to Korrin's giant feasting hall, where the rest of Jarl Halvar's command now sat at one of the farthest tables away from the king, next to the huge doors.

"Sit anywhere you like." Halvar made his way to sit at the head of the table nearest the choicest foods, as was the privilege of his rank. They scrambled to the remaining spaces at the far end of the table, but luckily for them, their gracious dwarven hosts passed platters of food down to their end.

The companions tucked in ravenously, and for long minutes, all that could be heard was the sound of eating, for the pies, meats, and creatively cooked root vegetables lathered in gravy even surpassed the fare of the Maiden's Beard. When they had eaten their fill, they slumped back on the benches with full stomachs and sluggish minds, only to be plied with a variety of brews that the dwarves specialised in. The drinks made friends of them all. Soon, some of the dwarves, who had eyed Brand apprehensively, howled with laughter as the Aerian recounted tales of battle, while others stared, eyes wide, at his huge blade, which was taller than half of them. He laughed as they sang drinking and battle songs in the Common Tongue, and the dwarves cajoled them all into joining in.

> Heigh-ho, to battle I go,
> With a full belly now
> And an enemy to show
> How deep my axe can plough!
>
> Heigh-ho, I drive deep and hard,
> Fast as the goat that leapt,
> Eager as the singing bard,
> As the fleeting elf that swept!
>
> Heigh-ho, 'fore our ranks they flee,
> Goblin scum dare not stand
> Where dwarf-kin rule undernea'
> High peaks in halls so grand!
>
> Heigh-ho, I strike fast to pierce,
> Brave as the maiden Lar,
> Like the great black bear so fierce,
> My enemies bleed far!

And so it continued on for many verses until Harper had quite lost track. Soon, Erika and Brand roared along with their dwarven hosts, weapons clashing in a smashing percussion with every verse. Aedon seemed at ease, too, happy to exchange banter with them on the many merits of elf magic and speed to his dwarven kin, whilst the dwarves insisted, most vociferously, how mistaken he was and that elves could not hope to compete with dwarven valour and strength. It was all in good spirit, and the insults thrown in good humour.

Harper sat quietly amongst them as she digested her meal —and the task ahead—unable to join in the merriment. A cold dread crept deep within her. Soon, they would be on the road once more and away from such comforts. Out there, somewhere, Ragnar awaited them—alive or dead.

Sooner than she would have liked, yet not at all soon enough, they left Keldheim, passing through the great gates onto the octagonal-paved road, down into the valley and east. Harper's shoulders already ached with the weight of the dwarven mail and her pack, and her feet stung from the hard road beneath them, but she ducked her head and jogged behind the rest of the dwarven scouts nonetheless.

It was a long and hard day of travel through the mountains, following the forested valleys as they meandered east. They were watched by the dwarf gods, whose stone likenesses lined the road at one-mile intervals. After a while, though, the blessing of the dwarf road became a curse. Harper was sick of the punishing pace and hard surface, all too glad to collapse by the side of the road that night as they stopped to make camp within the shelter of the woods.

Before dawn the next morning, Halvar called them to rise. They were so deep in the mountains that hoarfrost coated the entire camp, and Harper found even her cloak frozen solid. She was glad for the extra layer now, though, for her frigid breath billowed before her and the cold bit her face. Around her, the camp shook off the layer of rime that covered all in glittering white. After a warming brew and breakfast—dwarven travelling fare of folded pasties filled with gravies and meats—they were off, and Halvar set a punishing pace once more.

By the middle of the afternoon, Harper was so exhausted, and her body hurt so much, that when Brand asked her if she was okay, she growled at him. He lifted an eyebrow at the guttural sound. "I beg your pardon?"

"I think death... would be... preferable... to this," she snarled through ragged breaths.

He laughed, and Erika and Aedon turned to see what the fuss was about. "I'm afraid you're used to a more leisurely pace with us, Harper. You'll find no sympathy with our hosts!"

Harper groaned. Just as she envisioned curling up by the side of the road, Halvar threw a fist into the air, calling a halt. They stopped at once, and all hands fell to axe handles. The jarl surveyed their surroundings, slowly scanning from left to right and back again. Harper craned her neck to see over them. Not that she was not grateful, but why were they stopping? It was a valley much like any other. Evergreens filled the steeply ascending sides up to rocky heights and snow-capped peaks.

To either side of her, she felt Brand and Erika tense, waiting for the signal to draw their blades, their hands already on their weapons. As the lazy breeze blew, it carried the perfume of carrion. It was the scent of death and decay, and with a jolt, she realised what it reminded her of. Goblins. Fear shot through her at the memories of them. She drew her dagger, just as everyone else took out their own weapons to hold ready.

"Formation," Halvar commanded in a low voice. The dwarves spread out to cover the entire road, several layers deep. Brand, Erika, Aedon, and Harper filtered into their ranks, scanning the trees warily. Were they being watched?

"Remember, we are on a scouting mission *only*. We do not engage. We must remain undetected." The jarl surveyed them all before his gaze returned to the trees surrounding them. "I don't like this. It's too obvious. It's either a trap, or they're so confident, they care not that we could smell them a mile off."

As they slowly advanced, their first sign of obvious disturbance was the dwarf god statue smashed across the road. Covered in blood, mud, and faeces, the figure was shattered beyond recognition. The dwarves cursed at the desecration of their deity, and their curses only intensified as the next mile marker passed, then the next. The destruction grew worse, until the last god they encountered had been obliterated to nothing more than jagged rubble and dust. Jarl Halvar grew grimmer with every step. Harper almost pitied any goblin who crossed their path. Almost.

Around the bend, trees thinned to reveal the sprawling valley. In the distance, the city of Afnirheim rose. Like Keldheim, it was mostly within the mountain, but Afnirheim was like a city partly buried, for some sprawled upon the face of the mountain, too. Tiered levels spreading down into layers of green, crops that fed the city, were smooth against the jagged mountain from which they emerged. It was a spectacular view, even with the dirty smoke rising. The walls were dark with it. The forest smouldered, the valley scarred with black. That scent of smoke mingled with the strengthening stench of carrion.

They found the first bodies around the next bend. Harper vomited at the sight and smell of them, and she wasn't the only one. From the position of the bodies and the way they had been stripped of anything worthwhile and piled up unceremoniously, it was obvious the dwarves had not died a kind death. They had been dead for weeks, if Harper's knowledge of animal decay was anything to go by. She averted her eyes. Jarl Halvar murmured a prayer for them as he passed, which was echoed by his kin.

It was late afternoon, yet the sky had already begun to darken.

"We cannot stay outside the safety of Afnirheim with goblins about," Brand murmured to Erika. She nodded in agreement. It seemed that Halvar had the same notion, for he made for Afnirheim with singular purpose, chivvying them along. It was only when they drew within sight of the great door that he halted and his jaw tumbled open.

The land lay empty of trees and shrubs at the base of the mountain, which was a defence feature of the city, but it was clear no more. Afnirheim's standards were torn from the battlements and lay burnt upon the road. Blood spattered the doors, which hung ajar, and crusted between the octagonal stones. Carcasses—of dwarves and goblins alike—piled high, left where they had fallen.

The ornate carvings on the doors had been smashed in much the same way as the effigies upon the road. Overwhelming all was a great mark upon the door, daubed in blackened blood.

The Riven Circle.

The Mark of Saradon.

27
HARPER

Eyes wide, Harper stared at the destruction, her attention captured by the familiar mark. She closed her hand around the wrist with her bracelet upon it. Was it her imagination, or did the metal feel warmer to the touch than it ought to be?

Erika bounded forward with a snarl at the sight of the mark, but Brand pounced upon her and dragged her back, containing her within his strong arms. "Let me go!" she spat at him.

"Don't be an idiot," he snapped back. "We don't yet know what we deal with. Don't endanger yourself on a fool's crusade. It may mean nothing. How many times have we already seen his mark used in vain?"

After a futile struggle, she fell limp in his arms, but he did not release her.

With a sharp flick of his hand, Halvar signalled a retreat. Heart hammering in her chest, Harper followed as quickly as her screaming legs allowed.

Long into the night they ran, as though the goblins pursued them through the dark. Harper saw the golden magic Aedon dropped behind them, scouring their scent and presence from the road. She hoped it would be enough. She knew they had left the stench of carrion behind, yet it still clogged her nostrils, the image of bodies ever present. Every time she blinked—they were there. When they finally stopped, Halvar pushed them far off the road to a defensible spot. He spared no dwarf for a double watch that night, only allowing each a few scant hours of sleep, lest they be ambushed.

"What does this mean, Jarl?" asked one of the dwarves. Brand murmured to Harper, translating their language.

"It means it is worse than we feared, Torvaig. They have taken not just the road, but Afnirheim. Gods save our kin."

"They may yet hold out. Afnirheim is one—"

"Does it *look* like they held out?" snapped Halvar. He checked himself, blowing out a breath. "I apologise. That was out of turn. I hope it as well as any of you, but it does not look likely. Somehow, the goblin scum have overrun the place. We must return to the könig. He counts on us to report this, else he shall not know."

Harper swayed as everything blurred before her. Brand's strong hand grasped her upper arm to steady her.

"Th-Thank y-you," she mumbled, her tongue tripping over the simple words. She swayed again, her legs gave out, and Brand caught her as she fell.

In her mind, Harper continued to plummet, through the frozen earth, on and on, through the void. Brand's voice called from a distance, but she could not respond as she slipped further away.

Her wrist burned, as if her bracelet had become a loop of fire, searing her skin. Then up, up, up she rose, but this time, she ascended into Keldheim.

This is not Keldheim, her mind told her.

She looked around, blinking slowly. It was like Keldheim, but this dwarven city was in ruins. Instinctively, she knew she somehow saw inside Afnirheim, as it was at that moment. She flew through deserted and destroyed halls and corridors. Through caverns with smashed aqueducts plunging their liquids into the voids below. Through seemingly endless spaces filled with the dead of both goblin and dwarven races. She came upon a great hall, where the leader of goblins, one greater and more disgusting than the rest, sat upon the scarred throne, the head of a dwarf, still crowned by a bloodied circlet, hanging by the hair from his clawed hand.

The raucous din in the hall drove a blade into her brain as the shrieks and shouts echoed around the cavernous space. Goblins cavorted, many now wearing dwarven armour, holding jewels and finely crafted weapons. Others tore hunks of meat from... Harper looked no further, focusing on keeping the contents of her stomach contained.

A crack split the air. With a flash of light, a tall figure, far taller than the goblins, appeared before the king's dais. Harper drifted closer. An elf. Raven hair tumbled over his shoulders. As he turned to survey the horde before the throne, Harper saw a stern face, his dark eyes conveying wisdom, strength, and anger. Fine garments clothed him from head to toe. A jewelled sword hung at his waist, the pommel glowing red. He looked like he belonged in Dimitrius's royal court.

"Pascha," he said, and inclined his head to the goblins.

"Lord Saradon," snarled the goblin upon the throne, his mouth struggling to form the syllables.

A current shot through Harper. Perhaps she had misheard. It was so loud. But she stared at the elf all the harder, recalling Aedon's tale of the dark elf Saradon, whose mark she bore on her charm bracelet.

"You bring me no gift?" snarled the leader of the goblins.

The elf narrowed his eyes and turned back to him. He gestured at their surroundings. "I gave you Afnirheim. That is more than sufficient to show you my intent."

The pascha laughed, showing bloodied, pointed teeth, and waved at the hall before him, which teemed with swarming goblins. "Take what you want of the spoils, Lord Saradon."

"I do not need your loot. I need your scourge."

"And you shall have it." The pascha grinned wickedly. The scourge of goblins around them shrieked and cavorted with glee at the prospect of further conquest.

"Good." Saradon's lips curled into a mirthless grin. "I expect you to come when the banners are called."

The pascha hissed. "We do not take orders from Elfkind."

"But you will take mine if we are to succeed," said Saradon forcefully. He took a step forward.

The pascha's eyes seemed to unfocus for a moment as his gaze slid away. "Yes, we shall," he said dully, before he blinked rapidly and returned his attention to Saradon.

Saradon gazed around them. His lips thinned as he viewed the goblins with distaste. "I shall leave you to your spoils."

Harper floated away as the sounds, sights, and smells receded, fading into darkness once more.

She woke upon the ground with Aedon's cloak wrapped around her and a warm hand upon her forehead. She opened her eyes slowly. Above her, stars pinpricked the night sky.

The shadowed faces of Aedon and Brand, cast in the fire's glow, hovered in the fringes of her vision.

"Can you see me? Harper? Can you hear me?" Aedon asked.

"What happened?" she mumbled, closing her eyes for a long moment again. Her head pounded to the point it hurt to look around. She opened her eyes to slits—Aedon's troubled face hovered inches above her.

"I don't know," he answered. "You collapsed, and you've been twitching and mumbling for several minutes."

Harper slowly looked around. At the edge of her field of vision, she saw the company of dwarves lurking. Some openly looked toward her. Others glanced over subtly or pretended not to be listening.

She lowered her voice. "I saw something when I passed out. I don't know what it is. But I think it might be connected to the dwarves, the goblins, and Afnirheim. I just cannot make sense of it." She stopped, frustrated. *How can I possibly explain it?* It had already started fading at the edges of her memory, and she clung to it.

"You can show me, if you wish?" said Aedon. "I will be able to see what you saw. It might help us make sense of it."

Harper swallowed as Aedon reached his hands out. For some reason, she wanted to shrink away from his touch, despite them clarifying the boundaries between them. Instead, she forced herself to lace her fingers through his, as if there were nothing amiss.

The faint caress of his magic stroked through her, and she closed her eyes, sinking into the memory once more, trying to remember every detail. Aedon's hand grew tighter upon hers, until his grip became painful. Harper opened her eyes as the memory faded, and Aedon's grasp loosened. She pulled away. His pale face told her he had seen everything. She had hardly seen him so speechless before. A premonition of fear curled up her spine as he helped her sit up, then offered her a drink from his waterskin.

Halvar loomed over her. "Is she well?" he asked, frowning.

"Exhaustion," said Aedon with a reassuring smile that betrayed none of the consternation he had just shown Harper. "Humans, you know. Not as strong as you fine folk." The dwarves around them guffawed at that—and their attention peeled away, back to their own circles. "If we may have a healer at Keldheim check it is nothing more untoward perhaps?"

"Of course." Halvar waved his hand dismissively and returned to his own company.

"What is it?" Brand asked, a sharp bite to his voice.

"Far worse than we feared," whispered Aedon. "Harper, I believe you just had a vision—of inside Afnirheim." He swallowed, and his eyes darted around to the dwarves, who lurked close. "I cannot explain. Let me show you." He reached out to grasp Brand's and Erika's hands.

A few minutes later, looking at their faces, Harper knew they had seen what she had witnessed. She tugged her cloak closer as her body shook from fear and exhaustion. "What does it mean?"

"It means we must speak with the könig at once. Afnirheim is not only lost, but it is lost beyond their reach. *Saradon*," Aedon cursed. "Goblins are the least of our problems now."

"Was it really him?"

"Yes," said Aedon heavily. "I'd know that face anywhere. I've seen the portraits of him in the royal gallery of Tournai. A long time ago, of course, but one does not forget such a striking character. I do not know how he can be here now.

Maybe your vision was of the past, though I do not recall any record of him taking Afnirheim," Aedon said, a desperate edge to his voice, but Harper could see he did not believe his words. "We must report it. It appears... Saradon has returned."

DIMITRI

A black cloud hung permanently over Tournai, but it was not the storms of approaching winter. The city had become a dark and unforgiving place. The king's curfew was more easily kept now, for Kingsguard swamped the city, pushing their capabilities to the boundaries, and the people had not the strength to rebel against the king any longer. Anarchy had ruled the streets, but now it was a tired, cautious wait.

Food, water, and supplies dwindled as trade stuttered throughout the city, partly borne by rioting and looting, partly borne by a cessation of trade coming into Tournai. Only so many carts could enter or leave between curfews, and with the threat of the goblin scourge blighting the passes, trade had completely stopped from Valtivar and across the mountains from the east, decimating provisions.

The court was darker still. Toroth clung to his throne with mind and body, even as he wasted away from Saradon's Curse, which sapped his magic and strength. The queen hung on by a thread, and what nobles were left had grown increasingly suspicious and fearful for their own safety, both from Toroth's increasingly insane hands and from the affliction. It felt like all were only a breath away from death, either by dragonfire or disease.

The king had not purged the city again. Dimitri and Raedon had seen to it, though the king was unaware of their tenuous alliance. Dimitri was certain it was only that which held utter disarray at bay. The guild meets grew more rowdy and discontent each time, and it seemed it only needed the common people to have a chance to rise. Dimitri and Raedon both knew it. Dimitri imagined that was why Raedon doubled the Kingsguard patrols through the city, even though he could ill afford the increase in wages or rations.

Dimitri had not spoken to Raedon again about his obvious desire to rule, but he knew it drove the elf, who even now watched the king with a hidden gleam in his eyes. Raedon was a predator waiting to pounce—far too proud to serve a broken king and watch his hard work waste away, and now wondering on an unforeseen opportunity coming his way.

Indeed, the king had slowly become prey. Even the summer enchantments over the gardens, fed by his magic, had started to fail. The rose garden withered and died. The flowers had vanished. The leaves had fallen, covering the lawns in a blaze of fire—which now rotted into brown mulch. The gardens had become almost as lifeless and dreary as the court.

"The time to act is now, General," Dimitri said as he and Raedon stood upon the tallest tower in Tournai—the very same one from which he had allowed Brand and Harper to escape. Gusts of wind buffeted them as Raedon's dragon soared overhead, somersaulting through the steel-grey sky. It felt so different to when he had last stood there, under much calmer skies, urging *her* to leave. The thought of her was too uncomfortable. He focused on the slicing feeling of that unforgiving wind, and what he had to say to the general. No one would hear them, their words lost in the wind and shrouded by wards, whilst the court wasted away below them.

Still, Raedon stirred but did not speak.

Dimitri cast him a sidelong glance. "It matters not who rules in the end, General. What matters now is that the people can trust a strong leadership."

"Yet it will be seen as usurpation."

"Not if done the right way in order to stabilise the realm whilst the king sickens and wastes."

Raedon frowned. "What is the right way?"

Dimitri turned back to the battlement, looking over the city sprawling below them. "The right way is to notify the court, the city, and perhaps even the realm of what has transpired. The court is sick. All know it. Such gossip spreads like wildfire. It is the general's place to uphold order and peace. You are merely doing your sworn duty."

"I will not sit the throne."

Dimitri could not decide if Raedon sounded eager to do so, for the general guarded his tone.

"Of course not. Whilst the king and his kin live, the throne is not yours to sit. You will install the queen's throne below the king's. That way, you will sit by the seat of power, not in it. All will know what that gesture means."

It was Raedon's turn to give Dimitri a sidelong glance. "You seem to have all the answers, Dimitrius."

He shrugged. "It is my job to see all the possibilities to best guard the realm, Raedon."

The general pursed his lips. "You do not seek to take the throne yourself?"

Dimitri snorted and shot Raedon a look of disgust. "Certainly not. I'd have to put up with this confounded court all the time. I couldn't stand such a thing."

Raedon chuckled dryly. "I hear that. I cannot stand the bowing and scraping myself."

That wasn't the half of it, in Dimitri's eyes. Far much more sin passed there than that. To his credit, Raedon was one of the few who rose above such pettiness, who kept his reputation intact. But Dimitri did not say it.

"I will lend my support in any case, General," Dimitri pressed, for Raedon dithered. "I will stand beside you, in the shadows, and keep the peace."

Raedon shook his head. "I worry still about this curse. Is it truly Saradon's Curse, or is it mere rumour, blown out of proportion by a thousand mouths?"

Dimitri turned to Raedon, who stilled at the seriousness on his face. "It is Saradon's Curse."

"How can you know?" Raedon fired at him at once.

Dimitri regarded Raedon, choosing his words with care. "Saradon has returned. He is alive."

The general gaped at him. "No. That's *impossible!*"

"It is so. I have reports of unquestionable validity that say he walks once more."

"But it *cannot* be the case. He's a half-elf. Even if he had somehow lived, he ought to be dead by now."

Dimitri shook his head. "Saradon is as young and strong as the day he vanished."

Raedon took a long moment to recover. "You are *certain?* Beyond *any* doubt?"

"Yes."

The general looked out over the city in dumbfounded shock. "What should we do? Ought we tell the king?"

"Heavens, no. We must deal with this. Toroth is unfit to.

The mere mention of Saradon's Curse sent him into madness."

"But if this is truly Saradon's Curse, then—"

"All the more reason not to—not unless you wish him to burn the whole damned city to the ground."

Raedon's jaw clenched, and a muscle there ticked, but he did not contradict Dimitri, for the general knew he was right. "What of those afflicted?"

"They have poor prospects."

"They will all die?"

"Unless a counter-curse or cure is found. I have scoured the old records, and nowhere is any remedy recorded." The Dragonhearts had been the key when Saradon had risen before. Their power had scoured the land, obliterating his curse. And, as Dimitri and Raedon both knew, the king's entire stock of Dragonhearts was gone. Part lost in the escape of the Thief of Pelenor, and the rest to the king's selfish greed and paranoia. No one but Toroth knew where they were hidden—and Dimitri reckoned the king had lost so much of his mind even he no longer knew.

"We must tell the king."

"No!" said Dimitri quickly. "It would reduce him to tatters. We must stay his hand, contain him—neutralise him, if needed—before we deal with the threat of Saradon. If Toroth knows, he will not act in good sense and of sound mind. He is quite insane."

Raedon's ragged growl of frustration was lost as the wind snatched it away. His gaze slipped to the still blackened plains before the city. Toroth would purge everyone and everything he could if he thought it would help. Suppressing a smile, Dimitri watched Raedon come to the same conclusion.

"We will not tell him. For now," Raedon agreed at last. "I

will marshal my riders and the Kingsguard. We shall secure Tournai, then send riders throughout the land to spread news of the necessary measures we are taking to secure Pelenor."

"Excellent." Dimitri turned to leave.

"What of Saradon?" Raedon asked quickly. "Where is he? Does he possess assets? Allies?"

Dimitri mulled over what to share. "He has power that the old stories do not mention. At present, he is outside our borders, but not by far. I am informed of his movements."

"Then we shall go to him, attack him!"

Dimitri scoffed. "Do not be so brash, Raedon. Such rashness is what got your brother into the mess he's in now. Saradon already has the alliance of the goblins. They sweep across Valtivar, taking what they will. *That* is the truth of why the dwarven kingdom is in such chaos and why the passes are closed to our trades. The dwarves hold out, for now, but Pelenor will be next."

"Then I will mass our army. I will call everyone to arms."

Dimitri laughed without mirth. "What army? Given the talk in the city, the common folk will join Saradon just to be free of Toroth."

"They are bound to their king and country," Raedon growled.

"What will you do? Burn them if they will not fight for you?" Dimitri's stare was hard and cold. "No, I do not think so."

"I have the riders and the Kingsguard. They will stand for Pelenor."

"If there are any still to stand. I have seen your ranks falling, General."

Raedon winced. He had clearly hoped Dimitri would not know that, but he forgot the spymaster had eyes and ears everywhere, including inside the dragonhold, where riders lay abed, their dragons sick, as well.

"The academy and the keep are as yet untainted." The school of dragon riders and the stronghold of soldiers lay across the mountains from Tournai. New stock for Raedon's ranks, if all else failed. "We have time yet to see how this plays out. One step at a time, General. First, secure the court. Secure Tournai."

Dimitri made to leave, but Raedon stepped before him. "What will you do?" There was a slight glint of desperation in his eyes, Dimitri was pleased to note.

"Stay in the shadows, as always, and make sure this doesn't blow up in our faces." Dimitri walked away, enjoying the grim worry in the high and mighty general of the Winged Kingsguard. It is almost like playing a game of chatura. Except with living people, not wooden pieces, Dimitri thought. He rather enjoyed it.

On his way back to his quarters, Dimitri almost jumped out of his skin as Princess Rosella appeared from the shadows, blooming like a ghost in the shadowed halls.

"Oh, thank goodness. There you are, Dimitri." Rosella staggered forward and clung to his forearm.

He stared at her, quite dumbfounded as he took in her appearance. She looked ghastly. Her beauty had dimmed, her light extinguished. She was a rose no longer. Rosella's once shining sheet of golden hair hung lank around her shoulders. Her perfectly tailored dresses now sagged from her skeletal figure. He took in the jut of her collarbone, the twig-like fragility of her wrists, the high cheekbones that now protruded below shadowed, hollowed eyes which darted around with a hint of wildness.

Dimitri could not comprehend what she had been reduced to in mere weeks. "What do you want?" he said without thinking, yet she did not berate him, humiliate him, punish him, as she once would have for such impertinence. Instead, she clung harder to his arm.

"You must help us!" she hissed, winding her arm through his and pressing close. "Mother and father waste away. Father is quite out of sorts, and I worry I am ill, too. You must help!"

Dimitri untangled her arm from his and pressed her hand down to her side, away from him. "I cannot help you." His words were colder than he had anticipated, but how could he treat her any differently? She had been heartless to him over the years—he was never her lover, only her servant. And now she asked him for help? As she gazed up at him, aghast that he had dared turn her away, he smiled cruelly, turned, and stalked into his quarters, slamming the door behind him.

For once, he would not chase her, not hurry to meet her every demand, not pander to her every desire. For once, he turned her away. For once, he had the upper hand. Yet in the pit of his stomach lurked something quite unfamiliar toward her wretchedness. Something he could not quell. Pity.

DIMITRI

Even the stench of the city of Tournai was a far sweeter perfume than the rot of Afnirheim, clogged with carrion and goblin filth, but Dimitri did not show it as he bowed before Saradon, who had installed himself upon a giant, stone throne above the *pascha* and his seat of bones in the jarlshalle of the dwarven city—like a king. It was an unsettling feeling to Dimitri, watching him own that throne. Technically, Saradon had the right of blood to rule, for the royal blood of Pelenor ran through his veins, but a throne upon the bones of Afnirheim was nothing less than perverse.

Dimitri did not want to rule over this with Saradon. Not a kingdom like this. An empire of ash and bone. He clung to the thought of Pelenor—the open skies, the green lands. The vision Saradon had promised him. It would not be like the devastation, the blood and death in the dark mountain halls.

"What happened here?" Dimitri asked Saradon, his voice hollow. He knew he did not need to ask. The once thriving dwarven city was no more.

"The goblins wanted to advance their domain."

Dimitri eyed Saradon. "And you assisted them." The goblins, even with their numbers, had never before managed to overpower a dwarven dwelling. Dimitri had little reason to believe that had changed.

"It was the price of their alliance."

Anger curled in Dimitri's stomach. "You sacrificed an entire city?" Disgust and horror wrestled within him.

Saradon regarded him steadily. "It will be worth the cost."

"To whom?" Dimitri snarled. He clenched his fists beside him to stop his hands shaking.

"For us all. I see you find it difficult to stomach such warfare, but such is the price of peace."

"We did not need the goblins' alliance. The dwarves did not deserve this. Tournai and Pelenor are ready to fall without their help. The guilds will rise, and the Kingsguard will take control from the king."

"I am most glad to hear of it. You have done well, Lord Ellarian. The goblins are merely a *bonus*, shall we say."

Dimitri stared around the great hall. Columns soared into the dark heights. The banners that once adorned them were now piles of ash at their feet. It was utterly empty and silent, devoid of the dwarven life that ought to have had the very air thrumming with talk and warmth. Their blood still stained the floor, and Dimitri had seen the bodies piled outside. Saradon had not suffered to reign over corpses.

"Do you seek to reign over Valtivar, too?"

Saradon laughed. "Not yet. However, the *pascha* certainly aspires to do so."

Doubt curled in the pit of Dimitri's stomach. It was one thing to ally with the goblins—and, of course, change came with a price—but this was not what he had envisioned.

Nowhere did he think a city full of innocents would be slain for the wanton greed of goblins.

Saradon had confirmed his worst fears. The green and pleasant land that he had shown Dimitri in his vision was a lie. But what would the truth be? Would it be as bad as he was growing to worry?

"The court is falling then?" Saradon pulled him away from his thoughts.

"Yes, Lord Ravakian. It balances upon a knife's edge."

As Dimitri reported his work, a growing sense of dread crept through him. He wished he had been less successful at sowing discord, that the curse had been less virulent so he could have bought more time to figure out how to navigate the mess he now suspected he was in—and that he had unintentionally wrought on the kingdom he sought to strengthen. The irony was not lost upon him, and it tasted too bitter to bear.

"The king hovers on the edge of madness. The queen is almost dead. Even the riders of the Winged Kingsguard are falling. The people are troublesome and ripe for revolt. They are a spark, ready to catch ablaze when the time comes. They have no love for the king, and more spread word of how misunderstood and tarnished your name is."

Saradon clapped his hands together, the sound booming around the space, and let out a delighted peal of laughter. "Excellent! Clearly, I could not have entrusted this task to anyone more suited." His grim satisfaction was clear.

"So the goblins are unneeded, yes? The people will be enough? I also have the Winged Kingsguard in hand," Dimitri pressed, his eyes flicking to the blood-stained stone at his feet and back to Saradon.

He dismissed him with a wave. "You must trust me, Lord Ellarian. Do not doubt my plans." He rose from the throne and walked to Dimitri, standing before him. He raised a hand to Dimitri's shoulder and rested it there for a second. His violet eyes pierced him to the core. Dimitri strengthened his mental defences, ready for attack, but none came. "Remember our visions of Pelenor."

Green, peaceful, and prosperous… Dimitri could hardly forget, for it felt like a world apart from that now.

Saradon continued, "we are far from that. Peace always comes with the cost of bloodshed, but we shall see it done. From coast to coast, I will reign over a land so fair that none will seek to change it. I must go now. We have more allies to muster."

Saradon's gaze still pierced him, and Dimitri could not look away. He felt strangely hot and flustered. Dimitri blinked away the sudden haziness. "More allies? Who? Where?" he asked sharply.

"The Indis nomads were ever stalwart allies to my cause."

Dimitri could not hold back a bark of laughter. "You will find no aid there."

Saradon raised an eyebrow.

"The Indis nomads were hunted almost to extinction after their uprising for your cause. Even now, those few remaining are hidden from the world. I do not think you will find them welcoming."

Saradon smiled, a lazy curl of his lips. "Then you are a fool—and I would not think that of you. All the more reason for them to join me. *Revenge*. We seek it ourselves, no? It is a powerful motivator. They harbour hate for those who persecuted them—not I. They will come to my cause, whatever their numbers."

You are so sure? Dimitri questioned, but he did not dare voice it.

With a widening of his predatory smile, Saradon vanished into the ether.

Dimitri left a moment later, his heart pounding as he processed what he had found in Afnirheim—utter destruction. He had no desire to be in the halls of the dead with only goblins and death for company.

3 0

HARPER

The königshalle was silent as Jarl Halvar's voice stalled. It seemed that not a soul breathed. Even the könig sat in dumbfounded silence.

"It cannot be so," König Korrin finally said, a hint of hope to his voice that perhaps the jarl was mistaken.

"I am afraid there can be no mistaking it, König." Halvar's voice was hollow as he bowed to Korrin.

Aedon shifted but did not speak. His glance flicked to Harper, standing some feet away, before returning to the dwarven king.

Why isn't he speaking up? Harper could not fathom why Aedon did not talk. He had said it was urgent that the king know what she had seen in her vision. She stepped forward to take the matter into her own hands, but Brand's heavy hand upon her shoulder stayed her. She twisted to look at him, frowning at his warning glare. He shook his head infinitesimally, and she fell back into line beside him. His hand fell away.

169

It seemed an age before their conversation faltered and Jarl Halvar's attention strayed to Aedon, who he regarded with a troubled frown. Aedon had shared her vision with him in confidence. "There is something else I must discuss with you."

"Speak," Korrin said.

"If I may, König, this matter is for your ears only. Our guests bring grave tidings of their own."

Korrin looked over them all, drumming his fingers upon the arm of his stone throne. "Very well. Clear the hall." His fingers increased their drumming until the very last dwarf had left the space. When the doors boomed shut, he looked at Jarl Halvar. "Well? You have the floor."

"It's best if the elf shows you, König."

Korrin nodded. Aedon moved toward the throne, stopping a respectful distance away and bowing. He closed his eyes, and judging by Korrin's suddenly clenched jaw, Harper knew he now shared her vision. His mouth gaped soon after. Perhaps he now soared through the broken halls in his mind that she had seen. Harper felt a sick swoop in her stomach at the memory. Finally, Aedon bowed and stepped back, and Korrin's white, tattooed knuckles, clenched upon the arms of his throne, loosened at last.

"What is that?" he growled. His voice carried through the empty hall.

"König, I believe it to be inside Afnirheim at the present moment," Aedon replied.

"You have seen this?" Korrin asked Halvar.

"Yes, König. I believe it to be true. Seeing the carnage before the shattered gates and upon the road... Afnirheim has fallen."

"Gods help us." Korrin cast his eyes skyward, then to the

floor, before meeting their gazes once more. He rose slowly from the throne and approached them. "This must not become public... for now." His stern gaze held Halvar's.

"My men swore their secrecy, König. It will not be so much as whispered."

"Make it so." Korrin turned upon Aedon, Harper, and their companions. "Is she a seer?"

"Not that we have ever known, König," Aedon answered. "But the gift can strike any of magical blood, without true seer gifts."

Korrin's face fell and he paced back and forward, his movements sharp. It was bad enough to admit a city might have fallen, all those within dead, let alone that a power as dark as Saradon's had arisen. He deliberated, standing in silence for a moment, gazing at the ceiling. "I wish to have the vision verified. She will be sent before the Mother."

Harper's eyes widened. She glanced between Korrin and Aedon, but Aedon's face was blank. *The Mother? Who is that?*

"I can assure you the vision is true, König," Aedon said, "but if that is your will, so it be done." He turned to Harper. "Will you stand before the Mother? She is the Goddess embodied. She will see the truth of your vision."

That did not sound quite so intimidating, though anxiety still roiled in Harper's belly. "What do I have to do?" she asked in a quiet voice, hoping to avoid the king's ire—though he did not seem like King Toroth of Pelenor, quick to cruel anger, and that gave her hope.

"Nothing taxing, I promise," Aedon reassured her. "She will simply look at your vision and know if it presents the truth or not."

Harper swallowed. "All right." She straightened and bowed to the könig, unsure what else to do.

He seemed satisfied as he nodded. "Take her to the Mother at once," he ordered Jarl Halvar.

"Follow me." Halvar walked toward the throne, not the doors. After a moment, Harper followed, Aedon, Brand, and Erika trailing behind her. The jarl turned at the sound of their footsteps. "Not all of you, I am afraid. Only Harper will stand before the Mother. The rest of you may be at leisure. I will send for you when the Mother is finished with your friend."

Coldness spread through Harper. She didn't want to go alone. But Korrin nodded, so she knew that she had no choice. Still, she sent an imploring glance toward her companions. They only bowed to the könig, regarded her with inscrutable faces, and left through the great doors they had entered by.

The jarl turned once more to the back of the hall. "Come."

Behind the throne, a small door, seamless in the stone, silently opened at his touch to reveal a stairway descending into the mountain.

Down into the bowels of Keldheim they descended. The stairs went farther and farther, turning left every thirteen steps. No doorways provided an exit, the walls sheer and straight with nary a crack or fault. The air grew colder, the faelights more sparse, casting the stairs into shadows. The walls seemed to grow paler with every flight of stairs, until by the time Harper and the jarl reached the very last steps, the walls were white and ran with water.

The last step descended into a void. Jarl Halvar picked up a glass lantern containing a faelight that pulsed warm, white light, and led her into the dark. Beneath her feet, stones crunched.

She realised they were now in a cave. The white walls rippled, undulating and slick with water. It was so cold not even her cloak could keep her warm, but she tugged it tighter all the same, trying to ward off the insidious chill.

It felt like they trudged for hours, the long minutes lost in the dark. The caves trailed off in all directions, the true extent of them hidden behind white, dripstones hanging from the heights and snapping up from the ground, which Harper had never seen before. This place had teeth. It felt like being in a giant dragon's mouth. She suppressed the uncomfortable thought.

Somewhere, running water bubbled over stone, and the rock glowed with its own pale, ghostly light. Was it her imagination? Harper blinked, but it was impossible to tell. The faelight bobbed ahead of her in the jarl's hand. He stopped walking unexpectedly, just as she decided that it definitely grew lighter ahead.

"I can go no farther. The Mother will only see you."

Harper gawked at him for a moment. "I cannot speak Dwarvish. And—"

"It matters not. I may not take another step uninvited. You must continue alone. Go. I will wait here until she sends you back."

Harper swallowed and placed one foot in front of the other, forcing herself to continue. The jarl kept the faelight since she could now see, the way ahead of her gleaming in the pale light like a path in the moonlight. Who was the Mother? What did she want from Harper? Harper's nerves only brought more questions, but no answers.

The light brightened. Squinting, she realised, impossibly,

daylight lay ahead. Had they travelled under the entire mountain? It could not be, yet weak sunlight filtered into the cave, illuminating the space. In the final antechamber, before the stream tumbled from the mountainside in a rush of falling water, Harper saw a figure framed against the light, so still, it could almost have been stone itself.

HARPER

"Come closer, child." The female's voice was an aged croak. The dwarf's wispy, braided hair was so pale as to be almost transparent, and her eyes were as milky as the stone.

She is blind… How does she know I am here? Unease rose within Harper. Her legs were leaden and did not want to move.

"Come, Harper of Caledan."

Harper's eyes widened as she drifted forward, torn between apprehension and curiosity, forcing her unwilling legs to move past the rising fear gnawing in her belly.

"Sit with me."

Harper silently perched opposite her on a fallen tooth of rock.

"You may call me Vanir."

"H-Hello, Vanir," Harper whispered, feeling painfully awkward.

Vanir's wrinkled, weathered face split into a kindly grin at the tremor in her voice. "You need not fear me. I see all, and you are no threat to me, and therefore I am no threat to you. But you intrigue me. You hold visions of dark things and carry a token I have not seen in many centuries. I will see it before we are done here."

How old is she? Harper wondered.

"Older than you might believe," Vanir answered.

Harper startled. *She can read minds?*

"Only when you shout your thoughts for all to hear."

Harper blushed, resolving to think of nothing private whilst in the Mother's presence.

"I will verify your vision now. The könig must not be kept waiting." Vanir reached out her tanned, age-spotted hands to grasp Harper's. Somehow, she did not need to see to find them at once. Her skin was surprisingly warm and smooth, and a strange comfort to Harper. The Mother took a deep breath, then exhaled slowly. Instinctively, Harper did the same.

An instant later, she was suddenly no longer in the cold, milky caves, but the dark depths of Afnirheim. Her hands shook in Vanir's as she relived her vision. It was exactly like the first time, except she now knew what to expect. Nausea roiled in her stomach as she beheld the destruction once more. The vision slowly faded, and the chill swept in once more. Harper shivered, wishing the weak sunlight at the edge of the cave carried warmth. As if in answer, a flurry of snow danced into the mouth of the cavern.

"Your vision is the truth of Afnirheim at this very moment," Vanir said gravely. "I wish it were not so."

"What does that mean?" Harper dared to ask.

"It means that a dark power rises once more. One who ought to be long dead and banished. One who is in league with our gravest enemies."

"The goblins?"

"Yes." For the first time, Vanir's voice turned menacing. She cursed in her own tongue. "Yet there is one thing I must see before you leave me. I see you hold a talisman of significance. I did not realise it spoke of *him*." Suddenly, Vanir's grip was iron as she flipped over Harper's hand and pushed her sleeve up, exposing her leather bracelet and the silver bead upon it. The crone's thumb and forefinger rubbed over the stamped symbol. "Why do you have Saradon's Mark upon your person, Harper of Caledan?"

"I—I don't know," Harper stuttered. A familiar panic rose in her. The same panic of being utterly out of her depth and as helpless as she had felt in Tournai.

To her surprise, the crone dropped her hands, placing them in her own lap once more. Harper realised the woman held smooth, rounded, white stones of varying sizes in her lap, for she started to twiddle with them again, picking one up and running it between her fingers, caressing the worn surface. As they flowed through Vanir's fingers, Harper saw strange runes inscribed upon them.

"Your past is as interesting as your future," Vanir said with a sly smile that unnerved Harper. She shifted in her seat and clasped her hands in her own lap. Vanir cackled. "You will know what I mean. Eventually. Ah, if only you knew where you came from." She cocked her head. "I wonder how different your life might have been."

Harper fought a rising tide of curiosity—unsuccessfully. "What do you mean?"

"Do you know deep down, I wonder?" Vanir squinted at her and leaned closer, as if her blind eyes could see.

"Know *what?*"

Vanir sat back, looking at Harper with her head cocked, as if wondering whether or not to answer. "That charm you carry is hundreds of years old."

Harper looked at the innocuous bead with surprise.

"It was forged by the hands of elves."

She scoffed. Little surprise there. Aedon had already told her that her family had likely come from Pelenor.

"Did you never wonder why it has not tarnished over the years? Magic runs through that metal, girl. It is from Pelenor, from the time of Saradon's rising. It was made by the first son of Saradon."

"Saradon did not have any children," Harper said, though the moment she spoke, she realised she had no idea if that were true. Aedon had implied Saradon never had anyone of significance, save his mother—but she knew nothing more than that.

The Mother smiled, as if she heard Harper's doubt in her own words. "He did not have any children that the world *knew* of. His blood still flows today, though even he does not yet realise it. His line remains unbroken..." She paused, as if savouring the moment, "in you."

HARPER

Harper had not heard Vanir correctly. It was the only explanation. Saradon's line remained unbroken in her? A penniless orphan from halfway across the world?

"I ought to call you Harper of Pelenor. Harper of the House of Ravakian, by your proper birthright, though the name of that House crumbles into dust, and all others are long since dead."

"No. You must be mistaken." Harper shook her head and snatched her hand back from Vanir, clutching at the bracelet and the charm. "I'm a nobody from oceans away. I—"

"The water in your blood does not lie to me, child. You know you are half-elf, yes?"

"Yes…" Harper felt the now familiar curl of magic tingling in her belly, mixing with confusion and anxiety.

"Elves do not reign in Caledan. Nowhere over the Great Sea, in fact. That is the domain of men, those you know as Eldarkind, the faded puppets of the gods."

Harper frowned. She had no idea what Vanir spoke of.

"No. Your blood is Pelenori. You are the only remaining daughter of the Ravakian line. Your mother is Saradon's granddaughter, his only grandchild."

Vanir frowned. "She knew her heritage. I wonder why you were not afforded the same privilege. You deserved more than a life of poverty, despite the curse of your blood. Perhaps she sought to protect you, sending you far away with no knowledge of your birthright."

Harper had no reply, and for once, her mind had stilled of questions. Only one thing surfaced. She did not understand —and it couldn't be true.

"I promise you, I speak the truth. Drink of the wellspring and see for yourself." Vanir tucked her rune stones into a pocket, stood, and shuffled over to a ledge, where a stone chalice stood amongst other paraphernalia. She dipped it into the crystal-clear water and offered it to Harper. "Drink. See."

Harper obediently sipped. The water was ice cold, jarring her teeth. It carved a freezing path down her throat to sit unpleasantly in her belly. Her head fogged, overcome with dizziness, and Vanir's warm hands steadied her as she slipped away.

The woman's hand stroked the babe's forehead. She was slim and willowy, a curtain of raven hair obscuring the world as she cradled the swaddled child close. Her heart ached at the parting that was to come, and the one she had already made. But there was no choice. They came, and they brought death. She was already doomed, but her babe would live on.

"I wish I could have known you for longer, my princess," her soft voice crooned in the small space. She wished she had just a

little more peace. With him. With them both. Her love had already crossed into death to save them, but it had not been enough. She fingered the leather bracelet he had made her not long past, with the silver bead that had belonged to her father upon it, and tucked it inside the swaddling. "At least you will have something of your past."

She shifted, unable to find comfort on the rocks, and retreated farther into the cave, circling her pack carefully. Its contents would be her daughter's salvation. Outside, cool moonlight filtered in, as the stars twinkled coldly overhead. They watched her, but no longer watched over her. That time had passed. Now they would see as she met her demise. "But they will watch over you, and I with them, daughter," she promised, and her voice caught. "We both will. I—I will miss you with all my heart as I watch you grow."

She said it knowing that it was a lie in the hard depths of her heart. When death came—that would be it. The end. Obliteration. Gone. But her heart would shatter if she thought on it, that she would not be there to protect their daughter. She was afraid of death, as much as she tried not to admit it to herself. Long had she known this day might come, but it did not mean she embraced death, or walked to it willingly. She rebelled. Why else had she tried to escape? Yet now, there was nowhere else to run. Only beyond the realms of life, across the border into the unknown. She hoped death would not be painful—she begged the stars silently for at least that small mercy.

"I will meet him again—your father," she said to herself, infusing her voice with as much strength as possible. "I will pass into his arms." She still felt them around her, strong, warm, protective. Just as hers were now around their child. The thundering drew closer as wind battered the trees and mountains. She was surrounded. It was time. She swallowed.

"I will not die in a cave, cowering like a beast," she said with a juddering sob, as tears spilled from her eyes. "I am a daughter of

Ravakian." With one last, loving gaze, taking in every detail of her *sleeping baby—the wisps of dark hair, the round, peaceful face, the tiny hands—she kissed her forehead, savouring the tiny body's warmth. She forced herself to lift her chin and put one foot in front of the other, going to meet her death with a brave heart, no matter the fact that she trembled like a leaf and would sooner turn tail and run as far and fast as she could. They waited outside as she emerged from the trees and into the clearing. She had never been so close to one dragon before, let alone so many. Her breath caught in her chest as she stopped. She forced her feet forward and craned her neck up at them.*

"Ilrune, daughter of Arven of the line of Ravakian, you are charged with high treason against the realm and sovereignty of Pelenor," said the rider atop the largest dragon in the centre of the ring around her.

Her lip instinctively curled at the sight of him in his grand armour and plumed helmet. "It matters not to you that I am inno-cent, Raedon?" she sneered, despite her fear. She held her ground as his dragon rumbled at her.

"You have been found guilty on al—"

"I am not guilty for my grandfather's sins," she shouted. "My blood is not a measure of my ilk, rider."

"I do not come to bandy words with a criminal," he snarled back. "Our orders are clear, and retribution will be sought."

His dragon's throat glowed as molten fire brewed within it.

She trembled, struggling to maintain herself. She glanced down at the baby, the comforting warmth in her arms. "I do this for you, my sweet princess," she murmured.

"I beg your pardon?"

*She looked up with hate-filled eyes, wishing that the venom of her look could strike him down. "You took him from me, but I will see him across the border in death. She will not die with us this day. You will **never** find her!" Ilrune closed her eyes and sucked all her* *power into her core. She had drained every Dragonheart she had collected on her meticulous travels, every magical artefact with any remnant of power. She glowed from within, until the riders before her shielded their eyes.*

She pushed it all into the babe, then thrust her as far away as she possibly could, sending the child into the unseen plane where magic flowed like an endless, rippling ocean. She wished for warmth, love, and care, seeking it out for her daughter, but she only had a moment to act. There was no time to think about the coldness of her empty arms. No time to fear what would happen a moment later. She only hoped that she sent her daughter to a safer place and loving arms.

"No!" thundered Raedon as the babe vanished.

His dragon's maw opened and a jet of white-hot fire arced toward Ilrune. But with a smile upon her face, her life's energy utterly spent on the salvation of her daughter, Ilrune had already crumpled to the ground. By the time the dragon's flame consumed her body, her soul was already gone.

33

HARPER

Harper awoke with tears burning down her cheeks, half-leaned against Vanir's legs as the old woman sat, once more tumbling rune stones though her fingers. She blinked the world into focus once more. She was Harper, yet still Ilrune. Was the pain she felt her own? Her heart was shattered. The stink of burning flesh lingered impossibly upon the chilled cave air. Her ears rang with the roar of dragons.

"Interesting," muttered Vanir.

"W–What was that?" Harper asked, but she did not need Vanir's answer, she realised. She knew she had just witnessed her own mother's death, and her own salvation. Vanir did not answer as she regarded her with a kind, sad smile, her milky eyes filled with tears.

"It's true?" Harper choked out. Her throat seemed stripped raw, as if she had been shouting, just like Ilrune. *Ilrune. My... mother.* The word felt strange.

"That was proof, girl. The truth indeed. I told you your past was as interesting as your future." Vanir cackled, but she patted Harper on the knee with a sympathetic smile. "You do not have to decide what that means for you right this instant. It is a lot to learn." Her hands continued rubbing the stones from finger to finger.

Harper could not answer.

"I did not see *that* past for your bracelet. My, my. She is long dead, but perhaps you may yet meet your great-grand-father. He is so very close in Afnirheim, and your friend is there, as well."

Harper's attention sharpened. "Ragnar is there?"

"Yes, child. Ragnar Dúrnir is deep beneath Afnirheim. The water tells me all."

He had been taken much farther than any of them could have anticipated, but he was *alive*? Hope soared in her heart, even as much as it felt shaken by her vision's revelations.

"How can we save him?"

Vanir's face was grave. "Rescue may not be possible, child. But drink of the river. It may show you the answer. Focus on Ragnar Dúrnir to see what you will."

Even though the thought of another vision churned her already nauseated belly, Harper did as Vanir bade her. She hurried to use the chalice to scoop more bitingly cold water up and take a gulp, sloshing it down her chin and onto her chest in her haste. This time, she sat and braced herself against the rocks, ready for the swooping darkness.

That darkness crushed her. Harper could perceive nothing and no one. Her eyes hurt with the strain of looking for anything to mark her location. The vision tumbled through the shadowed, shattered halls of Afnirheim once more. Ruins and bodies loomed in the murk as she passed. Her gaze did not waver, and she set her lips

against the whimper of fear that sought to escape, clenching her fists to stop them from shaking. The prickles travelling up her spine did nothing to ease her anxiety.

Shadows and light cast by the sickly red glare of fires danced in the distance as she crossed voids and offshoots to the tunnels. Down she went, farther into the dark. The smell of decay, festering wounds, and excrement found her first. Next, she heard the moans and shrieks. They were not all goblins. She feared what she would find.

In the depths of the mines, dwarves huddled in pits, some covered with iron grates. Goblins crowded around each open pit, shrieking with excitement and amusement as they threw rocks at their captives, whipping and tormenting them. Harper did not want to look too closely. Panic rose in her, stealing her breath. The goblins' filed teeth and fetid claws were within inches of her. They could not perceive her, she reassured herself, but all the same, she kept a keen eye on them.

Harper floated over the pits. There were hundreds in a grid pattern. Most contained dwarves. It was where the dwarves kept their goblin slaves, she realised. She searched each pit as she passed, squinting in the poor light. It was hard not to stop and stare. Each dwarf barely passed as a living being, for they had been tortured beyond all recognition. She held in a retch as she passed a pit where several dwarves lay, obviously dead.

Please, let him be alive, she pleaded silently. It seemed too much to hope that Ragnar was unharmed. How many days had he been gone now? It did not bear thinking about. Then she saw him. It was only by chance, for her gaze had passed over the pit twice already. He huddled in a deep, dark corner under a slight overhang, head on his knees and eyes shut. Close by, other dwarves huddled or lay in piles of their own bodily fluids.

Her heart leapt. Was he alive? The vision wavered, then moved her along, past the pits, until she could no longer see him, even by craning her neck.

No! she longed to say. Stop! Go back!

It was fruitless. The vision carried her where it willed. On she passed, beyond the reach of the flames and into the darkness, where only the stale air awaited. Suddenly, a cold tendril of air caressed her cheek, pulling her onward. Forward and up it went, and she with it, breathing in the gift of the clear, crisp air that stripped the stench from her lungs. Stronger it grew, but the caves became narrower, until she squeezed into a tight fissure. In the distance, a crack of daylight was her only clue that the end was nigh. Through the stone, she passed into blinding light. As her eyes adjusted to the clear, cold day and the weak sun shining down upon her, she turned in a circle. She stood outside the mountain, a sheer, stone cliff behind her, yet no hint of a cave or fissure.

Harper frowned and drew closer to it. With ethereal fingers, she traced upon the moss-covered rock until she found the almost invisible crack. It was only the thickness of a hair, but she traced it up, where it bent horizontally to form the top of a doorway. A door into the mountain. Excitement fluttered in her stomach, as well as hope. Hope that she knew where Ragnar and the remainder of his kin were kept. Hope that the secret door would allow them safe passage. With a shudder, she recalled the goblin-filled halls and the carnage within. It would be suicidal to try to fight through the dwarven city.

The mountains grew hazy and faded as Harper surfaced from the vision. She looked at Vanir with wide eyes, gasping a deep breath.

"Do not delay, child," Vanir said. "You have seen the way. Go. They depend on you."

Harper stood—but swallowed as she hesitated.

"I am here when your questions seek answers," said Vanir simply.

"Thank you." Harper now had a pressing task, but it only just held back the tide of uncertainty within her. She bowed to Vanir, turned, and ran.

34
HARPER

The jarl looked disgruntled when she returned to him, but he brightened when she told him, between short, gasping breaths, what she had seen of Ragnar and his kin. "You describe a thirl door."

"What's a thirl door?"

The jarl set off at a jog, and she hastened after him. "It is a secret door, several of which are built into every dwarven city, that allow in good times for smuggling and illicit affairs, and more dire days for escape if the city is lost," he said as they ran back to the königshalle to speak with Korrin. "Our kin from Afnirheim should have used them to escape, but maybe they did not concede defeat until too late, or perhaps they were cut off. We cannot know. To my knowledge, a thirl door has never been used for entry, but perhaps there is nothing to stop it." With that, he hurried them both back to the königshalle, summoning her companions to join them.

König Korrin paced the hall, his brows furrowed, as Jarl Halvar finished recounting Harper's time with the Vanir—and her accidental discovery. "You are certain?"

Halvar nodded. "From what the girl describes, it can only be a thirl door."

"How many of our kin did you see there?" Korrin asked Harper.

Surprised by his attention, she bowed hurriedly to give herself a moment of composure. "Hundreds, König. All in a terrible state."

"We cannot abandon our kin," Korrin said decisively. "I thank the Mother for her vision. Now we are armed with knowledge."

"What will you have us do, König?" the jarl asked.

"For now, Jarl Halvar, I will muster Keldheim's forces. We will rescue our kin and determine the true scale of the rot in our once fair city." He glared at them all balefully. "Then I will muster every dwarf in Valtivar, and we will retake Afnirheim. The goblin scum will pay for their sins, and we will defeat them once and for all. The *pascha's* domain will be no more in *our* mountains."

Harper took a step back at the vehement hate and determination in Korrin's voice.

"When will you have us ready, König?" Halvar asked, his own visage grim.

"At once. Call every dwarf to arms. Those we do not take will defend Keldheim in our absence. We leave three days hence, by the tunnels and our own thirl doors. We stay away from the roads. None but our own kin will know of our passing. The goblin scum will not know until our blades fall on their necks. I will lead us to victory." Korrin gripped the head of the ceremonial axe belted to his waist until his knuckles whitened.

"We could not have asked for a better outcome." Brand heaved a sigh of relief.

Aedon bounced on the balls of his feet with impatience as they made their way back to their quarters. "I wish we could leave now."

Erika nodded in agreement, her mouth set in a grim line, but she did not speak. Harper felt nauseated by both prospects: staying, or going.

"These things take time. Three days is quick for an entire city to arm," Brand mused.

"Not quick enough," grumbled Aedon. "Will you share your vision with us, Harper?"

"W–What?" Harper stammered as he disrupted her thoughts, which had once more strayed to her vision of Ilrune.

Aedon frowned at her. "Are you all right? You seem quiet."

"Yes, I'm fine," she said, willing the heat from her cheeks, unsuccessfully.

Aedon's frown deepened. "Will you show me your vision of Ragnar?" he asked again.

"Yes," Harper said with relief. She willed herself to calm down. They did not know of her other vision. But ought she tell them? Once upon a time, she would have found it far-fetched to claim, but she was slowly beginning to accept that in Pelenor, the ridiculous was true more often than not. And yet if she told them, it would create such a rift between them when she had only just started to feel secure in her growing friendship—and place in their group. Already, a gulf had begun to grow between her and Aedon. After what had happened, he had stepped back, his friendliness strained. She had no idea how Brand felt. It was clear Erika hated all Saradon stood for, though Harper still had no idea why. Harper didn't need Erika to like her any less, Harper thought, suppressing a snort.

"Let's not delay then," said Brand. "Let's see this vision, and go train. We'll need every ounce of strength we have to survive a horde of goblins." He cracked his neck. "I need to smash some steel."

In the privacy of their quarters, they sat on the floor, cross-legged, hands interlaced. Aedon's magic mingled with Harper's and teased out the vision—but she kept the *other* vision tightly locked away.

"I will be glad when he is with us once more," Brand said heavily after the vision faded. "Let's go. Ragnar needs us to be as strong as we can for him." Erika and Aedon jumped up to fetch their weapons, but Brand grasped Harper's wrist as she rose, halting her. "You're not yourself. What's wrong?" he asked in a low voice as the others left. His gaze searched hers, but she dropped her eyes.

"Nothing," she said.

"I will not ask again, Harper. You can trust me. Whatever it is. You are one of us now. To compromise you is to compromise all of us."

Harper squirmed in his grasp.

"Distraction could mean failure. Ragnar is counting on us."

She swallowed. "There was another vision."

"What was it? It must have been grave to disturb you so."

Harper nodded, pleading eyes raising to Brand's. "You mustn't tell anyone else. Please."

"I swear it, unless it will harm any of them."

"It won't," she said quickly. "I… I found out who my mother is. Or rather, was."

Brand waited expectantly.

Her voice was so quiet, he had to lean closer to hear her. "My mother was Ilrune of the House Ravakian. Saradon's own granddaughter."

Brand's hand slipped from her wrist and he stilled with predatory grace. She felt the weight of his full attention crash upon her. "It cannot be."

Hot tears pricked Harper's eyes. "It is. I saw her die. I saw her send me to Caledan." She shook her head, trying to shake away the memory of the dragonfire as it obliterated all. Her hands trembled as she closed her palms over her eyes— unable to spare herself reliving it again.

"Skies above," swore Brand quietly, as the others returned noisily from their rooms. Harper sniffed and straightened, wiping her face clear of any expression that could betray her secret to them. His lips thinned. "Speak no more of this now. Later."

Relief bloomed in her. Head low, she raced off for her own knife and sword, not meeting Aedon's or Erika's gaze. But Brand stared after her and she felt the weight of his brooding upon her retreating back. She hoped she was right to trust him.

35

HARPER

For the rest of the day, they trained at full pelt in the training pit near the armoury. Harper was glad for the distraction. They pushed until every muscle screamed and her mind dulled with fatigue. She had reluctantly partnered with Aedon that day, and he was unusually distant with her. It left her like swirling water, confused and unsettled. Hadn't they agreed to be nothing more than friends? She hated the awkwardness that hung between them.

She pushed all thoughts of Aedon and that kiss to the back of her mind, as difficult as it was with the heat of his body so close as they locked in mock battle time and again. Instead, she relished practising, using magic with her blade, charging the dead metal with speed and accuracy, even flames and lightning... much to the delight of the watching dwarves. She now realised the truth of Aedon's insistence that magic was instinctive. It was like a warm river flowing through her. She only had to will it to harness it. The limit was her own strength, dictating how much or how long she could channel it.

"We'll stop there for now," Aedon said, though he was only breathing slightly more heavy than normal.

"I can continue," insisted Harper. The magic made her feel alive, exhilarated, and buoyed her strength and agility.

"It's best that we do not push you too much too soon. Not with what is at stake."

"What happens if you do?" Harper asked as she lowered her blade and let the magic fade away. Glowing blue flame along the dagger faded into nothing.

Aedon lowered his own long, slim blade. "The magic will suck the very life from you, and you die."

Chills flooded Harper. Before her, she did not see Aedon anymore, but Ilrune crumpling to the ground. *It wasn't the dragon that killed her. She used everything she had... to save me.*

"Harper?"

She blinked herself back to the world. "Yes. Sure. I'm going to get something to eat."

"Harper, wait up," said Brand as he parried Erika's strike. They disengaged and he ambled over, covered in a thin sheen of sweat. His chest heaved with each breath. "Aedon and Erika, you spar. I'll go with Harper. I need a drink."

Aedon shrugged and turned to Erika—who frowned at Brand, eyed Harper, then whirled to block Aedon's strike.

Brand walked beside Harper in silence to the all-day feast in the königshalle. The hall was busy, but not overly so. Many still trained at the various arenas around Keldheim. They each grabbed a bowl of stew and a beaker of water, then perched at the end of one of the long trestle tables.

Harper tucked in with gusto, savouring the rich meat and tangy spices, but Brand ate slowly, his eyes never leaving her face. "So," he eventually prompted. "Will you tell me more?"

Harper met his gaze for a moment—serious and kind, as

always—before looking away. "Only if you promise to hear me out and not change how you view me. I'm still the same person, just not sure how to make sense of any of this."

"I swear it. I will not judge you." Brand returned to his food.

The words tumbled out. Harper told him every detail of her vision. She remembered it with such vivid clarity, as if it had been permanently etched upon her mind. When she finished, Brand's food sat forgotten as he gaped at her. She squirmed under his scrutiny and folded her arms.

"Well?" she asked, having no idea what she wanted him to say.

He shook his head, blowing out a loud gush of air. "In truth, I do not know what to say. I would not have believed it, but I know you would not lie about such a thing. How would you even know to?"

He shook his head and ran a large hand through his messy locks, then dropped his voice to a whisper. "So, you are Harper, daughter of Ilrune, granddaughter of Arven, great-granddaughter of *Saradon*?"

She nodded.

"Wait… Who was the dragon rider you mentioned?"

Harper thought a moment. "Raedon, I think she said."

Brand's dark skin paled. "Are you certain?" he asked, a little too quickly to be casual.

"Yes. Why?" Her eyes narrowed.

Brand stared at her for a second, impassive. "We must tell the others."

"Why?" Her voice rose an octave. Nearby dwarves turned their way, and she fought the volume down, and schooled the anguish from her face. "I'm not ready. I don't even know how. Aedon will hate me, and Erika… Erika will *worse* than hate me!"

"I will see that she doesn't," he growled. "And as for Aedon, you shouldn't care."

"I'm not ready to tell them," she insisted.

"You must."

She refused to lower her gaze this time. "I shan't unless you tell me why."

His eyes darted around. Their disagreement had begun to earn attention. He leaned toward her, lowering his voice. "Raedon is the general of the Winged Kingsguard. He is also Aedon's eldest brother."

Harper gaped. "What?" she breathed.

"It's true. You are… What? Twenty or so summers old? Raedon has been the general of the Winged Kingsguard since before you were born. It makes sense. He would have been personally tasked to exterminate the line of Ravakian, if no one except for Toroth and his predecessors knew it had endured."

"Aedon's brother killed my mother?" It could not be.

Brand nodded, his face grave. "And that is why we must tell him."

Harper sat back, her own food forgotten, feeling sick to her stomach as the roaring of dragonfire consumed her once more. Yet again, she saw Ilrune's lifeless body fall to the ground.

36

HARPER

Erika was on her feet before the vision ended, pointing at Harper with a shaking finger. "*You* are his kin?" she snarled. Brand rose and placed himself between them as Harper and Aedon scrambled to their feet in the centre of their living space. She ignored Aedon, pretended not to see the frown he cast her way, but it pierced her none-theless.

"Erika," Brand said in a warning voice. "Do not be blinded. It was not her sin."

Erika swore in a harsh tongue. "I have been travelling with *you*—with *his* blood—all this time." She was pale, her body shaking with suppressed rage.

"It is not her sin, just as it was not *your* sin," Brand said through gritted teeth.

Erika's hand flattened the roughly cut fringe over her forehead.

"All I know is my mother died to protect me," Harper said in a low voice. "I don't know anything about her other than her name."

Aedon stilled beside her. "Saradon…" he trailed off. Erika flinched at the name. "In the beginning, he was a revolutionary. He fought for the greater good, for the people, against an oppressive and greedy elven king. Toroth's father. Somewhere along the line, his intentions grew less noble. He did not care who he harmed. For his sins, his entire family was executed. No one knew that he had any surviving children."

"Except the king," Harper said.

"Yes. Who knows how he found out. Toroth and his father continued the purge. They hunted Saradon's House… *your* House… to extinction, for fear it would happen again."

"My mother couldn't help who she was," Harper said softly. "Was she guilty of no other crime?"

Aedon shook his head. "We have no way of knowing."

"But Raedon killed her anyway," Harper said, her voice flat.

"When you are of the Winged Kingsguard, you follow any and every order," Aedon spoke softly, but with steel in his voice.

Harper stared at him. *He defends his brother?*

"As the general, even more so. You *are* the king's will."

Harper finally began to piece it all together. Why he hated the king so much. Why he was an outlaw. Aedon had once filled that role, as well. She fleetingly wondered how many orders Aedon had been forced to fulfil that he otherwise would have refused. She wondered how many he had killed on the king's orders, against the will of his own heart. She did not ask. She did not want to know. She felt sick. Harper gripped the back of a chair to keep herself upright.

For a moment, she looked at him in a new light. Aedon, the general of the Winged Kingsguard. Stern. Unflinching. Emotionless. She didn't know if she'd be able to see him as simply Aedon, the cheerful and charming outlaw anymore.

Simple, friendly, open Aedon. Or... the individual that she had danced upon the line of feeling attracted to, drawn by the alluring sense of freedom he offered her. Fleetingly, Harper felt grateful it had not been he upon the dragon's back. She had no doubt the outcome would have been the same. His brother was bad enough, but for it to be him... Her heart would truly break.

If that were the case, my time with them would be over.

Even so, she knew deeper in her bones than before that she could never pursue him, knowing what she now knew. She looked at him with fresh eyes as he stared back impassively, wondering how she had ever been attracted to him. Wondering how she had not seen the dark side, the shadowed past, that all his merriment concealed. She knew so little of him. Her attraction to what he offered had been nothing more than wishful foolishness. It sealed the certainty within her utterly. Her attention slid to Brand. As he calmly watched her, she knew he understood what was in her heart.

"I do not judge you for your blood," Brand said to her, then turned to Aedon. "Just as I do not judge you for your blood—or your past actions."

"Neither do I you and yours," Aedon murmured with a half-hearted smile that did not reach his eyes. His gaze dropped to the floor.

Brand turned to Erika, his eyebrow raised.

She pursed her lips, as if trying to keep the words in, then blew out a breath. "I will not judge you by your blood," she growled and shoved past Brand to storm from their quarters. Harper watched her go. The door slammed after her, shaking dust from the ceiling.

"She will be back," Brand promised. "You know she is quick to anger and needs to burn off that energy before she can see clearly again." He usually went with her, but now he lingered, as if unwilling to leave Harper and Aedon alone. Grateful, she drifted toward him.

"I think I'll call it a night," she said. "I'm not hungry, and I don't want to train anymore today."

Brand laid a hand upon Harper's shoulder. "As you wish, friend." The word sent warmth through her, and she smiled up at the great warrior gratefully. "I, too, have had enough of the day, but I had best go see that she is all right." He jerked a thumb at the door.

She did not acknowledge Aedon as she made her way to her room and barred the door. She heard Brand retreat, too, leaving Aedon alone. Harper quickly washed herself in ice-cold water and dressed again to sit cross-legged upon the bed, the scratchy but warm bedspread around her shoulders. Placing a candle upon a plate in front of her, she watched the fire slowly consume the tallow as her mind slipped to another time and place.

She had so many questions, but one nagged at her repeatedly.

Who am I?

37

HARPER

"I want you to understand why you're not dead." Erika's voice loomed behind Harper in the dark corridor. She jumped and whirled around, her pulse instantly thundering and her chest clutching with panic. Erika lurked nearby—a threat shrouded by shadows.

"What?" Harper stammered, conscious that she did not even have her knife upon her and the others were beyond shouting distance. She backed into the wall, fingering the rough texture of the stone behind her.

"If they had not been there to defend you, you would already be gone," Erika said. Harper could hear the scowl in her voice.

"I haven't done anything wrong." Harper straightened and stepped forwards again. She refused to cower, even though she was no match for the nomad woman.

"I know. And that's why I'm sorry."

Harper gaped.

"Anything of *him* is a reminder." Erika stepped into the

faint light, her hand lifting the fringe she always kept flattened over her forehead.

Harper gasped.

For the first time, she could see the scar marring it. Saradon's Mark, branded into Erika's forehead.

"How? Why?" she breathed.

"This is why I hate him so," Erika answered in a low voice. She swept her fringe down again, her attention fixed upon the floor, in another time and place. "I am one of the Indis, the warrior nomad tribes. Five hundred years ago, most of my people bound themselves to Saradon's cause."

Erika bared her teeth. "When he was defeated, our people were hunted and exterminated like vermin, almost to extinction. To this day, some support his ways. *Fools*. So our persecution never ended. One day, they came for us."

Harper stayed silent, transfixed.

"They killed any who were not useful, and those who were a threat. The matriarchs, the men, ones who would not bow to them or change their ways. Submission is not in our nature. The Indis win—or we die. That is our way. They branded the rest of us and sold us into slavery. My mother was killed. My father. My brothers. In *his* name. I was nine."

Harper sank against the wall. "I'm so sorry."

Erika let out a harsh bark of laughter. "It's not your fault. I eventually got my revenge. In a way, you are just like me. We have our ancestors' bad blood, but we are not them." Erika looked at her, her hard eyes glinting. "You are one of us. I will fight with you, defend you. But if you ever betray us, if you ever take up his cause, I *will* kill you. Do you understand?"

Harper narrowed her eyes. It surprised her to feel relieved, not scared. She understood that Erika now trusted her, truly, for the first time. "I do." And now... Now Harper knew where she stood with the nomad woman. And why Erika was as hard and unforgiving as she was. She had suffered unimaginably as a result of Saradon, however indirectly.

Erika turned and strode away without another word. When she had gone, Harper let out a deep breath. *I did not see that coming.*

Their departure was upon them in no time. A company of dwarves led by König Korrin's own command, as well as Jarl Halvar's group, assembled in the halls of Keldheim, ready to depart through the thirl door. Harper fell in with Brand, Aedon, and Erika amongst Korrin's dwarves. Korrin stood before them all, resplendent in his full armour of many-hued plated metals, embellished with enamel inlays of wolves, dragons, and gods across his body.

"We travel silently. We strike hard and fast. We return with our kin." König Korrin's voice rang through the silent hall. The entire room saluted him at once, fists to chests.

Harper wished she could have spent more time training. She could wield her slim blade with better skill than before, and her magic had come on in leaps and bounds, but she had seen what awaited them beneath Afnirheim and was under no false illusions that her paltry skills would see her through. She was glad for her companions now more than ever, knowing what they journeyed toward.

It took hours of tramping through dimly lit caves and up a steep incline before they reached Keldheim's thirl door. At the king's touch—Harper could not see much, trying to crane her neck over those standing in front of her—the thirl door opened, and light and fresh air tumbled in. The breeze was so cold, a welcome change from the moist, warm, stale air of the caves, that Harper pulled her cloak tighter, grateful for the thick wool. After walking through the thirl door, they followed the könig's men down into the thickly wooded valley, where the sky was lost to the green canopy above and, once more, the confining darkness under the evergreens consumed them.

At midday two days later, with little rest, they approached Afnirheim. The mountain stood as silent as any other, but the könig took no chances. His scouts melted between the trees, weapons out, in a wide, sweeping line before them. Up they climbed to where Afnirheim's most obscure thirl door nestled right at the top of the tree line, tucked into the cliff and shrouded by the towering pines. The narrow stairs, cleverly hidden amongst clefts in the sheer faces, forced the dwarves to ascend in single file. The host dithered impatiently at their foot, waiting to climb.

Just as Harper had seen it in her vision, it was an innocuous cliff with no hint of a door, but Korrin knew where to look. At his touch, light flared briefly, illuminating the outline of the door. When he placed his palms upon it and pushed, it clicked open.

"I'll need your help with the könig's plan."

Harper startled at the sound of Aedon's voice in her mind. She had not become entirely at ease with being able to speak into another's mind, though Aedon had her practise until she could manage it. It reminded her far too much of Dimitrius. And it still felt far too intimate for her liking. She still could not bear to be near Aedon, knowing what she now knew of her mother and his brother.

"Yes?" she answered dutifully, waiting for her turn to file through the open door into the darkness of Afnirheim.

"Goblins thrive in the dark. They almost have night vision, like an owl. Dwarves, on the other hand, need light to see, which goblins abhor. So we, dear Harper, are going to make sure our friends can see. You'll just have to follow my lead. All right?" She heard his grim glee as he looked toward the mountain with antic-ipation.

She, in contrast, felt sick to her stomach. *"Yes."* She focused on trying not to vomit.

It was their turn. The way was wide enough for three to pass abreast, so she filed in with Aedon and Erika, whilst Brand took up the rear, his wings taking a row by them-selves. In silence, they tramped inside, led down the smooth way by Aedon's dim faelights. The farther they descended, the more the stench grew with the heat, until Harper felt nauseous with that, as well. She was glad for an empty stomach for a change. She had barely been able to eat that morning through worry about what they were to encounter —and what they might find. She concentrated on Ragnar, seeing him in her mind.

Unexpectedly, Korrin halted, summoning Aedon and Harper. They pushed through the ranks of silent dwarves to find the way in front of them branching off into six different passages. "We are nearly upon Afnirheim's lower levels," Korrin murmured. "I need you to sense ahead, tell me precisely where the goblins are, as well as Ragnar and the dwarves."

Aedon shook his head. "I'm afraid it is not so easy, König. We have nothing of the dwarves or the elves to trace them by."

"Wait," said Harper, struck by inspiration. "I have some-thing of Ragnar's." She looked at Aedon. "You can trace him using it, yes?" she asked, then spoke into his mind. *"Just like you traced me using my knife."*

He nodded. "Yes. What is it?"

She unshouldered her pack and rummaged through it, to the sound of the könig's impatient tsking. "Here." She passed Aedon the one thing she had of Ragnar's—the tiny *chatura* piece he had given to her.

He smiled sadly, nodding. "This will be perfect. König, we can find precisely where Ragnar, and your kin, are. With them, I suspect we will find the goblins." Aedon passed it back to Harper, much to her surprise. "You've done this before, with the Dragonheart. You know how."

She swallowed. Did she? It had been different with the Dragonheart. Instinctive. Ragnar was another matter. Everyone looked at her, silent and expectant. She swallowed and closed her eyes.

Ragnar... Think of Ragnar. She held the wooden piece tightly between her hands, feeling the ridges and contours. She had watched Ragnar carve it. Watched his stiff hands shape it, like fat spread with a knife. He made it look easy, sitting there calmly while his hands worked.

Harper could smell the smoke of his pipe that always seemed to linger, but it was a pleasant, fragrant smoke. In her mind, she replayed him carving the *chatura* piece, then stopping and looking up at her, smiling in the way he always did—warm, friendly, genuine, the skin around his eyes crinkling. She pulled toward it, holding every part of Ragnar she could recall. Slowly, the niggle built, just as it had with the Dragonheart.

"This way," she whispered, pointing to the fourth passageway.

Korrin turned and led them farther into the mountain. If nothing else, the growing stench told them they were on the right track. That, and the faint sounds of shrieking and chattering that Harper had hoped never to hear again. Dwarves drew their weapons, most bearing an axe of some kind—some large, some small, some double-headed, some with short blades. Harper had never seen such an array of different axes. Some dwarves held staffs with long blades upon the end, and others gripped hammers. Despite being fully armoured, with clanking metal plates and weapons, the dwarves moved with surprising stealth, using the goblin's din as cover for their own movement. All had been warned to hold the element of surprise. Still, the order came too soon for Harper's liking.

"Now!" thundered Korrin—and burst forth. The dwarves surged behind him, pushing Harper along in their midst. Aedon firmly grasped her hand and pulled her to one side.

She felt the magic flare in him, then added her strength, focusing upon coalescing the light into being. Aedon's large faelight eclipsed her small, winking mote, but slowly, hers gathered strength, merging with his and soaring up to illuminate the cavern in blinding white. It took the dwarves a moment to adjust to the brightness, but they threw themselves back into battle with relish. The goblins' shrieks soon became wails of pain as the light seared their eyes and dwarven weapons struck them down. Still, more swarmed from nowhere, jumping over the grated pits to fall upon the dwarves in great numbers. Brand and Erika, smiles on their faces, stood back to back in the middle of the fray, killing all who came within reach.

"Don't stop focusing your magic!" Aedon said with gritted teeth, even as he pulled his blade. "Come. We have to find Ragnar!"

They leapt forward as the last of the dwarves spilled into the caves. Sheathing their weapons, they rushed to the pits, hauling up injured dwarves and carrying them through the passage, up to the thirl door, and out to safety.

Harper followed the tiny thread of Ragnar's essence through the maelstrom, while Aedon danced around her, his blade a blur as he cut down goblins. She joined in as little as possible, smashing her blade against any who dared get too close. The goblins were small and quick, popping up from seemingly nowhere. Her blade squelched into the guts of one, slurping as she pulled it free, the body falling to the ground, lifeless. She bent over, vomiting.

"Harper, we don't have time! Hurry!" Aedon said.

Brand and Erika fought their way closer until the four of them stood as a knot once more.

"Here! He's here!" Erika's triumphant shout emerged.

Harper rushed over to the pit with the overhang and saw Ragnar huddled at the bottom, staring up with wide eyes. He exclaimed at the sight of them, and Brand wrenched the grate aside. He leaned down to grab Ragnar's hand and haul him out with ease. The dwarf crumpled onto the ground before them, his face blanching and twisted in pain. Brand swore and picked Ragnar up. He launched into the air and dove for the cave exit before landing, tucking his wings in, and running up the tunnel to pass Ragnar off. Erika, Aedon, and Harper helped two other dwarves out of the pit, sending them on their way before moving to the next one.

They were halfway across the cave when the entire mountain shook. At the far side of the cavern, Saradon emerged in the giant opening, wreathed in glowing, purple light. Magic flickered in his palms.

38
HARPER

Aedon swore, only to be drowned out by Erika's screech of rage. Brand landed beside her, slamming into the ground, and bodily held her back to prevent her from leaping toward the elf. Everything around them ceased. Even goblins cowed before Saradon. Bedraggled, injured dwarves flinched away. Their battle-weary brethren gripped weapons tighter, but grave faces poorly masked their apprehension.

Harper stilled, captivated by Saradon, whose penetrating gaze swept the cave. Part of her felt fear, just as the rest of them did, but it was different for her. *He is my kin*. It felt strange, abhorrent. Shadows moved beside him. A figure emerged. And time stopped for Harper. Harper's jaw slipped open, and her eyes widened. She knew that silhouette before he stepped into the light. The clean cut of his dark, fitted robes. The dark, disdainful frown.

No.

It could not be. Her fragmented attention collided full force with Dimitrius, as though he pulled her in, as though he were the centre of her world. The very individual she knew that she ought to never see again—but the one individual she had secretly wanted to cross paths with more than anything. But not like this. Not there. Idle magic danced in Dimitrius's palms as he stood beside Saradon and beheld them all—but the blood drained from his face as he found her in the chaos, as though his attention too had been magnetised to her by some force greater than either of them. Without a doubt, it was him. Even if he had a twin, she would have known him by the way he so clearly recognised her.

Korrin's horn sounded the retreat, and the wave of dwarves turned, running toward the tunnel. Aedon, Harper, and Erika followed suit, swept along by the tide. Saradon attacked. Magic arced toward them, blasting aside goblins and dwarves alike. They were hurled into rocks, smashed into pits, or smote where they stood, falling to the ground in a jumbled tangle of blackened limbs.

It broke the spell. Harper wrenched her gaze from Dimitrius's and turned, even though every part of her wanted to move towards him, not away. The area became a stampede as dwarves lowered their heads and sprinted toward the tunnel. The thunder of their charge jarred until Harper could hear nothing else. The injured were dragged along, held upright by the crush; otherwise, they would not have made it out alive.

Aedon pushed through the bodies to one side, resisting the flow. When his hand ripped from hers, Harper turned back, swept forward inexorably. *What is he doing?* With a determined look, he forged back down the passage and flattened himself against the wall, holding out of everyone's way. With a great rumble, the mountain shuddered beneath their feet. Aedon's complexion whitened, and every muscle coiled in his body as he fought to channel enough magic. He attempted to break the stone—to bring the mountain down upon them! She paled. He could not face it alone.

"Erika!" she screamed. The woman turned, and Harper jabbed her pointed finger back at the elf.

Erika immediately understood. "I will defend you! Go!"

Harper pushed through the throng of dwarves with Erika on her heels, and rushed to Aedon's side, grasping his blood and dirt covered hand to lend her magic to him. He drew from her hungrily, slowly pulling at the very energy of the rock and worming himself between every crack he could find. She wove with him, prising open fissures deep in the rock, weakening, pulling, as the last dwarves cleared the doorway and her vision blurred.

The stone cracked and split around them, the sound jarring their ears. Aedon started running, pulling her along with one hand as he snagged Erika with the other. The magic snapped free, and the rumble grew.

"Run!" he bellowed, as the tunnel collapsed behind them.

Harper ran as fast as her burning legs could carry her, while the thundering stone avalanche chased them toward the thirl door. The rumbling slowed as the cave diminished behind them, but Aedon did not reduce his speed.

"We're the last!" he shouted as they broke into the fresh air, a cloud of dirt and rocks puffing out behind them. Harper breathed deeply, coughing on the choking dust.

The thirl door slammed shut behind them, and Korrin sealed it once more with his touch. "Come. We must flee at once," he growled. "We will only be safe when we return to Keldheim."

Long into the night they ran, without stopping, knowing Saradon would not be far behind. Harper staggered until her muscles were numb, her feet blocks of stone, and her chest burned. It was not only Saradon's eyes chasing her in the waking nightmare they endured, but Dimitrius's.

Why is he here? Why is he with Saradon? What is he plotting?

She had no answers. But the depths of Dimitrius's betrayal—of the person she thought she had known—sheared through her chest.

39

DIMITRI

Harper. It was her. And that was impossible. But it was *her*. Dimitri reeled from the unexpected sight of her in the midst of such carnage and destruction. She had no place there. He could hardly breathe with the shock of it. With the worry for her. He had sent Harper away to keep her safe from Toroth—how had she wound her way into something even more dangerous?

And more than that, it had struck him just how much she had affected him—far more than he had realised. He had felt a bolt of worry for her so deep at the sight of her that the incandescent terror of it cleaved him in two. He had to find her, had to warn her, had to make her *leave*. She could not be caught in what was to come. He should not have cared. She was nothing more than yet another bystander—a casualty if necessary. Yet he knew he could not bear that.

He sent a curse up to the heavens, to the gods who had made him weak. Because now he realised that he cared for her—he could not deny it to himself any longer—and worse still he wanted her, this brazen young woman who would not cease challenging him. Even her gaze had burned him from across that cave, though they had not shared a word. That look had seared him where he stood, and if looks could have killed, he would be dead.

"Lord Ellarian!" Saradon snapped.

It broke Dimitri's reverie, and he startled, coming back to the great hall of Afnirheim once more. Saradon glared at him —judging his silent lapse. Dimitri straightened.

"The *thirl door*." Saradon tested the unfamiliar words on his tongue. He curled his lip, irritated. At a slice of his hand, the dwarf before him crumpled, dead before he hit the ground. Beside Saradon, Dimitri held himself rigid, wiping his thoughts blank. He turned as Saradon addressed him.

"Of course, the rats have a secret entrance. Confound them! But it matters not. The goblins have what they want, a dwarven city, though less sport to enjoy now, and the thirl door is destroyed. The dwarves will not venture here again, and when the time comes, I will show them how we treat unwanted guests."

"I have no doubt," Dimitri murmured. He knew Saradon thought of the dwarven king, a fearsome killing machine in his impregnable armour, wielding his giant, double-headed axe. But Dimitri's thoughts lingered on the unexpected familiar faces in the crowd. Aedon. The nomad. The Aerian. And—something in his chest tightened anew—her. Harper. Why were they there? How? He could not understand how their paths had collided under such impossible circumstances—again. More fool him, but he still felt a shred of compassion, a shred of responsibility for her safety. There would be no keeping her safe from Saradon if she crossed his path. He pushed her from his mind as Saradon huffed.

"And the others," Saradon mused slowly, pacing back and forth around the grand jarlshalle, the centre of power in

Afnirheim, second only in grandeur to Keldheim's königshalle. One of the only spaces he had not permitted to be desecrated. The *pascha* had not taken kindly to that instruction, or Saradon's destruction of his throne of bones.

"The others?" Dimitri tried to keep his voice neutral. Luckily, Saradon was too engrossed in his own musings to snag on his discomfort.

"The Aerian, the human, and the two elves. Who are they? What were they doing with the dwarves? What unusual company to keep—they stuck out sorely. They must be of some note."

"I do not know, Lord Saradon." Dimitri was entirely truthful on that at least. He had no idea why. Only that they had rescued some of the dwarves the goblins had kept for sport. He suppressed a shudder of distaste. Ghastly creatures. He had no love for the dwarves, but they did not deserve such treatment. This had not been part of the bargain. Dimitri knew there was a cost to any war, casualties, but this was past the line he wanted to cross. It was too late now, he told himself to try and alleviate the creeping guilt beginning to gnaw at him.

"The girl…"

Dimitri froze. He could only mean Harper.

"She sang to me," Saradon murmured, as if in a daze. "It was as though my mother's blood called to me once more. Why, had I not known better, known it to be impossible, I would have thought her my kin." He frowned, staring into nothingness.

Dimitri swallowed. "It could well be so, Lord. Perhaps she is a distant relation. You know how the Houses intermingle."

Saradon met his gaze, steel in his eyes. "I do indeed, yet the line of Ravakian is ash, dead and buried. There could be none of my blood."

Dimitri squirmed. "If I may, Lord. I do not believe you to be correct. I have been the king's spymaster for decades. I have known his innermost business, his most secretive thoughts... things that could have destroyed him over the years. There was one secret I knew that he only shared with perhaps one other."

Saradon did not speak, but his attention commanded Dimitri to continue.

"You had a son, am I correct?"

Saradon stiffened.

Dimitri held up his hands to placate him. "I know it to be true. I know nothing more than that of him. I suspect no one living, save perhaps the king, knows any more than that. Your son had a daughter before he died, and no, I do not know the means of Arven's passing. It was before my time. The daughter, Ilrune, was killed on Toroth's orders."

Dimitri shook his head, sensing Saradon's anger growing. "I played no part in it. You may examine my mind to know I speak the truth," he added hastily. Saradon gave a sharp nod for him to continue. "The general of the Winged Kingsguard saw that Ilrune met her demise upon the king's orders. Afterward, there was just one question I heard the king ask that the general could not answer. Ilrune perhaps had a child. Her lover was already dead, but the child, a babe in her arms... No remains were found for the babe when Raedon executed the pair of them. It will be some twenty-five years past, give or take. No one could find the child. Not the king, not the general... not me."

But now, Dimitri had a growing sense of dread as he finally, painstakingly, connected the dots. A mysterious woman of elven blood, about twenty-five summers old, from a land where she should not have existed... A missing baby twenty-five summers hence, sent far away by her mother in order to protect her. The Dragonheart finding *her*, instead of coming to *him* to bring about Saradon's rise. How it had brought her home to Pelenor before she ever knew she belonged there. The charm on the bracelet that linked her to Saradon, to the line of Ravakian. As everything clicked, he wished he had never spoken the words. Even before Saradon declared it, Dimitri knew it to be true, and the blood drained from him.

He could not take his words back.

"The girl is the babe." Saradon exclaimed, his eyes alight with an excitement Dimitri had never seen before. "Fate drew her here. Her blood called to me. That is why. She is the blood of my blood—my sole *heir*, no less—I must have her," he hissed, whirling on Dimitri, fervent in his desire.

Dimitri's knees threatened to fold as he stood, hollow, whilst Saradon celebrated the survival of his bloodline. *She cannot be his blood*, he thought desperately. It would irrevocably change her fate, change her safety. Now he had no way to keep her from Saradon's attention.

"I have an heir!" Saradon crowed. "What a gift."

Crushed, Dimitri bowed. He did not dare speak.

At that moment, the *pascha* and his chieftains burst in, cavorting across the jarlshalle, all drowning in dwarven armour, jewelry, weapons, and other spoils. Saradon's jubilation tempered upon their arrival. Dimitri knew the *pascha* wanted more. More than Saradon was willing to give. Their disagreements never ended beautifully. Saradon's magic always won. Dimitri had no desire to get in their way.

Using their entrance as a distraction, Dimitri slipped away, his heart thundering, into the ether, racing as far and fast as he could. Yet no matter how far or fast he fled, he could not outrun the doubt and panic crescendoing within him. Harper was Saradon's kin—that was the missing piece of the puzzle—and now she was in more danger than ever, because Saradon knew it. The unfamiliar beast of his conscience haunted him, jarring in his bones and bitter upon his tongue. She had been safe. Without his meddling, she would have lived her days in Caledan, none the wiser. *Dimitrius, you fool! This is all your fault.*

HARPER

Upon their return to Keldheim, König Korrin immediately set about fortifying the dwarven stronghold, whilst Afnirheim's surviving casualties, Ragnar amongst them, were treated in the city's infirmary. Harper and her companions crowded into Ragnar's sick bay, unwilling to leave his side. After the traumatic and exhausting retreat from Afnirheim, it took another day before he regained consciousness. His breathing deepened and colour slowly returned under the ministration of the dwarven healers and Aedon, who gave Ragnar what magic he could to speed his healing and take the pain away.

Harper tried to push away the lump in her throat. Ragnar was a shadow of his former self. Tucked into the deep, dark coverlets, he looked pale and frail, his strength diminished. His once beautiful beard had been roughly hewn, some of it torn out. His face was swollen and bloodied. She had not seen the rest of his body, but Aedon had grimly informed them all that the rest of him was in no better state.

Worst of all, he now had two fingers and part of his

thumb missing on his dominant hand. The wounds were dark, swollen, and infected. It had taken all Aedon's concentration to draw the poison and infection out so the wounds could heal. Harper's heart ached. With those injuries, Ragnar might never carve *chatura* pieces again as he so loved.

After the fearful exhilaration of the retreat, their high spirits had diminished upon realising what—or, rather, whom—they faced, as well as the health of their friend.

"He's still alive at least," Brand murmured, frowning. Despite Ragnar's state, they knew it could have been far worse.

"We were lucky," said Erika, her voice hollow. "So many others did not make it." They shared a moment of silence. It was unlikely they would see any of the dwarves left behind again. Harper privately thought death would be a better outcome than remaining as a prisoner in the now goblin stronghold.

Aedon stirred, but did not speak, his attention fixed upon the rise and fall of Ragnar's chest under the beige linen shift. His bandaged hands rested atop his belly, the wrapping clean compared to the dirt and blood that had covered his hands when they found him.

"What is *he* doing?" Erika asked. They did not need to know who she meant.

"I do not know," said Aedon. "We can only presume that, somehow resurrected, he means to continue his old mission, to sunder the wheel of society. It is a dark day indeed if he starts by seeking alliance with the black hearts of the goblin scum."

"Why would Dimitrius be with him?" Harper asked, an edge of desperation cutting through her voice that she crushed immediately, lest it betray her. "Is he a prisoner?" A part of her wanted to think the best of him. He had been kind to her, after all. Saved her. Let her escape. And that he was a hint of the person she had started to see behind his reputation—not that the masks were the truth of him after all, and she had been so foolish as to fall for the deception that he was anything but calculating and evil.

Erika snorted scornfully. "Did he *look* like a captive to you? No. He's connected somehow. I'll wager he's a part of it. I wonder if this is the king's doing, or whether Toroth has any idea."

"Shall we ask him?" Aedon asked, raising his eyebrow and flashing a scowl that quickly faded. "I know. I know. Just jesting. It's over our heads. This is an age-old war between the goblins and dwarves. We take no part in it. I would wager it's an old feud between elves of the royal line, too, since Saradon seems to be very much alive again. We take no part in that, either. We need to get Ragnar mended, then get out of here. Maybe it's time for us to try lands to the east, across the mountains, for a while." When his glance caught on Harper, he swallowed, quickly looking away.

She raised an eyebrow. She still felt the void between them, despite their cooperation during the rescue in Afnirheim. It had been easier to distract herself when faced with a horde of goblins. She suppressed a shudder at the thought of that. "You're worried my connection to him will jeopardize us all."

His lack of a reply was all she needed. Her lip curled, even as indignation burned in her throat. It was true—now she worried for a different reason, that somehow, she was corrupt as a result of her heritage. It didn't bear thinking about now she had seen the company Saradon kept and what they did for fun with their prisoners. To her surprise, Erika stepped in before she had a chance to retort, even though she was not entirely convinced he was wrong.

"That's bullshit and you know it, Aedon." Erika folded her arms. "She's not suddenly going to turn into a bad apple one day on account of her blood. I'd know. I haven't turned into a wild savage despite my poor stock, have I?" She narrowed her eyes, as if daring him to reply. He did not. She smirked and flashed Harper a wink. "Exactly. She'll fail or succeed, and it won't have a damn thing to do with who she's related to."

Harper blinked. Since when had Erika been so amiable? She caught Brand's quickly hidden smile. "Well, since we're going to agree to give her the benefit of the doubt, can we eat? I'm famished," the big Aerian complained.

I think I'm one of them now. All it had taken was a horde of goblins and an evil elf for a great-grandfather. It sounded so ridiculous, she could have laughed. Life had changed so much in such a short span of time—mere months—since the Dragonheart had spirited her away from Caledan.

Ragnar moaned faintly. All their attention turned to him, even Brand, stomach forgotten. Slowly, he twitched. His lips moved soundlessly. His eyes fluttered open, blinking once, twice, thrice, before he opened them and stared up at the ceiling.

"Welcome back, old friend," Aedon said softly. Harper placed her hand upon the coverlet.

Ragnar's smile widened as he beheld them all. "I'm alive?" he croaked.

"You are indeed, master dwarf," Brand said. Harper could have sworn she saw a tear in the big Aerian's eye before he blinked it away.

Ragnar lifted his hand to grasp Harper's, but his face fell as he beheld his bandaged digits. He swallowed.

"It's all right, Ragnar. Everything will be fine," Aedon said, his tone low and soothing. "Don't worry about that just yet. You're healing well. That's all that matters."

Ragnar swallowed and nodded. He lowered his hand back to the coverlet. But he did not tear his gaze away from the bandage. "What happened?"

Aedon, ever the storyteller, recounted their escapades since the moment Ragnar had been taken, including Harper's visit to Vanir and the visions at the Mother's wellspring. When he finished, the question hung on everyone's lips, but no one asked—what had happened to Ragnar?

"Thank you, friends," Ragnar said heavily. "But for you, I would be certainly dead once they had no more use for me. I can hardly believe what has passed—for all of us." He glanced at Harper as he said it.

"What was it like?" Erika's eyes burned with emotion.

Ragnar swallowed. "I cannot speak of it. It is too much. But the elf, Saradon, is alive!" Ragnar tried to sit up, but he was so weak that he could barely lift himself off the bed.

"The könig knows," Aedon said, pressing Ragnar down, sending glowing magic into him as he groaned in pain and paled. "Korrin is determined to retake Afnirheim eventually. I am sure this will make him all the more determined, but perhaps, knowing who his enemy is, he will be careful."

"If I were him, I would send envoys to Toroth," Brand said.

"Certainly," Aedon acknowledged. "Saradon is not an enemy I would want to face alone."

"I will have to attend Korrin." Ragnar sounded reluctant.

"You can afford to delay. You must heal first," Brand said. "Korrin and your duties can wait. He has what is needed in hand, and that is what matters for your kin at present."

"Yes. We must get you fighting fit once more, friend. Ragnar Three-Fingers is a fearsome nickname, in any case.

You'll certainly earn some ales with that battle scar." Aedon grinned at him, trying to cheer him up.

Ragnar smiled weakly, unconvinced, but he *had* smiled. Relief filled Harper that they had found him, and that he was alive and would be well in time. Yet, it was tinged with something darker, more volatile, and heavier in the face of all that she now knew—all that now tangled together, crushing the breath from her chest as she fought rising overwhelm. Aedon's own brother had executed her mother. Worse still, Harper was Saradon's kin—and Dimitri was his ally.

41

HARPER

The königshalle was deathly silent. All heads turned to look at them as they entered. Or, rather, look at Harper. She would have quailed before the collected attention of the stern dwarven jarls, still clad in their intimidating armours, had she not been flanked by Erika and Brand. Aedon led them. Ragnar still lay in the infirmary.

"My cousin does not join you?" König Korrin greeted them, raising his bushy eyebrows. They placed their fists to their chests and bowed as one.

"No, König," replied Aedon. "At present, he is still too infirm, but will heal."

Korrin nodded and gestured to his jarls. "I summon you to stand with mine own kin. I doubt ever a couple of elves, a mortal, and an Aerian have ever been thusly welcomed to one of our councils. Yet I must express my gratitude for your help within Afnirheim, for without you, I suspect many more of us might not have returned."

His face grew stern. "Now, we have seen the truth of the

horrors that have passed there." His glance hesitated on Harper. "The Mother's vision was correct. My concern is her *other* vision." Korrin stared at her pointedly.

He knows. A thrill of fear rushed through her. Of course, Vanir had told him. Her allegiance was bound to the dwarves, not her. *She is one of their gods, after all.* Harper swallowed.

"Did you know of this before you entered our halls?" he asked her quietly.

"No, König." She met his gaze and tried not to flinch.

He shook his head and frowned. "I see no resemblance, yet Vanir would not show us falsehoods. How can we trust you, blood of his blood?"

"I have nothing to do with him, König. I hail from lands far away, where I have lived as long as my memory recalls. I know nothing of this land or its history, and nothing of my kin. I have been an orphan all my life. This changes nothing." *My mother is still dead.* That cut at the wound in her chest anew.

"So you say, yet I do not know that I can trust the word of an elf related to *him*. You saw as well as we did what he has done."

"And I was just as horrified as you all were," insisted Harper. "I came to tell you of the Mother's vision of Afnirheim the moment I saw it. If I were somehow in his thrall, would I have done that?"

Korrin narrowed his eyes at her, unconvinced. "Spies can bluff as many times as they need to in order to gain trust."

"I will vouch for her." Brand's quiet, even voice rang through the space.

"And I," Erika said, stepping forward.

"And I," said Aedon.

Warmth burned up her throat and a lump formed there.

She blinked hot wetness away from her eyes, raising her chin. She would not cry, no matter how glad she was not to stand alone.

Korrin surveyed them. "The words of Aerians, mortals, and elves do not count for much here, but I will let your good faith stand. Her actions are on your hands. If there is any hint, any at all, of something untoward, I shall see that Keldheim is protected at any cost." His stern voice left nothing to the imagination as to his intentions.

"We shall see it done, König," replied Brand, bowing. "Our friend is trustworthy. You have nothing to fear."

"I do not fear her," Korrin sneered, uncharacteristically arrogant for a moment. "But I will do whatever it takes to protect Valtivar." The jarls raised their fists to their hearts at his words.

"Then there is the matter of Ragnar Dúrnir." Korrin's sour tone showed his feelings on that. "With my cousin's return, his affairs in Keldheim must once more be raised."

"With respect, König," Aedon interjected quickly, "Ragnar does not wish to stay. His affairs may remain as they were before his arrival. We shall leave as soon as we may."

Korrin scowled. "He cannot outrun his fate for all eternity."

"We cannot speak on that, König." Aedon bowed.

"No, you cannot," replied Korrin flatly. "He shirks his duties as my kin, especially when the *pascha* and his horde plagues us all. He shames the line of Dúrnir."

"He shames nothing!" Harper said before she could stop herself, stepping forward in her indignation. She froze as all eyes turned to her.

"You dare to speak against me?" Korrin glared at her.

Harper straightened, quite sure she had made an enormous mistake, but not willing to back down. *I held my own in*

Afnirheim, just like everyone else in here. I helped light the way. I helped ensure our safe escape, she reminded herself. "Ragnar Dúrnir—" the word felt strange on her tongue, "—is a good dwarf, one of the best people I know. He seeks only to do what is right, and he knows that his place is not here."

She knew she had struck a nerve when Korrin scowled, but she refused to quail before him. "I will not speak to the likes of you on such matters, elf girl."

Jarl Halvar and another arrived then, distracting the König. "Reinforcements from Himmelheim have arrived, König," the jarl said.

Korrin's scowl split into a wide grin. "Praise the gods," he said, banging his own fist to his chest. His jarls copied. "This will be the first stage of our attack whilst we await the rest of our brethren. I will not suffer those *scum* in our lands a moment longer than we must."

"You seek to retake Afnirheim, König?" Aedon asked.

"Yes," Korrin said grimly. "Can we count upon your arms?" From their conversations on dwarven culture, Harper knew guests could not be called upon to fight, even for as much use as the four of them had already been in Afnirheim.

"Yes," said Erika with grim determination. "You could not keep me away from that foe." Harper felt nauseated by the pledge. She did not want to return to those halls.

Judging by his curious frown, Korrin wondered at her words, but nodded and thanked them before turning back to his jarls to discuss the finer points of their strategy. Harper and her companions drifted closer to listen to talk of war. All the while, anxiety built within her. To speak of a return to Afnirheim was bad enough, but now she knew what awaited —goblins, Saradon, and Dimitrius.

Harper had had enough talk of war, goblins, and Saradon. Her head echoed with it, jarring her already overwhelming headache. She needed fresh air. Jarl Halvar had pointed her to the way out—after a fashion—whilst the others ate. There was no true outside space in Keldheim, but it would do. Harper had trekked up the winding stairs until the void appeared. Spanning the void between two jutting peaks that joined obscure parts of the rear of Keldheim, the bridge was utterly open to the elements, yet so isolated as to be impregnable by outside forces unless dragons were involved.

Harper recognised the area. She was near where they had left Keldheim through the thirl door. She stepped onto the stone bridge, to be immediately buffeted by a cool gust of late afternoon wind. Already, the sun fell toward the horizon and had long disappeared behind the peaks, though the peach skies told her it had not yet set outside the mountains. Even so, she leaned on the waist-high stone wall, grateful for the fresh air that helped to banish the staleness from her mind... and all horror of Saradon's threat. The wind receded, leaving her in a pocket of stillness, though she still wrapped herself in the warmth her magic afforded. Harper admired the view, not thinking about anything for just a few moments. Below her, rushing water was all she could hear. Vanir's wellspring, she realised, or rather, where it emerged from the mountain.

A familiar, sharp, fruity aroma laced with musk hit her a moment before the realisation of who that belonged to. Eyes wide, she whirled around to see a figure emerge onto the bridge.

42

HARPER

The yawning shadows of the fading day made Dimitrius look drawn and worried. They pooled in the hollows under his eyes and carved gauntness into his cheeks. But it was his eyes that stopped her dead because they burned with such intensity—and the way his attention fixed so singularly upon her that it made the world fall away.

"How did you…" Her voice trailed off as her chest tightened. His citrus and musk scent surrounded her, and with every step that drew him closer, she trembled more. His presence was all-consuming.

"Miss me?" He smirked at her, cocking his head. For a second, the raw need in his eyes vanished as his mask slipped into place. The cocky, arrogant spymaster she had first met.

Her gape turned into an indignant scowl as fury fired inside her. "Never!" Fury was good. Fury was safe. Honed like a blade of fire, it carved and burned away this thing that threatened to engulf her, because to have him so close, to be reminded of the intoxicating power of his presence… oh, what she had thought she had felt towards him had only grown in his absence, and she despised herself for it.

"The lady doth protest too much," he said, his sharp teeth flashing in the gloom as his grin widened.

Already, her anger had peaked and receded, because damn him, even the masks he wore lured her in. But she had to know—had to rip off that mask. "Why did you come? How did you find me?"

The façade dropped away and that haunted stare of his returned as he crossed the final few steps to her. "Are you alone?" He looked both ways across the bridge, and then the full force of his attention was on her as she backed to the parapet, beyond which was a precipitous drop. She was glad not to be able to see into the void behind her. He was threat enough as he followed her. It knocked the breath from her to have him so close. His shadow crossed her. She could reach forward and touch him—and she wanted to, despite everything. She could not afford this.

"Why do you want to know?" Desperate hostility spiked from every syllable. She sought comfort in her magic, revelling in the feeling of power coursing through her—an anchor to this madness that wanted to sweep her away.

"You needn't do that, Harper, I mean you no harm. Put your magic away—though I am glad to see how much you have grown, little huntress."

The nickname sent an unwelcome thrill through her. "Don't call me that!"

The lazy smirk he sent her threatened to stall her breath. She held onto the magic brimming in her, fighting past the warmth that gathered in her core. His amusement faded. "I came to warn you, Harper." He swallowed, and his eyes slipped shut for a second.

She watched him warily—watching for any tell of a threat

—but he seemed a mess. It was an odd feeling. He *was* a threat, after all, yet they previously had had to cooperate so intimately that she did not view him as one. She trusted him —he'd saved her, protected her, even sent her away to keep her from danger, when he owed her nothing. It felt strange to fall back into such animosity. And now, when she felt as though she knew him, she felt like she could say with some certainty that the male before her was nothing close to cold and calculating. He was not, if she judged soundly, wearing any of his masks now. So why *had* he come?

"You need to leave Keldheim—leave Valtivar. Go far from here."

She did not know what she had expected—but it was not that. "Why?"

"Isn't it obvious? I saw you in Afnirheim. You know what's happening." He gritted his teeth.

She raised an eyebrow. "Do I?"

"You know enough to understand Valtivar is not safe for you."

"Why? What's happening that I need to be so worried about?" she challenged, stepping closer and jutting her chin out in defiance as she looked up at him.

"Gods, woman," he snapped, but a thrill rose in Harper as he glared down at her. He uttered a sound of frustration in the depths of his throat, and his hands fisted at his sides. "You delight and yet incite me with your wilfulness. You will not simply listen, will you? I know you saw *him*. This isn't just a goblin uprising. It spreads beyond that." He leaned closer, his voice dropping. "War is coming, Harper. Do you know what *his* mark means?"

That he would not utter Saradon's name sent a prickle of unease down her spine. "The Riven Circle?"

"Yes."

"It's a broken wheel."

"Yes, but it's so much *more* than that," he said impatiently, stepping back and running a hand across his hair. "He's returned, Harper. I won't lie. I played my part in it—" she stilled at his words, "—but you know the rotten depths of the sinful court I seek to topple. Surely you can imagine the better Pelenor I desire more than anything to build. The time fast approaches, Harper, when there will be little choice in the matter. Soon, he will be the master of Pelenor, and a new age of peace and prosperity will dawn—"

The blood drained from her. "Are you *insane?*" she shouted. "This is *your* doing?"

"Well, I—"

She jabbed her finger at the mountain beside her. "My *friend* is in there. He suffered unimaginably at the hands of those… those… *monsters*. People *died!* I saw inside the mountain, Dimitrius. I saw what they did to all those dwarves." Now she felt nauseated. She swallowed, and her tongue darted out to moisten her lip. "Please tell me you didn't take part in that. That is no better than Toroth. In fact, that is worse. *Please.*"

It was a plea for so much more than she could voice. He could not be complicit, willingly a part of that, surely. If so, she had misjudged him entirely and she was a fool. For all she had disliked discovering Aedon's hidden depths, she had known quite how vile Dimitrius was. Or at least, she thought she had. Thought she had at least appreciated the honesty with which he presented his callous shards.

"It's not like that," he said desperately, stepping forward again. "There are always casualties of wa—"

"No! I won't hear it. I thought… I thought you might be different. Decent. You were so kind to me. You protected me." She looked at him as though he were a stranger. "But you're just like the rest of them. Greedy and self-serving. Willing to do whatever it takes, *hurt* whomever you need to, in your race to the top." She shoved him away, wanting and despising the solid bulk of his muscled torso, but he yielded, perhaps in surprise, and she stormed past him, back to the mountain—knowing full well he would not give up.

"I'm *not* like that!" he snarled, and his steps chased hers. He grabbed her arm as she entered the hollow of the tunnel and spun her against the wall. Rough rocks bit into her back. "For heaven's sake, Harper, *listen.*"

This close, she saw the raging passion in his eyes, the desperation with which he implored her. Even though the cold wind stole every shred of real warmth it could from her body, the heat of his magic burned her right to her core. With his hand on her body, pinning her upper arm into place, a conflict of an entirely different kind raged within her. She hadn't realised that in the heat of the moment, she had grabbed a fistful of his shirt in her hands, and she released the luxuriantly soft fabric, clutching her hand to her chest as though it had stung.

His next words came more softly but no less filled with fervour. "I promise you, it's not like that. That's not who I am. That's not what I want." He closed his eyes for a moment, then sighed. At his slumped shoulders, the stiff resistance in her limbs melted away. This was no threat—he was in agony. This, whatever it was, gutted him. She did not understand him at all. His hands slipped from her shoulder, and he braced on the stone to either side of her. When he opened his eyes, he flinched at her hard expression, but she *was* listening.

He shook his head. "I'm not sure I can stop him now. It's like a river tumbling over a waterfall, picking up speed. I'm trying to steer it away from disaster with what power I have.

I just—I had to warn you. If you stay, you'll all be caught in the middle. I cannot protect you from what is coming. And…" His voice dropped so quiet that she could barely hear him over the rumble of the river in the canyon below. "…I want to." He hung his head, so close his forehead almost touched hers.

She wondered at his choice of words. A dangerous feeling took a hold deep within her as she stood, cradled in the cocoon his body created around her. "Why do you care?" she asked quietly, the stinging vehemence gone from her voice. The warmth of his breath caressed her cheek.

He opened his mouth. Shut it again. Swallowed. "I shouldn't," he admitted. "I shouldn't care at all. But I do. Just as I suspect you do, because you are brimming with magic and you have not yet attacked me as you ought to, if you knew what was good for you, even if the chance of you besting me is utterly futile. Somehow, you make me lose all reason, Harper. You offer me a sliver of brightness in this hell of an existence that I want to seize and not let go of, even though I have no damned right to deserve it."

It was so honest, so free of his confusing masks, that it felt too raw for her, speaking to the deep, piercing ache building inside her chest and closing off the breath from her chest. However much he meant well, however much she felt the bitter truth to the agony of his words, his actions spoke of a different story. One in which he was complicit in horrific acts. What did it make her if she wanted a monster? If she pitied him for the consequences of his ill-intended actions? If that made her feel only more conflicted, not less, by his shades of grey?

"He may kill me if he finds that I am here with you. Warning you." Dimitri groaned. "And yet, I still cannot stop myself. This is how much you affect me, Harper, and believe me, I despise myself for it. I despise that you make me so weak. I do not beg anyone—but I will beg you if I must, to see you safe. Do not make me."

He would *beg*? Did it thrill her to see him this utterly broken at her expense? Or horrify her? She would not yield to it, for that way, madness lay. "I cannot go. I will not go. There is too much at stake, and I am no coward," she said, raising her chin to look him directly in the eye, the tip of her nose threatening to brush his. The shock of his violet gaze searing into her so close clutched at her chest, and now her legs threatened to buckle at the not at all unpleasant swoop in the pit of her stomach.

"Of course, you can't. Of course, you won't," he murmured, the words dropping from his lips to hers. "I would not be so consumed by you if you fled."

Consumed. The shock of that confession stopped any retort.

He let out a bitter laugh. "Oh, Harper. You will be my downfall." He hovered there, and the only sound was the sawing of their heavy breathing. His eyes flicked to her lips and back again, and his neck corded, his jaw clenching as though he restrained himself at great cost.

Harper felt as though she were aflame and utterly lost to common sense and reason now. What hung between them, intense and charged, lured her in. If he stooped to kiss her now, she did not think she wanted to push him away, much as she knew she ought to. This was the forbidden fruit she had thought of, after all. A taste lay right before her, ripe for taking. The moral conflict of that lay heavily over the desire coursing through her. The energy thickened between them until she could have carved the tension with a knife, like a bolt of lightning needing the release of discharge to clear.

"Dimitrius…"

He groaned. "Damn it. Do not utter my name. I shall lose all semblance of control."

Harper took in a shuddering breath as he leaned closer still, just one fraction, showing his slipping leash. And she did not resist as she should have.

"Oi!" The wind lulled, revealing clattering footsteps heading their way. Dimitrius pushed away from the wall at once, snarling at the intrusion.

"Harper?" Aedon's voice carried across the bridge. "Is that you?" He emerged into the light, stopping suddenly at the sight of them. "Get away from her!" Aedon surged forward, magic lighting his palms.

Dimitrius looked at Harper and stepped back.

Harper's pulse thundered with something more primal that cut through the haze of desire. She sprang away from the wall and from Dimitrius as though they had burned her. To her surprise, she found herself moving in front of Dimitrius, holding up her hands.

"Stop!" she ordered Aedon. "It's all right."

Aedon halted, but the magic in his palms kept flickering. Suspicion darkened his face. Harper turned to Dimitri. What had brewed between them was shattered with Aedon's arrival, the spell broken. Yet he still gazed upon her with such intensity it stalled her breath anew.

"Heed my words, Harper. *Please*," he murmured to her, too soft for Aedon to hear. He raised a hand to her arm, but Harper stepped from his reach. That was far too dangerous. She narrowed her eyes, stared at him for a few seconds more, then turned on her heel and strode away, steeling herself against his intoxicating presence.

"You shouldn't have come here alone," Aedon hissed at her as she strode past him.

"I don't take orders from *you*, Aedon," she spat, throwing the wrath she felt at her own shortcomings in his face.

His face fell and he flinched at the savagery in her tone before his expression hardened. "Why is he here?"

She did not answer Aedon. She whirled around, searching for one last look at him before they disappeared into the tunnels—and stumbled to a halt. The bridge was empty. Dimitri was gone. Something bigger than her punched the air from her lungs. Before it could overpower her, Harper ran into the bowels of the mountain—but she could not escape what had just happened.

43

HARPER

Of course, Aedon soon caught up. He peppered her with questions. What did Dimitrius want? Why had he come? How had he managed to penetrate so far into the dwarven stronghold? How had he found her? Why was she there? Then his tone became more suspicious. Such an isolated spot... Had she conspired to meet Dimitrius? They had been so close in Tournai. Was she in league with him? At that musing, Harper abruptly halted. Aedon almost ran into her. She whirled around, shaking, and slapped him across the face as hard as she could.

"Still your tongue, Aedon!" she snarled. "For once, be quiet! I know little more than you. Leave me alone! I need to be alone." Without another word, she stormed away.

It was hours later that she gravitated towards company again. She eventually found Brand and Erika in the great hall, drinking and laughing with a table of raucous dwarves, but at her arrival—and her thunderous expression—they set down their tankards and slipped away from the mirth.

She told them what had transpired, ignoring Aedon, who arrived not long after her. She had a sneaking suspicion he had continued to trail her, but she did not have the energy to confront him. The shock of Dimitrius's appearance had drained something vital from her. Aedon's cheek, she was part viciously pleased and part ashamed to note, remained red. But, he did not remark upon it as he slid onto the bench. Without looking at him, she told Brand and Erika what had happened from the moment Dimitrius had appeared—taking care to leave out the parts that made her feel painfully exposed. She fought down the rising warmth in her cheeks with deep breaths.

"So, he wants us to leave?" asked Brand. His gaze repeatedly strayed to Aedon's scarlet cheek.

"It seems so. He wanted to warn me—genuinely, I think —that if we stay, we will be involved in the battles to come."

"And why did he take the time, I wonder, to warn you?" Brand's gaze was all too discerning.

Harper stilled under his attention—anything to stop the guilty squirm that wriggled through her. "After Tournai—" she left the implications of that to hang, because there was so much she had not and would not share with them from that time, "—I think he feels guilty, perhaps. He did not have to let me go—but he did. And perhaps now, he does not want to see me hurt. Who knows what his reasons are." She tried not to think about how close Dimitrius had been. How deeply his words had cut to her core. How compelling his presence was.

Brand leaned back and folded his bulging arms across his chest. "I don't trust the slimy bastard."

"Hmm." Harper's reply was non-committal. "Whatever his motive, he wants us to leave."

"Then let's go." said Aedon. "Once Ragnar is healed, let's travel as far from here as we can. Maybe across the mountains to the lands beyond."

Erika glared at him. "I'm not going anywhere yet. I have a score to settle."

Brand's gaze flicked to her, but he held his tongue. Harper saw how he pursed his lips, as though he wanted to appeal she not do anything foolish, but she knew he had already said such things and been rebuked for it. "If you will not go, I will also stay."

"It seems this is the only place I can find answers," Harper added softly. "I'll stay, too." She tried to shut out what that might mean. *Keldheim will not go the same way as Afnirheim,* she reassured herself.

Aedon sighed. "We're not fighters. We don't have any part to play in this."

Brand gestured at the door. "Then go." He sighed, his voice softening. "We have followed you far over the years, Aedon, even when you have led us into folly. We ask you, this time, to follow *us*."

Aedon squirmed, but he had no choice. "Fine," he muttered, staring mutinously at Harper. "I'm still not happy, though," he added rebelliously. "Dimitrius has never been selfless. No doubt this is one of his schemes. He's always plotting something, and whatever he wants is *not* to our benefit."

"I'm sure," said Harper, surprising herself with the certainty of her tone. "I know deep in my gut, that he means me no harm."

"You cannot trust him," Aedon scoffed.

"No," she assured them quickly, even though uncertainty

swirled within her. She had not told them of the open doubt she had sensed in Dimitrius, seen written on his face, and the change there too that remained unspoken and hidden between his words. Dimitrius had realised what folly he had gotten himself into, she reckoned, what trouble he had become involved with—and he regretted it. That felt important to her. He had overflowed with remorse.

And, despite the danger to him, he had put himself at an even greater risk by coming to warn her. Despite how badly everything had gone… that meant something to her. Something she didn't quite know how to untangle. He wasn't as bad as he appeared from the outside—of that, she had already been quite certain. Now, despite his misdemeanours, and the terrible movement he seemed to be caught up in, she could not think the worst of him. Not having seen a sliver of the truth of his character.

She cleared her throat. "I think you might be surprised to find us working alongside each other in the future. I think our aims might be aligned."

Aedon scoffed at that, and the others murmured their doubts, but Harper only shrugged. "I just have a hunch. You'll see."

Over the coming days, Keldheim's fortifications grew. Dwarves poured in from across Valtivar until the city was full to bursting and every bed occupied. Harper, Aedon, Brand, and Erika had been moved to the könig's own halls, where Harper and Erika shared, as did Brand and Aedon, for their old abode now housed ten dwarven warriors from Himmelheim.

Brand and Erika were alive with the hum of war. They

held a new energy, a vibrancy, that had not been there before, and spent every spare hour training in hand-to-hand combat with the dwarves, amongst whom they were starting to earn quite the reputation. In the fighting hall, which rang with the clash of blades, Harper and Aedon partnered. He had said no more of the slap she had dealt him—she suspected it had stung his pride at the very least—and she conversed no more than she had to. Instead, they sparred in near silence, dancing and whirling in a kaleidoscope of light and colour as they attacked and defended against magical assaults. Harper's blood thrummed with the force of magic rushing through her, setting her afire in energy.

Finally, Aedon called a halt, wiping a glistening brow on his sleeve. "That's enough for now. I'm going to spar with one of Jarl Halvar's men to keep my blade true. I suggest you do the same." He nodded to her and turned away.

"Wait," she blurted, stepping toward him.

He halted, turned back to her, and raised an eyebrow.

She could have laughed, though mirthlessly, at how their relationship had changed. At first, she, nothing more than a mortal nobody, captivated by the handsome, light-hearted elf. Then discovering her own magical talents, set afire with lust for him and daring to pursue it—before realising that he was not what she wanted, and she did not have to settle for him, regardless of what—who—she did want. She had been naïve and foolish to seek comfort in the first one to show her kindness. But that did not equate to the footings of a rela-tionship, or a healthy one at that. Now she felt they were on an equal plane, perhaps at long last, and found herself utterly indifferent toward him, now he had shown his true heart.

"Yes?" he prompted, still waiting.

She wiped the small smirk from her face. "I have a ques-tion. About Dimitrius." *I couldn't ask him when you arrived,* she thought with no small amount of irritation. How much else had been left unsaid? She would never know.

His own expression became closed, guarded.

"I don't know how he found me in particular, but how did he reach Keldheim? Where I was… It was impregnable. I mean, elves can't fly, but if he could, I would have seen him come from either end of the bridge. He seemed to appear out of nowhere." She frowned, recalling his scent washing over her, and something curled low in her belly at their closeness as he had pressed her to the rock—and she had let him. "I can't fathom it." *Any of it.* It haunted every step. She looked over her shoulder and around every corner for him, expecting his searing attention upon her, but Dimitrius had not appeared again.

Aedon shifted. "I don't know," he said eventually. "I'm an elf. Magic is innate, but that doesn't mean I can do or know everything. There's much I do not know of magic, and darker magics beyond that. He has skills I'm not privy to." By the way he gritted his teeth, the confession seemed to annoy him, but it only intrigued her. Dimitrius was more powerful than any other she had met. Perhaps it stood to reason that he possessed different magics. She had no doubt she would see him again. When she did… *I will ask him myself.* One way or another, she was determined to find an answer.

At that moment, Jarl Halvar strode through the melee to their side. "Harper of Caledan." He bowed to her.

"Jarl Halvar." She replied in kind, raising a fist to her chest in the dwarven sign of respect. He was pleased by that, judging by the little upturn of the corner of his mouth, but his face remained grim.

"You are to speak with the Mother. At once. She commands it."

Harper frowned, but nodded. *What could Vanir want with*

me again? She could not refuse, but part of her wanted to. She had discovered life-shattering revelations in the white caves. She didn't know if she could take any more.

HARPER

The white-haired crone awaited her. Seemingly agitated, Vanir paced beside the wellspring, her shoulders bowed and hunched with age.

"Oh, child. Come. Sit. *Sit!*"

Harper bowed and did as she was bidden, kneeling on the hard, rocky ground. Vanir scooped up a cup of the icy water and pressed it into her hands. "Drink it now. Girl, the fates tell me more is yet to be known, and if you do not know *now*, they warn me you shall never!"

Harper drained the cup, dribbling water down her chin in her haste. Vanir's firm, knobbly hands caught her as she sank into dreams.

Deep voices droned around her, a choir singing, but their song was a lifeless dirge. Before her, she saw greenery wither and livestock crumple to the ground in death, all burning. The sky was dark, and

a wind rose, whipping about her. Magic sparked in the distance and a fire grew, its smoke casting over her with the wind, forcing itself up her nostrils to choke her.

A light in the darkness, a pinprick against the onslaught of death and despair, tugged her closer. In the maelstrom, the tiniest thread of life pulsed, bright and clear. She fought to reach it, kneeling in the scorched, blood-soaked earth to pluck it from the ground. As she touched it, the light flickered before brightening around her, thrusting outward, beating back the dark. Harper's eyes widened. In her palms, she held a Dragonheart radiating all hues. Its iridescent surfaces shimmered as they reflected its own light in fractured beams.

Suddenly, she felt a gentle hand upon the top of her head. She glanced up to see the ghostly form of an impossibly tall, ethereal woman towering over her. Her golden hair flowed over an elegant gown of pure, white light, and her face was too bright to behold.

"Fated one, thou hast chosen well. Thou shalt seek the fulfilment of my vision. Half a millennia have I waited for this moment. Valxiron's legion spreads anew... in Saradon, his disciple. It was spoken. The Heart of a Dragon shall resurrect Him, and the Heart of a Dragon shall cast Him down. Thou shalt come into the midst of a storm thou cannot seek to comprehend. As it was before, so it will be again. Thrice as hard willst He attack, and thrice as deadly will the toll be. Thou art a pinprick of fading light against the onslaught, yet if thou standest true and with faith unwavering, thou shalt triumph over Valxiron's servant. Beware the Tainted Star and heed the Shadow."

The voice faded, the ghostly touch leaving her. Harper opened her mouth to ask for more, for none of the words made sense, but no sound emerged. Then she was flying herself, up and away, the Dragonheart clutched in her hands. She passed out of the storm and into the dark of night, where the veil of stars glittered above her, clean and pure.

All blurred. She sat in Vanir's cave once more. Her first instinct was to look to her hands. Empty. No hint of anything having lain in them.

"What is it, girl? Let me see!" Vanir demanded impatiently. The crone grasped Harper's face between her hard palms and stared into what felt like Harper's very soul with her milky eyes. Harper suddenly knew she could do as the elves did—see into another's mind. Vanir's sightless orbs widened as she beheld what Harper had seen.

"Twelve blessings," she whispered in awe, her hands slipping away from Harper's cheeks. "*She* has gifted you. I knew it must be of significance when I felt the summons for you. *Valxiron...* I have not heard that name uttered in an age, and ever should it remain unspoken." She muttered to herself in Dwarvish. Harper did not understand, but Vanir had already creaked to her feet and shuffled deeper into the cave, muttering to herself. "Mother have mercy upon us all, if *she* is involved." Vanir turned to Harper. "It seems you are racking up quite the clutch of titles, girl. Harper of Caledan, of Pelenor, of House Ravakian, Mother Blessed, and Fated One. I ought to call you *Frelsa*, not *girl*."

"Frelsa?"

"Saviour. You will save us all from Valxiron's disciple."

"I–What? Nonsense. I cannot. I don't understand!" Harper spluttered.

Vanir cackled and moved close to clasp Harper's hands and draw her to her feet. "It matters not, *Frelsa*. Don't you see? *It does not matter.* It will come to pass if you heed her words."

"But I don't know what they mean! Who is she?" Harper protested.

Vanir laughed, rich and throaty. "Oh, I did not say they would make sense. But nonetheless, heed them as best you can, for Erendriel's words will save us all. You may not wield the blade that severs the serpent's head, but you are a puppet of greater powers. Trust them to move you as they will."

Erendriel? Valxiron? Chills crawled down Harper's back at Vanir's words, and for a moment, she felt an icy sheet of panic drench her. This was not a game of *chatura*. She was in charge of her own actions. There was one simple problem—she had no idea what to do.

In the dark, eerie cave, with only the babble of the well-spring—which spoke in its burbling, hissing voice—it was easy to see wraiths and threats. Hastily, she bid Vanir farewell, rushed past the curious Halvar, and fled to the bridge above the cleft. Dimitrius was not there. It was only when she stepped out onto the stone bridge that she realised that was the cause of her sinking heart, because somewhere in herself, she knew what she had really sought was to ask him. Knowing that he would have told her, if he could.

In solitude, she breathed in the cold air as she sat and leaned against the wall that guarded the abyss. Below, Vanir's waterfall tumbled. Harper closed her eyes, reliving the vision over and over, trying to recall every last detail, each word the strange woman had said, and Vanir's own cryptic offerings. She could not help but wonder whether Dimitrius would appear again—or decipher whether she sought or dreaded that. It was almost dark when she rose on stiff, aching, chilled limbs… with no answers.

She could tell the others thought her vision almost silly, but the dwarves—for the könig was told all of the Mother's prophecies at once and already knew of her vision—took it far more seriously.

"We cannot allow you to come with us." König Korrin glared at Harper, who stood before him, outfitted in one of his smith's own fine mail shirts.

"With respect, König, I am not one of your subjects. Thus, you cannot command me," said Harper. She stood tall, but her heart hammered, and she had to lock her knees to stop them from shaking. To speak to a king thusly! Toroth would have struck her down where she stood, but she had taken the measure of Korrin and knew he was not the same.

He narrowed his eyes and pursed his lips. "The Mother's visions do not lie. If fated She says, fated you are. If you are the one who will save us all, it is too much to risk you."

"You would lock me up to prevent harm coming to me?" Harper's lips curled in derision. *What a load of tripe.* "Vanir—" Gasps rang out at her disrespect, and she checked herself. "The Mother told me to trust where the visions willed me to go."

It served her own ends to use Vanir's words to buy her freedom. Korrin wouldn't imprison her, surely. It did not seem like the kind of deed the dwarves would commit. It was that gamble she bet on, holding her breath unconsciously as she waited for his reply. She could not be certain, after all. Not after she had seen how they treated their slaves, the *tikrit*. The pits in Afnirheim had been their true home, after all.

Korrin ground his teeth together. "No," he admitted. "We would not do that. You have committed no crime. You are free to come and go as you will, as a guest of Keldheim and my hall."

"Then with respect, König, I will go to Afnirheim. I have a vested interest in what is there, as we all do, as the Mother has seen," she added pointedly, bringing her fist to her chest to show him respect in her defiance, glad she knew at least this one small custom of his people. He subsided at her gesture, but she could see he was still unhappy.

"Are you sure this is wise?" Brand murmured to her as the könig dismissed them to speak more with his jarls on their forthcoming strategy and inevitable battles.

"No," Harper admitted. "But I don't know what else to do. There are so many questions and no answers."

"I will find answers. And *revenge*," said Erika gleefully, smiling darkly at Harper. "I have waited a lifetime to repay the suffering of my family. Now that I find the one who caused it is within my reach, I will see it done."

"You cannot presume to take him on single-handedly," said Brand, exasperated. "Saradon is an elf, a most powerful one now, it seems. You are strong, but none of us would get near him."

"I don't care. I'll die trying. I'll try, even if none of you come with me."

"I will always come with you," Brand said in a low voice. Harper pretended not to hear. Aedon walked in stony-faced silence beside her. She was still not truly speaking to him.

"We're all going," Harper eventually said. "When the dwarves depart for Afnirheim next week, we will *all* go with them. Erika, we will stand side by side with you, come what may." She felt the weight of the nomad's surprise upon her—and then her warm hand on Harper's shoulder with a silent squeeze of thanks before it dropped away.

Vanir's words weighed on her. The mysterious vision of the one Vanir called Erendriel. Somehow, Harper was just another body in this, yet something more. She shivered as the dark clouds and scorched, ruined land of her visions teased her. The stakes could not have been higher, if what she had seen would come to pass should she fail. They could avert a catastrophe. Or they could die.

45

DIMITRI

Keeping busy was the only way Dimitrius had managed not to dwell upon what had happened with Harper. If he did, he would crumble, and he could not afford such a calamity. And so, he polished his masks and made sure not a chink presented itself in his defences as he surveyed the throne room of Tournai.

King Toroth's throne stood empty for the first time in centuries as the high council congregated in the hall without him, all silent and expectant. Not even a whisper rustled through them, their attention fixed upon Raedon, standing one step down from Toroth's throne, and Dimitri, standing one step farther down from him. Their rank in this could not have been stated more clearly. Commander and advisor.

There had been surprise and fear at the beginning, rippling through the court in a hail of rumours. Why were they being summoned? Was it one of Toroth's latest fits? More than a few faces were absent, for fear of their own fates in the king's volatile hands. They would find out what had passed soon enough and no doubt come flooding back.

For now, however, there was only confusion. Raedon and Dimitri had ever been on opposite sides of a bitter personal vendetta. Now they stood together before the empty throne. Dimitri suppressed a smile at the riddle with which he and Raedon faced them. Dimitri nodded to Raedon, who cleared his throat and straightened.

"We have summoned the full council today for a matter most urgent. It has been coming for a while, as I am sure you are all aware, though none of us would have dreamt to utter it. The king is no longer fit to sit the throne."

A muttering rose amongst them, whispers chasing around the room.

"Until such time as His Majesty, or one of his heirs, is once more fit to rule, we must act to preserve Pelenor. As general of the Winged Kingsguard, I will step in to keep the peace across the realm, in the king's name—"

He was cut off by a bark of derisive laughter. "You presumptuous, greedy upstart!" the king's aged treasurer cursed Raedon, before he bent at the waist, taken over by a coughing fit. He, too, had been struck by Saradon's Curse, which slowly wasted him away.

Raedon fixed him in a steely glare. "I do not seek to sit the throne, Treasurer."

Dimitri stirred. "Nor I," he added. All eyes turned to him, glaring and full of disdain. "The queen will soon be dead." Gasps rang out through the hall, echoing into the vaulted heights. "The king follows her, unless he miraculously recovers. Their children and many members of this court, as well." He glanced around the hall, which was far emptier than it ought to be. Cold shadows crept close.

"Saradon's Curse lives once more, feeding from the greed, corruption, and sin in this ghastly pit. Notice how the good general is untroubled by this affliction?" Dimitri gestured to

Raedon. "He stands above such pettiness with his virtues, and so the curse does not feed on him. You ought to take a leaf from his book." He fixed the treasurer with his own scorn. Before he could retort, Dimitri continued.

"All the passes east through our borders and Valtivar are closed. Pelenor wastes from within and without. No supplies come, and none leave across the mountains. The scourge of goblins, under their *pascha*'s leadership and with the aid of Saradon of House Ravakian, seeks to crush the realm of dwarves. Already, Afnirheim has fallen to them. It is sundered and barren, and I fear all other dwarven halls in Valtivar will soon follow suit, unless we help the dwarves."

"Why should we help them? Never have they risen for us," a callous voice called.

"That is not true. Though we have not needed their aid for a millennia, we have been allies for as long as our two nations go back, into the depths of time. We should not forsake them now. Would you have them fall, alone, because the enemy does not come for you?" Dimitri challenged them all. "If first he comes for the dwarves, and you do not stand beside them, where next do you think he might look? If then he turns to us, who will stand beside us? Not the dwarves. They will be ash and dust. Not the tribes of the Indis, who we have already shown our enmity to for centuries. Not the free dragons, for we have enslaved their kin for generations. They would sooner burn us. Not the elves of Tir-na-Alathea, who care for none. They will flee to their halls, and we will hear no more of them. No. We will stand utterly alone, and we will fall. Unless we stand with our neighbours."

Whispers chased the hall as his words ignited fear within those before him. Dimitri pressed on. "To ensure our own survival, we must seize control of Pelenor's own fate. Saradon is coming. Tournai is but one small part of Pelenor.

One small part of the web of disarray and strife that now spreads. Long has the court, the king, ignored the common peoples. If we allow it, Saradon will take them as his own and they will rise against us all. Toroth's answer will be to burn us all in dragonfire, for he is insane. It cannot be so."

"You speak treasons," the treasurer called, getting a murmur of agreement.

Dimitri laughed. "I will speak and commit them, if it is to save Pelenor," he said simply, fixing him in a steely gaze. "At least I will have earned my death. Will you have the courage to do what is right? Have you so quickly forgotten the burnings?"

The treasurer winced.

"I thought not. What of the last ones? All of them false traitors. You all suspected, yet I can confirm it. Not *one* supported Saradon, and their crimes were borne of the king's madness and greed. Toroth framed every last one of them to secure their assets for his failing funds, and his good favour on the centenary of Saradon's defeat."

Now, open consternation ripped through the ranks before him. Dimitri smiled, tight-lipped, satisfied. He had waited what felt like a long time to play that card.

Raedon fingered the handle of his sword. "Enough." His voice was quiet, commanding. "The Winged Kingsguard is taking command of Pelenor, in the name of the king. The guilds stand with us, and they command a vast amount of the people. If you disagree with this, I will deal with you. As for the rest of you, we will present a united, strong front to the people. We will go to the aid of the dwarves as soon as we are able. And we will rule Pelenor, keep her strong as she always has been, until such time as the king or his kin can take up their duties again. Whether Saradon's rise be truth or rumour, he will not succeed now, just as he did not succeed before. Leave now and attend your duties."

The court descended into irretrievable disorder. Raedon, his gaze sharp and determined, caught Dimitri's eyes. He nodded once to Dimitri, who replied in kind. It was done. Toroth would rule no more, guarded in his sickbed night and day by one of Raedon's finest. All of his kin, be they sick or well, would also be kept secure in their rooms. Raedon would assume command, as was the military right of his rank, with Dimitri by his side as the king's eyes and ears, to ensure nothing in the kingdom or beyond its borders escaped their notice.

If only they knew what a spy they had in enemy courts, Dimitri mused. Even Raedon had no idea just how closely they were both tied to Saradon. Dimitri was pleased as he left the hall, which was filled to the rafters with worry. Toroth was deposed at last. Yet his satisfaction soon soured in his stomach. It was not Raedon who ruled in Toroth's stead. Not truly. They were all puppets of a greater power.

Sooner than Dimitri liked, Saradon would stake his claim to the kingdom that balanced upon a knife's edge, ready to fall in confusion and disarray. No matter that Dimitri had been the one to raise him, Saradon would take all, with none to stand against him. And what had once filled Dimitrius with exhilaration and anticipation, now filled him with deep seated dread. What had he unleashed?

46

HARPER

"Who is Valxiron? Who is Erendriel?" Harper asked now they had retired to one of their rooms in the könig's halls, hoping one of them knew. But she was met by frowns and shaking heads from Brand and Erika.

Aedon, however, shifted at her side. "Are you sure those were the names you heard, Harper? *Exactly* those?"

She met his gaze and nodded, taken aback by the uncharacteristic seriousness. "She said, 'Valxiron's legion spreads anew in Saradon, his disciple.' And that we 'shalt triumph over Valxiron's servant.' It was Vanir who said the name Erendriel."

"'Valxiron's legion spreads anew.' That does not fill me with confidence."

"Who is Valxiron?"

Aedon's stare became baleful. "The Darkness of Altar."

"The… Darkness?" Harper murmured. A prickle of unease rippled through her.

"Let me tell you the tale of the Darkness of Altarea, my

friends," Aedon said solemnly, just as he had many nights past to recount the tale of Saradon.

"I will tell you the tale. In the beginning, there was Altarea, world of the elementals. Those many races know as gods, though by different names and faces. The elementals created all life in Altarea. Everything you see and know, everything you have not yet experienced, the spirits of the elements made it all. They created a master race. The Eldarkind." Aedon looked at Harper, who nodded slowly. The Eldarkind were deeply ingrained in the lore of Caledan. An ethereal, fair, nearly immortal magical race that had disappeared from Caledan, along with the dragons, centuries ago.

"The Eldarkind governed all in the elementals' stead, for the day came when most elementals disappeared, leaving few to roam Altarea. They were balance. It was their sole purpose to ensure the cycles of life and death continued in balance all across Altarea. That fairness came to all living things. In the earliest days of our world, where our realms—Aurauria, Pelenor, Caledan, Valtivar, and many more—did not yet exist, or were in the infancy of their years, the Eldarkind ruled all. Noble were they. Fair. Just. Had they continued their governance, I have no doubt Altarea would have remained as noble, fair, and just as they. Yet it was not to be so."

They all leaned closer, barely breathing, in anticipation of his words. Harper hung on his story. Here was a tale she had never heard before, but it had every promise to be as grand as any of the wandering bards' stories.

"There was born one Eldarkind, Valxiron, who did not share his people's vision. Valxiron was malcontent with being a lesser Eldarkind with no power amongst his kind. He sought power so he could win over Erendriel, whom he desired above all else. It is said she was the fairest Eldarkind maiden who ever walked the world. Her hair was starlight, her eyes the sky. Her soul was as pure as a babe's, and all she blessed turned to wonder and joy.

"Valxiron saw the Eldarkind as weak, not fulfilling the duty for which the elementals created them—to keep order in the world, or, as he saw it, to *rule* the world. Valxiron pursued Erendriel, but she rejected him and his rhetoric, to his humiliation. He refused to accept that it was her right to do so. That she was entitled to disagree with him. Erendriel did not believe that dominion over all else was most important, and Valxiron's ideology caused great consternation amongst his people.

"Valxiron scried the world at the seeing pool. He saw how much the Eldarkind seemingly turned a blind eye. War and strife were plentiful. Surely it was their duty to prevent such things? He was angry. In his eyes, his people ought to be ashamed for their failings. News of discord arrived, but Valxiron had already seen and awaited, wondering what his elders would do. They had to act. Yet they did not. Valxiron, furious, confronted the elders, imploring them to intervene. It was their duty and purpose. However, they would not listen. Valxiron realised that unless he took matters into his own hands, it would never come to pass.

"Valxiron visited the Heart of the World, the source of all power. It was intoxicating. He decided to tip the balance himself. To rebel against the elders for the greater good. Erendriel and the elders tried to stop him, to no avail. Valxiron was determined, his respect and obedience to them broken. He drew from the Heart of the World, unable to resist the alluring call of its limitless power, but such power was beyond his ability to harness and it broke what little was left of his sanity. The Eldarkind banished him from their lands, and from the Heart of the World.

"Drunk on power, he hatched a daring scheme to accomplish his ends. He would create more strife and chaos in the world and let itself be torn to pieces. Only then could order gain hold. Only then could he rule over the vision *he* desired for Altarea… once he had overthrown the elders, who he thought were too feeble and cowardly to stand against him. He vowed to fulfil the potential of their race, as it was meant to be. To hold dominion over all life.

"Valxiron found allies wherever he could, those who sought the advancement of their own peoples and dominions. In the dragons, the goblins, mortals, and more besides did he find those who promised themselves to his cause. He gave his allies power from the Heart of the World to accomplish their aims, but also used it to bind them to him. Erendriel sought Valxiron out and begged him to stop. He was anxious to please her and persuade her to his cause. She rejected him utterly. Desperate, Valxiron forced her to his will, but broke her spirit when he did so. She was nothing more than a hollow shell, and he could not undo what had been done.

"Valxiron was overcome with fury and grief. He blamed himself, but his emotions quickly turned into condemnation of the elders, for it was they he truly held culpable for all that had passed. Were it not for them, he would not have been forced to any of the extreme measures he had taken. Were it not for them, Erendriel would still be. His mind was clear. There was no going back from that point. The elders were not worthy. He, alone, would rule.

"Valxiron continued manipulating the various peoples around him to increase conflict as far and wide as he could, building his base of allies. He fully intended to betray many who followed him. They were unsavoury, beastly creatures, with no honour or merits, like the goblins. Whilst his machinations proceeded as planned, resistance grew from the elders. They pursued Valxiron, and it seemed his luck had changed. The Eldarkind captured Valxiron and returned him to their homeland, breaking their banishment upon him to do so, to imprison him there. They were distraught at what he had done to Erendriel, yet they still exacted no vengeance upon him. Valxiron's machinations were at last halted.

"Valxiron was taunted by his failings when he was brought before the seeing pool to see how chaos had been averted. The elders once again tried to explain that all was a cycle. That all would right itself as it was meant to. Valxiron, haunted by the loss of Erendriel, teetered on the brink of insanity. Valxiron claimed repentance. The elders were convinced of his sincerity, blinded by their hope and benevolence. He was freed, and though they welcomed him back cautiously, he was liberated entirely. Their forgiving and trusting natures would be their undoing."

Harper hung on every word, hardly daring to breathe.

"Valxiron struck. Fuelled by the everlasting power of the Heart of the World, he killed the elders one by one, then created a prison of the Eldarkind kingdom. No longer did he desire to fulfil altruistic aims. He was driven by anger and grief. He saw the world had righted itself but refused the elders' message to not meddle. The last elder, instead of defending himself, stripped his entire race of much of their power and sent it where Valxiron would never find it, but he had made one grave mistake. Valxiron cared not, for he now possessed the power of the Heart of the World. He killed the last elder.

"With his death, the last of the true Eldarkind, the all-powerful, immortal beings, disappeared. Those few who still remain in their hidden pockets of the world are but a paltry shadow of their former selves. Valxiron claimed the Heart of the World as his own. It gave him the power to have ultimate dominion over all. He had no love or loyalty to anyone, save himself. From that day, a darkness spread over all.

"His dominion lasted for an age and nearly tore the world apart. But for Erendriel, who ultimately cast Valxiron down, it would have endured to this day. It took another age to recover from the darkness he wrought—" Aedon looked at Harper, "—the likes of which I believe you saw just a hint of in your vision of Erendriel, Harper."

Unease flickered through her.

"However, his mission continues. Ever have there been pockets of malcontents who seek to revive his work, seek to continue his legacy. If Erendriel appeared in your vision, she speaks truly of Saradon. That he is somehow Valxiron's own servant. It would explain, perhaps, how Saradon, a half-elf with no magic, became one of the strongest mages in Pelenor seemingly overnight, and also how he can find servants or allies in the goblins. Perhaps even now, the Dark One's magic and his malicious will still endure." Aedon shivered. "I don't enjoy telling that story."

Brand scratched his forehead. "What does this mean for Saradon now? For Afnirheim? For us?"

"I'm not sure. Only that he is far more powerful than we know. I fear Afnirheim is not the worst he could do. We shall have to tread very carefully indeed."

"But if this is a prophecy, we're going to win, right?" asked Harper.

Aedon laughed. "I don't think that's how prophecies work, Harper. You cannot just sit back and wait for the outcome. You still must take part in your own destiny. You must 'stand true', 'beware the Tainted Star', and 'heed the

Shadow', whatever that means. And it seems we might need a Dragonheart, which is nigh on impossible—"

"Thanks to you," said Erika.

Aedon glared at her. "You're welcome! We would not have escaped Tournai alive had I not used their energies for our benefit, nor cured that accursed plague. How were any of us to know we might need such a rare substance again?"

"Regardless, we've given our word that we will follow the könig to battle, for better or worse," interrupted Brand. "At least forewarned is forearmed. We cannot be quite sure what we are dealing with, but he is clearly more powerful than even we thought. We ought to be more cautious on that basis."

"I'm not sure we can be cautious facing a maniacal half-elf who has the magic of the Dark One and a mountain full of goblins," said Aedon sourly.

Harper was inclined to agree, but they had given their word. They were to go to battle—and the inexorable conclusion before them.

47

DIMITRI

With all affairs taken care of in Tournai and a lull in what distractions Dimitri could find, he could not help but check upon Harper. Dimitri's heart sank when he found her outside the safety of Keldheim, camped upon the road amongst a great dwarven host that sprawled into the forest. Their purpose was unmistakable, albeit hopeless. They had come to retake Afnirheim—and Saradon would kill them all. If they even reached Afnirheim, that was, for the *pascha* planned to send out a great host of his own to further expand the reach of his domain.

Dimitri dithered on the fringes of the valley, hidden by the ridge of trees. *Do I warn her again?* Even as the thought occurred, he knew it to be hopeless to resist it. *Do I force her to leave?* The feeling in his stomach soured further. He had already implored Harper to leave, but now it was even worse. Now she walked to her certain death. He could not have it on his conscience. Never mind that everything else seemed to be spiralling beyond his control. This, he could avert. They did not need to die. *She* did not need to die. His heart twisted painfully at the mere thought. He looked over the valley and the thousands of dwarven warriors. He had to try.

He sought her out, flitting through the veils of the world until he came upon her, once more in the company of the confounded elf and their other companions, though the dwarf was absent. He waited until she excused herself a little while later to relieve herself, following her through the trees and melting into the shadows far enough away to give her privacy and dignity. On her way back, he appeared before her, stepping out of the darkness into a shard of moonlight on the game trail.

She swore and stumbled back, her hand reaching for her dagger before she recognised him. "Gods! I wish you wouldn't do that," she snarled. "Stop following me! What do you want?"

He longed to make a sarcastic retort but checked himself. There was no time. "Harper, I came here to warn y—"

"I'm not going anywhere, Dimitrius," she said, crossing her arms and glaring at him.

He could not help but smile at her stubbornness, foolish though it was. It spoke to the desperate and foolish part of him that still held hope. "Clearly. But you have to listen. You're walking into a trap. The goblins plan to march from Afnirheim to Keldheim. You'll run straight into them readying for battle. It will be a massacre—and not in your favour."

"Why tell me? You're a part of this," she said accusingly. Her gaze seemed to strip him to his core. "Are you trying to trick me?"

"No, I promise." He faltered, dropping his gaze. For a moment, he gaped, before he swallowed and spoke, meeting her night-darkened eyes. "Look. Perhaps I'm foolish. I don't even know why I care. Perhaps I feel I owe you after what happened."

Harper narrowed her eyes. "What do you mean?"

"*I* stole the Dragonheart from the king," he admitted, his gaze dropping to the ground.

She stiffened, her eyes widening. "That's why you sought us out, kept me safe. That's the reason you let me escape in the end, isn't it?"

He nodded.

"Why did you take it? And why send it to me?"

"That part was an accident," he said sheepishly. "I didn't mean to send it to you. I stole it to—" Dimitri frowned and faltered. "I was chasing rumours, I suppose. But in the end, for better or worse, I released Saradon. I was blinded by it all." His voice dropped to a whisper. "I think I made the wrong choice." Heat rose to his cheeks. Why was he standing there babbling on like a fool— admitting his deepest fears, cutting his soul open—to *her*, of all people?

"You're a bloody idiot," she snapped. He was glad she saved herself from shouting, though just barely, knowing they were too close to the camp for comfort. Instead, she closed the gap between them and jabbed a finger into his chest. "Did you have any idea what that would unleash?"

His stomach lurched. "Of course not! I wanted to build a better Pelenor, but not like this."

"Then you need to fix it."

"Believe me, I wish I could. I'm bound to him now, Harper. I gave my word and my magic. I cannot." With a sinking feeling in the pit of his stomach, he realised the true implications of that. He was bound to Saradon's will, whatever the cost.

She scoffed in disgust. "Typical. You're just like any other noble. Wash your hands and be done with it. Someone else's problem. Did you *see* inside Afnirheim?"

"I did," he said quietly.

"Did you help him?"

"Of course not! I had no idea. I never dreamed he would ally with *goblins*, much less sanction that. I was furious with him, but he does not care one whit for my opinion. He owns me." Dimitri hung his head. It was true. He had given his servitude in good faith—and now it bound him to a cause he did not want to champion.

"Don't you *dare* feel sorry for yourself," Harper hissed, whirling upon him. She slammed her palms onto his chest with a noise of frustration. Her grey eyes flashed with ire. "My friend nearly *died* because of you. A city full of his kin *did* die because of you. We are going to fix your mistake, and you'd better not get in our way."

She made to push past him, but he grabbed her arm at the elbow, not allowing himself to be shaken off. "You won't heed my warning?"

"We gave our word to the dwarven king that we would help them in whatever way we could." Her voice shook—just a little, but he caught it. She was scared but would follow through regardless. He admired her pluck.

Dimitri turned her towards him, so she would feel the full impact of his next, devastating words. "They will kill you all, Harper." How much more clearly could he put it?

"Not if the könig knows they're coming. Have you not seen how many thousands he has massed? The goblins stand no chance."

He hoped she was right, for the dwarven warriors held a fearsome reputation, but he had seen the *pascha's* horde—a never-ending flood of unearthly creatures passing through Afnirheim's halls and onward to battle. "Why are you so invested, Harper? This has nothing to do with you or your companions."

Doubt flashed in her eyes, which she swiftly covered with defiance. "It has, more than you know."

He stilled, an unfamiliar lurch in the pit of his stomach stirring into life. He had hoped to be wrong about her connection to Saradon, but was he? Did she know?

"My companions have dealings with him, of a sort," she said. "My connection is of a more… personal nature. I admit, I'm partly curious. I have to seek the truth."

"The truth of *what?*" If one of them did not speak in riddles, it seemed the other did.

"I am Saradon's kin."

He sucked in a breath. "I beg your pardon?" Icy dread consumed him. *It cannot be so!* She had spoken his worst fear —because now there was no undoing her part in this. And no way he could spare her from Saradon.

48

DIMITRI

"I am his great-granddaughter. The dwarven seer, Vanir, showed me." She trailed off, as if there were more she did not wish to say. Or perhaps she wondered why she shared such deep things with him.

"Beyond any doubt?" he asked, desperate for any shred of hope that it wasn't true—that she would not be pulled into the middle of the maelstrom with him. Desperate for her to continue, because hearing her speak was a balm after nothing but hate and conflict in his ears since he had last beheld her. Her palms still rested on his chest, her hands so delicate and light they felt as though he could break them with a thought. Her fragility terrified him.

"Beyond any doubt," she whispered.

His insides twisted. This was all his fault—he kept making it worse, instead of staunching the flow. His unwitting thoughts had led Saradon right to her. Dimitri grasped her shoulders and met her gaze, trying to instil his urgency. "Then you *must* go. It is all the more reason to flee! He must not find you!"

She struggled in his grip, but he did not release her. "I don't understand."

"He *knows*, Harper. Even if he is not certain, he has strong suspicions. Enough for him to seek you. He wants you. If you go to him, you walk to your own doom. I cannot shield you from him. Please heed me. Please leave—with or without the dwarves."

"Why do you care?" she asked him again desperately, her fingers winding into the silks of his shirt. It undid him.

"Because you made me!" he retorted before he could help himself. "Because you make me want to protect you from the tide of darkness that has been unleashed. Every damn thing you say and do makes me want you more—and I can take it no longer!"

"What?" she breathed, her face pale in the darkness. "Say that again. No lies."

"I want you," Dimitri growled, backing her into a tree. "I want you even though I know it is dangerous. I have wanted you since the moment you pulled that bow on me, and I saw the true colour of your spirit. I wanted you more when you held a knife to my throat and I realised fear would never fell your spirit. And I want you yet more every time you open that defiant little mouth of yours to call me out. I hate that you challenge me so, huntress. I love it. I desire it. I need it. And the peril we are in only makes me need you all the more, for if I am to die on the morrow, I want to die having known what it feels like to have tasted you."

Compulsion crawled underneath his skin, urgent and consuming. He could hardly breathe past the torrent of it. His hands slipped inside her cloak to circle her waist, and she gasped at the contact. So did he. She felt even better under his hands than he had imagined. He would excise this demon from himself. Indulge this reckless want and purge it from his system. It was a kiss—just one. A harmless kiss. That would free him from this madness. This was nothing more than wanting what he could not have, and once he quenched that urge, it would be satisfied. Wouldn't it?

And yet, as he felt her lithe body melt under his touch, he knew with deep certainly that it would not be enough. Far from it. The opposite. This would not quench the flames—this would ignite an inferno. Judgement on himself be damned, Dimitri wanted her. And one kiss did not cover what he wanted to do to her—but he would take it and anything else she would give him.

Dimitri drew closer, so close that every heaving breath of hers pressed against the beat of his own heart, and lowered his head, so that their noses brushed. She froze in place, silver eyes gleaming at him. Those beautiful lips of hers were so painfully close it sent every nerve ending alight within him, longing to fuse that final hair's breadth. But he would not. Not without her permission. Because there would be no going back from this.

"Tell me no, and I'll stop," he said roughly as their breaths mingled. He trembled from the restraint. Part of him wished she would deny him. Part of him desperately wanted her to have some self-control where he did not, to end this madness, so his feelings did not endanger either of them any further. But instead, Harper tilted her mouth up, tightened her grasp on his shirt, and tugged him to her waiting lips. And Dimitri unleashed himself upon her.

49

HARPER

arper had been lost the moment Dimitrius had confessed his need for her—and beyond salvation the moment his hands had circled her waist and the burn of his palms had imprinted through the fabric. Her legs had buckled—and only the tree and his hold kept her standing. *This* was what desire felt like—a potent storm without edges or end that consumed every fragment of her. She made her choice without hesitation, and as his lips crashed into hers, the world disappeared.

She opened to his punishing request at once, and his hot, wanting tongue slid into her mouth, wrestling with hers as her hands found their way up to tangle in that perfectly coiffed hair of his, utterly wrecking him the way he devastated her. This was no gentle kiss but a battle of tongues and teeth, licking, suckling, biting, and nipping with desperation. His hands planed up her back and down again, his nails digging in with a delicious bite of pain that edged her pleasure in something even more intoxicating. Dimitrius squeezed her buttocks and groaned into her mouth, and the sound sent fire chasing through every vein until all rational thought had fled her.

Tree bark scraped down her cloak as he hoisted her up. Harper spread her legs, locking them around his hips as he held her suspended there with the strength of his rigid arms. He pinned her between the tree and the hardness growing between his legs that nestled right into her centre. She writhed against it, her core molten with need, and he rocked into her with matching demand. She wanted more. Needed more—before common sense, guilt, and shame had air to breathe and grow. Never had someone ignited such passion within her, and now she had him between her legs, the fabric sliding between them was a barrier to it all.

Dimitrius broke the kiss, his voice ragged. "You are more than I ever could have dreamed of, Harper. One kiss will never be enough. You will be my ruin."

She groaned as he rocked his hips against her once more—and then he swallowed that groan with another kiss. But then—

"Harper?" Brand's deep voice rang through the trees.

She stiffened, and Dimitrius froze against her too. Her head whipped toward the direction of camp. Intense need still coursed through her—but darkness pushed in, bringing an edge of fear to the waves crashing through her. Reality. It had interrupted again. *Saved* her again. From the irresistible temptation before her. "I have to go."

They were chest to chest. That need of his still pressed between her legs. And gods, she wanted more. She wanted all of it. But she pushed him back and staggered on shaking legs to the next tree, leaning heavily against it for a second to try and catch the breaths she had let him steal from her.

"Don't. Please," he said, his dark eyes glittering in the shadows of the trees as he followed her. "Let me take you somewhere safe." He circled an arm around her waist, and it nearly undid her anew, but her palm upon his chest froze him.

She had to stop this. No matter how incandescent it felt—how much she now realised the power that pure desire promised—Harper had to walk away now, or she would not be able to at all. She brought a trembling hand to her gloriously swollen and stinging lips, touching her fingertips to the skin there. The ghost of his touch still burned her. The cold void of night air upon her skin felt an abhorrent replacement for his heated kiss.

"I can't," she whispered. "I cannot leave my friends. I cannot abandon what we must do."

His hand slipped from her waist, his gaze searching her eyes—but whatever he found made him step back. "Please leave, or at least warn the dwarves. I cannot be any clearer. To continue spells disaster."

"Harper?" Brand's voice rang out through the woods—closer this time.

Dimitri cursed violently under his breath—and she felt the same wave of frustration at the interruption, but it did not sway her. "We cannot be found like this—go. Please. I will pass on your warning. That is all I can promise."

"Be safe," he pleaded.

She could not promise that either. Harper swallowed and turned away, before she lost the will to leave. He faded into the shadows as the glow of a burning torch through the trees grew closer. Harper stared at him for a moment, before moving toward the light, gratefully gulping down painfully freezing breaths to cool the heat bubbling inside her.

DIMITRI

Dimitri reeled. He had kissed Harper. *Kissed her.* And she had let him—more than that, she had unleashed a furious passion so equal to his, it shocked him. One kiss would not suffice. He knew it deep in his bones.

From the first moment he had met her that day in the woods—a half-starved young woman with no idea who he was, with no preconceptions about him, who had without a second thought drawn a bow and shot an arrow straight at him—he had been curious about her. She had been so refreshing in his world—one that was otherwise filled with treacherous liars and danger in every shadow.

At what point had that curiosity turned into attraction? He could not pinpoint it. The way she had pulled his own knife on him had excited him—that was without question— but had he wanted her then? No, he decided. Still, she had been too novel, too unknown. He had cared more than he ought to when her death approached in the vaults—and he had credited his intervening action to uncharacteristic nobility at the time. But, no, not then.

He had known—without realising, because he had been locked with such denial then and after the fact, he now saw with hindsight—it had been that moment on the parapet. When Harper had pushed past the protection the Aerian warrior offered her to stand before him to demand answers, that fierce challenge in her gaze, he had cared then. Enough to send her away. But enough to want her back. He was never supposed to have seen her again. That was safe. That was for the best. And yet, he had been foolish and desperate enough to seek her.

On the bridge, he had known for certain. He—Dimitri, spymaster, *fool*—was attracted to her. Heart, body, and mind. This woman was no mere curiosity, no casual plaything—but a force to be reckoned with who would not let the small matter of her youth and inexperience hold her back. He was in awe of her, he realised. All the power he held—and yet he was such a coward, skulking in the shadows. Her—practically defenceless, and still, she threw herself into what was right regardless of the odds stacked against her favour.

Now, that weakness in him was even more desperate for her—and she was more determined than ever to place herself into harm's way. He despaired at it. At the boldness that both made her so special and yet endangered her so much. The time approached when he did not know if he could pluck the strings of fate enough to see her safely through the other side of what lay ahead.

Dimitri watched Harper leave, though every fibre of his being wanted to go to her. To continue what they had just started. To spirit her somewhere safe—far away from the hellhole this army advanced upon. But he did not move. She had told him what she wanted, and he would not take that choice away from her, even though he thought it beyond folly.

He stared until she had long disappeared between the trees. The icy chill froze him now, all that raging desire cooled to ashes. Now he had a moment free of her intoxicating presence muddying his thoughts for it to sink in. *She is Saradon's kin.* He could not begin to fathom what that meant, only that it spelled disaster if Saradon obtained her. Now he had all the more reason to keep her away from him, to keep her safe. He hoped she would heed his words, but he did not hold out much conviction. He disappeared to run back to his unwittingly acquired master. It would not do for him to be discovered helping the enemy.

But Dimitri knew with certainty. One kiss would not be enough. She would be his ruin—and he would go to it willingly. For her. Because though he had decided to allow her the power of her own choice, he would not allow her naivety to be the death of her. No. One kiss would *never* be enough— but it had to be. He could not allow it to happen again—for himself to lose control like that again—for he would only endanger her all the more.

The force of how much he needed her threatened to drive the breath from his lungs and the reason from his mind. He could not make her choices for her. But he could make his own. And the greatest gift he could give her was safety when the jaws of darkness threatened to tear them apart. He would put himself in her place before he allowed that to happen. It would never make amends for what he had done—but it was one good deed to end with.

51

HARPER

"What's wrong?" Brand asked when he saw Harper's frown and her distraction. "You were gone a while."

She looked up at him but did not answer. Her chest caved in as that desire evaporated into the cold dread of reality that stole her breath for an entirely different reason. They marched to battle—to death. And she did not want to die. She wanted to *live*. She wanted her friends to be safe. She could not bear to see any more of the death and destruction they had witnessed already in Afnirheim. And she wanted time to explore whatever this thing blooming between her and Dimitrius was, without the threat of such dark tidings hanging over them.

"Harper?" Brand's expression became more guarded, and his stance shifted defensively as he scanned the woodlands around them.

"Dimitrius just appeared," she whispered.

"What?" Brand growled, his hand falling to the handle of his dagger.

"He came with a warning." It was the only truth she could give, because the rest of it felt like it would damn her.

"Where is he?"

"Gone." That was the truth too, she hoped.

He stopped. "Come. Tell us all."

"Away from the dwarves," she urged. They did not need to hear of it—at least yet. He nodded. She staggered after him, her legs jelly after what had just happened—and with the threat that Dimitrius had warned of sending her molten with fear. With every step the cold air seared her lungs and cleared her mind. She forced herself to steel—she had to compose herself. She could not admit what she had just done. Her cheeks burned with the shame of them discovering it. No matter her own murky feelings on the matter, their's would be quite clear, and she did not need the complication.

Motioning her companions to a quieter corner of the camp, she recounted the bare minimum of their encounter, omitting how she had told Dimitrius of her heritage, his admission of stealing the Dragonheart—and that earth-shattering kiss. They were too overwhelming to mention. Even skirting around the edges of it left a raw ache in her chest. She reeled inside after what had just passed—for more details returned to her with every second of thought. Dimitrius, revealing he had stolen the Dragonheart from King Toroth! She had not seen that coming. That he had mistakenly sent it to her—which meant he was the reason she was here at all. Harper had no idea what to make of that. It complicated everything yet more. And Saradon knew she was his heir. The danger of that made her stomach roil. She dropped her head into her hands for a brief moment.

"We cannot leave them now," Brand said. "We gave our word."

"As I told Dimitrius," Harper said, folding her arms so no one saw how her hands trembled. It hurt to say his name, scratching at that new rawness in her chest.

"We must tell the dwarves."

"How? They cannot know that I met with him." Already, guilt leeched into her very bones. She had done more than that alright—and wanted to go even further. What did that make her? She was no traitor—but she wanted Dimitrius. There was no denying it. And the fact he wanted her too only made it all the more impossible to resist.

"A vision," said Aedon. Her attention slid to him, her expression carefully blank as she forced the writhing mess of thoughts deep down inside her and closed the door to them. "It's the only way. You have seen a vision of a great goblin host in the valley before Afnirheim. You saw it once. You can describe it again."

She nodded, though a coil of unease stirred. She did not want to lie—but it was the only way to pass on the spymaster's warning without inviting dangerous questions she could not answer. "But won't they want Vanir to verify the truth of it?"

"We are far from Keldheim now. There is no time to dally," said Brand. "The könig will not wish to delay, lest the element of surprise be lost."

With her agreement, they rushed to Jarl Halvar, who camped nearby with his command. When Brand murmured their purpose to him, he took them before the könig at once. Harper recounted her "vision" in short order to the könig, who did precisely as predicted—ground his teeth and vowed to press on.

"I thank you for sharing this warning with me, Harper of Caledan." He still refused to call her by her house title,

Ravakian, though she could understand why, since the name was tied to Saradon. "It changes our path not, only that we are now forewarned and forearmed. We knew there would be battle. Better it be upon the open fields where we may form ranks and sweep the blight away. If they are to be drawn from Afnirheim, it means the halls will ring empty—for *our* return."

He sounded far more confident than Harper thought he ought to. He had discounted Saradon entirely, which she felt was a great oversight. Dimitrius's unease and the open shreds of fear and doubt he had shown her were a far greater testament of the true danger of the half-elf than anything else. Did the könig realise Saradon's power? she wondered.

Dismissed, they returned to their belongings to bed down for the night on the fringes of Korrin's forces where their belongings marked a small camp for them. Her companions sat in a circle to talk—around where a campfire would be, were fire not forbidden—but their words were a haze. Harper mumbled her excuses and retired to her hollow in the mossy ground. They were almost surrounded by dwarven forces, but she felt utterly alone as she stared out into the forest, watching for any hint of movement—searching for those violet eyes. She found nothing. Only still darkness and unbroken silence, for the creatures of the forest fled with the size of the force disturbing their home.

Conflict raged inside her. She needed Dimitrius to return. Needed to see him again. Needed to finish what they had started. More than that—she needed answers. Her questions only piled higher, and the deserted forest gave her no reply. It was so late that her body ached and her head drooped with the weight of her fatigue. The thrill of her encounter with Dimitrius, which had chased all weariness from her bones, had faded. The excitement of that had been replaced with a constant simmering nausea that would not settle at the prospect of what awaited them as soon as tomorrow—a battle in which she would be on the opposing side to Dimitrius, and in which both of them were quite likely doomed.

5 2

HARPER

Confirmation arrived the next morning with the return of Korrin's scouts—Harper and her companions were summoned just after dawn to attend the king. Harper skulked at the back of their group, exhausted and shivering after a long, cold, and sleepless night, haunted by spectres of Saradon and Dimitrius.

The king was especially grim-faced that morning. "Your vision was indeed true. We did not need Vanir to verify."

Relief and then terror swooped through Harper.

Unaware, Korrin continued, "A great goblin host skulks—thrice our number—massing on the plain before Afnirheim. Though they will retreat into the dark halls with the return of day, they will as surely return when cover of darkness strengthens their daring."

"We are still to march, König?" Jarl Halvar asked what they all dared not to, what was not their place to question. That they would fight, despite the dubious odds of success.

König Korrin grimaced but nodded—and Harper let out a shaky exhale. She had not realised that secretly, she had been hoping that battle somehow could be averted, and they did not approach an inexorable conflict. "Aye. I know the lay of the land and the halls of Afnirheim. The scourge of goblins stands little chance when we know when and where to position and manoeuvre. Form up, Jarl Halvar. We march at once. I want every dwarf in position to strike after next dawn."

A tangle of nerves twisted through Harper. Halvar bowed and departed at once to send runners through the camp with the könig's orders.

That night, there was no merriment in their new camp. Precipitous cliffs hemmed them into a narrow offshoot of the valley that felt altogether too confining and reminiscent of where Harper and her friends had camped the night Ragnar had been taken. Fires were prohibited once more, lest their position be given away to the scourge of goblins that screeched through the peaks. Their harsh calls ricocheted off the cliffs, until it seemed they came from all directions. Everyone was subdued by the sobering reminder of what tomorrow could bring.

Sleep would not be had that night. Though Harper sat in a tight knot with Aedon, Brand, and Erika between the trunk of a giant tree and a rocky overhang, she did not count herself safe. The rhythmic rasp and scrape of Erika sharpening her twin blades was the only sound from their little group, though the clanking of other metal elsewhere in the camp signalled that she was not alone in her ministrations. Brand had laid out all his weapons—the giant blade none of them could hope to lift, plus a surprising number of knives he had concealed upon his body—on the rough ground before him. He checked them all meticulously, cleaning and sheathing them to check he could draw them all with ease. Harper clutched her dagger—the one Aedon had gifted her what felt like an age ago—and a slim, short blade she had briefly trained with in the dwarven halls. They remained in their scabbards before her.

"Are you all right, Harper?" Brand murmured, pausing for a moment.

"No." Shame burned a path through her belly as she admitted it. "I want to throw up." She was terrified, though she did not dare to voice that implicitly.

Brand chuckled quietly. "I understand that. Even for me, the time before a battle is filled with no small amount of apprehension."

"It's just…" Just what? Was it the threat she knew they were to meet? The risk to them all? The risk to her friends? To Dimitrius—and herself? Or merely the dark of the night amplifying all her fears out of proportion? "It's just *everything*," she decided.

"That's normal. The scouts watch with extra vigilance tonight. We are safe. Tomorrow with the dawn, the threat begins, but we will stand together, as we have always done, and we will weather the storm." He glanced at his other companions and gave a small smile. Harper knew they had fought together many times before.

"What if we don't?" she whispered. To voice her worst fears aloud scared her even more.

"Then, Harper of Caledan, an honourable death in battle we shall have had. But I will do all in my power to see it is not so. My time in this life is not done yet. I have more to live for." His eyes flicked to Erika and back again, almost imperceptible in the dark. Perhaps Harper had imagined it.

"As do you," he added. "What did Vanir call you? Harper

of Caledan, of Pelenor, of House Ravakian, Mother Blessed, and Fated One? The *Frelsa*?" He gave her another small smile. "It would seem *you* are most blessed of us all to survive."

"I'm not half the warrior you are. Or a quarter. Or even a hair's breadth," she said. In the face of death, that threatened to liquify her insides. She could not hold her own in battle—of that, she was deadly certain. Why had she signed up to this foolish venture? What utter madness had possessed her? She clutched the scabbard so tightly her knuckles whitened.

Brand laughed. "We will stand with you, Harper. And sometimes, standing together is the only kind of courage and faith we can muster when the outcome is uncertain, but it is enough."

His words did not comfort Harper as she tightened her cloak around her and braced against the tree trunk to try and snatch a few scant moments of rest. Tomorrow, the king had decreed—they were to go to battle. Tomorrow, she would see the sunrise. But would she see the sunset?

53

HARPER

D awn—and battle—arrived too soon for comfort. The dwarven host, uncharacteristically silent, stood in unbroken lines threading through the trees above the cleared land before Afnirheim where the battle-dead still lay. A stench wafted across the valley—of death and the scourge of goblins—further turning Harper's stomach. Already, she trembled, unable to contain her nervous energy, not even with Brand's reassuring presence beside her. The goblins' shrieks still echoed across the valley though, with the rising sun, many retreated into Afnirheim in disorder, trickling back into the dark halls.

Dwarven horns rang out—rich, strong, and fierce—and with that summons, their forces charged. It was a slow build of pace as the line of Korrin's army, all infantry, swept forward as they descended upon the valley floor, roaring their attack. The melee was upon them all in short order as the shrieking goblins, caught off guard by the sudden and unexpected attack, met the charge, spilling forth from Afnirheim with haste and urgency. They emerged in greater numbers until the valley before the dwarven city was full of bodies, din, and a stench that made Harper's eyes water.

Behind the dwarven king, who led the charge, and the front ranks of König Korrin's strongest warriors, Harper and her companions surged forward, meeting the goblin defence as the front lines married and the first of both sides fell. Brand's great blade emerged, sweeping away all before him, whilst Erika's twin blades were a blur, soon spewing black blood into the air as she felled those who dared come close to her. Aedon's own blade darted out like a serpent with each strike. Between the scything dwarven axes, they crunched and squelched in fleshy targets.

Harper stood between them all, wielding her own blade where needed, charging it with magic that burned and sizzled her targets as she struck, sending them either squealing to the ground or falling back in retreat—saved by desperation and luck, rather than skill. In the midst of battle, there was neither time nor energy to waste on fear, for every step brought a fresh challenge. That terror was lightning through every vein as she moved at speed to evade death.

Harper soon lost herself in an uncharacteristic haze, somehow finding all her senses overloaded, but having a clarity of mind and rhythm in her limbs that seemed a strange, deadly dance. Somehow, all her training seemed to come to some kind of fruition. She tried not to think that the goblins were hardly an organised opponent, and their disarray aided her far more than her paltry skills. Rather instead, that she had enough grace, skill, and nerve to attack and defend with a semblance of competence, enhancing her attacks with magic that bit into the onslaught of goblins.

The ground ran slick and muddy with red and black blood, until the host of dwarves had no choice but to clamber and stumble over the corpses. It made for a difficult advance, but Korrin's banners called them all forward as he progressed the dwarven battalion upon the fallen city. Their assault was inexorable, pushing back the goblins, who hated the growing daylight that made their vision barely passable, just as Korrin had said. Still, goblins spewed from the mouth of Afnirheim, and Harper found herself wondering when the horde would end… *if* the horde would end.

She sensed a turn in the tide when she could see the back of more goblins than their fronts. They stumbled into the dark halls under the growing light and dwarven attacks. Korrin's forces advanced upon the mountain, their triumph buoying their pace. However, the fortunes of battle changed once more. Storm clouds grew until the sky darkened to a dim gloom. The shrieks of the goblins cacophonied anew, for the darkness was their domain, and they flourished within it.

Once more, they poured forth from Afnirheim with such force that the dwarven lines were halted, then rebuffed, and suddenly, the goblins had the advantage on the slightly higher ground, the chaos of the battlefield behind the dwarves providing no sure footing or place to form effective ranks. Now, the dwarves no longer seemed strong and inexorable, no matter their weapons, armour, and order. The feral goblins, as slippery as smoke, held the advantage, moving easily over the carnage. As the dwarven lines thinned, Harper once more felt true fear carve into her when she saw the gaps begin to widen as dwarves were forced to retreat under the onslaught and regroup—or try to—behind the muddy, bloody battlefield.

She acted upon instinct—the true benefit of Brand's, Aedon's, and Erika's training becoming apparent—the ingrained movements saving her neck on several occasions. Despite her fear, it gave her joy to know that she was no longer helpless, and she revelled in the feeling, channelling her fear and energy into magic and battle. She used every part of it to hold the goblins back. Fire and lightning flew at them, charged upon her blade. It sent them fleeing, shrieking and smoking. She drifted farther along the line, leaving her companions behind as she sought out targets.

Korrin's horns sounded just as the dwarven lines fractured under the seemingly endless onslaught. *Retreat! Retreat!* The dwarves fell back, across the quagmire of the dead, to the far slopes of the valley, where they would once more hold the advantage.

Harper continued to move with a knot of dwarves, barely registering that she could no longer see Erika's whirling blades, or Brand's wide wings, or Aedon's darting form. During a lull, she looked up to view the battlefield. No matter that the valley piled high with twisted goblin bodies covered in black blood and grime, far higher in numbers than the fallen dwarves, the goblins kept coming, flooding in a constant torrent from Afnirheim's fractured gates.

She did not see the goblin until it was too late. He fell upon her with speed, brandishing a cruel, jagged blade in his claws, teeth bared. There was no time to raise her blade. Prophecy be damned, she was as good as dead.

Thunk.

54

HARPER

The goblin's head flew from its shoulders as Brand's giant blade swung before her, the big Aerian seemingly appearing from nowhere.

"I was fine!" she maintained, shouting across the maelstrom. He rolled his eyes before cutting another goblin clean in half. She knew her sting of annoyance was only aimed at herself, at her lapse. "Thank you!" she shouted, turning away again.

"Stay close!" he thundered. "Stay *together*!"

"I can handle myself!" Had she not already proven it? *I'm alive thus far.* The rush of self-protection singing through her was an antidote to her fear.

He did not respond. Perhaps he had not heard, for the din still raged around them. She could not even hear herself over the ringing in her own ears and the pounding of her heart.

Yet she could not mistake the figure wreathed in shadow and flame who appeared before the doors of Afnirheim. Saradon stalked from the city, casting his gaze and his magic this way and that. With every step, he blasted those around him indiscriminately, and goblins and dwarves alike fell before him. Harper quailed, riven to her core by fear. She turned, forging her way closer to Brand, even as he battled to make a path back to the rest of their companions. Now, she realised how much she needed them for her safety. All stilled for a moment as Saradon's raw power crackled through them all. She was not sure if she had imagined it, though, for in the next instant, all was as before—the onslaught and the din unrelenting. Dimitrius's warning rang in her ears, but she had a sinking dread that it was far too late to heed it.

Her heart skipped a beat when she saw him, too, standing in the shadows behind Saradon. But Dimitrius made no move, neither to aid the goblins nor the dwarves. His gaze slid to the giant Aerian, then to Harper. From across the distance, she saw his flash of gritted teeth, saw how his face paled, and he sprang to attention, straightening with the shock of seeing her. She knew he had perceived her—reckoned he probably hurled a curse her way for not heeding his warning, which had been given at such great risk to himself. She was glad she could not see those eyes of his. They could lecture her without a single word.

Harper noted how pale and drawn he was. She had not noticed it in the dark when he had sought her. He looked sick with apprehension. The tight lines around his mouth and eyes scared her more than anything. He was more powerful than any of them, save perhaps Saradon and his dark magic. How much worse was Saradon for *him* to fear?

She suddenly realised the flow of the battle had changed. Even as the dwarves retreated with renewed vigour at Saradon's appearance, so the goblins advanced with new purpose. A great knot of them surged for Harper and her companions, just as Saradon locked eyes with her across the valley. She saw the gleam of white teeth as he smiled with open satisfaction.

There was no way to hold them off, for the scourge of goblins was so overwhelmingly huge. The dwarves around them either fell away in retreat or were cut down where they stood. Rough, clawed hands dragged at them all, overpowering them, even Brand, with the sheer weight of numbers. But they were not torn to shreds, though the goblins made no effort to be gentle.

Instead, Harper and her companions were pulled and dragged—sometimes in opposing directions until her muscles and joints strained—heaved in a great, writhing mass, deafened by the shrieking that was far too close for comfort. They were prodded and poked all the way to Saradon's feet. With a flick of his finger, they fell to the ground, where he immobilized them with half a thought, so they lay unable to defend themselves in the blood and dirt.

Harper turned her head as far as she could, looking up at Saradon, who glared down at them all with grim glee. Her attention flicked when Dimitri loomed beside him, his face marred by barely concealed worry as he met her gaze—and then looked away, as if fearful Saradon would see his attentions upon her.

Saradon spoke in a harsh, jarring tongue, his attention straying to them for a moment before the goblins once more leapt upon their prisoners and rushed them into the dark of the mountain. The clutch of their claws bit her arms once more as they dragged her away. The last thing Harper saw before the darkness enveloped them and the ruined doors boomed shut was the last of the dwarves fleeing into the tree line.

The jarlshalle of Afnirheim, ruled by a dwarven lord rather than a könig, was smaller than the königshalle of Keldheim. It was made even smaller by the darkness within. Columns loomed in the space, but above them was darkness. No faelights shone in the tall, thin alcoves at the side of the hall. The floor was dark with ash and blood, and the emptiness stank of death and decay.

Saradon awaited them, like a king standing before his throne. Dimitrius was nowhere to be seen. Harper did not know whether to be comforted or more terrified by that. With a single word from him, their captors hurled them to the floor, then rushed out in a cacophony of shrieks and snarls. The doors boomed shut, the sound echoing from the bare walls, until all fell to silence. Unconsciously, Harper drew closer to her companions as they tightened their knot, all warily eying the dark figure standing on the dais before them whilst they knelt on the bare rock.

His raven hair—so like Harper's, she realised with a shock —was an even darker black in the dim light, but his skin glowed an unsettling red in the ruddy light of the braziers burning about the hall. They belched smoke that added to the stench of the tainted halls, but it at least covered up the worst of the death blighting the air. However, the dark could not hide his piercing violet glare. His attention sent her skin crawling as she inched closer to Aedon, Brand, and Erika, wishing she had paid more attention during the battle. Perhaps if she had stayed closer to them all, if she had not strayed so far, they could have escaped. But as Saradon's gaze swept over and through her, she knew she could not blame herself. The moment she had set foot upon that battlefield, she had sealed her own fate. She would not have outrun him. Perhaps she ought to have heeded Dimitri's warning.

Even though she felt as weak as a fawn before Saradon, she was grateful for her companions. At least she could find strength in their presence. For the first time, she truly realised how much she needed them, relied on them for her safety. Terror sawed through her already shredded nerves as Saradon advanced. The raw tang of his power preceded him, whipping and crackling through the very air until it hummed with the strength of it. It felt wrong in a way no other magic did, turning her stomach and tainting her own well of power in a way she could not explain. As he drew closer, she realised how very small she felt, for he towered over her in both height and imposing presence.

"Daughter of my blood, I welcome thee to my halls," he said to Harper, baring his teeth in a terrifying smile which curdled dread in her belly.

DIMITRI

Serpentine fear slithered through him, sending his nerves on edge and making it almost impossible to stand still. But Dimitri had a role to play. So, like a statue, he stood at the fringes of the hall behind Saradon, not letting the chasing trepidation take him—or allowing Harper to see him. He lurked beyond her perception behind a column. It cut him to see her, but he knew that all would be lost if she saw him, for she was painfully transparent to a flaw. She was in no true danger, whether she knew that or not—yet. He would intervene if that threatened. His own skin be damned, Dimitri knew he would not hesitate if it came to it.

Harper and her companions lay upon the floor, bound where Saradon had restrained them with invisible bonds of magic after the hulking Aerian and the feisty nomad had tried to attack him. Dimitri knew it would have been fruitless. It irked him. Were they so ignorant as to believe such folly had any chance of success? They should have protected themselves better—protected *her* better. He despised them for placing Harper in more danger. Yet he could not miss the desperate glint in their eyes. They knew what they faced, but it was not within them to die anything other than a warrior's death. He respected them for that, as futile as it was. They were better, braver, nobler individuals than he.

Not like me. Skulking in the shadows, playing games of intrigue and deception. Coward.

He shut down that critical voice without mercy. He could not afford to falter—if he broke now, he would endanger her, and he found himself caring for that as much as saving his own skin. He knew Saradon's intentions, but he could do nothing as Saradon advanced on Harper, raising her with his magic so she hovered before him, though she could not move a muscle. Harper glared at Saradon with defiance—a brittle mask over the fear Dimitri sensed lurking beneath. Pride and respect soared in Dimitri, that she could somehow scrape together bravery in such a moment, but all the same, his nails bit into his palm as he fought the urge to interfere.

"I will have the truth, girl," threatened Saradon. "Better that it be what I seek, for if not, none of you are any use to me."

Harper went rigid, her muscles cording, eyes bulging, and nostrils flaring, as Saradon dove into her mind. Dimitri stiffened, barely stopping himself from taking a step toward them, from raising his own powers against Saradon. Partly in defence of Harper. Partly because he feared what Saradon would see in her mind of him. Of *them*. He held himself ready—to attack, to flee, to react in whatever way he needed to.

After several moments, Saradon laughed delightedly. "It is as I suspected! She is my kin!" He whirled on Dimitri, baring his teeth in a wild grin.

Dimitri gave him a tight-lipped smile in return, relieved that Saradon had not seen anything to incriminate him. Yet.

"I have seen. She holds a vision of it from the dwarven hag seer. This girl is my heir."

Dimitri wanted to crumble—now Harper was in danger, as the sole focus of Saradon's attention. Now, Dimitri dreaded that he would not be able to protect her.

The invasion into her mind was not like her conversations with Dimitrius. It was not the gift of a vision or a shared discussion, a gentle and respectful brush through an open door, but a shattering intrusion, a perversion of that privilege which left her feeling violated. It made her shake and the urge to vomit became overwhelming, as though the visceral reactions of her body could expel his touch like a bad meal.

Saradon turned toward her once more, spreading his arms wide and taking in Harper with a different sort of attention, one that seemed to see her for the first time. She was not sure it was better. He viewed her with wonder—but to her, it felt as though the attention of a predator had snared her, and every nerve was alight with fire as it urged her to flee when she could not.

"I could not have dreamed it. What fate must it be to stumble upon the last of my flesh and blood. It gives me fresh faith that perhaps my machinations were meant to be so long stalled. You were meant to come to me."

Harper scowled and spat, a great globule, as far as she could at the half-elf, though it landed far short of him. A detestable habit, one she abhorred—and one that felt appropriate as the only defiance she could show him.

He glared at her, but his glee could not be stymied. "No matter. No doubt you know not of your heritage. Girl, you will be the *queen* of an empire after me. Pray, what is your name?"

Harper regarded him in silence for a moment before she raised her head, jutting out her chin as she eyed him boldly. "I am Harper of Caledan, of Pelenor, of House Ravakian, Mother Blessed, and Fated One, named *Frelsa* by the Vanir."

Saradon clapped his hands together. "Oh, you have my fire, daughter. Oh yes," he said with a knowing smile. "You are a born *lady* of my House now. A princess in your own right, if your true lineage be accounted for, for I shall be king of all these lands soon. But, one step at a time. I release you from your bonds."

He slowly lowered her to the floor, where she stood shakily.

"Together, we will avenge my son's and granddaughter's —your mother's—deaths." He rumbled with a flicker of anger, and his brow darkened at the thought. "I saw the death that was wrought for your mother, and I will discover what happened to my son—and who is responsible. I promise it will be avenged. Come. You have no need of them now." Saradon gestured at Aedon, Brand, and Erika, turning away.

Harper moved between Saradon and her companions, crossing her arms. "I go nowhere without them."

Saradon's attention slid to them, glancing over them in more detail. "You travel with curious companions, daughter."

Harper squirmed at the word. "Don't call me that," she said, scowling.

Saradon pursed his lips. "Who do you travel with that you would guard so? Do you bring me more allies?"

"Never," Brand spat from behind her.

"Come, you cannot reject me," Saradon said, his tone honeyed, but with a dangerous venom. "You do not know me. Only rumours that have been twisted for half a millennium."

"We know enough, *see* enough, to know that we will never ally with you," said Harper, calling on her magic.

Saradon snuffed it out in an instant without even twitching. His form darkened once more, and the entire hall seemed to darken with him. Even the flames within the iron braziers flickered out for a faint moment before sputtering back to life. "Do not be so foolish, daughter. I will wrest it from all of you if I must. Whom do you travel with? I will decide their use."

"I travel with Aedon Lindhir Riel of House Felrian, Br—"

Before she could finish, Saradon hissed. She was shoved aside by his magic, and Aedon dragged forward to sprawl before him.

"*You.* You are of House Felrian? How relate you to *Raedon*, he who killed my granddaughter?" Saradon snarled.

Aedon did not answer, but Saradon had it a moment later when he seized it from Aedon's mind. His attention wholly focused on the elf, he advanced, seeming to grow by the second, shadows building behind him. "Oh, it was indeed fate that brought you here, foolish elf. An eye for an eye shall be taken, the blood price exacted. I will relish your slow punishment. You will pay for the pain caused to mine own, elf."

Aedon held his head high and his jaw firm. His eyes darkened, showing no apprehension at the half-elf's words. He hid any fear well. Had Harper's own body not coursed with fear, she would have felt a flutter of respect, but it was crushed under the torrent of terror that rampaged through her. How would they ever escape now?

At that moment, the doors crashed open. The stench announced their company before Harper could twist to see who joined them. Her heart leapt into her throat. The biggest, ugliest, most foul and dark goblin she had ever seen advanced through the hall. He wore dwarven armour in a mockery of their style, for it had been ripped and patched to fit his grotesque form. As he approached, loping with an unbalanced, animalistic gait, she saw his necklace was of the metal and jewel dwarven beard embellishments she had seen Ragnar and his kin wear... and bones. She dared not wonder whom they belonged to.

He was too close for comfort as he prowled past them, taking no small interest in the small knot they formed in the centre of the hall. His goblins followed, cavorting, chattering, and shrieking as they flooded into the space, surrounding them. Harper froze, barely daring to breathe. She had her dagger, but her dwarven sword had been lost in the heat of their capture. She had no idea whether her companions held any of their own weapons, and she did not dare take her attention from the goblin to look. It mattered not, for they were still bound in their magical bonds. There were so many —if the goblins turned upon them, Harper and her companions would be dead.

With a word from Saradon, barked harshly and loudly across the space, the goblins retreated, grouping by the doors.

"I will have an audience," said the *pascha* in twisted Common Tongue. He stood firm, though his kin deserted him under the threat of Saradon's crackling magic. "These prisoners are *mine*. Give them to me."

Saradon snorted with derision. "You presume too much, *pascha*. They belong to me, and I will not yield them."

At his words, the goblin chieftain hissed and settled into a crouch, his clawed hands twitching as though he wished to attack Saradon but did not dare.

"I will remind you," said Saradon through gritted teeth, "how I have already delivered you conquest beyond your greatest desires and capabilities. You shall have nothing more of me through greed. I take my own conquest. They are *mine*."

The goblin scuttled forwards on all fours, hissing and gnashing his teeth.

Harper's attention flicked between the goblin and the half-elf.

Saradon raised his hands, which now contained crackling, dark flames. "I will not warn you again. You intrude upon my business, *pascha*. I will not suffer it. This hall is mine. You will not come here again without my permission. Leave now, and do not think of these prisoners again. They will be beyond your reach. Go and find sport with your other captives."

The *pascha's* eyes, hazy and unfocused, slid over Harper and her companions. To her surprise, she watched as he turned and ambled away, almost as if in a daze. At a crack of thunderous magic from Saradon, the rest of the goblin horde shrieked into life and fled, too. The doors boomed shut. Saradon's crackling magic still lurked, as if he were too angry to let it go.

"Those confounded savages," he cursed. "Would that it be soon I have no need for them."

A shock coursed through her as Dimitri stepped from the

shadows. "Indeed, Lord Ravakian," Dimitri replied smoothly. He refused to meet Harper's gaze as she turned to him, ire rising within her.

"I will see to it that there is no chance they touch a hair on your head," Saradon said to Harper, his dark attention falling to her. "For now, until I have no further need of them, your companions are mine. You are a curious lot, and I will know you all more intimately before I am done with you."

She did not like how he smiled with dark glee at that, but she could not reply, for his power clutched her wholly once more. It strangled the breath from her chest and smothered her senses. The world fell to darkness and Harper knew no more.

57

HARPER

When Harper next awoke, the world did not exist. There was no air, no light—nothing but darkness and a chill that seeped into her bones. Disorientated, she blinked furiously, but the darkness did not abate. Rising panic engulfed her and Harper clutched at it, forcing it down. She moved her hand, which remained invisible before her, her mind faltering with the strange feeling of disconnection from her limbs without light to orient her.

Ground. There was ground beneath her. Her palms skimmed it. Hard. Rocky. Sooner than she had expected, the stone rose. Harper followed it up, until it was out of reach of where she sat. A ragged sob broke from her when she realised that she was entirely entombed within hand-hewn rock, judging from the angles that scarred the surface. The space was only just large enough for her to stand.

No light permeated it. Only a small, hairline crack signalled a possible door, also made of stone, that did not yield when she threw the weight of her body or magic at it.

No air moved in the space either, but the cold somehow found a way in. It flowed through the very stone, freezing her where she stood. Her bones ached with it, her cloak and boots no protection, and she could hardly feel her fingers. She pressed her hands against the door once more and heaved with all her might, to no avail.

Time stretched endlessly beyond measure in the tomb of stone, only marked by Harper's failing legs when she became too tired to stand any longer. She reluctantly huddled on the floor once more, leaning against a rough surface of rock that dug into her back. She had already determined there was not even enough room to lay down. Any sleep she had—if any came at all, for nerves still charged through her and she did not feel like she could afford to close her eyes and rest—would be taken uncomfortably hunched up against the stone.

As she sat with her senses open, faint shouting permeated the stone. Their direction was impossible to discern. Was it her companions? The prospect of that made her chest tighten. The timbre sounded so familiar—enough for her to take a chance. Harper sucked in a lungful of stale air and bellowed until her throat hurt. After a few moments, others answered—one, then two, then three—albeit muffled. Definitely familiar. Relief blossomed warmly. Knowing they were alive gave her courage in the darkness as she sat alone. A light against the ever-present embers of terror writhing in the pit of her belly. What was to become of them all?

An indeterminate length of time later, light flared, and the hairline crack of a door illuminated before her. Harper staggered to her feet, heart leaping at the faint hope—and then fear—of what approached before the urge to escape the claustrophobic space surged over her common sense at whatever awaited her outside. She pressed her hands and face to the slim crack, trying to force herself through the gap but the stone remained inexorably sealed. Harper scrambled backwards as the burning light of a torch flooded in, teasing her with the tenuous promise of freedom as the door inched open.

A familiar voice spoke through the gap, one that made her legs want to fold with the sheer relief that the illusion of safety greeted her, not more danger. "I told you not to come. Why did you not listen?" Dimitrius's words were quiet, with an edge of desperation that cut straight to her core.

Her throat closed around all the words that longed to erupt. The last time they had seen each other, it was days—but it felt like years ago. The way Dimitrius had pressed her against that tree and taken every ounce of passion from her, turning it back on her in a way she had never felt before… The way that they had communicated with so much more than words. She heard that passion now in his voice, and she was not sure whether she hated herself or him more for it. How could she not have come? He knew as well as she that she could not abandon the right thing to do, no matter how hard or dangerous. No matter that it had landed them all in harm's way.

"Where are my friends?" she asked quickly, as the door opened fully, and light bloomed. She could not bear to look at him and closed her eyes against the brightness blinding her. "Are they well?" Asking that was easier than scratching at the rawness inside her which longed to ask deep questions she suspected she would find no happy answers to.

"They're here. Unharmed."

A sigh of relief gushed past her lips, and she pressed her fingers against the cold stone, so relieved for a second that dizziness pressed in from all sides and she forgot to breathe. Suddenly, his hands were at her elbows, steadying her, and her breath failed for an entirely different reason as that beautiful lively scent of his banished the stench of death from the air.

"You should have fled. For goodness' sake, you should have fled." His tone held a bite of frustration, but she could not tell to whom it was directed. Her or himself. It made her indignant either way.

She sucked in air once more, if only to spit it out at him. "I make my own choices. I told you I could not."

To her surprise, Dimitrius chuckled, though he shook his head—and she hated how that rich sound made something pleasant twist in the pit of her stomach. She could not see his face, so deep were the shadows cast over him. His presence engulfed her in the small space. "I don't know whether to admire you or shake you. You ought to be trembling with fear, yet you still have defiance burning within you. Are you brave or foolish, I wonder?" His hands still circled her arms. She shook him free. She could not think clearly with him touching her.

"You're calling *me* foolish?" Harper's eyebrows rose. "This, coming from the moron who decided it would be a great idea to resurrect a dead, evil elf?"

"He wasn't dead, and I didn't know he was evil," protested Dimitrius. "Not then. I—"

"Oh, I'm not going through this again. You're a *fool* for doing it, but we are where we are. I don't much care, as long as we get out. Where is this place?" She peered past him now her eyes had adjusted to peer at a dimly lit stone hewn hallway.

"You're in the mines. These are some of the old stores for the blasting powder they used to expand the cave systems. Don't worry. Saradon has kept this area free from goblins. They won't come here."

At his words, Harper shuddered. "Good." The darkness

was made worse by thoughts of goblins creeping toward her. Goblins with their pointed teeth, sharp claws, and cruel intentions. "What's going to happen to us?"

She hated the way that her voice carried an edge of fear, but if he detected it, Dimitrius did not remark upon it. He did not answer at all, in fact, which only made her feel all the more desperate, unable to quell the seething worry that chased under her skin as he looked at her with such stricken fear in his gaze that she could bear it no longer. If he fell apart too, there would be no hope. No matter her feelings for him—and whatever he felt for her—her friends' survival, and her own, depended on him. And she would fight for them with whatever resources she had. Right now, that included him.

"We would never be in this predicament but for you," she growled at him. "You and your grand schemes. Our safety rests in your hands, and I don't know whether to cry or scream at that!"

"I told you to leave! I made it expressly clear that you ought to. Do not blame me for your own folly in coming here, Harper."

Hurt stung her, but she cut off his next words. "But for you, none of this would be happening."

"As you have made quite clear," he snapped, stepping forward into her space. She did not yield but stared mutinously up at him, setting her jaw in a furious scowl and willing her quickening pulse to settle. "Skies above, you will not be biddable even to save yourself and it infuriates me so! I cannot change it now, which *I* have made quite clear. In any case, there is no time to dally. He has summoned you."

The anger drained from her, fear surging in its place.

"Will you run?"

She looked at him, but he was unreadable. Did he truly

care? She dismissed the thought—he was there, pleading with her, wasn't he? And yet, he planned to deliver her like a beast for slaughter to Saradon all the same. It made a lump form in her throat that she did not have the strength to unpick. "Do I have a choice?" she whispered.

Tight lipped, he shook his head. "I would not try it."

"What am I to do?" Her head bowed and shoulders caved. She shook her head at the floor, eyes stinging with hot, indignant tears at the hopelessness of the situation. She sniffed loudly and straightened. No matter what, she would not flinch. She would not flee. She would not falter.

When she met his eyes again, deep amethyst pools darkened by the low lighting, they were soft. "We must go. I am bound to serve him, but I will not harm you. You know this."

"I'm not scared," she retorted, but she knew as well as he it was a lie.

"You don't have to put that wall up for me. Not here. I will keep you safe." His throat bobbed as he swallowed. Slowly, gently, he brought a hand up to her cheek to tuck a strand of hair behind her ear, grazing the sensitive skin of her neck.

Harper stiffened at the contact, for it sent a sensation shooting down her throat so at odds with the fear that strung an exhausting and agonising melody through her body. "You cannot guarantee that," she forced out.

His hand dropped. And he did not deny it. That absence hit her like a blow to the stomach as he backed away, leaving the way clear to run, if she chose. No. She had learned by now that most things Dimitrius said or did were deliberate. His omissions were as carefully crafted too. He could not guarantee her—or any of them—safety. That did not give her much hope.

She found herself wondering what that meant for

Saradon's intentions. They could not be good if even Dimitrius worried that he could not keep her safe. In her solitude, she had slowly concluded that to survive, at least for now, they would all have to make themselves useful... somehow. Because running was not an option either. The time for that had passed. They had walked into the jaws of death, and now they would have to cheat it.

58

HARPER

Dimitrius reached a hand to steady Harper as she crumpled anew—feeling struck with despair that she had been so naïve as to walk into this and dream that there might have been the chance of a single positive outcome. Harper threaded her fingers into his giant palm, her eyes slipping shut as she sank into the poisoned comfort of that touch. His hand was warm and reassuringly firm. Her eyes flickered open. Perhaps he too was nervous for what was to come, because his touch lingered three heartbeats longer than was necessary before he dropped her hand, clenching and unclenching his fist, as if to rid himself of her touch.

They still stood before each other, she a footstep away from his chest, confined by the small hallway. His gaze burned her. He spoke into her mind, making her start and she almost flinched into him from the unexpected sensation of his voice inside her. *"I can help. He must believe that we do not know each other at all. It is something and nothing, but any connection can weaken us. May I protect those memories we share?"*

"I don't understand." Saradon had entered at will. Yet Dimitrius… asked? She didn't understand any of this at all.

"*It means he will not be able to see that which is hidden.*" He sent a flood of mental images her way, of their first meeting, their time together in Tournai, and the kiss they had shared. To watch them from his perspective—to see herself through his eyes and to feel so viscerally his kaleidoscope of emotions—made her intensely uncomfortable, as though they stood skinless before each other, their very souls on show.

And yet it was dangerous too, because she felt his emotions like a torrent that wanted to slam her into the wall with the force of them—at how conflicted he was to want her, and the depths of his desire. They stirred something wild within her as she relived those intimate moments, knowing he watched them too and feeling all too bared before him. Never mind his masks, she longed to don one of her own, to hide from the weight of feelings on both their parts that she did not feel able to face.

"You think it will help?" she managed to choke out, staring into the dark fabric of his chest, because she could not meet his violet gaze without becoming entirely lost.

"At the very least, it will not damn us."

Her throat had closed. She nodded.

Dimitrius shifted just a fraction closer. Heat radiated from him, a fiery contrast against the frozen stone at her back. With the movement, a warming, sighing caress slipped into her mind. It was different than Saradon, who ventured there without her permission, but even so, it was unpleasantly violating and deeply intimate. Somehow, she knew where he looked inside her, and how carefully he trod only the paths he needed to hide what he had promised. Not one memory more. Or less.

"I didn't realise you disliked me so much," he murmured as he drew closer. Those eyes captured her, filled with depths in the barely lit tunnel, and captured in their gaze, something pulled in her chest. She was grateful for the dim light to give cover to her scorching cheeks. At his side, his hand flexed. Fingers forming a fist and then opening once more. "I suppose I did not give you any reason to endear me."

He leaned in, so close that his breath caressed her ear. Her own stilled, overcome by that bittersweet scent of his and the promise of this unspoken weight between them. Unbidden, she arched back, exposing her neck to him. Gods above, how she wished this were all simpler—that the lives of her and her friends did not depend on every moment going in their favour. "But I *am* glad you think I'm the most handsome male you ever did see." She heard the smile in his voice.

She gasped and recoiled. "I—I! No!"

As her face heated anew, he laughed. "You cannot deny it, for now I have seen the truth etched upon your soul."

"That's not fair!" she protested.

His smile was savagely mischievous as he dropped his gaze to her lips. She wet them, her tongue darting out. "Alright. Since I have seen one secret of your heart, I shall give you one of my own." And with that, he leaned right in, so that his lips grazed the side of her neck.

Harper froze, her hands upon his chest between them, her senses raw with the proximity of him.

His whisper was barely audible over the drumming of her heart—and his thundered under her palms. "If we had not been disturbed, I would not have stopped kissing you against that tree, Harper. I would have taken that as far as you let me."

Harper gasped as he pressed his lips to her neck, and his tongue darted out to lick a line up the column of her throat to the base of her ear. She arched into him, and he groaned, the sound muffled in her skin.

"Oh, how I wish we had the time for all the things I would like to do to you." He sighed and pulled back, his gaze dark and heavy as he dragged it away. Her hands fell from his chest. "Come. We've tarried too long. He does not like to be kept waiting."

"Wait. Just one thing." She braced herself on the rocky wall behind her, begging her breath to steady, her pulse to slow, and her legs to firm. He turned, silhouetted by the torch behind him. "You said you sent the Dragonheart to me by accident. How did you raise Saradon without one?"

The prophecy had mentioned that a Dragonheart would raise Saradon, and cast him down. As far as she knew, the only other Dragonhearts in existence had been burned in their escape from Pelenor or hidden by the king.

Dimitrius chewed his lip, and she stilled at the shrewd look he shot her. "You were not the only ones in the king's vaults that night."

Her lips parted. That, she had not expected. "You were there? That's impossible."

"Not all those who wander are seen, Harper. But I saw everything that transpired, from the portcullis lowering, to your fall, to the elf and his dragon magic."

Her breath caught. *No.* He could not have been there, and yet, he spoke truths only someone present would know. "What were you doing there?" she whispered, though she had a feeling she already knew. *I need to hear him say it.*

"I took my own Dragonheart that night." Dimitrius said. Harper couldn't breathe. She knew it, but to hear him admit it felt magnitudes *more.* Quite what she felt—to know that he was there whilst she and her companions had fought for their lives, and that he had done nothing to intervene one way or the other—she was not sure. But those feelings were dark as they rose to a tempest within her. She had nearly *died*, and he had taken for himself and left.

"And you let us escape." Her palms pressed to the cool rock behind her, anchoring her from being snatched away into the storm within her. All the desire of moments before cooled to ashes. She was a fool to feel anything for this dangerous elven male—because he would not stop at anything to get what he wanted. He had been willing to let her die.

"With you gone, far from Tournai I presumed I would never run into you again. I did not care that you had a Dragonheart, or that you had destroyed the rest. It was greater cover for me. You would be blamed for all their thefts, and I would escape with my prize. We were never supposed to meet again." His eyes met hers, his gaze serious and steady, and that weight hanging between them in the air charged with his attention. "But you were there, that night. I saw you about to die. And something inside me snapped."

Clarity seared through her anger. She had nearly died—but for what she had deemed inexplicable chance. She had not killed those soldiers—someone else had. In the heat of the moment, she had thanked every god and goddess she knew to pray to for her good fortune. But... "It was you."

"Yes."

"You killed them." Without hesitation. She had been instants away from death.

"Yes."

"To save me." She couldn't breathe.

"Yes."

"Why?"

He huffed, and a rueful smile twisted his lips. "I think we both know why, Harper. Because I cannot bear to think of a world without you in it. Because… more than that… I want you for myself. However selfish that makes me. I would have burned down that mountain for you. I'm not as ruthless as you think, Harper. Not when it comes to you. I will be ruthless for you. I will never be ruthless to you."

She opened her mouth, but no words came. His were so soft, it stunned her.

"Come. Saradon awaits." His tone hardened, brooking no argument, and he stalked away down the dark halls, taking the torch and the only source of light with him—and the tenuous thing growing between them was gone, like a spider's web dashed through by a hand. With the threat of goblin-filled shadows nipping at her heels, Harper chased after him, her pulse dizzyingly fast, as she reeled on his revelations.

5 9

HARPER

Harper steeled herself as they returned to the cursed jarlshalle where no jarl now sat. Saradon greeted them, sending the *pascha* and his scourge of goblins scurrying away. To her surprise, he stood with his arms wide at her entrance, a beaming smile upon his face —as open and friendly as his dark visage could manage. A tingle of suspicion curled through Harper.

"Daughter of my blood, welcome."

Even as he spoke, beckoning her—Dimitrius helped her along with a subtle nudge in the small of her back to propel her forward—she felt the subtle fingers of Saradon's mind invading her own. It brought a dull, throbbing ache that sharpened into stabbing probes which had her gasping for breath with the impact of each lance deep within her. She stiffened but kept walking. Dimitrius's hand did not leave the small of her back. Saradon gave no sign or hint that he invaded her, clasping his hands together as his lips closed over gleaming white teeth, though his grin remained wide.

Through her mind he stalked, rifling through memories,

from her time in Pelenor with Aedon and his companions, to her incarceration in Tournai at Toroth's hands, to her time in Caledan with Betta and the years before… which she spoke of to no one. Harper stumbled and fell to all fours, her hands clawing into the stone-flagged floor. She bared her teeth at Saradon in a feral scowl as he touched those memories, but as much as she gathered her magic to push him away, she could not budge him from his possession of her most secret memories. Her back arched as the pain intensified, but she would not be defeated. Harper forced her screaming body to move. One inch closer at a time, she crawled across the floor to Saradon.

Finally, he rifled through the most recent memories, until he saw the burned land and the pale figure of Erendriel. She felt a flicker of fear, but she was not sure whether it was her own or his, so entrenched in her mind was he. It was all she could do to see the stone beneath her as her vision swam in and out of focus.

Harper halted before Saradon with Dimitrius close beside her. His presence lent her comfort and strength, a familiar anchor in the dark hall. A part of her hated to find strength in him, because he still felt far too much like an enemy, but it was true that he was the closest thing to an ally she had in that cold place. She dared not wonder if he knew what Saradon did to her at that moment. Surely he must have, she reckoned. There would be no other explanation for her reaction—and his lack of one. Saradon withdrew, and Harper sagged, shuddering. Nausea rolled over her. She was glad for an empty stomach.

Shadows moved as Dimitrius dropped to a knee beside her. "Allow me to help you," he murmured. Perhaps it was the only kindness he dared to offer her. She allowed herself to take his hand, and he bore her weight without a word as he helped her to her feet. Her legs felt molten. Her limbs shook. She felt as though she had been tortured physically, not just mentally. Dimitrius did not let go, but stood there silently—a lifeline, although she would not admit to it—until she reckoned that she could stay upright. No matter what, she could not afford to show weakness before Saradon. Harper withdrew from Dimitrius, and, impassively, he turned back to Saradon as though nothing had happened.

They waited. Moments stretched into lifetimes. Saradon's hard gaze bored into her as he picked apart her memory of Erendriel's vision—and prophecy. "Well met, daughter of my blood," he said more softly, cocking his head as he sized her up anew. "It would seem we have *many* things to discuss, and your whole life to catch up on. We will spend much time together henceforth, I think."

That filled her with horror and trepidation. It was obvious she would be no challenge for him to overpower at any opportunity. She knew that no matter what Saradon said, she would never trust him. Yet something within her remained desperate, defiant. "I'd rather not," she said, scowling as much as she dared.

Saradon laughed, delighted at her defiance, but his eyes remained predatory, dark. "Whyever not, daughter? You are of my blood, and I yours. The last of our line—the end of our house. Whyever ought we not be close? You shall inherit my legacy." Saradon paced slowly around her. Harper shifted, never taking her gaze from him, but Dimitrius remained still. Perhaps he was used to it, but she did not dare take her attention from Saradon for fear of what he might do. It felt uncomfortably like she was a rabbit in the sole attention of a wolf about to pounce.

"Is this how you treat your family?" She looked down at herself for the first time, and her own lips curled in disgust.

She was filthy. Not just with dirt, but with blood and gore. She already felt immune to the smell of it, for which she was grateful, for the stench of the battlefield had been enough to make her want to vomit.

Saradon paused before her, raising his eyebrow and cocking his head. "What do you mean, daughter?"

"You keep your family in filth and squalor? I have been locked in a windowless, airless tomb for heavens knows how long. You would treat me so, yet desire my respect, my loyalty, my familial love?" She scoffed at the ridiculousness of the idea.

Saradon drew himself up, and Harper felt the crackle of his anger in the very air. "You will not disrespect me again thusly, daughter. Yet I will be merciful. I will show you the kindness which you so clearly do not expect to see. You will be moved to better quarters at once, as befits my heir." He nodded at Dimitrius to make it so.

Harper narrowed her eyes. "Will you do the same for my friends?"

Saradon laughed. "No."

"I demand it!" she said, puffing out her chest with far more bravado than she felt.

His brooding anger cracked like a whip around them, as though lightning rove the air. "Do not presume your status grants you the right to act with such impunity."

Her own anger rallied against his, but his was the weight of the mountain, quashing hers.

"Why care you, daughter? They are no one. Forget them. You are where you belong at last. With your kin."

"I'd rather be anywhere else." She turned to leave, but he froze her where she stood. She screamed in frustration. "Let me go!"

"Not until you learn respect for your elders and your

betters, daughter," he hissed. "I own you and your loyalty. I shall have it, whether you will it or not." His bared teeth mirrored hers as he drew closer, bending until they were level, their eyes locked.

Panic clutched her chest at his words. His power clamped down upon her until she could not so much as blink of her own volition, and even her chest ceased rising and falling. Dizziness swooped over her as he held on, like a wolf to her throat, slowly starving her body of air. All at once, his control vanished. She crumpled to the floor, smashing against the stone. Harper lay upon it, gasping, as her vision cleared and her body stabbed with pain.

"Rise." His command was laced with magic. Her protesting body slowly forced itself to kneel, then stand. Dimitrius still stood immobile beside her. Why would he not help her—say something? But she knew the answer. He did not dare.

"Will you give yourself to me, daughter? Or must I show you the error of your ways and the righteous path?" Saradon's tone was hard, brittle. When he drew himself up, she realised just how tall and imposing he was.

I am a fool, but I will not yield, she thought. She said nothing, forcing herself to stand properly—to straighten her shoulders, hold her head high, and stiffen her limbs. Last of all, she walled away the fear, which sapped at the dregs of her depleted energy.

"Answer me," Saradon growled. Darkness clung to him as the shadows deepened.

"I will not serve you," she answered through gritted teeth.

HARPER

Fury flashed across Saradon's face, which was swiftly veiled. He stepped forward and struck Harper across the cheek, sending her sprawling to the floor once more. Her ears rang from the strength of his impact, and her jaw blinded her with pulsing pain. She heard his voice as if from a distance as inky blackness wrapped itself around her and tendrils of his power seeped into her.

"You *will* serve me, daughter, whether you will it or not. I will not see the words of Erendriel hold sway over my destiny." His voice darkened and deepened, crackling with a power the likes of which she could not fully perceive. It blanketed the space, smothered her—and sent her heart into a frenzy at the prospect of her impending demise.

"Get her out of my sight," he commanded. She realised that he spoke to Dimitrius. "I have more work to do persuading the Indis to join us. I will return to continue this. I expect you to have managed her better the next time I lay eyes upon her."

She felt Saradon's gaze, even with her eyes closed, as

though it pierced into the core of her soul. She cowered before it, curling away from his attention. Then it passed and Saradon, along with his power, was gone, but Harper had nothing left to give. She faded into the welcome, cool, dark embrace of unconsciousness.

Soothing, wet warmth bathed her forehead. Gentle hands stroked the pain away, passing the soft cloth across her cheeks and back to her forehead again, moving in a slow, comforting sweep across her brow. Magic chased it, the welcome tingle calming as it banished away the angry pain in her jaw, along with the dull aches and jarring hurt elsewhere in her body.

Hands grasped hers, soft and warm. The wet cloth passed over her fingers and between them, across her palms, as whoever tended to her meticulously cleaned her. Her hand was gently placed back onto her stomach—onto a coverlet there, she registered a moment later, soft and warm—before the other was picked up and the same treatment administered. Light, gentle and warm, filtered through her closed eyelids. A familiar scent drifted across her, though she could not place from where. It was too much to open her eyes. She slipped into the darkness once more.

When next she came to, the same hands once more bathed her forehead. She felt burning hot—the wet cloth cool upon her brow. She moaned a little, turning her face into the cloth. Now she could feel the soft, smooth, woollen coverlet beneath her hands. Her fingers circled lazily upon it, relishing the comfort. The light was brighter this time. Everything still hurt, though the tingle of magic still ran through her, banishing the worst of it. She slowly cracked her eyes open, one at a time, for even the dim light felt oppressively bright after her descent into the dark.

Her lips curled into a faint smile as she slowly turned her head to behold the hands that had tended her. She froze when she saw who they belonged to.

"Hello, Harper," said Dimitrius evenly. He sat on the bed beside her. His hands lay in his lap, the cloth in his grasp.

"*You,*" she croaked with as much vehemence as she could inject into her feeble tone.

"Yes, me. I have a name, you know. Call me Dimitri." He rolled his eyes, but his voice held no bite.

Her hands clutched at the coverlet. "What are you doing? How dare you! Did you? You didn't?" She had no boots on—they were neatly by the door. As far as she could tell, she still wore her pants, her shirt—now untucked—and her cloak hung over the back of the chair Dimitrius sat upon.

He seemed to understand and grinned with a hint of his usual arrogance and cockiness. "Don't worry. I used my magic. I didn't peek. I can, though, if you like."

Harper tried to retort, but only an indignant croak emerged. She hoped he was telling the truth. That he had not removed her dignity or worse as she slept. She wished she had the energy to throw something, anything, but she sank back onto the pillow instead. She still hurt too much, and her limbs felt leaden.

Dimitrius winked suggestively. The top of his unbuttoned shirt slipped open as he shifted in the seat, revealing those dark tattoos that wound up his chest and the side of his neck. She could have sworn the markings moved as she watched—

and blinked harder, dispelling the sleep in her eyes and berating the poor light.

"You're welcome," he drawled, a hint of a twinkle in his smile. The smile she hated and desired. The one that presumed he could have whatever he wanted.

"I don't need your help. Begone, you fiend!" All the comfort of that tender touch had vanished, and anger filled the raw hollow it had stripped from her defences.

"Oh, good. You must be alright if you're cursing me," he said, looking at her lazily from under his lashes. His smile widened as he crossed his legs and leaned toward her, dropping the wet cloth on the coverlet. "Go on. Try out some more insults on me."

Sapped of strength and will, Harper scraped together what little she had to pick up the cloth and throw it into his face. It slapped wetly against his cheek and plopped into his lap, wetting the fine anthracite fabric. He blinked in surprise before recovering his customary swagger—and laughing. A belly-deep guffaw, confound him. "Feisty. I like it."

Harper swore at him again, her face burning and agitation crawling under her skin at how vulnerable she found herself. "Get out!"

Dimitri pushed himself up from the bed and sauntered out, laughing. "You're welcome."

Harper glared after him, noting the quiet click of the door as it shut and the snap of a lock. She was determined to stay awake, to make sure he did not return, but exhaustion assailed her again, and the blackness called to her. It was as though some of Saradon's magic lingered. It filled her limbs and mind with heavy sluggishness and pulled her down into the darkness, where dreams swirled of goblins and Saradon and Dimitrius with that cloth. She gladly fell, because the nightmares seemed better than the waking reality.

HARPER

The next time Harper awoke, Dimitrius sat beside her again, holding the cloth and a warm, fragranced bowl of water. Harper considered tipping the water over but was too tired to berate him. Questions assailed her —and she needed answers more than to antagonise him again.

"What happened?" She struggled to sit up, propping herself up on shaking arms.

"You've been drifting in and out of consciousness for a day or so now. I was hoping you would wake soon. I am sorry—I did not anticipate he would use such powers upon you. I would have intervened." Dimitri's smile was tired, but the fury that lined his eyes was razor-sharp. His familiar scent of him—sharp, sweet, and the hint of musk—teased her. It had been Dimitrius caring for her all that time. She did not quite dare ask why. The truth of that was too uncomfortable to face. "You haven't been lucid much, mind. Incoherent mumbles at best."

The back of her neck prickled, and her cheeks heated. Oh

goodness. What had she said? She dreaded to think. "Where am I?"

"In Saradon's own quarters." His voice was quiet. Dimitri's assessing gaze swept the room. He caught her wide eyes as she glanced down at the bed—wondering if it was his. Bile filled her as revulsion reared. "He has the jarl's wing. You're in one of the other suites—as far from him as I could settle you. You're safe here. As safe as you can be. I promise."

I promise. Did that reassure her or not? Harper swallowed past the nausea and took a moment to examine the room. She reclined in a large bed—wider than she was tall—finished with thick coverlets. The stone-flagged floor was set in a diamond pattern tooled with geometric designs. Smooth walls held tapestries for warmth and alcoves for windows, each holding a stained-glass window that backed onto stone, with a faelight in a sconce to cast warm light over the room. A large fur on the floor—a bear of some kind—provided a touch of comfort, and at the foot of the bed was a closed chest of wood carved with knots and dragons. Through a rectangular archway, she saw a curl of steam emerge. A bathing chamber? She frowned and her gaze passed on, snagging on a wooden armoire and a desk—Dimitri sat in the matching chair, she realised.

Much like the quarters at the königshalle in Keldheim, it was practical but comfortable, but she could tell these were furnished for a higher class than their spartan quarters. Windowless, though. She fought the ever-present current of claustrophobia at the realisation of being under immeasurable tons of rock.

"Why are you here?" she asked. She drew her hands over the coverlets, clenching the fabric.

"I promised I would see us both through this. I don't know how, I wish I did, but the least I can do is ensure you are not wholly at his mercy." Dimitri twisted the cloth in his hands. His throat bobbed.

"Thank you," she said softly, looking away. "Where is he?" She did not want to say Saradon's name.

"Away." Dimitri's tone was hard. "He seeks alliances wherever he can find them. At present, he's with the Indis peoples."

"The warrior nomad women?" Erika's people.

"Yes." Dimitri looked at her sharply with a frown, then nodded. "Of course. The elf's companion. You would know. There are few enough of them left, but they are a fearsome people. He hopes to leverage their anger after half a millennium of persecution in his name against those who hunt them."

"Erika would never fight with him." Harper was utterly certain.

"Then let us hope the remainder of her kin feel likewise, but I fear it will do little good. He will enslave them regardless." Dimitri's shoulders slumped. "This is madness. I see the chaos approaching, yet I feel powerless to do anything. This great storm shall devour us all."

His voice was devoid of hope and strength, in a way she had not heard before. It dawned on her then. "You stay because you have nowhere else to go, yet you feel bound to try, don't you?"

He nodded but did not speak.

"Perhaps I can give you a reason to hope." Erendriel's pale form hovered in Harper's mind. It was nothing more than an impulse born of instinctive compassion, and he did not deserve it, but she reached out. He startled as she grasped his hand, laced her fingers through his, and pushed Erendriel's vision to him. Dimitrius felt so reassuringly warm and solid amidst the uncertainty, and she enjoyed the contact more than she knew she ought to. Guilt twinged her at the realisation. His face slackened and he grasped Harper's hand until his knuckles whitened. Only when the vision faded did his grip ease.

"What was that?" he breathed.

"Perhaps our only hope. I can't decide whether it's madness."

"All has turned to insanity, Harper. And yet you are still here, living, breathing—hoping." Dimitri gazed at her with ferocity—and the way he looked at her, as though she were the sun in the sky, stopped her breath. Did she imagine the fragile stroke of his thumb across the back of her hand before he pulled away? She could not ignore the low sweep in her belly at this thing growing between them.

"If that vision be true, higher powers than us are at work. Valxiron and Erendriel... Legends indeed. It makes sense now. How the half-elf with no magic now has power beyond measure—and darkness within. It is so much worse than I could have ever feared, yet if Erendriel herself speaks, acts, through you—if you are the light against the dark, then I have more hope than I have yet found. Perhaps there is a way to somehow unmake all of this by the magic of the Dragonhearts."

"I don't know how to make it come to pass, though," she admitted, shivering at the recollection of the dark place within the vision that was scorched and dead.

"I would trust to Erendriel's words. 'If thou standest true and with faith unwavering, thou shalt triumph over Valxiron's servant.' Let that be your guide, whatever is to come."

"What do you think she meant when she said, 'beware the Tainted Star, and heed the Shadow'?"

Dimitri just shook his head, looking at the stone walls all around them. "You must hope that becomes clearer, too."

"Can we not leave whilst he is gone?" she asked, disappointed, but struck by sudden inspiration.

"It is not so simple. We are bound now. I gave my word to him, and you cannot defy his strength. My blood and magic are his to command. We could probably walk through the very gates, but if he commanded it, I would have no choice but to return and he could drag you back, no matter how much we tried to resist. We would be punished savagely for it." He scowled. "For now, we must remain wherever he commands us."

Harper closed her eyes in frustration. "There must be a way."

"There may be," Dimitri acknowledged, but his reply was half-hearted. She realised why a heartbeat later. If there was a way, any loophole at all, he would have already found and exploited it. "Do not lose hope, Harper." He rested his palm atop her hand with surprising softness before standing. "Come. I've drawn you a bath. You'll feel better if you're clean."

Something warm settled in Harper's chest. He had thought to do that for her?

"I will leave," he said quickly. "As long as I can make sure you're in there safely. I have done my best, but I do not know what lingering hurt may remain."

He looked at her with an open question in his gaze, and his expression neutral—carefully so, she reckoned. Her eyes flicked to that coiling steam and back again. She nodded and swung her legs from under the coverlet. A groan escaped. She *hurt*. Every inch of her was stiff and painful. Harper took his offered hand and staggered to her feet.

"Thank you," she muttered. The rub of his thumb across her knuckles was his only answer—and it did nothing to lend steadiness to her legs.

"In here," he said, drawing her through the archway. She gasped. Inset into the floor was a stone depression as wide and long as the bed—and it was filled with hot, steaming water covered in white foam. It smelled *delicious*. Floral and fresh, it was a world away from—she caught a sniff of herself and grimaced, the back of her neck prickling with discomfort at the state of herself.

"Can you undress yourself?" he asked evenly, but the look he shot her was loaded with heat.

"Yes," she forced out. She could not—would not—let him help her. Not in this state. Not ever. That was too dangerous. Harper tugged her hand from his.

"I'll return in an hour."

"Please don't leave." The words escaped before she realised. His lips parted. She licked hers. Her voice fell to a whisper. "I don't want to be alone here." Her attention flicked to the door. She did not trust—not at all—that she was safe here. Except with him, she realised.

"Of course. I'll remain in there. Out of sight." He nudged his head towards the bedroom.

Harper did not dare reply. Dimitri pulled a tall wooden screen across the entry to the bathing room, and Harper noted the large dark towel slung over it. She took a long, steadying breath, her body torn between fighting and submitting. She would be completely at his mercy, with just that flimsy screen in the way.

And yet, this felt so different to the first time they had met in close quarters, when he had offered her the common decency of a wash and clean clothes. Because now... her throat closed, and she swallowed past the thick lump there. Now she trusted Dimitrius, she realised, in a way she trusted so few others in her life. She had no doubt that she could take a bath there and he posed no threat to her—rather the opposite. Now, she felt as though she could count on him to defend her. That felt altogether too complicated. She tugged her stinking shirt over her head and kicked off the close-fitting leggings before she could delve into the danger of that thought and crossed to the bath.

She sat—gasping at the cold stone—upon the edge and swung her feet in. She could not see under the white foam. As her feet touched the bottom, Harper surmised that the depression was only knee high. In she slid, groaning with delight at the hot water melting the tension in her body, and the soft kiss of the bubbles that popped against her skin. A build-up of pressure threatened a headache, and agitation lurked at the fringes of her mind—this kept both at bay, and she was glad for it.

"Are you quite alright in there?" Dimitrius called from the other room.

Something clenched within her. "Yes," she forced back. There was a scrub and a bar of soap across the other side of the vast bath. She sloshed to them, grabbed both, and set to cleaning herself as vigorously as possible, until every inch of her gleamed and the soreness of her limbs had been banished to a dull ache.

A quick duck under the surface with her eyes scrunched shut rinsed the suds from her hair and she erupted from the water, surging to her feet with renewed vigour. The stone bottom of the bath was warm and smooth under her feet, and the water sluicing down her body a sensory pleasure in contrast to the grit and grime that had ingrained itself in every pore. This felt *delicious*. She let out a sigh of relief. Dimitrius had been right. She did feel better for being clean.

At the thought of him, she whirled around, clutching her hands over her chest—but he was not there. The screen remained in place. Beneath it, no shadows, no hint of his feet, nor anything untoward. It was quiet—so silent, her ears rang. "Dimitrius?" she called.

"Yes?"

The panic clutching at her chest receded and she took a deep breath. "Nothing. Sorry."

Harper squeezed the water from her hair and padded to retrieve the towel from the screen, leaving a trail of watery steps behind her. With brisk strokes, she dried herself, grateful for the warmth of the steamy room, because already, chills bumped across her skin.

"I don't suppose there are any fresh clothes out there I can use?" she asked, staring regretfully at the pile of dirty garments next to the bath. Even if she washed them now, they would take a day to dry, if not more. Harper finally felt deliciously warm for the first time in goodness knew how long—she had no desire to don cold, damp, battle-damaged clothes.

The chair in the bedroom scraped as Dimitri moved. A drawer screeched open. The armoire doors clunked. "Hmm." His voice was muffled as though he rummaged inside it. Harper wrapped the towel around her chest, tucking a corner in to secure it so it covered her to her knees, and pulled back the screen slightly to watch him.

Dimitrius had his back to her. He'd taken off his dark jacket, and she could see the hint of his muscled form beneath the midnight shirt he wore. He had dropped to one knee, elbow deep in the chest at the foot of the bed and pushing aside throws. Something clunked against the wood. As he withdrew his arms and huffed with annoyance, she drew a sharp breath at the sight of his sleeves rolled up to the elbows, and the flex of his forearms—covered in more of those exquisite, dark tattoos. She had not realised they stretched all the way from his neck to his wrists, and some irrational, primal part of her wanted to see them all.

At the sound, he turned to her—and his eyes instantly darkened. His voice, when it emerged, was carefully even. "I've found a tunic I think might fit you, and some leggings. They might be a little large, but there's a belt." He held it up.

"Thank you." Harper slipped from the bathing room and padded across the fur on the floor towards him. It was deliciously soft and warm on her feet in contrast to the cool stone.

Dimitri rose to hand her the garments. She took them—freezing as his hand tightened on her forearm to stop her turning away. He drew her closer, running the tip of his nose up the sensitive skin on the inside of her wrist and inhaling deeply. "Your scent is exquisite," he murmured, his breath hot on her skin. Her heart skipped a beat to be this close to him again, with nothing between them save for their own decisions. Dimitri's dark eyes took every inch of her in. "You're making it *incredibly* hard to be a gentleman right now, Harper."

"Maybe I don't want you to be," she breathed. That pressure was building inside her, a desperate need for some release in the face of such overwhelming darkness and a loss of control over every other part of her life.

Dimitrius laughed harshly. "You are going to be my ruin. Say the word, and I will do whatever you let me. I am yours to command."

He was so close. Close enough that her nose filled with citrus and musk, and his warm, firm hand upon her stole away all reason. In that moment there was only her, him—and the choice hanging between them. "Then kiss me."

62

HARPER

Dimitrius grinned wickedly and a rumble escaped him as he hooked an arm around Harper's waist and pulled her closer. In the next moment, his mouth captured hers with a bruising kiss of need and want. Harper moaned as his sinful lips teased hers apart and the velvet warmth of his tongue brushed hers, delivering instant release—and a rush of liquid fire that chased through every vein.

Harper's body moulded into his and the clothes fell forgotten from her hand as she raked a hand up through his perfect hair, undoing him as he undid her—scraping his teeth across her lip as he took it into his mouth, sucked, and released. Pressure built in her core. Her body felt aflame with his touch—one hand holding her waist firmly through the towel and the other sliding up to grip her jaw. That firm hand tilted her up to him so he could devour her. Her toes curled into the thick fur under foot, and had he not been holding her up, her knees would have given way. Her towel fell between them as they moved with each other—and when he realised and withdrew, leaving a cold absence on her glistening lips, he froze.

The noise he made was utterly feral as he glanced down to see her naked form before him. His indecent gaze raked down her, from the slicked wet hair trailing over her shoulders, to her bare stomach and below—snagging when he swept his attention up again and found her hard nipples pebbled against the shock of cool air.

A yelp escaped her as Dimitrius swept her into his arms, lifting her so her chest was level with his face and his hands gripped her bare backside. She clamped her legs around him, squeezing harder than she intended to and letting out a ragged cry as his hot mouth found one hard nipple, enveloping it in warmth and wetness. He swirled his tongue around it, grazing it oh so lightly with his teeth. It was an explosion of sensation that blinded her for a second as every nerve lit incandescent with pleasure at his attention. She arched into his touch, pressing closer, but Dimitrius would not be rushed as he switched his focus from that breast, lavishing just the same on her other nipple as he feasted upon her.

Then, they were moving—and the world tilted. The soft bed rushed up to meet her as Dimitrius laid her amongst the covers and settled between her legs. The divinely solid weight of him took her breath away for a moment—and then he pressed into her, an unmistakeable hardness bulging into her core. She whimpered, so sensitive even that graze of fabric felt like too much. His mouth covered hers and stole the sound away. Propping himself up on one elbow, his other hand found her breast and he palmed it. A finger rubbed over the tip of her nipple, sending lightning through her, and then he squeezed, edging that pleasure with pain.

Fumbling with the buttons on his shirt, Harper let out a

sound of frustration against his lips. The clasps gave way, and she plunged her hands into the depths of his shirt to run her palms over the planes of his inked chest and shoulders, revelling in the dips and peaks of muscle and bone she found there before her hands rose of their own accord to tangle in his hair and pull him closer still. Harper could not kiss him fiercely enough to convey the need raging through her—this was everything the kiss against the tree could not have been. Here, there was no need for secrecy and silence, no need for swiftness and no room for shame or guilt. As he consumed her mouth, with every despicably irresistible flick of his tongue and nip of his teeth, she came undone yet more.

This was *nothing* like the fumbling and inexperienced encounters she had shared with Alric where her feelings for him had outweighed the pleasure he had served her. He had been a boy barely into manhood then—but Dimitrius was undoubtably a male, and he knew how to play her body like an instrument. Even the mistaken kiss she had shared with Aedon had held none of this promise of flamed desire.

Aedon.

The thought of him sent her blood ice cold. Aedon. Brand. Erika. Ragnar. Her friends. Suffering at the hands of their captor—whilst she selfishly took her pleasure in relative safety and comfort. All the desire raging inside her ceased at once.

"Stop!" she gasped against all the instincts of her body which had writhed under his touch and come alight at his attentions just moments ago. She pushed at him—but she could not budge his bulk. And yet, at her word, he stopped instantly.

"Are you alright? Did I hurt you?" he demanded, evaluating her quickly, efficiently—and finding nothing wrong.

"What is it?" His hand slipped from her breast to cup her cheek.

Her eyes fluttered closed as his touch—now so gentle—threatened to undo her anew. But guilt coiled inside her, feeding on her doubts.

"I can't do this." She let out a bitter laugh. "Oh, I want to, even though I shouldn't—but I can't. I could not live with myself, taking my pleasure with you, here, now, whilst my friends suffer."

Dimitrius quickly masked his disappointment, but she had seen it slide across his features. "As you wish." His words were restrained as he pulled away and stood, leaving her naked upon the bed. She scrambled off it to retrieve the towel, wrapping it around herself. Still, his attention ensnared her and she felt pinned in his gaze. It made her skin crawl as the discomfort bubbled to an unbearable strength, as though it would claw itself free of her skin if it could.

Her eyes dropped to his fingers. They deftly rebuttoned his collar, hiding away the shadowy ink on his chest. "You're a better person than I. I would have taken you all the same." His admission sent a thrill through her. A dangerously tempting one. "Why should you deny yourself pleasure for the terrible things outside your control?"

She shook her head and folded her arms across her belly. If he tried to unpick her, she would spiral into madness. "I'm sorry."

Something ticked in his jaw. "No. I'm sorry. I should not have taken advantage of you."

"You did not. I gave myself freely." And she did not regret it, which only made the guilt coil around her heart all the tighter for her selfishness. She wanted him—truly—but she could not.

"Hmm. This was a mistake—clearly. I shouldn't have

allowed myself to lose control. It won't happen again." Dimitrius stooped to pick his jacket from the back of the nearby chair and draped it over an arm. "I'll take my leave. Rest now. Soon, he will return, and you will be summoned. You have said you will not obey him, yet I do not think you will have any choice in what happens next. I will protect you when I can, but neither of us can defy him."

Any hint of desire was quenched with the mention of Saradon. The ever-present trepidation squirmed around her stomach at his words. As Dimitri left, she wondered what would pass when she was next brought before Saradon, but quickly pushed the thought from her mind. The fear of it was as bad as the event itself. It would not do to dwell on it.

No—now she had something more consuming to worry about that seized her body with an entirely different symphony of feelings. She had nearly just given herself to the Spymaster of Pelenor. And what was worse? She still wanted to, despite the fact that it was definitely a mistake, which he had admitted. With a groan she toppled face first into the bed. But even the covers could not silence her angst and the empty room had no answers.

63

HARPER

Harper had slept for goodness knows how long when she awoke with a start. She listened for a long moment, but there was nothing untoward. Dim faelights danced in the alcoves, casting a warm hue over the space. Silence reigned within and without. But now, she was awake, and she could not return to slumber. She was glad for the oblivion, however long it had lasted. It had saved her from agonising over her captivity at Saradon's hands, the state of her friends, and the calamitously intimate experience with Dimitrius. Calamitous because she had no idea how it would work out, like everything else—and there were no good outcomes she could see for any of it.

She had stopped their kiss—stopped it going any further, much as she wanted it to, too overcome by guilt and shame at her own selfish greed in taking pleasure with Dimitrius when her friends suffered somewhere in the stones under that mountain. Unable to bear the feeling chasing under her skin, Harper slipped from the bed and padded to the bathroom to dip a finger in the bath—flat cold. So, it had been hours at least, then. Her stomach growled. There was no food to be seen. When had she last eaten? What time was it? It was impossible to place time under the mountain, free of natural light. When had she last seen daylight?

As she returned to the bedroom, she halted. Something rested draped across the chair where Dimitrius had sat. She crossed swiftly to it. A dress of delicate diaphanous fabric. As she gingerly picked it up, a piece of paper slid to the floor. She bent to retrieve the scrap. A note in looping handwriting awaited.

"Wear me. –D."

D for Dimitrius. Something low in her belly stirred, a remnant of that desire. A part of her could still feel the ghost of him upon her lips. She glanced back at the dress. It was yards of fabric.

Harper had slept wrapped in the towel. She shed it now, hooking it over the armoire door, and held up the dress by the shoulders. It seemed a simple enough affair, thankfully free of any corsetry or lacing which would have stymied her. She pooled it upon the floor and stepped into it, shimmying the fabric up and over her hips before slipping her arms through.

There were no mirrors in the suite, so she did the best she could of adjusting it on her body—it was slightly loose and slightly long—until it felt as though it hung correctly on her frame. The fabric was so soft every ripple of it moving across her skin was a soft, sighing kiss. It made her want other things—forbidden things—that she definitely ought not to indulge in again with a certain spymaster, she reminded herself sternly.

At first hidden under the dress, Harper had not noticed the box upon the chair. Inside, she found a hairbrush, hair combs and clips, and some bracelets. She wondered who they had belonged to with an uneasy ripple and closed the box abruptly. Some silk slippers hid under the chair. She eyed them dubiously—they looked too insubstantial to protect her feet from the chill or the rough stone. She beat her boots together over the bath to get rid of the mud crusting the soles and shoved them on instead.

A knock at the door made her startle. She called her magic forth in a rush and spun, crouching slightly—thanking her foresight to put on boots and lamenting the fabric of the dress which would open her up to any number of vulnerabilities. She did not have a weapon, save the hairbrush which was next to useless. But, a familiar voice had her releasing her pent up breath in a gush. "Harper. It's me. Are you awake?"

Her heart fluttered for an entirely different reason. "Yes." She straightened as Dimitri opened the door and stopped. His nostrils flared as he took her in, his lips parting at the sight of her. It took a moment for him to compose himself. Perhaps her rejection stopped him from making any further advance. "If you don't mind, I took a little liberty."

Her attention dropped to his hands, where he held out a silver bangle to her—new, but with a familiar item upon it. Her little silver charm with Saradon's mark stamped upon it.

"You seemed very attached to it, and so I thought I would give you an upgrade. Fit for a princess now."

That title made her stomach flip unpleasantly, but she offered her wrist, touched that he had thought of her at all— especially after she had essentially rejected him at his most vulnerable moment. "Thank you," she said past the lump in her throat, reeling at the warmth radiating through her chest —and other, more dangerously treacherous parts of her body —as those fingers of his, so gentle when they wanted to be, slipped the bangle on her wrist.

"There. Perfection," he murmured, meeting her glance for the briefest moment before he dropped her hand and stepped back. Before she could think of any way to respond, he added, "It's time. Saradon has returned and we must attend him."

Hope guttered and her spirits plummeted. But she gathered herself and tucked a strand of hair behind her ear, before fiddling with the rest of it, twisting it around her hand and letting go so it fell as a rippling sheet across her back. She did not open the box to use the jewelled clips—she had no idea how. Her idea of hair was a braid. Practical. She had no idea how to dress in a royal court. That thought threatened to overwhelm her.

She followed him in a daze through the corridors, almost immediately lost in the unfamiliar hallways. When she stumbled over a crack in the paving, Dimitrius took her hand without a word, slipped it through the crook of his arm, and continued to lead the way. She dared to glance up. He looked stern. Worried, even. That concerned her more than anything else.

When they reached the vast space of the jarlshalle, the cool air rose bumps across her skin. It was empty. Dimitri led her quickly across the stone floor, her boots tip-tap-tip-tapping across the surface. He drew her up the steps onto the dais, to the smaller of the two thrones, slightly below and off to the side of the largest one.

"Must I?" she turned a pleading gaze upon him as he gestured for her to sit there.

The hard line of his mouth softened, but he nodded. "I'm afraid so. You are his heir. He will see you recognised as such." His touch was gentle as he helped her sit in the chair without becoming tangled in the drape of fabric. The armless dress draped across her shoulders, falling down her seated form to the floor, where the fine, thin fabric pooled around her hidden boots. Her hair had fallen across one shoulder in waves, and her silver charm perched on her wrist, now upon the fine metal bangle.

Shivers crawled down her spine. This garment was no protection against the insistent chill of the place. The braziers to the side of the hall were cold and dead, offering no respite. A moment later, they raged to life—and a shadow loomed from the corner of her eye. Dimitrius stepped back to a respectable distance and bowed at the waist.

Harper's eyes flicked to the dark form gathering just to the side of her. Through a swirl of shadow, Saradon came into focus—and her mouth went dry. Her hands gripped the arms of the stone throne so hard her knuckles whitened. Saradon's poisonous magic still clung to her, as if it slowed the very life through her veins—but the power of his presence chased that from her with pure, abject terror.

When he spoke, his deep voice rang clear. "I bid thee welcome, daughter, on this most auspicious day." He sounded malevolently gleeful, adding to the chills wrapping around her. "Eat! We have much to be thankful for."

She glanced to one side of her chair, to see Dimitri placing a small table within arm's reach. Fine foods—the likes of which did not belong in spoiled halls overrun by goblins—piled high upon it.

Could it be poisoned? Her stomach grumbled, tight and empty. If she was to escape, she needed strength—and she reasoned if he wanted her dead, she already would be. She fell upon the offerings without a further worry of any taint upon the food. It tasted like ash in her mouth, and her stomach roiled with nausea, threatening to expel the lot of it, but she ate regardless. She had no idea if and when her next meal would come.

"Good, good," Saradon said approvingly as he settled on the throne to her other side and picked at his own private pile of food. Dimitri stood still, like a sculpture.

"How goes Pelenor, Lord Ellarian?"

Dimitri stirred. "Events progress apace, Lord Ravakian. I have not attended court in some days, to make sure things here are… managed. The court continues to crumble. The king is primed to withdraw, and the general of the Winged Kingsguard to assume temporary regency to maintain order. The curse spreads through the court as planned. My allies are poised and waiting, though scared, to shore up control of the court."

Harper did not have enough wit to truly take in his words and the level of deception and scheming Dimitri was involved in—and the master of—and nor did she want to.

"Excellent. I thank you for the sustenance, Lord Ellarian. Much nicer fare than the carrion amongst these halls."

Dimitri bowed and murmured his welcome.

"Now, daughter, this day is for you. I want to use all my time to become familiar with you." Saradon smiled, and Harper's heart sank. She dropped her gaze, not wanting to meet his piercing violet eyes.

"Tell me of your life, daughter." His voice was silky smooth, inviting. The magic in her blood, his magic, coaxed her.

Tell him. Oh, wouldn't it be so nice to tell him? She shook her head. "N-No," she stuttered, forcing her will to shove against his. "You already saw it." Why did he need to hear it from her?

"But, daughter, I wish to hear tales from your own lips, hear your voice. You have the sound of my own dear mother, may she rest in peace. In you, I hear the timbre of her voice. I miss it so."

An aching sadness filled her at his loss and grief, eliciting sympathy and a desire to comfort him. *He's controlling you,* she told herself doggedly. *Don't give in.*

"You must give him something," Dimitri said into her mind. *"Else he will shatter your mind and take what he will. Then you will be good to nobody and nothing."*

A lazy, slow apprehension reared at his words. "I don't know what you want," she said dully, her tongue feeling large and clumsy, sticking in her mouth, as though she were a drunkard. A warm rush of magic stroked over her—a gift from Dimitri. It banished some of the fuzziness within her mind and her limbs seemed to lighten. She sat up straighter. "I am a nobody. My life has been boring. Meaningless." *And it's none of your damn business.*

"And yet *you* are hardly meaningless, are you, daughter? The bearer of Erendriel's own edict." He spoke with honey in his voice, but she could not miss the spike of venom at Erendriel's name.

"I don't claim to bear anything," she said guardedly.

"I saw the vision. Erendriel, for all her faults, does not lie." He watched her out of the corner of his eye.

What did he want her to say? Did he want her to admit that she was some prophetic chosen one? Harper did not even know what Erendriel's words meant. "Then you know more than I." Harper lifted her chin. "I've been nothing but a pauper, scrounging from the land. I've spent more years starving than I have full, and never more than a couple of coppers away from destitution. There's nothing gifted in that."

"Those who made it so will pay for the crime, do not worry, daughter. I will see them suffer several times over that you did not have the life you were entitled to as my heir." Saradon's voice was dark once more, and his displeasure crackled through the halls.

Harper's skin crawled. She knew who had killed her mother. She knew who he would make suffer. *Raedon. Will he punish Aedon for Raedon's crimes?* She pushed the thought from her mind as quickly as it arrived, though she was certain Saradon already knew. She sent a desperate plea to the heavens that Aedon would not be punished in Raedon's place.

The doors swung open and a band of writhing goblins dragged in two bedraggled figures. Saradon clapped his hands together, the sound booming around the hall. "Ah! Excellent. Our entertainment arrives."

Harper's shoulders sagged with relief that his attention had diverted from her, then suddenly straightened again when she perceived who their "entertainment" was.

"No!" she cried out involuntarily, jumping up.

64

HARPER

Saradon frowned and motioned for the goblins to bring Brand and Erika forward, even as he froze Harper.

"Sit!"

His command forced her to sink onto the throne once more. Brand and Erika's attention snapped to her at his command. She shuddered against his will, her limbs locking, but it was no use. Their eyes widened when they saw Harper seated next to Saradon. She knew they would be wondering at her presence—and her place beside their captor.

Harper tried to surge forward, but Saradon's bond held her in place. Slowly, despite her strangled screams of anger, her body subsided onto her chair once more. Saradon's magic forced her to sit, back straight, even raising her chin so she glared imperiously at her friends below her. Furious tears streamed down her cheeks, and she raged against the magic that held her there, to no avail. Her companions were almost unrecognisable—beaten, bruised, and dirty. Erika's furs were crusted with dirt and blood, and Brand's wings were tattered and covered in gore.

The goblins did not dare get too close, it seemed, for they kept Brand and Erika in their centre and at bay with the pointed ends of the various weapons they held. Brand and Erika had nothing but the clothes on their backs, but it did not stop them from standing back-to-back, as though they could protect each other from their captors. Her friends' wary attention darted between the goblins. They looked like prey. They bore hunted looks in the dark hollows under their eyes and the hopeless set of their mouths. As much as Brand swung at any goblin who came too close and Erika ducked and wove between their feinting attacks, Harper knew they could not succeed. They were too weakened and vulnerable—and vastly outnumbered.

The cruel scenario reminded her of the caged bears that had visited her local town, Glymouth, with the travelling shows that occasionally came to her home county. She recalled how the animals had been much the same— doggedly tired, malnourished, and battered, yet still dangerous enough to kill… and provide good entertainment. She hated the spectacle before her now as much as she had hated that. Brand's and Erika's bodies were peppered with small cuts and nicks that were meant to draw out suffering, rather than kill. How could anyone bear to watch or enjoy such cruel sport?

Her friends lashed out at the goblins who harried them, though they were in no fit state to defend themselves. Their chests rose and fell raggedly with each uneven breath, and their lowered stances and delayed reflexes only allowed the goblins further successes, until they shrieked with glee at their torment of the Aerian and the nomad. The cacophony drilled into Harper's already tired mind until her head pounded, but she fought through it, determined to throw off Saradon's control upon her body so she could help them.

"Please, stop this," she implored, but Saradon only waved his hand, sealing her mouth so she could not defy him further. Before her, Dimitri watched the spectacle before him with hard eyes. She knew he could not help, for it would damn them all.

It seemed Brand and Erika had resigned themselves to their fate, and though they would not give up, their defences grew slower and more laboured. Eventually, one goblin got too close. Brand lunged forward to grab the goblin from amidst his cohort with his giant arms. They bulged as he crushed the goblin into his chest—snarling and teeth bared, he looked as feral as they. The goblin stilled, and as Brand released it, the goblin's patched armour was dented and crumpled, and its body twisted out of proportion.

Brand lifted the goblin by its neck and ankles. With an almighty roar, he flung it toward the goblins surrounding them. The unexpected assault wiped out half a dozen and scattered the rest. Brand lunged forward to try his luck again, managing to stamp on the helmed head of another goblin, who did not rise, before he and Erika were once more hemmed in by the now vengeful horde that bristled with even more blades than before.

They were repaid tenfold for their rebellion. The goblins set upon Brand and Erika like wild beasts, hacking and slashing with cruel serrated blades, teeth, and claws. Brand crushed Erika close to his body and hunched over, closing his wings around them both and bowing before the onslaught. Slashes marred his wings, and he bellowed in pain, but did not yield as the goblins' blades bit deep and rivulets of blood ran down him to pool onto the floor.

Harper refused to shut her eyes, refused to let Saradon

win, but tears streamed down her cheeks at her friends' plight. Her strength ran thin against Saradon's endless reserves. She could not help, no matter how much she wanted to. Saradon seemed to sense her submission, for the shackles upon her loosened—though not enough for her to move or use her magic. But now she had enough room to twitch and to breathe fully, though she did not want to take in the air from the tainted hall.

She flung herself from her chair with all her might, the most she could manage with hardly any control over her limbs. She crashed onto the stone before Saradon, on her belly and at his mercy.

"Please! I beg you, stop this!" She looked up at him from the wide step of the dais, her cheeks wet and eyes brimming with fresh, angry tears, willing for some ounce of compassion in him, but as she searched his cold, hard gaze, she found none. "I'll do *anything* to make it stop. Please!"

He raised an eyebrow. "Anything?"

"Yes. Please, make them stop!"

"It will be so." With a sharp slash of his hand and a crack of magic, the goblins fell back, shrieking, though they still cavorted around their prisoners, albeit now at a distance—as though they wished to continue their sport rather than obey their master's command. Saradon rose from his throne, slowly and with relish. Harper scrambled to her hands and knees, caught in the folds of the dress, and her heart palpitated with relief at the sight of Brand and Erika, now unharried by their tormentors. The cold stone seeped into her hands and knees, numbing them, but Harper did not miss the unmistakeable twist of magic writhing around her.

"You offered me anything, so I shall take what I will of you, daughter. I choose your *obedience*. I bind you once. I bind you twice. I bind you thrice. You shall follow me in all I command, until you learn that my way is the righteous one and follow me of your own will. It is for your own good. Your wilfulness has no place in my court."

Harper felt the magic bite sharply into her as he bound her to his will. Her own was suppressed, forced down within her until she felt like she was trapped helplessly at the bottom of a well, yet she could do nothing to defy him. Horror filled her. She knew she was entirely under his thrall, and she had delivered herself there without even securing her friends' releases. What had she done?

True to Saradon's word, he called the goblins off, banishing them from the hall and sending them away with a touch of his own malign cruelty so they shrieked in pain for his pleasure. "Detestable creatures." His lips curled as he turned away to reposition himself on his grand throne.

Harper rose by his will, and dipped into a graceful curtsey, which she would never have been able to execute without him, her puppeteer, then slipped into her own seat beside him. Dimitri refused to catch her eye, but his clenched fists were not lost on her. Her friends still huddled upon the floor, beaten and broken, but their will was not so entirely sapped that they were defeated. Brand still hunched over Erika, though now they half-lay upon the stone. His eyes caught Harper's. She tried to fill her gaze with urgency and hope, but he stared at her impassively.

I tried to help. Please believe the best of me, she begged, knowing her message would not reach him. Even if, in the end, she had accomplished little but prolonging their torture. Her stomach churned with nausea at the thought of all their suffering and her uselessness.

"Who are your dear friends, daughter?" Saradon's fingers, steepled under his chin, rubbed together as he contemplated the sorry prisoners before him.

She could not deny him. "Brand of the Aerians and Erika of the Indis."

"Ah, the *Indis*. Of course. I have just returned from your lands," he said to Erika, who glared at him through the crack in Brand's wings, as though wishing she could rip him limb from limb. Erika bared her teeth and spat at him. The bloody globule fell far short of the dais, splattering upon the already sullied stone. Saradon without magic would have been no match for a fit and healthy Erika. A pang of anger rippled through Harper. *One day, she will get her vengeance upon him. Somehow, I will see it so.*

His lip curled. "Your kin were far more welcoming and respectful. You will be most pleased to know that they once more join my banners." Worry chased through Harper at his crowing admission. "I shall give you the chance, of course, to stand with your kin under my rule."

Erika spat at him again.

Using his magic, he pressed her to the floor, crushing her face against it as he made her bow in submission. "Foolish," he snarled. "You shall not receive a second offer. Die in the darkness with your *defender* instead." Saradon sneered at Brand, who had collapsed beside Erika, slowly weakening as his lifeblood left him through the great gashes in his wings. "Be the sport of the goblins for the rest of your miserable lives. I care not." Saradon summoned the goblins once more, and Brand and Erika were hauled away, leaving trails of scuffed dirt and blood in their wake—and then nothing but silence.

"The Indis agreed to ally with you, Lord?" Dimitri's quiet voice broke through the deafening silence.

"They did indeed, without any real need for coercion. Their hate runs deep, as I knew it would." Saradon sounded confident. "When the time comes, they will join me. Already, they travel west over the tundra and the mountains to join us upon the low plains."

"Excellent," said Dimitri, but Harper could hear how devoid of emotion his voice was. She wondered if he felt as scared as her.

"More than excellent. The Indis were some of the strongest fighters under my banners. If they are any remnant of their former selves, they will serve us well, though their numbers have dwindled. With the fury of the Indis, the disarray of the goblins, and the righteousness of the common peoples of Pelenor, all united against the crumbling court that dies from within, our victory shall be swift and certain." Saradon turned to Harper with a half-smile. "I have already seen it, like your own visions. Come. Look." He waved his hand, palm down, before him, and a great, flat mirror coalesced and hovered by his hips.

Harper rose and padded over to join him, though her whole body wanted to shy away from being so close to his presence. She gasped as she beheld the scene within the mirror.

"The old and much forgotten Eldarkind gift of scrying, daughter, of my own foresight. Behold what will come to pass."

It was disturbingly similar to her visions from Erendriel. Saradon smiled, and she wondered whether he knew what she likened it to. Eyes wide and mouth clamped shut, she advanced, resting the tips of her fingers upon the edge of the mirror, as though she could reach into the vision underneath the smooth, silvered glass. A blasted earth passed beneath her, as though from a bird's view. Burning and charred piles were partly obscured by still rising pillars of smoke that twisted in the winds to cover almost all. The dead were a flood upon the earth.

"What is this?" she breathed. Beside her, Dimitri also stood, watching silently. As he shifted his weight from one foot to the other, the smooth fabric of his sleeve touched her bare arm. A minor reassurance. She was not alone.

"Victory," Saradon hissed. "Victory at last. Five hundred years have I been denied, but no more. The wheel shall be riven, and I shall build a new Pelenor from the ashes. Pelenor will fall, with Valtivar soon to follow. Slowly but surely, my dominion will spread as far as the land passes east and west and north and south, until it can go no farther. All will fall under my banners and obey my rule. No more will there be war and strife. All will serve."

"The land is barren," said Dimitri, his voice hollow.

"War has a cost, Lord Ellarian, as you well know." Saradon glanced at him sharply. "The land will recover, as always. The peoples, as well."

Gripped by his will, Harper felt a giddy swoop of excitement that was not her own pass through her, though she was horrified by his intent, despairing by the second that there was any hope. His excitement mixed with the nauseating fear that would not leave her belly, making it all worse.

"I could not be more pleased with how all progresses," Saradon said, drawing up with a satisfied smile. "It will not be long now before the sword will strike and I will be king of all." Saradon turned to Harper, smiling with a cruel glint in his eyes. "And you, daughter, shall be first by my side in all things."

Harper had no choice as his will forced her to curtsy before him deeply and remain low, with her head bowed and her gaze on the floor. "I will serve," she intoned, fighting every word he made her speak.

65

HARPER

Dimitri escorted Harper to her chamber in silence. She tried to take note of the twists and turns and the many levels they climbed until her legs burned, but was quickly lost. Harper glanced at him as they strode, their steps echoing down the dark and deserted halls, but he stared resolutely ahead, his jaw set. She did not dare speak. Not with the darkness nipping at their heels beyond the glow of the faelight he cast to illuminate the way. Not with their master close by.

They returned to the jarl's sprawling quarters, high in the mountain fortress. There, the air was not marred by war. Fine tapestries still hung from the walls, containing some sparse warmth in the space, and nothing was damaged, desecrated, or looted. Harper was most thankful there was no sign of death. She had seen enough and could bear no more. She was surprised to see in her wing that she had not just one room, but a suite of her own, with a living space and a dining room, in addition to the bedroom and bathing room. In her haze, she had not realised its breadth. It was much like the rooms she, Aedon, Brand, and Erika had first shared in Keldheim. It felt comfortingly familiar, though too large and empty for her liking.

She did not like to think who this set of rooms had belonged to—because other people's belongings scattered the space. A pair of boots here. A cloak there. Books upon the shelves. It clutched at her heart when she saw an open book propped on the dining table next to a mug—both abandoned as though left in a hurry. Their owner was no doubt dead. It threatened to tear a hole in her chest. She blinked away the rush of prickling heat in her eyes and turned into the living room so that she could not see. Dimitri slumped onto a cushioned armchair before her, as though he was a sail that had lost all its wind. He looked depleted, which concerned her.

"Are you all right?" she asked hesitantly, lurking by the arched entrance.

Dimitri waved her to a chair adjacent to his own. "No," he said dully, running a hand through his hair and ruining his coiffed look.

Harper perched on the chair arm, arranging her dress around her, and waited, staring at him expectantly. She could not relax into the chair, too agitated by the situation they found themselves in, what had just happened to her friends at the hands of the goblins, and by the kiss—and *more*—that the two of them had not spoken of. For all the closeness she had felt between them, now it felt like a gulf. *This was a mistake.* His words echoed in her mind. Harper steeled herself, walling the hurt away—it would not help anyone.

He stared at her, taking in her unusual appearance for a long moment, before his eyes flicked to hers, then dipped away. "We are bound to this runaway stallion now, and I fear we cannot untie ourselves."

"The mirror…" Harper twisted the fine fabric of her dress between her fingers.

"Yes. If that were truly foresight, then it does not bode well. I would go so far as to say it is quite hopeless." Dimitri shook his head and stroked his lips with his forefinger and thumb as he stared into nothingness.

"But what of Erendriel's vision?" Harper leaned forward. "She said there was hope—if only we could remain faithful and follow the way."

Dimitri laughed. "How do you propose we do that, Harper? Hmm? Because you just as good as gave yourself away!"

"You're angry at me?" she asked incredulously. "I'm trying to get us out of this mess! The mess *you* created!"

"Yes, I'm angry—no, I'm *furious*—at your lunacy!" He stood, unable to contain his energy, and stormed to the opposite side of the chamber before turning to stride back, eliciting a thrill in the pit of her stomach. "You gave your freedom for *nothing*, and without it, we are as good as damned, Erendriel or not!"

"I gave it to save my friends!" Harper stood, too, squaring up to him, though she had to look up to meet his stormy gaze as he towered over her.

"Yet you did *not*! They live merely to die another day," he said, scowling down at her. "If anything, you only prolonged their suffering."

His words speared right to the certainty in her that knew the self-same, but Harper would be damned before she admitted he was right. "Then how can I help them?"

"You cannot," snapped Dimitri. "You gave your word to him. You don't realise what you've done, do you? You have condemned *all* just for the chance—ill-used—to save *two*, and you did not even manage to spare them!" He threw his hands into the air, punched the wall, and leaned heavily against it.

"*You* condemned us all by raising him!" She advanced upon him.

He wheeled on her with a snarl, and the darkness in his eyes made her heart pound as she ceded one step, and then two, until her back was against the wall. "And it was a mistake that cannot be taken back! I know now that power does not lead me to my desires. When will you cease putting me through the wringer for it? Must I be reminded of it at every turn? We are where we are. We must react, adapt, survive… then maybe we can undo this. You cannot be mad at me for wanting a better life."

"For yourself, or for others?" She glared at him.

"Who says it cannot be both?" he muttered rebelliously, glowering at her under lowered brows. His breath caressed her forehead, and the cage of his arm resting above her head on the wall a contradiction to the anger that flickered between them in the charged air. She was so close to those lips—the lips that had kissed her and made her come undone. The same lips that had admitted it had been a mistake. Hurt warred with rage inside her, quelling the desire that threatened to rear.

"Argh!" He pounded the stone above her head, glaring at her, his jaw set. "I hate the way that you undo me so, woman —how you crack every defence I have built, how deeply you force me to face the darkness of my own conscience despite my best attempts to wall it away, and how I both loathe and love it, this chaos you unleash upon me! You give me hope that we are not doomed, and I do not know whether to hate or thank you for it."

His anger thrilled her—and incited her. She was no longer afraid of him, despite the power he wielded. She raised her chin to him, and his gaze dropped to her lips, sending a swooping rush through her. "Someone has to keep you from believing your own horseshit, Dimitrius. I will never give up—not whilst I still draw breath—and whilst you hold the power to change this, I won't let you give up either."

Wordless, he stared at her for a long moment. She still could not fathom him. He was not evil—of that, she was quite sure. Misguided? That fit him better. He seemed to have been trying to do what he thought was right and best, however ineptly he had orchestrated it. Or perhaps, he was simply plain selfish. Somehow, the anguish in his eyes, in every hard line of his body, spoke of the former not the latter as the fight within him drained away.

He swallowed. "Never stop, Harper. I need you." Those three whispered words pulled at something raw inside her. "I need the light and fire you bring—without you, I would see nothing but the darkness." His eyes slipped shut, and when he opened them once more, she recognised with frustration the calm mask there—because she knew him well enough to know he was anything but serene inside. "I'm sorry, Harper. I shouldn't have taken this out on you—not when I am far more to blame. Anger won't get us anywhere."

Harper sank into her chair and covered her face with her hands. She needed to hide from the world—just for a moment. She had no bravery left. Despite his words, she felt damned near hopeless too. "What will?" she asked in a hollow voice. If he was right, what hope was there? What small chance she may have believed they had was surely gone if she had given herself to Saradon without thought.

He knelt before her, taking her by surprise, and gathered her hands in his, pressing them gently. Her breath stalled at the contact. "We are alive, for one," Dimitri said, but she could hear the bluffed confidence in his tone, the attempt to rally her.

"If this were *chatura*, we would be out of moves." She slipped her hands from his and folded them in her lap, her heart pounding and unease circling within her belly anew.

"It might seem that way, but whilst we still draw breath, we can find a way out of this."

Skies above, she could not look away from those violet eyes of his. She hated herself a little for it. That even in the midst of this chaos, she entertained any desperate notion of attraction. How bad a person did that make her, if she were attracted to *him*? Her heart sank. She closed her eyes to deny him. "But you don't have any ideas?"

"No," he admitted. She saw the shadows behind her closed eyes move, felt the air disperse and his presence recede, and opened her eyes. He sank into the other chair. "I don't. Not yet."

"We are safe by his side for now, though, are we not?"

"I'm not sure. I don't believe we are safe at all. But perhaps as long as we dance to his tune, we will remain outside his scrutiny—and the danger of that."

"Then that's what we will have to do to survive, isn't it?" She used his own words against him.

"Yes," he said heavily. "That's how I've felt since… since I raised him. All the while, I've been trying to discover a way out, a way to stop it all. I just haven't found one yet."

"Then we must find one together," Harper said, straightening, a curl of fire within her. Some hope that all was not yet lost. "If we are perhaps the only two close enough to him to know what he plans and remain below his regard, we are best placed of all to stop him."

"You may well be right, Harper." Dimitri stirred, gazing at

her thoughtfully. "In this, we must put aside any animosity between us and work together."

Animosity? Harper wondered at the word. Did he feel it toward her? An aching hurt lanced through her at the thought. Was that why he had chosen that word? She was not sure she hated him anymore, despite the harshness of their first impressions. Despite what had passed between them being a mistake, she still wanted him—even though she knew she should not—and she saw sides to him that she did not detest. Far from it. It unsettled her, for she felt like she finally looked upon him in a new light.

She was not there yet, she surmised, but she was close to gazing upon his true face. The one he hid under his masks. Those many masks—which were now being stripped away one by one for her. No longer was he the dangerous, dark mask. Not the cold, distant one. No more the haughty, sneering one. Nor the over-confident, cocky one. Not even the sly, cunning one. *How many masks are left?* she wondered. He now seemed vulnerable, and she was sure she could detect a shred of decency beneath his selfishness and foolishness.

"What?" he said at her silence.

"Do you feel 'animosity' toward me?" she asked quietly, not dropping her gaze. Had it been *merely* a mistake, a lapse in judgement, what had passed between them, or had she found herself falling for someone who hated her? She could not bear to think she had misjudged him so—and she knew him well enough to know that he would answer with the truth. No matter how painful. She needed to know.

He considered for a moment, and his lips twitched, though he did not smile. "Of course I do not," he said in a low voice, one that tugged something within her. Every word struck honest and true. She did not know what to make of that. "I feel far more for you than is sensible. I regret nothing between us, Harper, let me make myself crystal clear. What happened between us was a mistake in the midst of this madness—but that does not mean I do not want it and far more beside." She shivered at the promise in his words, at the intensity of his gaze that threatened to kindle that doomed fire within her.

He continued, "I meant animosity for you toward me. I have been so reckless—with what I have done, and with the way I behaved with such dishonour towards you. You, on the other hand, have only ever done what you felt to be right, even to your own detriment. How could I hate that? How could I do anything but bask in your glory that no matter what, you will not stop on your crusade for justice? You're a fool to give yourself so easily without thought to him, but aren't we all?"

Harper rankled at his words, but he laughed then, despite the gravity of the situation.

He held up his hands as though he sensed the rising indignation within her as she straightened, words leaping to her tongue to defend herself. "I know. I'm the biggest arse of them all right now." He stood to leave. "I'll go to your friends and see that they are well. That is the best I can promise." He nodded and strode toward the door, only slowing when she rose to her feet and he caught the movement out of the corner of his eye.

"I don't hate you," she admitted in a quiet voice, staring at the wall next to him. She could not meet his eyes. That thing inside her chest threatened to crush her. She did not hate him at all. Far from it. Mistake or not, those kisses—a desperate attempt to escape this hellhole—were the truth, and she still wanted him. If anything, she hated herself for that, not him.

"Well then," he said. "We may not be in such a bad partnership after all."

"Thank you for helping my friends."

"We must help each other."

She nodded. "If you can help my friends, especially if they can escape, I'll help you." They could work together, somehow. She had to believe it was possible for her friends to obtain freedom from Saradon, even if she could not see how it would come to pass.

He dropped his gaze. "Don't make promises you cannot keep, Harper," he said softly. "I'll do what I can." He left her in the empty chamber.

Harper sank into the chair slowly, rubbing her arms to rid them of the goose pimples that had arisen with the cold. Her eyes slipped shut for a moment. She was exhausted, only buoyed by nervous energy and desperation, but the deep-seated tiredness within her crept up relentlessly, sapping her remaining energy. The small spark of hope dissipated in her solitude.

All is lost, her mind teased her. *They will all die. It will be for nothing. You are no one. You are nothing. You will never prevail.*

The taunts were relentless, and she could not silence them, even when she covered her face with her hands and groaned into her palms. Harper stumbled to the bed chamber and toppled upon the covers, fully dressed, to drown herself in slumber and silence the insipid voices that prophesied doom.

HARPER

Her dreams were filled with Dimitrius and that tension between them melting—in her slumber, it had not been a mistake and there was no end to it. She could take what she wanted—and she did, indulging in finding a release with him, consequences be damned. Because he was right. They were in grave danger, and death danced with them each day—but that did not mean they should shy away from taking risks. No, if anything, they ought to burn all the brighter and take that light and pleasure where they could—whilst they had the chance. And so, she sank willingly into that realm of sleep that offered her deepest desires and asked for no price in return save the regret of waking to find it untrue.

Wake Harper did, with her hand between her legs wishing and half imagining it was his—Dimitri's—and her core swollen with desire. She sighed lazily, caught in the haze between sleep and waking for a moment as the disappointment of the fading dream mingled with the crescendo of reality. She lay upon her back, still wrapped in that thin, floating dress, with the covers smudged beneath her.

There was movement by the door. A rustle. Her attention snapped to it—to him. Dimitrius. Appearing as though she had summoned him from nowhere. He stood in the open archway staring open-mouthed at her—and looking utterly predatory. He wore his usual dark attire, though the top buttons of his shirt were undone, leaving the strong lines of his neck on show. One arm bulged, holding a wad of shimmering fabrics. His dark eyes—made darker by the dim lights—speared her to the bed, and his nostrils flared as though he could scent the pleasure upon her. Could he? A shiver, not at all unpleasant, curled through her. His free hand flexed.

"I heard a cry. I worried you were… My mistake. I see you are not in any danger at all," he said, that low voice of his curling something deep within her core. His eyes still fixed upon that hand between her legs. She pulled it away and his gaze tracked the movement.

"Only from you," she admitted. Because it was the truth. She was in no physical danger from him—but her mind was. Her heart was. It fluttered as she sat up on the bed, her legs within the folds of shimmering material that felt altogether too much as they slid across her sensitive skin.

His brows plunged into a frown. He dumped the bundle of fabric upon the chair before crossing the room. He towered over her, gripping her chin in his forefinger and thumb and tilting her face up. The violent intensity of the promise in his eyes consumed her. "You are *never* in danger from me. I would burn the world before I let harm come to you."

She had to know—and desire made her bold. She slid from the bed and stood, never mind that she still had to look up to meet the fire in his eyes. It made her braver to stand before him. "You said it was a mistake—what happened between us. I need to know if you believe that. Give me your honest answer."

"Of course not. I told you—I regret nothing. I will take as much as you are prepared to give me, Harper. I would take *everything*. But I will not take one kiss more than you wish." His thumb, still at her jaw, lifted, and he rubbed the pad of it across her lower lip. Her tongue darted out to taste it, swirling across the tip, and he shuddered, his eyes sliding out of focus for a second.

In the next moment, he seized her head with both hands, his palms at either side of her jaw and his fingers reaching around into her hairline. She gasped at the closeness, at his heat, at the throb beating like a drum deep inside her. Their breaths mingled as he bared his teeth at her, his eyes wild and bright, their lips almost touching.

"You want honesty, Harper? I have never felt this for anyone before. You are intoxicating. I am addicted to you. You *consume* me. You are the very air I breathe, and I want you to fill my lungs so I drown upon you. Never has someone put me in such danger before—and never have I tolerated having such a vulnerability. You are my weakness, Harper. I would die to keep you safe—and that terrifies me more than anything else. I respect what you want—what you choose—but what I want? If we are to die, I want to die having known what it feels like to bury myself in you, to wring every ounce of pleasure from you, to have you cry my name as you come. I would die knowing we had flown into the sun and perished in one glorious destruction. *That* is the honest truth of what I want, Harper."

She had stopped breathing. His words broke something within her, because every one of them speared right into her heart. She wanted that too—she just did not dare to reach for it. *Did* she dare? Could she? No matter what was to come, no matter what happened out there in the darkening world, all she had control over was what happened in that moment. Right there. In that room. With him. Nothing else was guaranteed. If they were to die from the peril they were in, she could know some pleasure and some escape at his hands before the end came.

That sealed her decision. Death be damned. She would have him. And she had never been as sure of anything in her life. Harper surged up to fuse their lips together. Dimitri groaned into her lips, but pulled away, those hands cupping her cheeks now holding her back. Uncertainty fluttered within her—not hers, but his. Did he not want it too?

"I need to ask you, Harper—do you desire this? Truly? Because this cannot just be a kiss. You do not know how hard I work to restrain myself. To walk in on you with your beautiful hand between your legs in the very place I long to bury myself... You may want a kiss and nothing more, but my self-control will not endure so far today, and I respect you far too much than to throw caution to the wind. I will remove myself, if I must, to respect your wishes. But this is not—cannot—be just a kiss for me. Not one. I will take them all and everything besides."

Pleasant warmth curled within her core, a tingle shooting through her at his promises. She spread her palm upon his chest, breathing him in, that intoxicating citrus and musk scent of his that primed her body for pleasure and sent lust stroking down her spine. "I want them all. I want you. I want this. I want *everything*, Dimitrius."

He gave it to her, surging forward to capture her lips. The kiss swallowed her gasp at his eagerness before he pulled away to pepper more along the hard line of her jaw and utter words that sent her even weaker at the knees. "Then allow me to worship you like the goddess you are, because to me, you are the coming of the sun and you banish all the dark despair from the depths of my soul when I am with you. Please let me?"

"…Yes."

He kissed down the column of her neck, cradling her skull in his palm, and pulled down the fabric of her dress draping across her shoulders so he could continue the trail across her collarbone. Her hands raked through his hair as the fabric fell, pooling at her feet. She was naked underneath. This wasn't fair. She had to even the odds. This was twice now that she found herself bared before him— and she would have reciprocation.

Pulling his mouth up to hers, Harper teased his lips open, and Dimitri yielded to her, those sharp teeth of his grazing her tongue as she explored him with her mouth and her hands. She tugged his shirt open, teasing apart the buttons one by one—until his hands met her in the middle, having started at the bottom, and off that shirt came to join her dress.

Pulling back momentarily to admire his honed body, she ran her hands up the hard planes of his abdomen, across his chest, and over his broad shoulders. Dark ink stained his torso in a glorious swirl of shadow that shifted as she watched—writhing around the muscles of his shoulders, chest, and arms as though they had a life of their own. She dragged her fingers over him in wonder, and he shuddered, leaning into her touch as she wound her fingers up his neck, through his hair, and pulled him to her mouth once more.

Now, she dared to go lower. Her hands dipped to Dimitri's waist, tracing over his navel—and continued until they found the satisfying warmth in his breeches. She cupped her hand there, squeezing against the growing hardness, and he gritted his teeth against her lips momentarily.

"Careful, huntress. Not so fast." Dimitri captured her wanton hands and slid his fingers up her arms as he drew both to hang loosely around his neck. "Let me. I need to touch you. Please." The need in his voice undid her.

"I'm right here. Touch me." Her daring sent a thrill through her that shivered with every pound of her wanting heart.

"As you command it." His mouth fused with hers again, his kisses hungry and passionate and his tongue and teeth a symphony of sensation as they teased her. He tasted of sweetness, spice, and everything forbidden. His hands palmed down her arms again and continued, briefly skimming over her breasts. She drew in a sharp breath at the contact—hot and sensitive—and then its loss to the cool air as he continued down and past her hips. His hands rounded her bottom where he squeezed, digging in his nails ever so slightly and sending a pulse of pain-edged pleasure through her. That warmth between her legs grew, and her breathing quickened. If he had yielded her mouth at all, she would have begged to be satisfied, for she wanted nothing more than for him to make her feel everything. Everything good to banish the all-consuming darkness that devoured them.

As if he knew her thoughts, one hand slid around to her front, caressing her belly and searching lower. A trail of shivers followed in its wake as she hissed with the unexpected sensation, and how intoxicating it felt wherever he touched her. His fingers slipped between her legs, and she bit his lip involuntarily from the explosion of feeling as he slid a finger along the sensitive folds there—and dove between.

Dimitri groaned. "You're so wet for me, my huntress." He rolled a finger around her slick clit, sending a crescendo of pleasure through her, as he pressed another kiss to her mouth and lavished her tongue with the attention of his lashing tongue in perfect rhythm to his hand. She attempted to draw a hand between them, but his free hand squeezed her backside in warning.

"Not yet." He peppered her jaw with kisses, licking and sucking down her neck. "I want to last as long as possible with you. I will take whatever time we have for this, Harper."

There was only a gasp by way of reply because she could not form words as he lavished attention on her breasts, taking one into his mouth, licking and sucking at her nipple, grazing it and nipping oh so gently with his teeth until it was hard and peaked for him, before giving the same thorough awakening to her other.

Dimitrius dropped to the floor. "Skies above, you bring me to my knees. I will never willingly kneel for another living thing. I will never yield in spirit to another. Only you." Still, his hand swirled between her legs, and as he kissed down her stomach, it was all she could do to remain standing, her hands clutching at his hair, because each wave of pleasure he wrought threatened to undo her legs. She parted her thighs at the unspoken request—the slight pressure of his hands teasing them apart—and gasped when he pressed a gentle kiss to her core, following it with a lash of his wicked tongue.

Her legs trembled, and it was the strength of his arms holding her up as that tongue found her clit and licked again, sending a jolt of satisfaction through her. She needed more. This was just a tease, and her body felt aflame, every part of her begging to be stoked to the point of no return and the precipice of release.

Dimitrius surged to his feet and walked her backwards, chest to chest with her, until her calves hit the edge of the bed. "Damn it," he growled, desire dark in his eyes. "I need you too much to be patient now."

She fought with the buttons of his trousers—and won—stripping the garments down his legs. He kicked them away. Harper paused for a moment to admire the sight of him before her, naked for the first time. Tall, broad, honed with lean muscle—and his considerable length rock hard for her with a bead of liquid gleaming at the tip. Her mouth dried—and there came a fleeting urge to lick it.

Harper reached for him, but he caught her wrist before she could do more than graze the sleek tip. He pulled her closer, until her body was flush with his, and that wet, hard length pressed into her belly—and his next words were forced through gritted teeth. "Absolutely not—yet. I'm going to wring every ounce of pleasure from you first."

Her stomach flipped and a rush of heat flooded her body at the sensuous promise of those words. She did not doubt him—and she wanted it with every pounding beat of her runaway heart. So, she let him push her back onto the bed, sitting on the edge and bracing herself on her hands, her head now level with that glorious cock standing proud for her. It vanished a moment later, for he knelt between her legs and pushed apart her knees. Her breathing quickened.

"Lay back." The instruction was quiet, sure. She acquiesced without a word. What was he planning? She had her answer when his palms planed up her belly and down again before settling at her hips, pulling apart her legs yet more, so she was bared before him and the apex of her legs was utterly at his mercy. His hot breath ghosted the sensitive mound of skin there with a second's warning before his mouth enveloped her clit—and she gasped at the sudden shock of sensation.

That ungodly tongue of his set to work, teasing and swirling around her clit, lavishing it with sleek broad strokes, every one of them sending her pleasure up to a higher plane. Then he quickened with needy laps, up and down her folds, before returning to that most sensitive spot at her clit. Her hands wound into the coverlet, twisting in the fabric as she let out a ragged moan. He sucked her clit into his mouth—and she went rigid, arching her back off the bed as he edged it with his teeth, sending a lightning edge through the rising tide of pleasure sweeping her away.

He hummed with satisfaction at her movement and the vibrations of his noise fused deep into her. His tongue followed. Down it brushed, and then into her wetness it speared—but his tongue was not enough. Not when it came to there. She gasped. "More. Please."

One hand slipped free from her thigh, and a finger teased her entrance as his mouth enveloped her clit once more, lapping there as that finger stroked her, before sliding home. A second joined it, relieving some of the pressure building in her and Harper shuddered as the throbbing rhythm within her crescendoed to a point of unbearable pleasure. He curled his fingers inside her, brushing a spot that sent her to oblivion.

She shattered upon his tongue. Over the edge she

plunged with a cry as he wrung her climax from her with every sweep of his hot tongue through her wetness and every pump of his fingers within her, curling them to hit that white-hot point inside that made her see stars.

It was not enough—still not enough. She needed more. She needed him. Harper pulled him up and he came, crawling onto the bed to hover over her. She kissed him fiercely, tasting herself upon his lips as the waves of her climax faded. Her thighs spread wide around him, Dimitrius settled between them, and she rolled her hips up to welcome him, melting anew as his hard length pressed against her soft, wet core that still ached for him.

"Mmm." He bit down on a moan, and his eyes were narrow slits as they devoured her. "Still eager for more, huntress? Did I not sate you?"

She sent him a wicked glare of her own, a playful spark dancing through her. "Oh, you did—but I'm not done yet." The need broke through her voice. "I want you. All of you."

His throat bobbed. "Are you sure you want this, Harper? Because there's no going back. Once we do this—you're *mine*, and I'm never letting you go."

She reached down between them and took his thick cock into her hand, her lips curling at the soft velvet feel of his shaft in her palm. He stopped breathing and his attention tightened upon her—the whole world fell away when he speared her in his gaze like that. She rolled her hips against him, feeling that slick, wet tip brush against her so deliciously, but he locked himself, holding firm, so she could have no more of him than that.

"Harper," he breathed, the words rolling hot onto her mouth. "I'm warning you…"

She lifted her head and licked along the length of his jaw.

He shivered against her. "Dimitrius," she whispered into his ear. "You talk about claiming me—but I claim you. You're *mine*. Now give yourself to me and make me yours."

A carnal sound forced apart his lips and he closed the gap between them, lining up with her entrance and edging in just his tip. It was an agonising tease, the promise of more.

"Now. Please. I can't take it anymore," Harper said against his lips. Dimitri swallowed her cry as he slid home, seating himself within her as he took her mouth with a punishing kiss. Harper took a shuddering breath as she adjusted to the shocking pleasure of him inside her. Gloriously, perfectly stretched, he filled her all the way to the hilt and she clamped around him, soaking in the ripples of pleasure as his cock twitched inside her. With a shift of his body, he pushed in yet further, as far as he could, grazing her swollen clit as his body connected with hers.

"Mmmm." He gritted his teeth, pausing for a moment as he hung over her, his nose nuzzling hers. "You feel so good. I never imagined it could be like this."

She felt so sensitive, it was as though she could explode once again, and it took her breath away. She needed this as much as him. The distraction. The release. The all-consuming inferno. "More, Dimitrius. Don't stop."

"As you command." He slid out, and the absence was a hollow void within her—but only for a moment, for he slammed home once more, burying himself. His pace quickened, rolling and deep, each stroke thorough and stoking something rooted inside her that promised that blinding glory once more. This was no gentle fuck, every stroke and every fierce kiss filled with desperation, urgency, and passion.

Dimitri thrust in and out, hitting that deep, primal spot

inside her with every pump as they fully coupled. His mouth found hers again, his tongue seeking as one hand pinned her wrists above her head. The other gripped her throat, softening to caress it and slide down to her breast to squeeze and roll her nipple between his fingers, making her gasp into his mouth. He sunk to his elbows, bracing on either side of her head as their kisses became sloppier, their breathing harder. The distance between them vanished, until they were so close she could feel the pound of his heart rattling through her chest as that glorious inferno rose again.

"I can't last much longer," he grunted. "Gods be damned, you are perfection."

"Good," she gasped. She could hardly breathe. He plunged into her again and again, and that white-hot obliteration threatened, the intense wave building inside her, on the cusp of sweeping her away. She gave herself to it gladly. "Come with me."

On the next thrust, Harper shattered again. She locked her legs around him and pulled him closer, calling his name as the world disappeared. Dimitrius groaned and stiffened as she broke on his cock, tightening and spasming around him —and he followed her over the edge with one last thrust, powerful and deep, as his own release found him and he gushed his seed into her. His strokes slowed as he buried his face into the crook of her neck, eventually stilling, but still fused with her body.

They remained like that, breathing heavily, their slick chests sliding together and with him still buried within her for a long moment. Harper's eyes slid closed as he placed tender kisses where he rested against her neck, revelling in the hazy after-effect of her climax, and relishing in the settled warmth of him on top and inside her. In that moment, there were no regrets or misgivings over what they had just done—only a deep, certain satisfaction.

But, they could not remain like that forever. The cold of the world crept in around the edges of that warm cocoon. Dimitri slowly pulled out and she sighed at the loss of him as his length vanished and slickness from their mingled pleasure slid down her thighs. It felt *glorious*, and she wanted more.

"You are extraordinary," he murmured, caressing her jaw with a knuckle. His eyes were bright with wonder as he regarded her. He leaned in to kiss her once more—so softly this time, it seemed as though it was someone else entirely. "If I die tonight, I shall go to my doom happy."

Bitterness crept around her edges. "Don't say things like that," she whispered, sitting up. "Why would you say that?"

His expression clouded, and he pushed back from the bed and stood. He did not answer for a long moment as he retreated and donned his trousers.

Unease curled, tainting the afterglow. She felt suddenly exposed. "Dimitrius?"

"I think you know me well enough to call me Dimitri now, princess," he said with half a smirk, but she saw at once it was one of his masks.

"Don't do that. What aren't you telling me?" She stood too, crossing her arms across her bare stomach.

His gaze flicked to the pile of fabric. "He's back," he admitted.

The white-hot fear that shot through her at his admission burned away the last embers of pleasure.

"He summons us both to attend to him."

"When?"

Dimitri had the good grace to drop his gaze. "Since we have made other use of our time... Now."

The walls closed in. Harper could not breathe. She sank onto the bed again. She could not bear to face Saradon—not again—and the walls closed in as her breath stalled for an entirely different reason. Any sanctuary she had found in those snatched moments with Dimitri was destroyed in the face of the truth. She was at Saradon's mercy. And she could not save herself from him.

6 8

HARPER

Her body carried a multitude of delicious aches from what they had just done—sweetest of all that lingering satisfaction simmering in her core. What *had* they just done? She reeled from it—the utter recklessness of what she had invited. Dimitri was right. There was no going back from this. She had fucked Dimitrius—spymaster, traitor, duplicity incarnate—however much he felt none of those things to her. But that did not mean she felt ready to face the consequences of her choices as they slammed her in the chest with full force. He took a daily preventative tonic—there would be nothing born of their union. But that did not relieve her, not with the magnitude of their choice. Now she was glad there were no mirrors in this suite. She wouldn't have to look herself in the eye.

Dimitri hovered, twitching with impatience between the living and dining areas as Harper dressed in the bedroom. He had filled the armoire in her room with elegant dresses from the elven court of Tournai—the bundle of shimmering

383

and sheer fabrics he had brought and dumped on the chair. Whose dresses she wore, she had no idea, but he told her, with no give in his voice, that Saradon had decreed she dress as befit her rank.

"I still prefer breeches!" she called to him, wriggling into a dress. "You have no idea how cold my legs get flapping around under these ridiculous skirts! It's winter!"

"You never know. I might," he called, a smile in his voice. "I might suit a dress, you know."

She snorted. "I'd pay to see that."

"I'll dress up—or down—any time for you, princess," he oozed in a sultry tone. It seemed his cocky, arrogant mask was back. Harper tutted. At least it meant he had recovered some of his spirit and resilience—and it helped keep the emotions simmering inside her at bay. She could fall back on bickering too.

"This... is... ridiculous!" she huffed, trying to pull the sleeves and neckline up far enough so she could button the back. "Argh! I can't get into this damned thing."

"You chose one that fastened in the back, didn't you? You do know they're the hardest ones to get into. You probably need a maid for that." She could practically hear his eye roll.

"Well, how would *I* know? I don't wear these blasted things. You ought not to have brought it!"

"Well, how would I know?" he mimicked her. "I don't know the first thing about dresses."

"Clearly you do..."

"I suppose. I'm an expert in taking dresses off, though, not putting them on. I'm *very* good at taking that style off." She could see his wolfish smile in her mind.

"Lech," she called, hating the jealous roar, hot and angry, that raged through her. He was an expert at taking off dresses, was he? She bit down on the questions that longed to unleash from her tongue. It was none of her damn business. She didn't even want to know. She didn't care. Harper shoved aside the lies to herself and pushed that frustration into the dress.

"I'll be whatever you want me to be."

Harper scrabbled at the buttons again and swore. "I can't get them. I have to change."

"We don't have time." The smile faded from his voice. "He's ordered us to be there presently. If we're late… Well, he does not wish for today's entertainment to start without you, he said."

Harper stilled. Her own amusement drained as reality seeped in. They were not in the elven court of Tournai, at Dimitri's apartments, relatively free. They were in the heart of the mountain at Afnirheim, captives of Saradon, with no chance of escape.

"Are you decent?" he asked. "Nothing on show you don't want me to see?"

Harper snorted. "After what we just did? Modesty would be hypocritical."

Dimitri strode in, a hand shading his eyes. "Turn around, back facing me. I'll do it."

"Oh, give over."

He lowered his hand and threw her a wicked smile. "Certainly, if it means I get to devour you—visually, of course."

She slapped his chest half-heartedly. "I think I'll find a way to manage without you, on second thoughts. Go away."

"You want to go out there half-dressed? I think not. I'm your only option—lucky me. Turn around."

She stuck out her tongue, but did as he asked, clutching the dress to her chest as the back gaped open. "I… Well… Hurry up then. D-don't touch me." Again. She did not have the self-control for that. Her cheeks burned and she angled her face away, not wanting him to see if her cheeks had reddened, betraying her.

Dimitri snorted and lowered his hand. "That's a little difficult, but I'll do my best. Do you know, the blush on your cheeks when you're embarrassed is adorable."

She whirled on him and froze as his hands caught in the fabric and threatened to tug it aside with the force of her movement.

"Careful, princess," he teased. "Else I'll be showing you just how well I can undress you—*again*."

Her belly swirled at the dark promise in his voice. Wrath spiked. Wrath at herself, at how good that little coil inside her felt. The worst thing was that she wanted him to make good on that promise and undress her—and make the world and all its dangers disappear for a few more blessed moments coupled with him.

She stepped closer, her hands crossed over her chest to hold up the dress. So close that with a heaving breath, she would press against his smart jacket. And how she hated herself as much as him for wanting it for real. Even if it was to pretend of an escape for a few scavenged minutes. Harper glared up at him, her smile all teeth. "Try it. I dare you. And see which part of you I skin first."

He laughed with delight. "Oh, I do so like your bite, huntress. But beware—you might know how to skin a rabbit. But I, darling, am a *wolf*." The smile he returned was all teeth too—but not the stinging bite of hers, the promise of something far more dark and sensual.

And with that, he dared to grasp her waist in those big, warm hands of his, and spin her on the spot until her back pressed against him. She stiffened. His head lowered, and she stifled a groan at the feel of his breath upon her ear, and then the slightest graze of his lips as he opened them to speak.

Harper squeezed her eyes shut, glad he could not see her face. Glad he could not know how much his touch and that promise of something *more* between them ignited something inside her she did not dare to face.

"Now, huntress, are you *quite* ready?"

A little sound escaped her, and her cheeks *burned* with the shame of it, as he squeezed her waist ever so slightly and then stepped back.

A soft chuckle emerged behind her.

Gods, she wanted to stab him. Stab him good and hard for making her feel this way in the middle of the maelstrom of *everything*.

Harper did not dare speak. She could not. She straightened, forcing her breath to even out, cursing the warmth flaring low in her belly, and bared her back to him wordlessly.

Dimitrius took that for permission. His fingers were silk at the base of her spine as he captured the fine fabric. With every touch, her skin pebbled as he gingerly lifted each button and loop, pulling the dress across her skin as he fastened each one by one from the base of her back to the crest of her shoulder blades. When he was done, he smoothed the fabric across her shoulders and down her back with a whispering touch, then stepped away, at last ceasing the sweet agony of temptation.

"There. All done." He sounded… regretful.

Harper released her breath and filled her voice with cold indifference, the only weapon she had, drenching the fire within her that longed to rip it all off and succumb to temptation. But she could not hide any longer. Not if Saradon summoned them. "Thank you. This will do, I suppose."

The rich, mid-blue fabric complimented her pale skin, and the light embellishments of silver threads at the neckline, wrists, and hem were muted enough to not draw atten-tion to her. It was a pretty dress, sitting just off her shoulders and sweeping down from her waist, over her hips to tumble to the floor, but it belonged on someone else. An elven lady, not a glorified pauper.

"Stop worrying. You look perfectly presentable. If I may?" He gathered up her hair, tucked each side behind her ears, and arranged the rest in a cascade down her back. "I ought to have brought some hair adornments, but alas, it will be fit enough for now."

Standing beside her in a suit of the darkest blue that was almost black, they looked a fitting couple... in any other scenario. *Anywhere but here*, Harper thought. She would stand beside him in Tournai thusly, if it meant she was free. She swallowed.

He smiled at her, but his eyes creased with worry as his smile faded. Despite his neat presentation, she had noticed the developing dark hollows under his eyes. *He looks like he is in mourning*. Perhaps he was. There was much lost, and much left to lose.

"He's waiting. Let's go." Dimitri offered her his arm, but Harper strode past him, back straight, kicking away the folds of the dress with every step.

She shivered at the frigid air that rushed around her legs, but she needed it too. Needed to put some distance between them, because she could not face up to the things he made her feel. Needed it to quench that heat rising within her and to ground herself in fear once more—because fear would keep her alive.

HARPER

They convened in the jarlshalle once more. Dim faelights gave no hint as to the time of day. Under the mountain, day was night and night was day in the everlasting gloom. Harper despised it. Despite the vastness of the space, there was a terrible sense of claustrophobia at not being able to see the sky and have the wind upon her skin.

She drew closer to Dimitri as they entered, though she still did not take his arm until they reached the dais, where the steps were too large to clamber up without tripping on the folds of her skirt. They bowed before Saradon—a flicker of displeasure showing on his face when Harper did not curtsy—before they advanced. Dimitri helped her up to her seat, the small throne beside Saradon's, bowing as he placed her hand in her lap. He turned away, face blank, to survey the empty hall, before retreating to stand beside her throne.

"When we relocate to Tournai, I will see that you are educated in etiquette and all things you shall require as my heir, daughter." Saradon frowned at her before casting his attention upon Dimitri.

"I am pleased with your progress in Tournai, Lord Ellarian. I took the opportunity to visit this night hence, and I am most encouraged. Rioting has once again commenced in the streets, and the Winged Kingsguard look harried and are too few to hold back the tide." He grinned menacingly.

Dimitri bowed his head. "I am pleased to hear it, Lord Ravakian. We are ready to move when you give the command. The general will swear in as regent any day now, and my allies are poised to overthrow his rule before it begins. The common people will rise to any banner that promises them what they desire—fairness, prosperity, security—revenge." His voice held no emotion. Harper turned over his words in her mind.

"Excellent. I shall offer them all, and more besides."

Dimitri bowed again and took a seat below the dais on the side of the hall. Saradon clapped once. At his unspoken demand, Harper looked up. It was as though a leash tugged her mind and body into place every time she thought or moved to defy him. Harper's heart sank as the great doors swung open and Saradon's latest sport was dragged in.

She did not want to look. Not as they dragged Aedon in by his bound legs, trailing his torso and head across the floor with no consideration for injury. Not as they scurried back at Saradon's command, kicking and clawing at Aedon as they retreated with his bindings and left him prone upon the floor. It was Aedon's turn to answer his summons. Saradon seemed determined to take his pound of flesh from Aedon for the death of his granddaughter, Harper's mother, Ilrune, for when he ordered Aedon to stand, Harper could not hold in a gasp of shock.

When he gradually pushed himself to his hands and

knees, Harper could see he wore only the remains of a shirt, but he was so blackened with dirt, blood, and bruises that she had not realised it at first. His trousers were ripped and tattered, the fabric trailing below his knees, and his feet were bare—and blue with cold. He slowly forced himself to his feet, with obvious pain in his shaking limbs. Shoulders slumped, he glared at Saradon defiantly, refusing to lower his gaze.

"Would that I could exact punishment upon your brother, but you shall do in his stead, whilst he is more useful to us elsewhere," Saradon said, his lip curling.

"My brother would have nothing to do with scum like you." Aedon's vehement hatred spilled to Dimitri as his glare flicked between the two males before him.

Saradon laughed. "So you say, yet he acts for me, whether he knows it or not. As I said, you will suffice. Besides which, you are his predecessor. What heinous acts have you committed, I wonder?"

Aedon's gaze dropped and he glared at the floor. Saradon stared at him in silence, and Aedon's jaw clenched. Harper realised Saradon invaded his mind—or tried to. After a moment, Saradon straightened and scowled.

"You would do well to not be so rude. I can make your suffering far worse, elf."

"You have no business prying into my affairs, half-breed," Aedon hissed at Saradon.

Harper gasped. Never had she known him to be so cruel. At the escape of air from her lips, Aedon finally saw her. His face paled as he stared at her in a daze, as though he had seen a ghost. Then his eyes slid away, like he had never seen her. *He tries to protect us both.* She wished she could protect him. After seeing Brand's and Erika's cruel treatment at Saradon's hands, she held no hope that Aedon would not suffer the same, or worse, for his brother's crimes.

Saradon advanced upon him, seeming not to have noticed Aedon's attention wavering. "I will not be called such by the likes of *you*." Black fire crackled from him, racing toward Aedon. Harper leaned forward, but Saradon's leash tugged her back. Aedon cried out as the inferno engulfed him.

70

HARPER

As the fire dissipated, Aedon stood, blackened but alive. Harper sagged with relief, though her heart still raced and she felt light headed, her breath frozen in her chest alongside the cry that longed to burst free.

Aedon laughed, baring his teeth in a defiant grin. "Your half-breed magic is nothing against dragon-blessed power!"

Saradon sent an even bigger blast in answer. Aedon howled from the midst of it. Harper tried to reach into her own well of magic to send any help his way, but it was trapped behind an impenetrable barrier. She cursed silently, jerking against the invisible bonds that held her, to no avail, whilst Aedon's own orange flames licked at the edges of Saradon's black fire, tearing it to shreds. Smoke rolled across them all, sending Harper and Dimitri into fits of coughing.

When the blaze cleared, Aedon was on his knees, breathing heavily, but still glaring defiantly at Saradon. The attack had taken much from him. Despite that, Harper knew he would not submit. "Is that your best, half-breed? No wonder they put you and all your kind down." Aedon bared his teeth in a feral snarl.

"Don't goad him, Aedon!" Harper cried without thinking.

Saradon turned to her, his eyes narrowed, before turning back to his prisoner. "Yes, *Aedon*, don't goad me. You have no idea who you deal with." His voice took on a dark tone, crackling like dark fire and lightning. Shivers crawled across Harper's skin as she realised the voice was not his own. From Erendriel's warning, she had an inkling whom the voice truly belonged to, but she dared not think what that meant.

Aedon ignored him, glaring at Harper with open worry. "Are you all right? Has he hurt you?"

She shook her head, not daring to speak again. His brows creased as he stared at her. She guessed what he wished to say. *Run. Flee.* And how impossible that was for both of them. Saradon stood between them, cutting off her view of him. "She is mine now, elf."

"She will never be yours, half-breed. Let her go. She is nobody and nothing to you in this fight."

"You know as well as I that is not true, elf, don't you?" She heard the dark smile upon Saradon's voice, which added to her heightened anxiety. "You know she is my true heir, and the machinations of fate have returned her to my side at the most opportune moment."

"You will never control her," Aedon spat.

Saradon only laughed and turned to Harper with a cruel smile. "Oh, elf. You have no idea indeed. She bound herself to me," he said gleefully. "*Willingly.*" He savoured every syllable, circling the fallen elf, whose limbs trembled from exhaustion.

"That's not true."

"I will show you, if you do not believe me. I will enjoy seeing your reaction."

"You lie."

"I will prove it."

Saradon snapped his fingers. His will tugged Harper from her throne, forcing her to stand rigidly, and glide down the steps to Dimitri. To her horror, and his surprise, she slid into his lap with feline grace. Her muscles strained in resistance, but her body moved of its own accord with no hesitation. Did Saradon know what they had just done? Or did he just taunt them with the complete control he had over the pair of them?

She sank into Dimitri's lap and leaned against his chest. She heard his breath catch, but instinctively, Dimitri's arms slid around her, cradling her waist and holding her legs so she did not fall off. The touch was light, formal, as though he only endured it, like she. But she felt the reassuring squeeze on her waist, light and gone in an instance.

It felt *wrong*. So wrong, this forced contact, a violation of the willing intimacy they had just shared, and the connection growing between them. This was a mockery of that, one that made nausea swim in her belly and revulsion crawl under her skin with every touch.

Harper met Aedon's gaze with hers, imploring him to understand her foolishness. That she had not given herself to his cause willingly, like he suggested, but had sacrificed her freedom to save their friends, however misguidedly. But Aedon could not hear her thoughts behind the impenetrable barrier he had constructed around his own mind to stave off Saradon's attacks.

Saradon was not done. At his command, she tilted her head back and leaned it onto Dimitri's shoulder. At his next unspoken bidding, Dimitri dipped his head to kiss her neck. Her skin shivered at the touch of his soft lips upon her, but this did not spark desire, knowing how his lips could undo her. This ignited revulsion and fear at the control Saradon had over them both. It was an abhorrence that could not have been more opposite to the intimacy they had begun to share.

"Stop it," Aedon growled. "You know she does not wish for that. Get the bastard away from her, *now*." Harper felt Dimitri stiffen underneath her at that, and her heart caved in for him. But Aedon's command held no weight. Saradon knew it as well as he, as well as them all.

Harper's hands slid around Dimitri's neck. One idly toyed with the hair at his nape, while the other cupped his cheek and brought his mouth to hers. Tears of fury and shame slipped from her eyes as Dimitri met her gaze and kissed her. Her core shrank away, her whole body wanting to close with this violation, and his eyes burned with the same feeling of helpless rage and shame. This was nothing intimate. A press of one set of lips against another. Nothing more. Just what they needed to do to act the part—and survive.

She knew he had to appear neutral, impassive, but his eyes, still locked with hers, filled with an intensity she could not translate. She wished she could understand what it was he thought and felt, what he was trying to tell her, but their mental communication had been severed by Saradon's control, and she knew he would not dare reach out to her then. His body was stiff against her, softening for only a moment into her lips—perhaps the only solidarity he could offer her—before he pulled away. He resumed staring into the distance, as though nothing had happened—but unseen by Saradon, his thumb stroked the small of her back in silent reassurance.

At last, Saradon's leash retreated, and Harper slid from Dimitri's lap. She threw herself away from him with all the force she could muster, snapping free of Saradon's command for a moment, catching him by surprise. She tumbled to the hard stone and landed on her hands and knees with a crash that winded her, her body jarring from the impact. Dimitri leapt to her aid, helping her to her feet. His iron grip on her wrists was an unspoken warning not to be so foolish before he let her go and retreated a pace to stand behind her.

"I hope you feel ashamed of yourself, bastard," Aedon cursed at him. "Do you feel good taking advantage like that?"

Dimitri gazed at him impassively.

Aedon spat onto the floor, a red globule of blood.

"If you are so willing to help me, daughter," Saradon crooned, "join me. I insist."

Harper walked toward him, rebelling against every step he made her take, until she stood before him. His finger lifted her chin so that she met his gaze—her stony rebellion against his cold ire.

He leaned close, so only she could hear, his hot breath fanning against her cheek. "If you decide to be so foolish again, I will only punish you all the more."

He pressed his knife into her hand, the blade a cruel and dark river of black steel. He stepped back. To her horror, she brought it to her own throat, tracing her skin with the cold edge of the blade, teasing it with the sharp point until he forced her to dig a little too deeply and pierce the skin. A droplet of blood ran down her neck, warm and prickling. She stood frozen, no longer rebelling against him. Her eyes met Aedon's, whose face mirrored her own horror. She saw the same terror within him. Harper did not dare move, lest that blade slip and cut her own throat. Her hand trembled.

71

HARPER

Saradon laughed and cast his attention to Aedon. "As you see, she will do as I bid. She will act how I instruct her, even if I command her to take her own life." He grinned at Dimitri, who smiled, a thin-lipped grimace that did not reach his eyes. The best he could attempt at sycophancy. Dimitri's attention did not leave Harper's—but she could not read beneath the stern mask he wore.

"I can even ask her to take *your* life. Oh, I am so tempted," Saradon murmured to Aedon.

With an unspoken order, Harper moved to Aedon. Her hand found his, pulling him to his feet. She tried to warn him, her eyes widening even more, that she did not act of her own volition. Only the tears streaming down her face were hers to control. She saw the moment Aedon realised—when the cold steel touched his blackened and bruised bare chest. Aedon's green eyes flickered to it before returning to hers, capturing her attention. They had never looked more serious. The light and sparkle of his laughing gaze was gone. Now his eyes were the colour of the brooding winter forest. Hard and cold. Not toward her, she realised, but toward the fate that might be his at her hands.

"You don't have to do this," he said in a voice so quiet that she thought she imagined it.

"I cannot defy him," she breathed back. Not in any meaningful way. With all her might, she uncurled her fingers, one by one, from the dagger. It clanged to the floor between them.

Saradon barked with laughter at her defiance, then yanked her leash tighter, forcing her to stoop and pick it up. This time, he made her press the point into Aedon's chest.

I'm sorry, she tried to tell him as the tip nicked his skin, but her mouth was not her own, and not a sound emerged except a whispered breath. He grimaced and pain flashed through his eyes before he masked it, gazing at her calmly and reassuringly. He flinched as she pressed harder. Yet Aedon did not push her away, did not blast her with his magic. Her heart hurt so much she would have screamed if her mouth were hers to command. *He will not defend himself no matter what I do?*

The dagger carved into his chest in a slow, lazy circle. Aedon's jaw clenched. He shook with the effort of keeping in the pain, not letting it show to Saradon, who watched keenly, nor Dimitri, who lurked behind them all, yet could not stop watching, pacing like a caged beast. "I forgive you," he forced out between flinching. "I know it is not you who acts."

I'm sorry, she managed to mouth. His words did not alleviate her guilt. This was all her fault. If she had been less foolish…

"*You are not bound to him as fully as you think you are,*"

Aedon hissed, breaking into her mind. *"Your blood binds you to him, it is true, and you gave your word, of a sort, but in that ambiguity you can find escape."*

"What do you mean?" she dared to ask, even as her hand pulled back the dagger to start a new line, a wave across his chest.

He grimaced in pain. *"Your magic is yours, and no one can ever truly control that but you, Harper. Think on it. You harness that which the world gives you. It does not come from within you, and thus, no one can shackle that."*

Gratitude welled within her at his solid friendship, his faith in her, though she wondered at his words. Was there a part of her that was free from Saradon? She had managed to throw off his control before, if only fleetingly. Could she escape his thrall completely somehow?

Before her, Aedon sagged in pain, but Saradon's magic held him aloft. Horrified, Harper realised what she had done. She stepped back, even before she realised she could move, and her hand, which had clutched the dagger tightly, loosened on the handle, almost throwing it away before she halted herself.

Saradon momentarily lapsed in his control of her as he admired her handiwork. She had carved his own mark, the Riven Circle, upon Aedon's once beautiful, bare chest. With a rush of grief and anger, her magic rushed up within her, raging to burst forth. In a chink of clarity, she touched Dimitri's mind, and he opened his walls to let her in. She communicated her thoughts in an instant. Dimitri rushed into her mind then, protectively encasing it in his own adamant wall against Saradon's control. It would not last long, but she hoped it would be enough.

"Go!" she screamed into Aedon's mind with every fibre of her being. Aedon's eyes widened—but he acted at once. He

blazed with magic, despite his broken body and tired heart, the dragonfire still slumbering deep within him.

Harper launched the dagger at Saradon. Caught entirely by surprise, he did not have time to move before it buried itself in his side. Yet, Saradon was far more powerful than all of them combined. As Aedon ran to the doors, blazing fire at any goblins in his way, Saradon pulled the dagger from his flesh, like a knife from butter. He would heal himself in a moment, Harper knew, but she hoped it would be distraction enough.

Valxiron's darkness grew as Saradon channelled his master's power to him. The true brunt of it took Harper's breath away. She was lighter and more inconsequential than a feather, pummelled by a storm of storms as he turned on her, rage visible in every line upon his snarling face. The hall doors slammed open—but this was not Saradon's doing. Aedon bolted for them immediately. Harper's heart stumbled and fear flooded her veins as a tide of goblins swept in. The goblins overran the hall as Aedon fled, but their shrieks were of fear, not predatory glee, and Saradon whirled to them as the *pascha* himself barrelled in amongst them.

"The dwarves are here!" Dimitri said into Harper's mind, his tone high with shock. *"Come. This may be our only chance!"* With that, he leapt to her side and grabbed her around the waist, disappearing into the ether as he spirited them away. Seconds later, they came upon Aedon. Dimitri grabbed the elf—who protested vociferously—by his arm, then once more took them into the nothingness.

A breath later, he set them down in a quiet hall. They heard the din not far away. When Dimitri grimaced, Harper knew why—because she felt it too, like a tug around her navel. His arm around her relaxed, then stiffened again. Saradon summoned them, as he did all those in his control. It was a summons they could not resist. The goblin horde would hurry to do his bidding, to meet the tide of dwarves flooding their ancestral home, determined to take it back. She hoped they would number enough, but against Saradon, who could triumph? Despair filled her.

"Go," Dimitri snarled at Aedon. "Get out of here."

"I'm not leaving without her. Harper, come with me!" Aedon reached for her. She saw exhaustion in him before, but only determination and desperation fuelled him now. She longed for nothing more than to go to him. For him to take her away from dark and brutal Afnirheim, for a breath of fresh air, a fine meal, and the company of friends whom she had taken for granted and now missed.

Tears pricked her eyes as she realised it would not—could not—be so. She stepped back, further into Dimitri's arm. "I cannot go. He calls for us. My very bones ache to go to him," she admitted. Shivers racked her, but not just from cold. From resisting his order that called for her body to leave at once.

Aedon gaped and glanced between them.

Dimitri's visage was serious yet tinged with sadness. "Aedon, I know you bear me much enmity. We cannot leave. I will protect her—I *promise*." He grimaced as the summons came again, stronger, and Harper blanched, too. He looked at her, and she met his gaze. "Come," he said softly to her. "The sooner we heed, the less the punishment will be."

"No!" Aedon leapt forward to grasp Harper's wrist, trying to tug her away from Dimitri.

But she pulled herself free, curling away from Aedon— and stepping backwards, into Dimitri's chest. He curled an arm around her—and the relief of the security she found in his arms was overwhelming for a second. With him at her side, she did not feel consumed by the dread that prickled in her belly. The blood drained from Aedon's face.

"Aedon, I cannot. Please, trust me. You must leave before the opportunity wastes. They are coming." Already, she could hear their infernal shrieks as they scrabbled up through the halls, even as the other end of the vast space started to fill with dwarves forming ranks to sweep through the city.

"Take Brand and Erika if you can." She sent him a flood of memories of their maltreatment at the goblins' hands.

He paled at the sight, then growled at her with a grimace. "Damn it!" They all knew none of them had any choice. "We will return for you. I swear it!"

"Go," she urged him again. "I am Saradon's blood. He will not harm me. I am safe, for now." She said it with far more confidence than she felt. But if it meant her friends were saved, her remaining was a small price to pay. She would remain—so they had a chance at freedom. She could not think what that would mean. She had seen her friends suffer most terribly at Saradon's hands. Could she endure the same? It was too terrifying to imagine what her punishment might be if she could turn his ire at their escape onto herself. *You must*, she urged herself. *Be brave.* They had had no choice but to suffer it. Ragnar, Brand, Erika, Aedon… They had all suffered at Saradon's hands. She had escaped lightly thus far. If that was the price she must pay to save them, then so be it.

Aedon glanced at the dwarven ranks, but instead of escaping that way, he dove straight for the heart of the goblins now pouring into the far end of the hall, blasting them out of his way as he disappeared into their midst and the dark caverns beyond.

"I must help them," Harper moaned to Dimitri, threading a hand through her hair in anguish, but his grip stopped her.

"You cannot. We must go. *Now*. Can you not feel his anger?" For the first time, Dimitri sounded fearful.

Harper sagged in his arms and turned to him. Her voice muffled as she spoke into his chest. "If I had not given him my word, my bond, this never would have happened. My friends would have been safe from him. From me." Harper balled her hands into fists until her fingernails dug into the skin of her palm painfully—but she did not stop. She deserved the pain. His arms tightened around her with wordless reassurance.

"Saradon would have taken it anyway," said Dimitri harshly. "He used his sway with the goblins to keep the *pascha* and his scourge in his thrall. I will do my best within my orders to help your friends, Harper, but I can make no promises. I am bound to do what he asks of me." Dimitri gritted his teeth.

The din rose around them as the dwarves charged from their end of the hall toward the rabble of goblins at the other. In the centre of the area, the noise was overwhelming, as overwhelming as the call to Saradon's side. Dimitri looked between the opposing forces to either side of them, clutched Harper close, and fled into the shadows, racing back to Saradon's side.

He was not far behind the goblin scourge. His magic filled the hall with charged crackling as he smote left and right, sending blasts into dwarven ranks and scattering them, leaving bodies in his wake. The goblins rushed forward, taking advantage of their foes' disarray.

Dimitri and Harper materialised before Saradon, whose scowl deepened. "Where have you been?" he snarled.

"I only sought to keep her away from the goblins," Dimitri said at once, but Saradon cut him off.

"I expect better from you, Lord Ellarian. Go forth and make sure my work is done. Kill them all!"

Dimitri bowed and vanished once more. The last thing to disappear was his reassuring hand on Harper's own. Harper quailed, her own power and defiance a tiny light against the dark of night that threatened to extinguish her.

"I will deal with you later," Saradon said threateningly. He extended a clawed hand toward her. Pain racked her body—and oblivion claimed her.

72

AEDON

Aedon limped into the depths of Afnirheim to where they had been imprisoned, where he hoped Brand and Erika still were. He was emotionally numb after the whirlwind of events—his torture at Harper's hands, her position in Saradon's captivity, the spymaster. He grimaced. A part of him relished the numbness, because he knew he would be overcome when it hit him, and he had to escape first.

Not for the first time, Aedon did not understand Dimitrius's motivations, or machinations, but Dimitrius had promised to keep Harper safe. The sincerity in Dimitrius's voice had given Aedon pause for thought—that there was more to this than the spymaster's plotting. It was Dimitrius he would hold accountable if any harm befell Harper. But there was no time to think on it. Aedon pushed the thoughts from his mind, focusing on not getting lost in the maze of tunnels down into the depths of the fallen dwarven city.

Aedon pleaded with the silent heavens for the dwarven reinforcements to buy them enough time. He was certain this would be their only chance. It was that or death. He had so much to live for and did not want to meet his end in dark caverns devoid of hope and life, far from the green woods and the open sky. It gave him renewed vigour and strength to run, despite his limp, for remaining would only bring doom on them all. He only hoped Harper would remain safe until they could manage her rescue, too.

Nothing could stand before Aedon's burning drive to leave. He blasted goblins, sending them crashing into the walls to fall upon the floor, still and prone. If nothing else, with the remnant of her fire, he could pretend Valyrea fought beside him once more. The thought of her gave him courage to defy the ordinary and manage the impossible. *You are the Thief of Pelenor*, Aedon reminded himself. He could escape from anywhere.

When he broke through the stone doors and into the lightless, airless prison, Brand and Erika greeted him with moans of relief. They emerged into the dim light on shaking limbs, as battered and bruised as he. Aedon grimaced when he saw them, a mixture of pity and anger consuming him at their state, but he did not have time to be righteous about it. "Come. There's a window of opportunity. We must go!"

"What of Harper?" Brand asked as he loped through the corridors beside Aedon, his face set in a permanent grimace of pain.

"There's no time. I'll explain when we get out. We'll come back for her. Trust me," Aedon implored. Brand nodded, his calculating gaze evaluating Aedon's unusual seriousness. Erika was in a better state than Brand, but Aedon sent what energy he thought he could spare to them both. It would not do for any of them to falter. They took any weapons they could from the corpses of goblins they passed. Brand lamented the loss of his giant blade, and Erika her two swords, but their loss would be a small price to pay for escape.

The three cut down any before them, lifted by their success, until they turned a corner and ran straight into a huge band of goblins. They scrambled backwards, bunching together as the horde turned upon them. Brand swore. There were far too many. *This is it*, Aedon realised with a sinking feeling that he pushed away. They stood no chance of survival or escape.

73

DIMITRI

Dimitri was grateful for Saradon's vague orders, for in their ambiguity, he had room for disobedience. "Kill them all." Dimitri grinned wolfishly. *He didn't say who.* He rushed through Afnirheim, obliterating any goblins he came upon with a wave of fury, but he found no solace in their deaths. Each extermination only fuelled the inferno burning within him. When would the damned scourge of creatures end? They seemed to pour from the very earth without pause, as if they spawned infinitely. Dimitri internally cursed Saradon for his foolish alliance as he smote another pack of goblins into oblivion before they realised he was there.

Up ahead, a huge rabble of them squawked and screeched, excited. *Who have they found to torture now?* Dimitri thought, disgusted. When he rounded the corner and perceived their prey, his snarl deepened. Brand, Erika, and Aedon were already backed into a corner, fruitlessly fending off the ever-boldening goblin attack. Dimitri's blast of magic sent goblins reeling, stunned, before they wheeled around, chattering with rage. At the sight of him, they cowed into submission as angry power roiled toward them.

"Run!" he commanded Aedon, who prodded a confused and suspicious Erika and Brand into action. They dashed through the deserted halls and out of sight.

At their victims' escape, the goblins let out a clamour once more, brandishing weapons and charging Dimitri. He curled his lip and sent out a giant blast of magic, bringing the tunnel down upon their heads in a cascade of thunderous noise and choking dust. Before the halls turned to silence, he was already gone—on to seek his next targets. One way or another, he would see the *pascha's* horde diminished.

74

AEDON

"There's no time for questions!" Aedon called to his companions as they straggled behind him. "Just trust me—and run!"

They dashed through the dark halls with the remaining dregs of their strength, up through the levels of Afnirheim, until the sounds of battle before them were deafening and growing by the second. Aedon changed direction at the last minute, circumventing the great space that had become a battlefield and treacherous sea of dead and dying, taking them higher to the galleried walkways. Shrieking and shouting behind them gave away their pursuers. Aedon chanced a glance back—too close for comfort.

He looked ahead once more. The stone doors at the other end of the bridge were too far away to reach. Natural light spilled in, calling them to freedom. Aedon dug deeper and sped up, though every muscle screamed. Behind him, Brand's thunderous steps quickened, too. Yet the goblins were faster, and before they made the door, Brand, Erika, and Aedon had to turn to meet the attack.

Their purloined weapons were paltry protection compared to those they had lost in the depths of the battle, but Brand and Erika were skilled enough fighters to turn any weapon to their advantage. Aedon was glad to stand with them as he brandished the broken blade he had taken. It was of dwarven forging but had been made less than noble by its goblin owners, who had replaced the handle with bone—whose, he did not care to wonder—and shattered the mighty blade so it was short and cruelly edged.

They spread out, three abreast across the walkway. Aedon darted forward, slicing through a goblin's arm and causing him to drop his trident with a shriek. His kin filled the gap, seemingly endless, as Aedon and his companions fought them off, all the while shuffling one step backward at a time to the door, and the possibility of safety. After a few minutes that seemed like an age to their faltering bodies, they passed under the great, stone arch. Before them, goblins trampled their fallen kin with no reverence, their sole attention on the three before them.

"We cannot make it," gasped Erika. "If we turn and run, we will be cut down where we stand. I will not die a coward's death with a blade in my back!"

"I will cover your exit. Go!" cried Brand, taking a huge, scything swing at the first of the goblins. It leapt out of the way of his blade—but the next one died where it stood.

"No!" said Aedon. "We leave together! Now!"

They launched one final assault to push the goblins back, then dashed through the open stone doors. As Erika and Aedon heaved upon them, closing them one painstaking inch at a time, Brand stood in the opening, pushing back the goblins, earning more injuries for his bravery.

At last, he leapt back and lent his strength to their efforts, shutting the doors with a boom. He wedged a broken length of wood in the place where the original bar, which was smashed and twisted upon the floor, ought to have gone, then bellowed for them to run. Run they did, up the huge flight of stairs that was wide enough for ten men to climb alongside, toward the faint light ahead that signalled the riven doors of Afnirheim, the outside, and their hope of escape.

Aedon's elven strength and Brand's Aerian power carried them up the stairs faster than Erika. All Aedon could hear was the pounding of his own heart and his ragged, tearing breath, as his feet pounded toward freedom—until the doors yielded behind them, splitting Brand's makeshift bar in half with a splintering crash, and the goblins surged through, faster than Aedon and his comrades could outpace them.

75

ERIKA

Erika turned. Her mouth fell open with dismay at the sight of the goblins pouring through the breach and up the staircase after them. She would not make it out. The realisation sent cold steel into her bones. She looked up at Brand and Aedon far above her. Brand's once beautiful wings were blackened and bloodied. Her heart ached fiercely that this would be the last time she saw him alive.

She let out a ragged sob of anger that it would end like this, in the dark halls, that her death would be at the hands of those who did not deserve it, but she refused to die a coward's death, straining to escape a fate that destiny crushed upon her. She turned and threw aside her blade, grabbing a dwarven double-headed axe that lay on the stairs. Other than a covering of gore and dirt, it seemed in perfect working order.

"I will kill you all in the next life!" she screamed and raised the axe before her as she met the bloodlust in their eyes with her own rage. The impact of her axe upon the first helm within reach fuelled her fire, and she screeched a battle cry that had them all clamouring to sing of death and blood. It deafened her, and her senses narrowed to only her sight and the feel of the wooden handle, smooth in her grip, as she swung the axe in a deadly dance.

But she was one against many, and they surrounded her in quick order. Those below her pulled and scrabbled at her ankles, until she could no longer kick them away. Their blades slashed at her limbs until with every spin of her axe, she trailed ribbons of blood, then that, too, was snatched from her grasp.

A great bellow sounded behind her, and the goblins were blasted back in a great ball of fire. To her left, Aedon, his face contorted in pain and anger, shot fireballs with every thrust of his clawed fist, and Brand cut down any before him with a long-bladed spear.

"You fools!" she shouted, though the clamour was too loud to hear her own voice.

Brand's feral grin and the spark in his eyes was enough answer. "We will not leave you to stand alone. We die together."

"I will see you in the next life." With that, she re-joined the fray.

The goblins suddenly shrieked and retreated down the stairs, just as a great shadow from above fell upon Erika and her companions. Dimitri's dark form appeared from the ether as they turned to face him.

Enemy or friend? Erika did not know, so she kept her guard raised, snatching up a new weapon in a moment of reprieve. It was a thick, short, dwarven sword, the type she hated to fight with, but it would take a life if she needed, even though the world spun, and she knew the last of her strength was fading. She would die with a weapon in hand—and no shame.

"You need to get out," Dimitri snarled. "I cannot keep them at bay forever." With every word, he sent blasts of power at the goblins behind them, sending them tumbling down the stairs in a heap. She did not understand. He was helping them? He raised his arms high and wide, bringing them down to the floor in his biggest blast yet. Dimitri wavered on his feet for a moment as his power reeled through her, stealing her breath.

The world shook as the staircase sheared off a dozen steps below them and crumbled into rubble, sending goblins tumbling into the depths of the great abyss. The door they had barred sheared in half and followed them into the darkness, as well as the bridge beyond it—showering those below with giant chunks of masonry that killed all they fell upon, as if the heavens smote them.

Aedon needed no more urging. He grabbed Erika's arm, tugging her after him. Her legs would not move. Instead, she tumbled forward, toward the abyss. Brand's giant arm caught her and their blood mingled, wet and sticky, as he pulled her close, sweeping her into his burly grasp and barrelling up the stairs. Each jolting step sent her further over the edge into darkness. Brand's jutting chin and curve of his wings loomed over her like a protective cave. Her fingers loosened. The sword fell from her grasp as she sighed and slipped away.

"Go!" Aedon urged Brand, who thundered up the stairs with Erika dangling in his arms, even as the remainder of the staircase shuddered beneath them, threatening to tumble them into the void.

Dimitrius stood before Aedon, blocking the way, with a hand raised to his chest. "Get out now, before it's too late. Take whoever you can with you. Warn the dwarven king. Do not return to Afnirheim. It is lost. Do you hear me?" He bent close, searching Aedon's gaze—breaching the distrust and hate Aedon lathered upon him. Aedon, taken aback by his vehement sincerity, nodded, speechless. "Tell them to make the rest of their kingdom strong. The *pascha* will come, and Saradon will aid him to take all of Valtivar. That is what will come to pass." He said it with such terrible certainty that it shook Aedon to his core.

"How do I know you speak the truth?"

Dimitrius shook his head, glaring at Aedon. "Do you not see?" He held his arms wide, gesturing around. "For fuck's sake, Aedon. This is about so much more than you or I now. Forget your petty hate. There is a *world* at stake. There is but the slimmest chance to stop him, if only we can figure it out. You managed to get the Dragonhearts once. Now we need them again. Erendriel herself calls Harper to a higher cause. This is greater than any of us. You must do what you can to help her stop him."

The staircase rumbled beneath them. Dimitrius grabbed Aedon by the arm, wrenching them both up the stairs as fast as they could go just as the rest crumbled into nothingness behind and beneath them. Dimitrius thrust them into the ether as the last of the bridge disappeared before they could reach safety, and Aedon's yelp was cut off as they reappeared, tumbling to the ground at the top of what was now a cliff before a yawning void in the mountain.

"H-How?" Aedon stammered, his face paling.

"There's no time. Go, *now*. Remember my warning. Swear you will pass it on. No more must die needlessly."

Aedon grabbed the front of Dimitrius's shirt, yanking him close as he took one last look at the broken mountain. "I will swear it only if you promise to keep her safe. Swear on your blood, your magic, your *life* that you will keep Harper from harm until we come for her."

Dimitrius met his hard gaze with a surprisingly sincere one. "I swear it once. I swear it twice. I swear it thrice," he said quietly. A slight breeze arose as the rush of magic swept around them, a bond of their word. For a moment, under-standing passed between them.

What is he playing at? Aedon wondered, not for the first time. For without Dimitrius, they would all have been dead. The mountain rumbled behind them with ominous warning. Aedon released his shirt just as Dimitrius pushed him away.

"I will see you soon." Dimitrius's words were a promise as he disappeared into the ether once more. With a last look at the dark mountain that seemed to shake with its own anger, Aedon turned and fled, following his friends from the bowels of the earth into the welcome touch of light and air.

77

DIMITRI

imitri watched Aedon go, wishing that he could leave, too—truly, without the leash of his master tugging him back. *You are a fool, Dimitri,* he berated himself. His eyes shut momentarily as he tried to swallow the guilt as best as he could once more, for it stabbed at him like a knife twisting in his gut. How many had already died because he had been foolish enough to raise Saradon? He could never undo that. Never make it right.

As he stood before the creaking, shattered gates of Afnirheim, watching a straggling line of dwarves flee—though he stood shrouded from them—his spirits sank. This was not what he had envisioned. A kingdom destroyed and overrun with barbaric creatures that had not one decent bone amongst them. Could he stop more dying if he stood against Saradon? Or had this grown so much bigger than him that that was a futile hope?

He had no idea if Aedon and his companions would survive their flight to Keldheim or another sanctuary, but his word to Harper was complete. He had helped them as best he

420

could. His conscience was clear on that matter. It was a small comfort in the face of such far-reaching horrors. He knew now with unshakeable certainty, that there was no room for cowardice—and he would rise to the challenge. Harper had given him the courage to do so, however hopeless it was to think he could stop this.

Slowly, Dimitri slunk back into the mountain, going the opposite way of the fleeing dwarves. Any goblins he met along the way, he killed to allow as many of the dwarves to escape as possible.

The end begins now. I started this... I must finish it.

78

AEDON

The refuge of Keldheim was a long-awaited relief. The silent halls were peaceful, the air clean, but it was still too dark for Aedon's liking. The giant faelight and scattering of lanterns could not replace the daytime sun, nor the wind upon his face. Korrin had granted them refuge, gladdened they had somehow survived, though filled with grief was he for the loss of so many of his kin in another fruitless mission to retake Afnirheim. The last for now, Aedon knew, for the dwarven forces were too spent to attempt a third. Winter would soon likely close any attempts to salvage the dwarven stronghold.

As much as relief filled Aedon at the prospect of his own safety, Brand's and Erika's trepidation matched his own. It had been a long time since they had felt so hopeless—and so helpless. They regrouped in the infirmary, where Brand and Erika rested near to each other in the now crowded space filled with as many beds as would fit, for the number of wounded was overwhelming and spilled out into the halls of the dwarven city.

The four—for Ragnar joined them, albeit on a crutch—sat in silence. They all knew. It was the calm before the storm. They had seen nothing of Saradon's—or Valxiron's—power yet. Inexorably, Saradon would come and do all in his power to lay waste to the lands and peoples before him. Do all in his power to stop the prophecy from coming to fruition.

What part would Harper play in it? None of them knew. None of them could know. Aedon's heart ached for the loss of her. *She gave herself so willingly for us.* That, above all else, proved their companionship. She truly had become one of their small family, their bond as deep as blood.

Her friendship had also brought him the peace he had sought over the years since Valyrea's death. Perhaps he could truly open up to her. *If we ever see her again*, his mind taunted. Somehow, just like the others, she helped heal him of a grief so old and deep, he never thought he would see the end of it. Now, he truly regretted being so casual and flippant with her own feelings. She had deserved better than that.

He winced, recalling how he had been so cold to her when all she had sought was some warmth and love. No more than she deserved after her own hardships and a life of cold loneliness. He chastised himself for not being as good a friend as he ought to have been—but she was alive, and there was hope to make amends. There could be no greater way to repent than to save her from the arms of their enemy.

Aedon watched as Brand slowly climbed from his bed to pour a goblet of water for himself and Erika. The Aerian's wings were a mass of bandages, and the rest of his body was patched with poultices over the various wounds and bruising he had suffered. Aedon hoped the Aerian would recover to his former strength. Erika was in an even worse state, her strength utterly spent and every limb in need of tending from the injuries she had sustained in their escape.

Brand hobbled to Erika's bed, lifted the goblet to her lips, and trickled it in, more tenderly than anyone would have thought possible of the huge warrior. She tilted her head up, taking the offering like a small, frail, helpless chick in the nest, all the while glaring at him fiercely. Aedon smiled, which deepened as Brand bowed to rest his forehead against Erika's. Both closed their eyes in unspoken solace.

Had he found redemption, too? Aedon wondered. Long had Brand carried the weight of Nyla's death upon his shoulders. The death of another was a heavy burden to carry. Aedon felt that only too well. Brand could never bring her back, as he well knew. Aedon wished his friend would stop blaming himself—and cutting himself off from love again. It was no betrayal to seek a second chance. Aedon had only just realised that himself, though too late to save any fragment of a relationship with any of his past courtships.

"You know, if you're going to be busy mooning over a girl, Aerian, you shall have no hope of winning *chatura* any time soon," Ragnar said, a hint of hoarseness still in his voice. He sidled up to Aedon and smiled warmly.

Aedon clasped his friend close in a one-armed hug, grinning. "Well met, my friend."

"Shut up, dwarf," growled Brand, then he kissed Erika upon the lips in front of any who watched.

Aedon laughed delightedly. "Oh, thank heavens! It's about time."

Brand grinned, his cheeks red at the unusual public display of affection. Erika's smile was hard but filled with her own brand of affection as her fingers laced through his.

As they talked into the night, Aedon found solace in his companions, until the healers sent him and Ragnar scurrying for fear of disturbing the other patients. Aedon missed Valyrea fiercely. It was an aching void that would never be filled. Something within him died with her that day. He wondered if he could ever truly love again, as more than a friend anyway, for none of his companions would become as close of a soul mate as his dragon had once been.

He had lost his chance with Harper, for he did not know how to love her when she had sought it. He respected that she had realised her own worth was far greater than he had measured it, with no small amount of shame on his part. He was grateful she still cared enough to sacrifice herself for them. After his treatment of her, it was more than he deserved. He vowed to get her back. A part of him hoped that now, in the arms of her enemy, she had at least one to call a friend, or at least an ally, temporary or not, in Dimitrius. She would need to find much strength before they saw her again.

"Are you all right, friend?" Ragnar, released from the infirmary to reside once more in the königshalle, paced beside him silently.

Aedon huffed, and scrubbed at his eyes which stung with gritty tiredness. "Just worrying, Ragnar. Just worrying."

At Ragnar's silence, he continued. "I mistreated Harper. I see it now. She's been a better friend to us than we deserved, even after we doubted her at first. I hope she is as safe as can be." His thoughts strayed to Dimitrius and his promise to protect her. Did he trust the spymaster? He had seemed so sincere, yet it had been many years since they had seen eye to eye. "And that our paths cross again," he said finally, his voice heavy.

"Against all odds, we are all here." Ragnar's voice was warm, reassuring. Aedon was grateful that his friend never lost hope. "We will find her again."

"More than that," said Aedon grimly. "We'll do everything we can to stop Saradon. I would not be doing my duty as a former general of the Winged Kingsguard if I did not stand up to protect those who cannot protect themselves from power such as his."

Ragnar looked at him in surprise. "You would take up your old position?"

Aedon snorted. "No. No matter the current situation in Pelenor, I would not be welcomed back into those ranks, but there is nothing to stop me acting of my own volition. I may have a dragon no more, but her fire burns in me, and I will no longer squander it selfishly. She would want me to fight, as we always did, for the peace of others."

Ragnar clapped him on the back. "I'm proud of you, my friend—my brother."

Warmth bloomed within him. Aedon nodded, but glanced at him sidelong. "You know, you could help the cause, too."

Ragnar scowled.

"Hear me out. No matter your personal squabbles with Korrin or anyone else here, your rank holds power. You know as well as I what good that can do. We must not permit suffering if we can avert it. Look at the sacrifices your people have made already, let alone our companions. Think of the suffering to come." Dimitrius's words weighed heavily upon him, his fervent promises of the destruction Saradon would wreak upon Valtivar. "You could stand against that," Aedon insisted.

"But how?" Ragnar's quiet voice held hope and desperation.

Aedon only shook his head. "Who knows, my friend. The opportunity will present itself, I am certain. Saradon's Curse spreads. Somehow, Harper is the key, as are the Dragon-hearts. But moreover, we must all stand as one against him. Nothing will spell our doom more surely than dividing."

Ragnar sighed. "I do not know if I can reconcile with Korrin."

"You can try, and that is all I ask you consider."

Through the rock of Keldberg Mountain and across the valleys lay Afnirheim, a shattered reminder of their fate should they fail.

"We must stop him," Ragnar said.

"Let us hope we can outrun the storm long enough."

When Harper awoke, it was to darkness, silence, and solitude. Heavy chains slithered and clinked as she moved in the small, confined space—but not too far, for she could do little more than sit or lay curled up, thanks to her restraints. The metal was freezing—and yet it burned her and made nausea swill in her belly.

With great effort, she quieted her panic and reached for her magic, which bubbled and simmered deep within her, as closed off as it had been since Saradon's subjugation of her obedience. Far beyond her reach. These bonds were made of iron, she knew with instinctive certainty—the antithesis to magic. Harper huddled, shivering and freezing in the dirty rags of the once fine dress, having no protection from the freezing stone all about her. Strangled, her magic could not help with that. The cold seeped in relentlessly.

She did not know which was worse—the waiting, or the not knowing who would come for her. Saradon? Dimitri? Or... someone else? Harper fired a silent prayer into the heavens that her companions had escaped somehow. On a second thought, she sent another, hoping for Dimitri's safe return. Out of all of them, he stood the greatest chance of seeing them both escape from Saradon's shackles.

For now, Harper had no inkling what had passed. They were all gone, far beyond where she could perceive, and so was the safety net she had found amongst them all. Now she was at Saradon's full mercy. Not that he possessed any. He had been *furious*. That was the last thing she remembered. That, and the pain that shattered through her. She shivered even more violently. She was certain worse would be her fate.

A wave of exhaustion rolled over her, threatening to completely fog her already drained mind. She was exhausted, bone crushingly tired, yet she did not want to sleep alone, vulnerable, and isolated. Not there. Her stinging eyes betrayed her anyway and slipped shut.

Soft fingers lifted her chin, and Harper blinked into the pure, bright light. A hint of a smile on the face too light to behold. The golden, flowing hair. The endless robes of white light. Erendriel.

"Be well, daughter. Rest at ease, and I shall watch over thee."

Harper struggled to stand, barely able to rise to her knees, the chains still binding her. "Help me! I must escape him!"

Erendriel bent low and cupped Harper's cheeks with her hands. "I cannot make it so. It is not your destiny to run, but to endure, child."

"Endure what?" Harper asked desperately, even though half a thought later, she was not sure she wanted to know.

"The trials that will make you. I can offer you no guidance. It is not fated. Yet I will give you my gift." Warmth spread through Harper, banishing the cold and the pain. "It is of utmost impor-

tance that you succeed, to be the flame forever lit against the darkness coming. It will be so very easy for you to fail, to be led astray. Do not let it pass. Do not let the mouth of Valxiron tempt you with foul sorcery."

"But I don't understand! If I am to succeed, you must help me."

Harper started to fade back into the darkness. Erendriel's cool hands found her own, squeezing reassuringly.

Harper felt an entirely different set of hands upon hers. Not cool and slim, but warm and enveloping.

"Wake up, Harper."

Harper jolted awake, pulling her hands out and shrinking away, disorientated and fearful after Erendriel's cryptic warning, before relief blossomed as she recognised the voice and blinked open her eyes to the dim light of Dimitri.

"Harper. It's me. Are you…?" Dimitri trailed off, and he swallowed, his lips thinning. "No. Of course you aren't alright."

She was still within the confines of those chains. In silence, Dimitri released her, his hands caressing the spots where they had sat heavy upon her skin and marked her. "I'm so sorry, Harper," he murmured, so quietly that she barely heard him.

When she did not reply, too numb from everything to form words, he rose, and then drew her to her feet. "Come."

When she shuddered, so cold that she could not feel her feet, he swore—and his magic bloomed through her, warm and comforting. She let out a sob of relief.

"It will be okay, Harper," he said, but she heard the desperate edge upon his voice—and knew he could not promise it. Folding her into his arms, he spirited them away into shadow and wind for a moment.

The jarlshalle rumbled with thunder as Dimitri and Harper materialised. The lights were dim, the entire hall cast in shadows and the acrid tang of bitter smoke choked the back of her throat.

Harper froze at the sight of Saradon, prowling through the hall with vengeance wrought upon him. Dimitri slid his arm through hers, tugging her into a bow at the door, then forward, into the hall, even though every muscle in her clearly longed to run away.

"What is the latest?" Saradon fired at Dimitri.

"The dwarves are gone, Lord Ravakian. No more left alive within a day's travel. The survivors made for Keldheim."

Saradon growled, and the thunder in the hall grumbled with him. "Curse them all! No matter. They will be gone from all Valtivar soon enough. I do not need them to come to me to die." He wheeled away. "The goblins suffered heavy losses. The *pascha* no longer wishes to ally with our cause."

"They will cease the alliance?"

Hope pricked at Harper.

Saradon barked a laugh. "Do not be a fool. Of course they will not break it. They will serve whether they will it or not." His lip curled as he turned to them. "As will you," he added flatly to Harper. She met his stare like a rabbit caught in a wolf's gaze.

Saradon advanced upon them, and Harper stilled at Dimitri's side. "I will suffer no more defiance from you. You are my blood daughter, and you are my heir. You will act as such. Do I make myself clear?"

"*Agree,*" Dimitri said into her mind. "*Placate him.*"

After a pause, Harper bowed her head. Relief bloomed in Dimitri and she felt it as if it were her own.

"We can get out of this mess later."

She hoped he was right. It stalled Saradon, who must have expected defiance, for he narrowed his eyes at Harper, then nodded, perhaps satisfied that he had broken her spirit.

"We are to leave this foul pit at once. I have had my fill of dark halls and death," said Saradon. "I will leave it to the goblins to fulfil my mission in Valtivar. They will kill every last dwarf in the realm until there are no more, then it will be mine."

"Where are we to go, Lord Ravakian?"

Saradon glared at him, but a grim smile broke through his stern visage. "Tournai. It is time to break the wheel, my friend, and may it bring death, devastation, and destruction to all those who oppose me." He savoured every word. "Let us go."

Dimitri shivered, and his voice rolled unbidden through her mind. *"I am not your friend."* Had he meant to say that to her? To let her hear the innermost of his thoughts? A wave of uncertainty rolled off her, and he held her closer as though he sensed it ripple through him. Had he? But he could not offer her any comfort, some reassurance that all would be well, for she knew he had no certainty of it himself. Despite their trepidation, they had no choice. As Saradon faded into the ether, Dimitri followed suit, holding Harper in his arms.

Dimitri

It could not have been more starkly clear.

The Saradon he thought he had raised... the visionary, the fair, the downtrodden... was gone. Whether he had ever truly existed was beyond Dimitri's ken. What was left was nothing more than the remnants of Saradon, held within the grip of a greater power, whose name had faded from memory for three thousand years.

Saradon was a servant of the Dark One himself, Valxiron, and nothing more than his puppet. Now, Valxiron would move, and Dimitri was certain they were all doomed, for there were no legends to step from lore to save them. Erendriel and all her kind were dead and gone.

He looked into Harper's eyes, as they appeared in the royal hall of Tournai beside Saradon and the screaming of the courtiers began, to see his own despair mirrored in her gaze. Dimitri had succeeded, and yet, he had failed. He had broken the wheel. Utterly beyond repair.

THE END

THANK YOU FOR READING

WANT MORE?

Thank you so much for reading *Court of Treachery*! If you want more before you read book three, *Heir of Darkness*, remember to join the *Heart of Shadows* Readalong Experience. Enjoy behind the scenes of writing the book, exclusive artwork, and more

Join the read along here: http://www.megcowley.com/heartofshadowsbonus/

Stay in touch!

If you want to reach out to me, I love hearing from readers. You can find me in the following places:

Follow me on Amazon, Bookbub, or sign up to my Romantasy Fellowship newsletter to be notified of new books/releases/sales/news/etc.

Say hi on Facebook, Instagram, or TikTok (find me at

@megcowleyauthor)—I love hearing from you and seeing gorgeous pictures/videos of books out in the wild!

Join my communities on Facebook for social chit chat and Ream for early access and additional story content that isn't available anywhere else.

Find out more about my books and links to all the above on my website www.megcowley.com.

Please leave a review

Thank you so much for reading *Court of Treachery*! If you enjoyed it, please leave a rating/review on your retailer/book site of choice. Positive reviews really help my books find new readers to love them.

What's next...

You're halfway through the *Empire of Blood and Malice* series, but there is *so* much more to come. The payoff for the steamy romance in book three, high-stakes battles in book four, and twists and turns ahead of you are absolutely worth the build up! Keep reading in the next book, *Heir of Darkness*...

Enjoy!
Meg

BOOKS BY MEG COWLEY

World of Altarea stories:

EMPIRE OF BLOOD AND MALICE SERIES

Heart of Shadows

Court of Treachery

Heir of Darkness

Promise of Ruin

A slowburn, steamy, dark, epic quartet with enemies to lovers, forbidden romance, a courageous and vulnerable heroine, found family, high stakes, and a morally grey hero.

TALES OF TIR NA ALATHEA: DARKNESS OF THE LIVING FOREST SERIES

Flight of Sorcery and Shadow

Ascent of Darkness and Ruin

Purge of Flame and Song

A dark and immersive romantic fantasy of unlikely allies facing and overcoming darkness within and without together. Sequel series to Empire of Blood and Malice series.

MARRIED BY STARFALL

A fade-to-black standalone beauty and the beast inspired romantasy retelling featuring redemption and healing. Sequel to Empire of Blood and Malice series.

BOOKS OF CALEDAN SERIES

The Tainted Crown

The Brooding Crown

The Shattered Crown

A coming of age young adult epic fantasy filled with magic, dragons, and adventure, that classic epic fantasy fans will love.

Other fantasy series:

RELIC GUARDIAN SERIES

Hidden Magic

Cursed Magic

Gathered Magic

Tomb Raider meets Indiana Jones plus magic in this fast-paced magical urban adventure fantasy, co-written with Victoria DeLuis.

ABOUT THE AUTHOR

Meg Cowley is a *USA Today* bestselling fantasy author from England, where she lives with her husband, son, lovable golden retriever, two mischievous cats, and myriad book characters.

Meg writes slow burn steamy epic fantasy romances with courageous and vulnerable heroines, protective and brooding males, and lovable and welcoming found family in stories that will steal your heart long after the last page.

Meg's favourite past times are reading, hiking, and cooking. She can usually be found curled up with a cup of tea and a riveting fantasy romance book, cooking up a fantasy-book worthy feast, or out walking the wild, windswept moors of Yorkshire dreaming up her next story.

Visit www.megcowley.com to find out more, discover Meg's books, find exclusive reader bonus content, and join her Romantasy Fellowship newsletter.